"This is a riveting, suspenseful story, full of vivid characters and stirring reflections on medical and genetic issues. . . . Cassella is a gifted writer, gorgeously animating her landscapes and the forces of nature, underlining her theme that even medicine cannot save her characters from mortality."

—*Seattle Times*

"A suspenseful narrative of emotional depth and moral complexity with a sharp little twist that binds the main characters. A practicing anesthesiologist, Cassella has keen, beautifully rendered insights into genetics, neuroscience, and medical ethics."

—*Boston Globe*

"A book at turns heartwarming and heartbreaking, it invites us to accept, if nothing else, that the only way to live is to 'cling to every moment even as you [leap] into the next.'"

—*Publishers Weekly*

"[*Gemini*] poses interesting medical questions and offers deepening mysteries to keep the reader turning the pages."

—*Library Journal*, starred review

"A compelling look at the collision of a physician's professional and personal lives. . . . A uniquely involving read."

—*Booklist*

"This engaging medical mystery makes . . . compelling points about economics and sociology."

—*Kirkus Reviews*

"Involving . . . [Cassella] writes with enviable authority about medicine and disease. . . . She also delivers wise and considered explorations of the way that Eric's life is shaped by his illness and Jane Doe's by her poverty."

—*Wall Street Journal*

"A gripping fictional narrative that will spark conversations about the very real moral dilemmas we face in this age of medical miracles."

—*Bainbridge Review*

"Cleverly but incrementally, Cassella—a practicing physician as well as an author—puts together the pieces of Jane Doe's mystery even as she ponders, through Charlotte, the Big Questions."

—Bookpage.com

"Those who love the drama and mystery Jodi Picoult always delivers will adore Carol Cassella's deep and heartbreaking new release, *Gemini*."

—*Huffington Post*

"Cassella delivers a mind-bending, emotionally charged story featuring tough medical and end-of-life issues. The plot slowly builds as we learn the backstory of a critically injured patient and the dilemmas facing her doctor. Not your ordinary mystery, this is an unusual plot and a great, thought-provoking read."

—*RT Magazine*, 4/4 Stars

"Overall, Cassella has created a work of insightful characterizations, finely crafted language, and socioeconomic contrasts that are detailed in almost Dickensian fashion."

—*Bellingham Herald*

"Cassella writes with urgency and precision, crafting a classic mystery's tension that keeps readers sleepless over the next development. Fortunately, her exacting style does not come at the cost of lush prose. . . . The world of Charlotte and Raney felt dreamy and mythic, yet as ordinary as the craggy sand beneath their feet."

—Bustle.com

"Once again, Carol Cassella has written a novel full of gorgeously rendered characters, fascinating medical detail, and tour de force plot twists. From its gripping first pages straight through to its stunning conclusion, *Gemini* is an unforgettable novel—a morality tale, a mystery, and a love story that will leave readers breathless."

—Maria Semple,
New York Times bestselling author of *Where'd You Go, Bernadette?*

"Carol Cassella's novel taps into the very core of every person's hopes and dreams . . . and their fears. Her beautifully crafted story explores the unbearable fragility of the human body, and ultimately celebrates the sturdiness of the human spirit. This book is a triumph of literary mastery and emotional resonance."

—Susan Wiggs,
#1 *New York Times* bestselling author of *The Apple Orchard*

"A natural-born storyteller, Cassella's vivid novel, beautifully set in the Pacific Northwest, creates a haunting backdrop for this spellbinding examination of how family, loss, genetics, and ultimately the triumph of love can connect and confound us all."

—Lee Woodruff,
#1 *New York Times* bestselling author of
In an Instant and *Those We Love Most*

"With big themes, an unforgettable setting, high stakes, mystery, suspense, heartbreak, human triumph, and rare insight, *Gemini* surprises and fascinates at every turn. Nobody writes about the miracle of the human organism like Carol Cassella. *Gemini* is a novel sure to keep readers flipping pages deep into the night."

—Jonathan Evison,
New York Times bestselling author of *West of Here*

"*Gemini* is an engrossing, compelling page-turner of a novel that will keep you guessing until the very end. Carol Cassella's expertly crafted story about love, genetics, loss, and the search for identity will resonate deeply with readers."

—Kristin Hannah,
#1 *New York Times* bestselling author of *Fly Away* and *Home Front*

"Carol Cassella has written a wonderful novel. A deeply moving story about the heartbreaking pursuit of happiness by a courageous woman without means. *Gemini* is a page turner I had a hard time putting down."

—Jan-Philipp Sendker,
international bestselling author of *The Art of Hearing Heartbeats*

"You will love learning the story of these two women and how their lives intersect and what brought them to that point in their lives. I couldn't put this book down!"

—*The Pilot*

"Book groups will devour this compulsively readable novel with thought-provoking themes. Perfect for readers of Jodi Picoult and Chris Bohjalian."

—*Libraryreads*

Also by Carol Cassella

Healer

Oxygen

GEMINI

A NOVEL

CAROL CASSELLA

Simon & Schuster Paperbacks

NEW YORK

LONDON

TORONTO

SYDNEY

NEW DELHI

SIMON & SCHUSTER PAPERBACKS
A Division of Simon & Schuster, Inc.
1230 Avenue of the Americas
New York, NY 10020

First Simon & Schuster trade paperback edition March 2015

SIMON & SCHUSTER PAPERBACKS and colophon are registered
trademarks of Simon & Schuster, Inc.

For information about special discounts for bulk purchases,
please contact Simon & Schuster Special Sales at
1-866-506-1949 or business@simonandschuster.com.

The Simon & Schuster Speakers Bureau can bring authors
to your live event. For more information or to book an event,
contact the Simon & Schuster Speakers Bureau at
1-866-248-3049 or visit our website at www.simonspeakers.com.

Manufactured in the United States of America

1 3 5 7 9 10 8 6 4 2

The Library of Congress has cataloged the hardcover edition as follows:

Cassella, Carol Wiley.
Gemini / Carol Wiley Cassella
p. cm.
1. Single women—Fiction. 2. —Fiction.
3. —Fiction.
PS3603.A8684 O99 2008
813'.622   2007037542

ISBN 978-1-4516-2793-0
ISBN 978-1-4516-2794-7 (pbk)
ISBN 978-1-4516-2795-4 (ebook)

For Lucie Rose Gendreau

Your light still shines

GEMINI

What are days for?
Days are where we live.
They come, they wake us
Time and time over.
They are to be happy in:
Where can we live but days?

Ah, solving that question
Brings the priest and the doctor
In their long coats
Running over the fields.

—PHILIP LARKIN, "DAYS," FROM *COLLECTED POEMS*

*"There is only one law in the universe that never changes—
that all things change, and that all things are impermanent."*
—BUDDHA

Part One

· 1 ·

charlotte

It is natural law that all complex systems move from a state of order to disorder. Stars decay, mountains erode, ice melts. People get off no easier. We get old or injured and inevitably slide right back into the elements we were first made from. The organized masterpiece of conception, birth, and maturation is really only two steps forward before three steps back, at least in the physical world. Sometimes when Charlotte lost a patient she thought about that and found it comforting—a reminder that she hadn't failed in what was ultimately an unwinnable game. But if she thought about it too long, she had to wonder if her entire medical career was an interminable battle against the will of the universe.

She resisted sinking into such rhetoric the night Jane Doe was whisked across Puget Sound in a medevac helicopter to Beacon Hospital's intensive care unit, to Charlotte. It seemed they always came in the middle of the night, the ones from the more remote hospitals on the Olympic Peninsula—West Harbor and Forks and Port Townsend. Charlotte could picture some overwhelmed doctor reaching his breaking point too many hours before the next sunrise, dreading a night of slumping blood pressure and low oxygen levels and erratic heart rhythms, finally picking up the phone to plead the case for a flight to Seattle. Not that anyone had to plead; they were never turned down.

Charlotte had her own survival plan for these long nights on call: get the critical facts over the phone, tend to the crises of her eleven current patients before the new one arrived, grab a Diet Coke and some Oreos from the vending machines, a blanket out of the warmer at the nursing station, then tuck into a ball on the love seat in the ICU's waiting room and listen. Listen for the chop of the helicopter blades, the rising pitch of the engine as it settled onto the roof with its cargo of impending death. Listen for the buzz of an elevator being held open, the swish of the automatic doors into the ICU wing. Sometimes the next sound was a "code four" alarm—someone who'd clung to breath all the way over the peninsula, the islands, the bay, giving up just when the medical mecca was reached, as if a glimpse of heaven in flight had convinced them to move on. Most often the next sound was her pager, confirming the patient had arrived. And then Charlotte was up, the blanket dumped in the hamper and her white coat buttoned.

She made her first assessment before she was even through the patient's doorway: weight, age, the color of the skin, the shade of the bruises, the number of tubes snaking from the body, sucking fluid away, pumping fluid in. By the time she was at the bedside she was ticking off which invasive lines would have to be removed, replaced, inserted.

Jane arrived just after 3:00 a.m. with no fewer than five tubes: one down her throat, another in her neck, two in her left arm, and one looping from her bladder. Jane's arrival was heralded by pages and alarms and a scrambling of personnel that stopped just shy of a code four. She came with a four-inch stack of medical records, a splint on her right arm, a scaffold of hardware stabilizing her right lower leg, and so much edema that her skin was pocked with the medic's handprints. But she did not come with a name. Not her own name, at least.

The medics rolled the orange transport gurney next to the bed and, smooth as a dance, coiled up all the lines and logrolled Jane onto her side to slip a plastic board underneath her. Charlotte stood at Jane's head and Anne, the nurse, held Jane's feet. On the count of three all the lines and tubes and wires and the sodden, bruised flesh of Jane Doe slid onto the clean white sheets of the bed that would become her next home. The medics talked while they moved, disconnecting the portable monitors, locking down the empty gurney. "Pressure dipped to seventy after takeoff so we upped the dopamine. Had her on a hundred percent O2 halfway across to keep her saturation above ninety." The taller of the two handed Charlotte a clipboard to sign, looking more relaxed now that Jane Doe was hooked up to the hospital's equipment and off his hands. They had met before, on some other transfer, though his name tag was half-covered by the bell of his stethoscope and Charlotte couldn't recall it. He tapped the stack of chart notes he'd brought. "I wasn't sure she was even going to make it across."

Charlotte looked at the monitors, her new patient's heartbeat racing across the screen. "How much fluid did she get on the flight?"

"Fifteen hundred. Pressure kept falling. Not much urine, though." The fluid in Jane's Foley bag was the color of rancid orange juice.

"Thanks for getting her here"—she nudged his stethoscope aside—"Harold."

"Harry."

Charlotte held her hand out, and he shook it. "Right. Harry. Sorry." She flashed her own name tag. "Charlotte Reese. Now, if only Jane had worn hers, we'd know who she is."

For the next two hours Charlotte's only goal was to keep Jane Doe alive. Her blood pressure was so low the monitor's alarm kept chiming, the numbers flashing in red. Jane's hands and feet were dusky blue, and the largest IV line had clotted off. Charlotte tied an elastic tourniquet above Jane's elbow and tapped the skin creases, hoping to feel a vessel.

"You want me to turn up the dopamine?" Anne asked.

Charlotte glanced at the numbers on the pump. "Call the pharmacy and get some Neosynephrine. And some fresh veins along with it. They must have forgotten to stick those in the helicopter."

Anne hung up the phone. "Ten minutes. They're all out of veins. You want to do a cut down?"

"Not yet. How'd we get so lucky to be working tonight?"

"No luck about it for me, baby," Anne answered. "I'm taking every shift they offer. Got no child support check again this month."

"Can't you get a judge on him?"

"Judge would have to put money in the man's pockets to do any good. Tryin' to get blood from a turnip."

Charlotte closed her eyes to focus every sense through her fingertips, pressing and releasing an invisible tension in Jane's swollen tissues. "There it is. Hand me a sixteen-gauge IV."

"Like I was saying."

By the time the sky was lightening, Jane Doe was stable enough for Charlotte to dig into the records the medics had left on the desk. If time didn't matter, if this were her only patient, she could spend the whole week sorting through what had been accumulated in four days. How many numbers and images could be spit out of centrifuged blood and spinal fluid and spinning magnets and X-rays? Hundreds. Thousands. She started by skimming the blood work completed just hours before they loaded Jane into the helicopter; her eyes caught the critically abnormal numbers as though they were in neon: Jane's kidneys were shutting down, her liver was stressed, her lungs were stiffening and filling with fluid, her bone marrow wasn't making enough blood, and she was infected with some unidentified bug, verging scarily near septic shock.

Anne looked over Charlotte's shoulder. "Any surprises?"

Charlotte turned toward the woman lying immobile on the bed. Anne had dutifully pulled the metal side rails up, as if there were any chance this patient would spontaneously move. "What you see there is what I'm seeing here. Not good." She flipped the chart open to the doctors' progress notes and started deciphering the handwritten scripts. Charlotte hated the auto-filled phrases pumped out by her own hospital's medical software, saw it as a shortcut around the methodical, personally described physical exam she had been trained to do. Once she had ripped a printed chart note in half because someone—she assumed a student—had clicked "normal exam" and the computer spit out exactly that for a patient with a subtle heart murmur, which had probably caused his stroke. Later she discovered the error had been made by the chief of surgery. But at least computer-generated notes were legible; her eyes blurred with fatigue reading Jane's chart.

Charlotte translated a summary for Anne. "Hit and run. A truck driver spotted her in a ditch beside the highway and called 911. Femur fracture, shattered lower leg. Broken elbow. It looks like she was conscious when she got to the ER but too disoriented to give a clear story or her name . . . her initial head CT was OK, so maybe just hypothermia. They rushed to the OR to fix her leg. And somewhere in there things really went to hell."

The doctor who'd called Charlotte to request the transfer four days after Jane's accident had sounded young and exhausted. Charlotte had caught the note of regret in his voice, almost defensive, anticipating blame. She knew they were begging for doctors out on the peninsula—towns built on timber and fishing now collapsing along with those industries, three or four hours and a million cultural miles from the city. The doctors they could hire were often new graduates, and the best of them burned out within a few years. And how much of every doctor's education happens after he leaves medical school? Half or more, Charlotte thought. More. The guy was in over his head, doing the best he could in a rural, underfunded hospital. Reading these notes, she felt almost as bad for him as she did for Jane. After they fixed her leg they'd taken her to the ICU, still unconscious, still chemically paralyzed by anesthesia drugs. A day had passed balancing her fluids, transfusing blood, and then another day weaning her off sedatives, trying to figure out why her oxygen levels were so low.

But she didn't wake up. Another head CT showed no bleed, no mid-line shift, nothing to explain it. And on the third day, when Jane was still unconscious, when her white blood cell count started going up and her lungs started getting stiff, a storm had blackened the coast-line and flying her out was impossible.

Charlotte paged through the lab reports and radiographs, waiting for one to pop out at her. Something unifying. Something correct-able. After fifteen minutes she shut the chart and cupped her palms over her eyes until the world was dark and small and calm and the thousands of bits of data settled. She was Jane Doe, lying beside the highway, cold, confused, in pain, lifted into an ambulance, rolled into an emergency room bay talking, apparently making enough sense the doctors were more worried about her bones than her brain. Then the blissful nothingness of anesthesia, the pain in her leg and arm and bruised body finally relieved. The bleeding from her open fracture stopped. Warm for the first time in hours.

Charlotte opened her eyes. "It happened in the OR."

"What?" Anne asked.

"Whatever happened." Charlotte flipped to the back of the chart, the tab marked Surgical Records. The operation had lasted more than five hours—two or three hours to put a rod up through the fractured bone of her femur and then another two hours working on her lower leg and arm. The surgeon's notes were boringly unremarkable, glibly dic-tated from memory, Charlotte could tell. She turned to the anesthetic record—three pages of dots and checks and Xs marching across the grid-lines noting blood pressure and pulse. Then, in the middle of page 2, a brief, sharp dive into scary-low numbers before they popped back to normal. So brief it might be written off as a few erratic readings from the automated machines, a kink in the tubes, a loose blood pressure cuff. But when Charlotte looked closely at the other numbers charted by the anesthesiologist, she knew it wasn't an aberration. He or she had given repeated doses of drugs to kick Jane's blood pressure higher. And one line below that, Charlotte saw Jane's oxygen and carbon dioxide levels. They, too, had taken a dive, quickly corrected but blaring like alarms.

Anne looked over Charlotte's shoulder. "What happened?"

"I bet she threw a fat embolus when they put the rod into her femur. Has to be. That's what hit her lungs."

"Was her oxygen level low enough to turn her into this?"

"Maybe. Or maybe not. Maybe some of the emboli got into her brain." Charlotte closed the chart and walked to the end of Jane's bed, watched the white sheet rise and collapse with each forced mechanical breath. She imagined the shimmering spray of pale yellow particles forced out of Jane's marrow when the metal rod was hammered home, coursing through her blood, across her heart or through her lungs, into the fine capillary network of her brain, where they lodged with the effect of a thousand tiny, toxic bombs. "Damn. Can't fix that one, Jane. Have to get the rest of you well and see if your brain still works."

Not a month earlier Charlotte had had a conversation with her boyfriend Eric, who'd more than once watched her throw the weight of modern medicine along with her single-minded will against all natural forces to keep a patient alive, only to lose in the end. Eric had challenged her on it that day. "Should quantity of life always trump quality? Maybe you set your goals too high."

She knew he was only giving voice to her own darker thoughts, but still she'd been miffed. "Maybe I'll repeat that to your doctor when you're lying in an intensive care unit someday."

"Maybe I'll get lucky and be in your ICU. I'm just saying it might not be the *number* of days that matter. Maybe it's the *one* day they need to fix whatever's standing between them and heaven."

"Said the guy who doesn't believe in heaven," she had retorted.

"Stay with me, Jane. It's going to get worse before it gets better," Charlotte said out loud.

"The Neosynephrine's here. What next?" Anne asked.

"Next I call the doctor in West Harbor and tell him to stop blaming himself. This one was an act of God. God and whoever slammed into her and drove away."

· 2 ·
raney

As should be the case with any memorable love story, the first time Raney Remington saw Bo she hated him. She didn't have any choice but to hate him, he was so beautiful. So foreign. After all, no exceptional thing can exist for long without a counterbalance—the weight of it would tip a life over. Raney hated Bo for his skinny frame, scrawny even for a twelve-year-old kid still shy of puberty. She hated his pale skin, as coddled as all the city boys who came out to Olympic National Park for summer camps and vacation Bible schools and "back to nature" classes. All of them soggy and miserable in their L.L.Bean boots and Eddie Bauer parkas. This boy must have borrowed his father's; the wrists drooped over his hands and the hem came nearly to his knees, his stiff blue jeans poking out all mud-splattered below. He was standing outside Peninsula Foods underneath the gutter, and a dam of leaves broke loose, spouting a cascade of rainwater directly onto his head. Any reasonable person would have stepped under cover, but this boy pulled his hood back and looked straight up at the stream like he might open his mouth and swallow. His skin was so white the shadows of his cheekbones were blue. That's how Raney would have painted him—how she did

10

paint him years later from memory, translucent and frail as Picasso's *Blue Boy*, black hair a mess of damp points and planes, rain running down his cheeks like tears. A blue-blooded member of the club that didn't want the likes of her. She stared so hard he finally looked at her, and even from across the street she caught the same ghost-blue color in his eyes. Then a woman walked out of the store and directed the boy to a scuffed red Malibu that Raney recognized from John Hardy's store, where her grandfather bought his feed, and there was Mr. Hardy at the wheel. She watched them drive down the street and around the bend in the highway until the exhaust fumes disappeared, and she knew exactly what she wanted: that boy gone from Quentin. She never wanted to see him again.

And she didn't. Not for ten days. Not until she was painting down in the ravine and caught him squatting on the opposite bank with his knees splayed apart inside his clasped arms and a book dangling from his hand, watching her like he'd paid for a ticket and had every right to be in her woods. Raney concentrated so fully on ignoring him she dropped her brush on the ground and had to pick pine needles and dirt off the bristles. She could swear she saw him smirk. She raised her middle finger at him. Bo, in turn, raised his first two fingers in the salute drivers around Quentin gave passing strangers on back roads. He nodded once and crossed his legs with the book facedown in his lap, as if she should pretend he belonged around here and go back to her canvas.

She worked from a row of baby food jars filled with house paints nabbed off porches and out of garages and construction dumps, a palette scrabbled from the poor taste of a poor town mixed into the colors she saw in these woods and water and sky. She dipped her brush into white primer and filled in the trillium blooming in the sword ferns beside Bo; lit the ridge of cloud showing through the canopy over his head. And then, with no conscious intention, she started painting his intrusive, unwelcome face, his doughy brow cut by his black eyebrows and the gray hollows at his temples. He needed a blood transfusion, that boy. She popped the lid off a sampler tin of Barn Red and painted a slash across his face, packed her brushes and jars into a tackle box, and hauled the whole lot down the slippery path to the creek bottom then back up the other side, where she stood over him, breathing hard with anger more than exercise.

"You here for the Bible church camp?"

"No."

"You don't belong here. Don't live around here."

"No."

She looked out at the ocean this stream bled into, waiting, until a fist of impatience made her ask outright, "So what are you doing here?"

"Watching you paint."

"I don't mean *here*, here. I mean here. In Quentin."

He squinted up at her so only half his eyes showed underneath his brows. "My aunt lives here. I'm staying with her for the summer."

"How come?"

"My folks are on a trip to Europe."

"So why didn't you go with them?"

Bo looked away like he had to give the question some thought. "'Cause I didn't want to spend all summer in museums and churches." He stood up and brushed dirt from his seat, lost his balance, and bounced awkwardly back to his feet. "I live in Seattle. You know where the Space Needle is?"

Raney wasn't about to give him the satisfaction of learning she'd only been to Seattle twice, the last time at age seven. Up this close she saw he must have had some blood running through his veins; he flushed pink at the corner of his nostrils and under his cheekbones while she stared him down. He reminded her of a china cup her grandmother had had—so thin you could see the shadow of your fingers through the bowl—he looked like he could break just as easy. It made her stomach go tight, this beautiful, breakable boy who lived in a house near the Space Needle with two parents lolling through France for a summer; this boy who did not belong to these woods and should know better.

"What's your book?" she asked him.

He flashed the spine toward her. "*Lord of the Rings.* Read it?"

"Only good one was *The Hobbit.*"

"Only easy one, maybe."

Raney felt the band tighten around her stomach again, a hot flush. She jerked her head toward the wide breach in the earth where the Little Quentin River had carved through twenty feet of cliff and the sky and ocean split the gloom of woods. "Anybody showed you the cave yet? There was seal pups in there last year—they might have come back. Follow me. Unless you're scared."

He chewed the inside of his lip, probably gauging whether she might be some of the riffraff he'd been warned against. That or he was just plain chicken, in which case the boys around here would make his life hell anyway. She might as well teach him how to fend for himself, she justified. She broke out across the duff and mossed roots that hinted at a trail. At the break where the earth began the steep dive to the beach she stashed her tackle box under a rock ledge, then grappled and slipped down to the beach, following the foamy waterline until she was out of his sight. When he hadn't appeared after five minutes she popped her head and shoulders out of a gash in the bluff above the wet sand. "You gotta climb up along the side. Over here." The lip of the cave was no more than seven feet above the beach, but he stood wary underneath her, like he was staring straight up the pylons of the Space Needle itself. Raney hooked one foot into a crevice just below the green stripe that marked the tide line, then dropped at his feet like a cat. "Over here. Hand me your book and take hold of the roots." She talked him root by rock up the bluff into the mouth of the cave. "I'm going back to get a flashlight—I heard 'em mewing toward the rear but it's too dark." Any color that had crept into Bo's face from the climb up the rocks paled, and Raney saw him winding up to protest. Frigid seawater lapped her bare ankles. She tucked his book under her arm and called up, "If you sit quiet a little ways inside you'll be able to see them when your eyes adjust. Last summer one practically crawled into my lap. Won't take me twenty minutes to go and get back."

It occurred to Raney to return to the beach and check on the boy in the cave before nightfall; it pricked her conscience enough she didn't eat much dinner and even after she'd gotten into bed she still tossed and turned, wondering if she was more irked at herself or at him. What idiot would follow a total stranger down a cliff into a tide-flood cave looking for seal pups? Just after midnight she pushed the covers back and pulled his soggy book out of her tackle box. The pages were stuck together and it smelled more of the woods than book glue and paper. Tolkien. Wouldn't you just know it? She lit the gas heater in the bathroom and propped the book on a trash can in front of it, flipped the toilet seat down, and sat with her chin in her hands watching it dry. The cobalt-blue dye of the book's cloth jacket had stained the pages a paler shade, not far off from the color of his eyes. If he had stayed missing all night, the whole town would know about it by the time the sun rose.

As soon as it was light, she bundled a thin sheet of plywood and a few clean brushes into a tarp, picked up her paints, and stomped out of the house. Not ten yards down the drive she turned around, climbed back upstairs, and shoved his stupid book into her pack. A fog had moved in, making the early summer day as wintery as December, the clouds so low to the ground it was like the ocean had spread itself thinner and higher until it blurred into sky. On days like this Raney sometimes painted the mood she felt more than the shapes she saw, shifting her palette to grays and greens that moved in waves rather than the sharp lines of sunshine and shadow. She propped her plywood up on a park bench across the street from Hardy's Store a good hour before it opened. She watched the lights come on upstairs and then in the back storeroom when the Star Food Service truck pulled up, and finally saw the shadow of Mrs. Hardy through the milky glass in the front door. A minute later Mrs. Hardy stepped onto the worn plank porch with a broom in one hand, her other hand planted at what used to be her waist, breathing in the foggy morning air like she expected no better from life but no worse either—just her usual sour acceptance of Quentin and its slow journey to nowhere. She didn't look panicked. Not like a woman who'd stayed up all night combing the woods for her nephew with the police. She saw Raney and nodded her chin. And damn if Raney didn't figure out then that she'd been holding her breath for the last thirteen hours.

An odd thing happened after that, which Raney would remember all her life. She began a painting of the main street of town: the empty two-lane highway that barely slowed as it passed the few storefronts and the elementary school on its way to the national park; Jimmy Tucker's shoebox Pan-Abode house beyond the intersection near the Baptist church, his dad's rusted trawler forever listing on its keel like it had been swept over his chain-link fence and deposited there by a great tidal wave. She painted Hardy's Store in the center and sketched in Mrs. Hardy stabbing at the doorjamb with her broom. But right after Raney started coloring in Mrs. Hardy's bulky figure and fleshy calves in their thick-rolled stockings, she suddenly dipped her brush into Commodore Blue and painted denim jeans on a skinny boy wearing Converse sneakers and a gray hooded sweatshirt with the sleeves pushed up. Not five minutes later Bo took the broom out of his aunt's hand and pushed the sleeves of a gray sweatshirt further up his pale arms. That was sufficient God-sign to last Raney all summer. She assumed she was forgiven.

She caught him looking at her, but she kept painting and he kept sweeping until it felt too ridiculous. She wiped the paint off her brush and pulled his book out of her backpack, marched across the street, and stuck it in his hand. "I tried to dry it out." She saw a tangle of scratches up both arms, one long red line under his left eye. So he'd climbed up the face of the cliff instead of risking the surf—City Boy didn't have enough fat on him to float, she thought. Or he didn't know how to swim.

He flipped through the clumped, wavy pages with one thumb, the broom tucked under his arm. "Guess you didn't try very hard."

That seemed to be as much as either of them could think to say; Raney wasn't about to apologize now that she knew he hadn't spent the night in that cave. They stood silent, watching two crows tear at a sodden bag in the gutter near her painting. The mist gathered itself into something more declarative, and he jerked one shoulder toward her propped-up plywood. "Your drawing's getting wet."

"Everything here gets wet at some point," she answered. He looked at her with a funny half smile, like she'd shared a secret, and she felt something prickly creep up her spine; something she wanted to avoid but it was already inside. "I know where there's an eagle's nest. Three babies still in it." She spit on two fingers and held them up in the air. "For real—I swear. No caves."

Bo stayed in Quentin for three months, the whole of his summer vacation and then some. If he missed his mother or father or anything else about his life in Seattle, he didn't say a word to Raney, nor did he ask about the topics she sidestepped. As if they had an undeclared truce on their private struggles, they talked only about what mattered each day—the book he was reading, the easel she was saving for, the model car he was building, what section of the town dump they should scavenge next.

After a week or so Raney decided that stranding Bo in that cave was the best possible beginning for their friendship, right up front doing away with any awkwardness about him being a boy and her a girl, him having money and her not. He was like one of those kid-napped kids that bond with their kidnappers and forget they ever lived a better life. And with Raney at his back the local boys be-queathed a grudging tolerance and kept their distance. Bo made a good effort to pretend that clawing his way out of the cave had been no big deal, but the forests and drift-tangled beaches around Quen-tin were as foreign to him as Paris would have been to Raney, and for the first time in her life *she* was the wise one, the teacher. One afternoon she took him up Mount Wilson to see the view of the bay and he spent a long time reading the forest service signs warning of cougars. Half an hour later she turned around to see him poking a stick at something in the trail, and he shot off like a shy horse when Raney snapped a branch coming back for him. She stopped at the pile of wet black cones he'd been inspecting. "What were you looking at?" He ambled toward her, shrugging his shoulders, looking embarrassed. "You thought it was cougar scat, didn't you? Cats bury their business. Anyway, if a cougar's following us you won't know till he's got his claws in your neck." They were already comfortable enough he could laugh at such a gibe.

Raney's grandfather, though, had a different take on her new friendship—he didn't like Bo from the get-go. One hot afternoon Bo was buying her a Slurpee at 7-Eleven when Grandpa pulled his truck across two parking spaces and got out with the engine still running. He stood in the middle of the walk between Bo and his bicycle, staring Bo down. "I am Renee's grandfather. You are . . . ?"

Bo looked at Raney and then looked back at her grandfather and dropped the Slurpee on the ground. He bent to pick up the cup, then seemed to think the better of it, wiped his hand on his pant leg, and held it out. "I'm Robert, sir."

Grandpa crossed his arms. "Well, Robert, you need a haircut." Then he turned to Raney like Bo was nothing more than a squashed bug. "Dinner at six. Small towns have big eyes, Renee."

After he got into his truck Raney picked up the half-empty plastic cup and stuck it into Bo's rejected hand. "You're not going to pee your pants, are you? He's not scary when you know him. He might get used to you." Later, a part of her mind figured Grandpa must have wondered what this twelve-year-old boy was teaching her, a thirteen-year-old girl, out in the woods all day. Grandpa didn't trust many people right off the bat, and Raney was the only family he had left to worry about, so he invested himself thoroughly in the job. As a consequence, perhaps, Bo only came to Raney's house once, early in that first summer, a day Grandpa had driven to Shelton to sell a gun he'd bought at the Bremerton Gun Show. Even though she knew he was sixty miles away, her hand was cold and sweaty opening the back-door latch; she kept hearing the cough of his F-150 every time a car came up the hill below their property, heard his boot step every time one of the dogs jumped up on the porch. She hardly ever invited people into that house—her few girlfriends were too scared of Grandpa to do more than call for Raney from the yard. Her nervousness seemed to infect Bo. He kept asking, Where was Shelton, how long was the drive, when had her grandpa left, how long did it take to sell a gun?

"You'd think he was buying a gun to use on you," she finally retorted, and it must have hit close to home, because Bo came right back with, "Well, would he?"

She told him her granddad liked guns well enough, but his philosophy was that the best protection when TEOTWAWKI comes is long-term survival. The gun hoarders would be out there killing each other off for a few months until the ammunition ran out, and then those who'd stayed alive and healthy would end up the better for it.

"When what comes?"

"TEOT . . . The End Of The World As We Know It." By the look on his face it was clear this was not something people on Queen Anne Hill in Seattle were worrying about. "Never mind. Watch out for the dogs—show 'em the back of your hand first."

Bo walked through the door ahead of her, and Raney followed his eyes around the sparsely furnished kitchen, seeing it for herself in a new way. Seeing how much she had forgiven and how much she had accepted without expecting anything more—a paucity of material goods that suddenly looked more like loneliness than simplicity. There was a long plank table in the center of the kitchen with two mismatched wooden chairs, a jar of washed silverware in the middle. They had four metal folding chairs in the pantry for guests, but they'd never used them, not as far as she could remember. On the Formica counter was a metal toaster, a half loaf of bread in a knotted plastic bag, and a row of gallon-sized glass canning jars with flour and sugar and coffee. None of her schoolwork or class photos were taped on the refrigerator, standard decor in her friends' houses she'd not thought to miss in her own. A shorter counter along the back wall held a deep porcelain farm sink under a wavy-paned window that looked across the yard and the shallow duck pond and chicken coop. On a clear winter day when the wild cherry and the bigleaf maple were bare, you could see the white cap of Mount Olympus, but now they made a green thicket. The view out that window had always been enough for her until Bo was sitting at their kitchen table running his fingernail down the greasy crack between two of the wooden planks.

Gif, their old German shepherd, butted his nose against the screen door until she let him in. He made a thoughtful assessment of Bo, lifting his nose to take in the boy's scent; then he leaned against Raney's leg. Bo reached out a hand but drew it back when Gif curled his lip and rumbled.

"Hungry?" Raney asked.

He only shrugged, which didn't surprise her; she'd yet to witness him eat anything that he hadn't packed from home and didn't look suspiciously vegetarian. So she noticed it when he asked, "You got any Coke?"

Raney stopped scratching Gif's ear and looked at him. "You drink Coke?"

"Well, no. Not at my house. But I thought maybe you did."

She shook her head. "Gramps doesn't believe in it. I mean he believes it exists and all, he just . . ." She petered off, unexpectedly self-conscious with him. "So why don't you drink Coke?"

Bo was looking at Gif, rubbing his fingers together like he might tempt the dog to trust him. For a minute Raney didn't think he was going to answer, and then he shrugged and said, "Sort of the same. My mom thinks it makes me sick."

"Sick how?"

"I had this spell last year. From eating too much sugar and pre-servatives."

"What kind of spell?"

"Like a fainting spell. How come your dog's so mean?"

"He's not mean once he knows you. I guess he only knows me and Grandpa. I could fix you some cheese toast."

"How long's your grandmother been gone?"

"A while. She died when I was about eight. Had the cancer."

"What happened to your mom and dad?"

Here it came. The question that always changed everything. It had taken him long enough—he hadn't brought it up once on the treks through woods and beach they'd already taken and Raney had gotten hopeful he'd never ask. She had a vision of that moment in *The Wizard of Oz* when Dorothy's world goes Technicolor. Raney knew that was the part most people liked best, but not her. She might love standing in the oil-paint section of the Port Townsend craft store touching the undimpled tin tubes of color she couldn't afford, imagining the mix of tints that would tell the truth about her own world, but in *The Wizard of Oz* she preferred the black-and-white part. Dorothy safe and sound with her Auntie Em and Uncle Henry and nobody giving a damn where her mother or father was.

She pulled a fork out of the jar on the table and started gouging at the filthy crevices Bo had picked at. "My mom left when I was four. She was sick. I don't remember it, but Grandpa says she left because she didn't want me to see her like that." Bo was staring at her like he was waiting for her to cry or something, and she had an urge to plant the fork in the back of his hand.

"What about your dad?" he asked like he couldn't help himself.

Raney squared her shoulders and looked straight at him. "I don't know who my dad is, which is fine with me. I'd rather have a grandpa who loves me than a dad who couldn't care less, right? We're the same blood, Grandpa and me. So don't go feeling sorry."

"I didn't say I felt sorry . . ."

She pointed the fork at his face. "You didn't say it but I could see you were thinking about it. My mom loved me plenty. I got letters for a while." She put the fork back in the jar and crossed her arms. "I think she's dead. Sometimes I wake up at night and know it for sure, down inside of me. You know how when it's black and quiet and

you're dreaming and then you go through that weird space of trying
to figure out if you're asleep or awake? Well, I think those dreams
might be truer than anything you think in the light of day. Like you
had one foot in the next world. I've seen her there, my mom. If she
could get back to me she would."

His mouth pinched tight and Raney shot him a challenging look,
ready to tackle him if he so much as smiled. After a long minute he
said, "My parents aren't on a trip to Europe. They're getting a divorce.
They didn't tell me that—nobody wants to tell me. But I know it
anyway."

Raney wanted to know if he got to choose where he'd live, with
his mother or his father, but she looked at his face and knew not to
ask. "You want to see the rest of the house?"

The living room was dark. Her grandmother had decorated it, but
Grandpa and Raney almost never used the room, so the smell of
mold came through like abandonment and the furniture looked
more like the props used in school plays than anything a person
might actually sit on. Bo asked if they could watch MTV and Raney
said Grandpa didn't believe in TV, thought it was the government's
way of stupefying the population so no one would rise up. There were
two pink velvet–covered armchairs, a matching pink sofa, and a dark
wood coffee table with glass over the top that Raney had tripped and
split her chin on when she was five. There was a bookcase with some
war medals and books about Korea and Vietnam and one oversize
book with pictures from the Metropolitan Museum of Art, which
had belonged to Raney's grandmother.

Bo kept his hands in his pockets, as if he was cold, moving his
eyes from one dusty object to the next without a word. Raney felt
like she was supposed to be telling him something about this room
where time seemed to have stopped, but she couldn't identify what.
She started to wish she had not brought him here. Then his eyes settled on a photograph of her mother, Celine. She was about fifteen
in the photograph, wearing a turquoise sweater with a big gold pin

in the shape of a rose—Raney still had that actual pin in her underwear drawer. Celine was looking right at the camera, which meant, of course, that she was looking right at Raney, and her mother's eyes were a complicated mix of brown and rusty gold and green, the same green Raney saw in her own eyes. The photograph was actually a black and white, but Raney saw those colors rich and saturated and they never faded, no matter how old that picture got year after year. Bo stood in front of it for a long time. He didn't ask who the woman was, but Raney saw him look at the picture and then look at her and it was pretty obvious.

"I can't show you my room. Grandpa wouldn't like it." Bo looked a little relieved, which for some reason made her want to take him upstairs and show him the quilted twin bed where she slept, the wooden desk Grandpa had built for her under the window that, in wintertime, let her watch snow pile up on the Brothers peaks. Then the dogs started barking and she got scared for a minute that Grandpa might be driving in, but then she did the math of miles from here to Shelton and back and knew it was just rabbits or one of the barn cats. "I've got another place I can show you. But you have to promise me you'll never tell a soul. It's outside."

Rex, their pointer, must have decided by then that Bo was no threat. The dog danced around the boy's legs as they went out into the yard, running to grab sticks for them to throw, bowing down on his front paws to drop them at Bo's feet like he was making offerings to a king. Raney could tell Bo didn't own a dog—he'd reach tentatively for whatever Rex dropped, like the dog might change his mind again and bite. But she granted that Bo had a pretty good arm for a boy who was so pale and skinny you wondered if they let children play outside in Seattle.

The sun had broken through the clouds and the yard was alive with jays and crows and the hum of dragonflies. A cluster of hot-pink hollyhocks seeded ages ago by Raney's grandmother swayed with blooms as big as saucers. Grandpa's long-dead Mercury rusted in a patch of morning glory at the edge of the woods and the faded

red paint and twisting vines with their white trumpet-shaped flowers, all illuminated in a beam of sunshine, looked more glorious than
decrepit to Raney. This was how she saw her house, their land, and
felt acutely awkward to know she hoped Bo could see it the same—
brilliant and vital and not at all lonely. And Bo was lit up, too, pitch-
ing rocks and plastic bottles for the dog, loosening his body more
with every throw like the sun had oiled his joints, whooping at that
hunter as if he needed any encouragement to race and retrieve. Later,
Raney wondered why she couldn't just enjoy the moment as long as
it lasted. Instead she did it to him again. She slipped inside the barn
and disappeared from Bo's sight.

· 3 ·

charlotte

Felipe Otero, one of Charlotte's partners, rapped on the metal frame of Jane Doe's sliding glass door before stepping inside—a small gesture of courtesy uniquely his own, Charlotte thought. Most of the other doctors breezed in and out of the ICU cubicles, barely pausing unless family members were present, subconsciously claiming this property as their own, this time their own, even the moment it took to pause at the doorway too valuable to squander.

"Full house today. You had a busy night." He nodded at Jane, still unconscious and immobile, and spoke in a half whisper barely audible over her ventilator and the bustle in the hallway and nursing station, filled with personnel as the nurses changed shift. "Want to sign out? I can take over."

Charlotte glanced at the clock. "You still have time for breakfast. Why so early?"

"Easier to be here than at home some mornings." He grinned at this reference to his teenagers, who Charlotte knew had been giving him hell. "Ethics board had a meeting this morning. I heard about the new patient."

24

"The ethics board is already discussing her?"

"No. Helen Seras asked me if I'd seen her yet. KING-TV called her."

"The accident was five days ago."

"Yes, but there's no TV station in Forks."

"West Harbor. Do us all a favor and keep Helen out of my way this morning. You know the whole story?" Felipe shook his head. "Hit-and-run pedestrian found beside the highway. No ID—"

"That much I know," Felipe interrupted.

"She was alert when the medics got her to the ER. Arm and leg fractures. And now . . . this." She looked at Jane's pale, bloated body. "I think she threw a fat embolism in the OR when they were fixing her femur fracture."

"Just pulmonary or to her brain? She's had an MRI?"

"I'm sure it hit her brain. She never woke up after surgery. MRI is at nine o'clock this morning. Echocardiogram this afternoon when they can fit her in. Her lungs are getting worse by the hour. She'll need a tracheostomy soon."

Felipe looked at the numbers on the flow sheet in front of Charlotte, then walked to Jane's bedside and in one sweep of the monitors saw enough to know that Jane would be here for weeks before they could guess her ultimate outcome—if they could keep her alive that long. Then he turned his face to the woman lying on the bed, limbs arranged doll-like at her side in their casts and bandages and braces. Charlotte saw him smooth the folded edge of the thin cotton blanket that covered her torso. "She's quite young," he said when he came back to the desk.

"Around forty." She almost added, "around my age," but it felt too personally referential—unprofessional to hint at any close identification with a patient even to someone like Otero, whom she considered a friend. As if he heard her thoughts, he smiled and looked Charlotte in the eyes. "Yes. Young. Lots to live for. Finish your note and go home to your garden. Call your boyfriend."

"Eric doesn't get out of bed until ten."

"So, join him." Felipe laughed at the face Charlotte made, a self-

mocking grimace that summed up how she felt after being awake and
working all night, her hair lank, her scrubs rumpled and smelling
faintly of sweat. Felipe was twelve years older than Charlotte, his outside life consumed by one particularly wild son and a perpetually
tempestuous marriage. But for four years they had shared patients
and call schedules and a mutual skepticism of hospital bureaucracy,
which proved to be the best possible stress relief in a job that was
often all stress. Felipe had championed Eric even before Charlotte
allowed herself to think about him romantically, when she was still
too angry at her prior boyfriend to consider any man with a forgiv-
ing heart. Or maybe Felipe just championed love itself, found its
unsteadiness a seductive twist to its pleasure—all the more alluring
when success was unpredictable and thus an ideal counter to his precision in the ICU, where Charlotte could sometimes *see* him silently
tick through all practical options for a patient, weighing hard choices
against statistical odds before setting a clinical course his emotions
couldn't impeach. Sometimes she envied him that.

She flipped through the notes she'd made about Jane Doe over
the last hours, looking for any missing test or order or medication—
and Jane was only one of the twelve patients she was managing, albeit
the sickest. Charlotte's eyes felt sticky and she recognized the lag between her thoughts and her decisions that always crept in after long
nights. "All right. I'll go. Come out to the nurses station and let's go
over the charts."

She called Otero twice on the way home, remembering details she
hadn't outright talked about even though she knew he'd handle
them: remind the echo tech to look for a septal defect in Jane's heart,
get a surgical consult for her trach, make sure Infectious Disease
sees her first thing today. It could be endless, this mental circling she
did around complex cases, knowing how drastically things could
change in one day. She stopped at Whole Foods for cat food, yogurt,
and some fruit but left with an enormous frosted cinnamon roll—
somehow they almost looked healthy sitting on their tidy brown

paper squares in a wicker basket. She thought about driving to Swansons Nursery for more lettuce starts. She thought about going straight to Eric's but decided to rent a George Clooney DVD instead, then circled the parking lot of the video store twice and decided to go home without stopping. The fog of fatigue, an entire, sparkling afternoon ahead with no obligations, it left her aimlessly wandering through a boggling plethora of options. She needed more hobbies, she thought. She needed sleep.

Puck, the tiny gray kitten rescued from a Dumpster and now grown into an enormous, belligerent hair ball, stood on his hind paws clawing at the glass door and pushed between Charlotte's legs before she'd even stepped into the kitchen. She dropped her purse and groceries on the table and opened the first section of the newspaper while she finished the cinnamon roll. She should sleep now, she knew, let her brain reorder itself so she could get something accomplished later. But the sun looked so nakedly yellow this morning, and the petunias she'd put into pots on the porch just beyond the open kitchen door gave off a pungent smell of earth, shouldering their fat purple and pink blossoms like they intended to take over the whole garden. And there was a certain luxuriance in being so thoroughly fatigued; an excuse to let her mind roll into whatever corners it chose, a day off from life as much as a day off from work.

She got a pot of coffee going and took a shower, and by the time she came back into the kitchen, Puck had returned and slumped onto the newspaper for a nap. He jumped off the table as soon as he heard Charlotte rattle the box of cat food, the top sheet of newsprint clinging to his fur so that it sailed to the floor. She stopped halfway to picking it up when a headline and a pencil sketch of a woman's face caught her eye: "Unconscious Jane Doe Still Unidentified." Charlotte was wide awake now. She skimmed the few paragraphs so quickly they hardly made sense and then sat holding the page in front of her, reading it line by line until it was clear that yes, this was Beacon Hospital's Jane Doe. *Her* Jane Doe, though the sketch was so generously ambiguous it could have been a thousand Caucasian middle-aged women. The article read more like a tantalizing "if it bleeds, it leads" than a plea for Jane's relatives to find her, which made Charlotte irrationally angry, strangely possessive—as if one of her own family members had been exposed just to sell copy. But when she calmed down and read it again, she realized that what she really felt was protective, as though bad press was as threatening as bad bacteria and it was her job to guard Jane against it all.

The paper told Charlotte only slightly more than she already knew, but the fact that it focused on the nonmedical questions—Why had no one reported her missing? Where had she lived? What were the police doing to find her relatives? Who had run her down and driven away?—made Jane seem even more vulnerable to Charlotte; more *human*, she was embarrassed to admit. She tore the article out and put it in a drawer with loose recipes, plastic spoons, and crayons she kept handy for her nephews. She stood outside with her coffee watching morning commuters stalled on the 520 Bridge, plucked a few faded blooms from the wooden flower boxes, then got the article out of the drawer, read it for the third time, and opened her laptop.

A Google search didn't tell her much more. No serious investigation had been started until three days after Jane's surgery, probably because they'd kept expecting her to wake up and tell them her name. It was as if her conscious, relatively stable status when she'd hit the emergency room had lulled them into taking their time about identifying her. They seemed to have few clues about the car that had struck her. No wonder Helen Seras was already asking about Jane; as the vice president who did most of the public speaking for the hospital, she'd be left to explain things if this turned into a bad PR trip.

Charlotte leaned toward the floor and rubbed her fingers together, tempting the cat to sidle near; he sniffed once and, discerning nothing edible, slunk beneath her attempted caress and wandered away. She loved the diffidence in that animal, quite irrationally; Eric teased that he'd be gone in a heartbeat the day she neglected to fill his bowl. Eric would probably still be asleep; she would call later and tell him about her night, hear what turn his book revision was taking. The closer he got to a deadline, the more he reversed his days and nights, often writing until nearly dawn. So they would both be exhausted, Charlotte figured. He got so immersed in the final stages of a project, she'd come to accept a temporary sense of distance—knew better than to take it personally and knew the same passion would be focused on her once the book was done. But this time felt different to her—not as clearly rooted in his work. Not as clearly rooted in him.

She thought of another three suggestions for Jane's care and called the nursing station in the ICU. But as soon as the secretary answered, she reconsidered—Otero was the best intensivist at Beacon, better than herself, in her own opinion. If he was half as busy today as she'd been last night she should give him some peace. Instead she asked the secretary if Jane Doe was still in cubicle 6, which meant that she was still alive. She repeated the same call every four hours that entire day, hardly aware she was holding her breath until she heard the reaffirming answer followed by her own relief.

· 4 ·
raney

From underneath the barn floor, Raney listened to Bo hollering for the dogs, listened to his low grunt as he heaved the stick for them again, the pause of its silent sail through the air, and then the thud of wood against packed earth. She held the trapdoor of the bunker cracked only a few inches open; dust and bits of hay picked up slits of daylight coming through the old walls and chinks in the roof. She heard Bo's footsteps change pace, circle back around, closer, and she let the hatch down with a soft thump. A few minutes later she heard his voice calling for her, echoing through the metal air shaft hidden behind a mock orange planted just for that purpose. Then he was inside the barn, though judging by the rising pitch of his voice and the pace of his Converse sneakers crisscrossing the floor, Bo didn't start to panic until he'd checked every corner and the hayloft to boot. Even then she waited until his steps came to a halt nearly over her head. When it got so still she wondered if he might be crying, Raney threw the hidden hatch open and popped out of the ground like a ghost springing from the grave. Bo dropped to his knees with his arms across his stomach. Raney would have climbed out to comfort him if she hadn't been laughing so hard.

"You going to puke?" she asked.

"No," he said, wiping his eyes and mouth. "But if I were I'd make sure to hit you in the face."

"Come inside. Watch the ladder—there's a weak step on the third rung." She sat on one of the two cots, watched Bo's feet feel for the steps until he was on the ground letting his eyes adjust to the low light.

"What is this? Your playhouse?" His voice was still shaky, but he had his thumbs crooked in his pockets like he was totally cool.

Raney let out a laugh, not that it was a ridiculous question. It was a house, of sorts. "It's a bunker. My grandpa built it." She turned on a lantern and settled back on the cot.

Bo walked deeper into the room and let himself down on the other cot, their knees close enough to tangle. "What's he use it for?"

"Survival. It's like a bomb shelter. Where you go if there's a war or something."

Small as it was, Grandpa kept this room meticulously organized. All four walls were lined with plank shelves that held stacks of alphabetically arranged cans: artichoke hearts and asparagus and beets and Boston baked beans and carrots. Hundreds of them. Raney had argued that it made no sense to stick to the alphabet, as when you are hungry you think with your stomach: meat first, then vegetables, and eventually Hostess Ding Dongs for dessert. But Grandpa took so much pride in his system she let it be.

Under each cot were tanks of water and oil and gasoline and kerosene, and under the shelves were packages of batteries and a gas stove, a sun shower and more water; plastic bins with blankets and tarps, a big metal can filled with packs of Burpee seeds and a sealed metal box of medicines—aspirin and Tylenol and Imodium and Pepto-Bismol, iodine tablets and alcohol and bandages and even some skin suture and needles he'd pinched from the Jefferson General emergency room once. He had hooks screwed into the wall holding ropes and hoses and an axe and maul and a shovel and trowel, various-sized lanterns and a fire extinguisher and a hunting rifle with shells in a waterproof case and several skinning knives. There was one shelf of books: a *History of War*, *Wilderness First Aid*, three Reader's Digest Condensed Books, and a complete volume of Shakespeare's plays. One copy each of the Bible and the Qur'an, and *The Tibetan Book of the Dead*, *The Communist Manifesto*, and a partial set of *The World Book Encyclopedia* he'd picked up at a garage sale. Also *Gone with the Wind* (which Raney had requested) and a spiral-bound *Boy Scout Campfire Cookery*. There was an unframed photograph of Raney's grandmother, Joy, tacked to the wall and beginning to curl at the edges. For the first time Raney was struck by her grandmother's awkwardly wide mouth and thick eyebrows and saw more of her own face there than her mother's. And just today, waiting for Bo to panic, she had discovered two new additions to the bunker: a Costco-sized carton of Kotex and a shallow Rubbermaid container Grandpa had filled with tubes of paint and various brushes and a few prestretched canvases. Genuine oil paints, with names like magenta and titanium, intended for canvas instead of a sheet of drywall. Raney had stroked the smooth paint tubes like they were bolts of fine silk. She wondered if he was hiding them here for her birthday or if he was thinking the end was coming sooner than expected.

Bo looked like he'd fallen down the rabbit hole. "Jeez, you could live in here."

"That's the point."

He leaned close to inspect the photo of Raney's grandmother. He stood up and touched the hunting rifle and knives, picked up a shortwave radio from the shelf. "So how does your granddad say the world is going to end?"

"Depends on his mood. There's that AIDS disease. He says that could be like the bubonic plague. The USSR might blow us up—they have missiles pointed right at the navy base over in Bremerton, you know."

"My dad says the Soviet Union is broke. He says it's going to fall apart 'cause of Afghanistan."

"What does your dad do that makes him so smart?"

"He buys and sells corn and stuff. Commodities."

"Corn. Your dad sells corn. In Seattle."

"Well, at least I've got a dad. He's rich too." Raney's face went stony, not believing he would put that shit on her. Bo turned all shades of pink. He took his hand out of his pocket like he might touch her, but she pulled back. "I shouldn't have said that. I'm sorry."

She shrugged, but wished now that she'd left him out in the yard still searching for her. She stood on the cot and pulled an oblong box off the shelf. It was filled with cartons of Marlboros. She took out a pack and tamped it firm against the heel of her hand like she did it all the time, unzipped the gold plastic string from the clear wrapper, and shook one cigarette out. "Go on. Take it." He looked at it like she was passing him a rattlesnake. "Can't bite you."

"Your granddad would kill me."

"He won't know. I'll just rearrange the packs so you can't tell one's gone." Bo slowly pulled the cigarette out of the red-and-white box and held it between his thumb and first finger, turning it this way and that. Raney took a lighter off the shelf and clicked it into a blue flame; the sharp scent of butane made her feel grown-up and brave. "Go on. I do it all the time." Bo put the filter in his mouth, and she touched the flame to the tobacco. Nothing happened. "You pull the smoke *into* your mouth, stupid. Breathe *in*, not out."

"I know. Just give me a minute." She clicked the lighter again, and Bo siphoned enough air through the cigarette for the paper to catch. Not two seconds later the hatch right over their heads opened up and Grandpa jumped down the ladder in three steps.

Raney had never seen him so mad. The truth, really, was that she hadn't much seen him mad at all. As gruff as he was with everyone else, he had never been harsh to her. Later she decided it must have been some protective instinct coming out in him, no different from Gif's growling at Bo. Bo ducked like he thought Grandpa might hit him, but Grandpa just stood there, a look of fuming fury on his face. The small room was getting hazy from smoke; Bo was holding the cigarette in front of him like a holy candle. For a minute Raney wondered if he was going to offer it to her grandfather. Finally she hissed, "Put it out, Bo."

Grandpa boomed, "You'll not waste a perfectly good cigarette on my property. Smoke it. Right here." Bo looked at Raney, like she would overrule her own grandfather. Grandpa took the cigarette out of Bo's hands and put it to his mouth. "I told you to smoke it."

So Bo took a puff, inhaling this time. He started to cough immediately, but Grandpa didn't budge. Nobody was leaving that room until the cigarette was gone. Tears were running down Bo's face and he coughed so hard he doubled over. After five puffs he bolted past Grandpa up the ladder and out the barn door and Raney heard him retching in the grass.

"I started it, Grandpa," she said.

"And he obviously didn't turn you down." He followed Bo up the steps and waited for him to stop vomiting. Bo wiped his mouth and backed away. "Oh, come on," Grandpa jeered, rolling his sleeves up his arms. "You're enough of a man to smoke. Break into my things. What else are you good at? Think you're strong?"

Bo looked half-scared, half-bewildered and fully hoping a second hole in the ground might open up for his escape. "I don't want to fight you, Mr. Remington."

"Hell, I'm not gonna fight you." He looked Bo up and down and then pointed down the hill toward the highway. "It's a half mile to that road. Half mile down and half mile back up. Tie your shoes first, pup."

Bo shot Raney a desperate look. She raised her eyebrows and mouthed, Just do it!

"That's right, kid," Grandpa said. "You're strong enough to beat the old man. You get a ten-count head start."

Bo pinched his mouth shut and then he took off. Raney couldn't tell if he was running to race or running to get away. Grandpa counted to ten with his hands proud on his hips, and then he shot off too. He caught up with Bo halfway down the hill and from up at the barn Raney heard him whoop. They kicked a cloud of dust between them that almost blocked her view. When they reached the mailbox at the highway she could tell Bo had taken up the challenge and was digging in; he slapped the square wooden post and skidded on the gravel in a tight circle. Grandpa was so close they looked like a single four-legged creature before Bo pulled away. He started back up the hill just as fast as he'd gone down. They were both calling out now, Bo with a victorious yelp and, Raney swore, she heard her grandfather let out a laugh. She started running down the hill toward them, saw Bo grow larger and closer and Grandpa slip farther back and then they both disappeared just below the short, steep rise at the last bend. When she saw them again, Bo was in full stride, pumping fast and smiling wide. But Grandpa was doubled over at a standstill.

Bo saw Raney's face change as she passed him. He spun around and sprinted back to reach Grandpa first. As bad as Bo had looked after choking on that cigarette, Raney's grandfather looked worse. He bent over his knees with a low moan, his eyes squeezed shut in a grimace and his breath coming coarse and quick. Raney knelt in the gravel beside him. "Grandpa," she said, then repeated with a cry of panic, "Grandpa!"

He shook his head once and then again. He put a hand on Raney's shoulder and slowly straightened his knees and then his back until he was upright. His face was the color of ash, stubble bristled over his chin. Had it always been so gray? He was sixty-one, but he looked old to her that day. Old for the first time. It took a while for color to return to his face.

Bo was as quiet as death through all of it. Finally he asked, "Are you all right, sir?"

Grandpa took a deep, clearing breath and pulled up so his greater height cast a shadow over Bo. He waved him away. "Go on. Both of you, go on. You're too scrawny to take advantage of her anyway."

Raney's grandfather started preparing for the end of the world the spring her mother, Celine, disappeared. Raney remembered climbing onto the kitchen counter so she could see the barn doorway through

the window, watching him drive a shovel into the still winter-
hardened ground, stamping his boot down onto the flange like he was
crushing evil itself. For days he clove and heaved pile after pile of soil
out of the earth. She remembered her grandmother washing dishes
at the sink with her mouth pressed into a hard white line, offering
Raney no explanation. And as young as Raney was, she understood
that he didn't need a reason to dig. He just needed a place to spew his
fury and a hole in the ground was as good as anything else. After all,
there's no bottom to it until you decide you are done. She didn't feel
rage herself. Later, much later, she knew that degree of anger was too
big for a four-year-old child. All she felt was a brand-new emptiness,
deep as that hole under the barn.

He pretty much quit going to work in the machine shop, maybe
so that if Celine came back he would be there to catch and hold her.
And she did come back once, a few months after Raney's grandmother passed. She came and went again so quick and quiet he
would never have known she'd been there but for the fact that this
time she took Raney with her. The summer after Raney's sixth birthday she woke up in the middle of the night and there stood Celine,
all the blowsy blond flesh of her Raney knew from the photo she kept
tucked inside a *National Geographic* magazine. She had wrapped the
picture in a foldout map of Africa, possibly by chance or possibly
because her mother was as exotic and foreign to Raney as that wild
continent with its bare-breasted, dancing natives.

Celine had already put Raney's clothes into a grocery bag. She
scooped her baby into her arms like they'd kissed good night just a
few hours ago, Raney still in half a dream. The dream and the real
never did fully sort out—what memories of that summer were true
and what were the longing of her motherless childhood. Even years
later she would recall the noise and color and smell of events that
couldn't have happened: a parking-lot carnival with every ride lit up
and spinning, arcade games whirring and gonging, but Celine and
Raney are the only two people there; Raney rides the Octopus standing on the seat with her arms extended wide to the wheeling sky

while Celine laughs and waves to her from the deserted gate in a deserted asphalt lot. A day later, or maybe a month, Raney sits between her mother's bare, tanned knees and pushes down the accelerator of a convertible sports car, trying to catch shimmering black pools on a hot desert road before they evaporate. That night, or a month before, or a week later, in a windowless room where it is always night, a man places a wrapped package in her lap and inside is a blue dress with a stiff petticoat—she will get a pink dress tomorrow if she stays quiet and lets her mother sleep.

Over time she learned a few more facts. Grandpa had come into her room to wake her and found an empty bed, empty closet and drawers. He waited two days to call the police, a delay that was criticized by some, but given that it was the child's own mother doing the taking, even the police were slow to call it kidnapping. And considering Grandpa's view of anything resembling government, Raney never blamed him.

They were gone for nine weeks. They took a bus down through Oregon and across Idaho, and after a stay in Denver they switched to cars driven by a series of men who all had the same unshaven face and ponytail. Then a loop through Kansas and Oklahoma and north Texas until Celine landed in Las Vegas, where they stayed long enough in one motel that it acquired the imprint of a home for Raney—a routine of waking up alone to powdered doughnuts and a carton of milk set out on the desk beside the TV, which was already tuned to the *Sesame Street* channel. The room had a small refrigerator with Oscar Mayer cold cuts and peanut butter and jelly. Their days and nights must have got swapped around, so by the time Raney awoke it was after dark, and by the time she heard a key ratchet into the doorknob, it was nearly dawn. Celine would take Raney down a steep set of concrete stairs where a swing set and a merry-go-round sat in a field with grass so tall she had red whip marks across her bare legs after playing, as if no other child had trampled that ground.

The police never found them—likely handicapped by the nebulous legalities of Raney's ownership. At the end of summer Celine drove her back to Seattle, and they crossed the sound on the ferry, a journey that stayed sharp in Raney's memory because, even at the age of six, she knew it marked her last day with her mother. Her grandfather wasn't home when they arrived. Celine deposited Raney in the kitchen with a bag of dirty clothes and a brand-new Barbie doll, and drove away. For the rest of time Raney would catch a scent of Jean Naté perfume or clove cigarettes, or the mustiness of an old canvas tent, the metallic tang of a Greyhound bus windowsill, and be emptied of gravity and grounding by the rogue wave of an emotion she could not name.

Raney didn't see Bo for three days after the race. She hung around Hardy's Store, reading *Tiger Beat* magazine at the rack near the stairs leading up to the bedrooms. She bought five-penny candies so she could see Mrs. Hardy's face up close, thinking that if her eyes were red it must mean something bad had happened to Bo. It never crossed Raney's mind to just ask outright where he was. And then on the evening of the fourth day she was in her bedroom and heard a whistle, opened the window, and there he was, straddling his bicycle in her backyard.

After thirty seconds pretending she couldn't care less, she went to the back door. "So where the hell were you?"

He squinted down the long drive. "My dad says girls shouldn't cuss."

"Well, I'll remember that next time I want advice from a corn farmer in Seattle. I thought you'd gone home."

"My dad took me camping in the park for the weekend. I didn't know he was coming until he showed up at the store." He looked down the drive again, and Raney realized he was checking for her grandfather's truck.

"What? Did you hide in the bushes till my grandpa drove off this afternoon? He won't be home for a couple of hours." Bo swung his leg over his bike and they started toward the path that led through the woods to the bluff. Once the house was out of sight, he parked his bike against a fir. The path narrowed, so they couldn't walk side by side, and Raney led him down a deer trail that skirted a clear-cut where the fireweed and yarrow grew thick and hummed with bees. She gathered a bouquet of the purple and cream flowers and showed Bo how to choose the ripest, bright-orange huckleberries from the top of the bush, still bittersweet this early in summer. Above the clearing a red-tailed hawk screamed and Bo searched the sky. "I heard a bald eagle," he said.

"You've been watching too many westerns. Eagles sound like this . . ." Raney tried to imitate the high, broken *kre-ee* of an eagle, less imposing than the smaller hawk's cry. "Well, not like that. But not like they sound in the movies." She slapped his arm and he jerked it back. "Mosquito. They're bad this time of night." She pinched a feathery leaf from one of the yarrows still in her hand and rolled it between her fingers, then pressed the crushed greens on his mosquito bite. "I always wonder why so many animals hunt at dusk. Mosquitoes, snakes. Coons. Filling up without a worry in the world they'll be alive and on the go tomorrow."

"That is just the kind of thing you would say, Raney."

"What does that mean?" She let the flowers fall to the ground and started back toward the house.

"But he's okay, isn't he?"

"I was just talking, Bo. You're the one who's making a big thing about it. My grandfather's fine. That was indigestion."

Bo hop-skipped till he caught up with her. "Does your grandfather hate me?"

"As a matter of fact, I asked him that. He said he likes you fine. He just likes me a lot better."

Bo closed his mouth in a tight line and considered. "So I can keep coming around?"

"Yeah. If you can get over being scared of both of us, you can keep comin' around."

For the rest of that summer they lived in the woods and the ravine and the cove, running wild as hares. For Raney it was little in the way of new, but Bo was a prisoner set free, starting that summer off in a tight fist and every day between him and his parents' fights letting a little more light inside. His pale, blue-white skin became blushed in days of sun. Someday, Raney decided, she would invent paints that came with permanent scents: greens that smelled of fish and seaweed; yellows that smelled like lightning strikes and crushed cedar and wet bark stripped from hundred-year-old firs; creams and whites that smelled like sand sifting through your fingers. By the end of that summer Bo's portrait would have smelled like all of those. Even his body changed. His muscles began to fill his lean height, which had seemed like a cumbersome gift he couldn't coordinate.

Bo had a whole list of books he was supposed to read that summer, and when the rain kept them inside he'd pull one out of his pack. They might have been assigned, but Raney could tell he liked reading them. Often she found them left behind in the bathroom or on a kitchen counter, and he made no effort to reclaim them, pointedly leaving *The Catcher in the Rye* a second time and asking if they read "that kind of book" at her school. She was stung at first, but the books collected on her shelves and slowly she began to read them.

Raney's school started before Labor Day, but Bo stayed around another week until his father came to take him to his new boarding school in Connecticut. His last weekend in Quentin was over a full moon, a tide high enough to swell the brackish lagoon near the mouth of the river. At its crest the flood of fresh and salt water in the pool was more than eight feet at the deep spot. Years before, kids now full grown had strung a rope off the angled branches of a big madrone. The bound knot was as thick as a thigh and so weathered it had petrified into a solid mass—impossible to trace one lap of rope around another. No grown-ups ever checked it, but the town was small enough that any broken necks or backs would have been famous, and so the swing was universally accepted as safe. Most things are until a disaster occurs.

In late July, Bo had tried the swing once on Raney's dare, but he'd dropped a single second too late in the arc of fall and his gangly legs had struck hard against the bottom; the shock jerked his breath away and zinged through his spine. Raney had waited for him to inhale, made a shallow dive, and pulled him to the ladder of roots that climbed the steep, muddy bank. After that, somehow the tide was never high enough, or the day warm enough, or the mood right for them to try the swing again. It became an event they both remembered and pretended had never happened, which made it as much a pact of loyalty as slicing their fingers open and touching blood to blood. Maybe it was that bond, or the full moon, or knowing Bo was heading to another world two thousand miles away. Or maybe it was the combined force of all. On his last full day in Quentin, Bo looked at the tidemark on the cliff and said, "The lagoon is right for the rope swing if we go now."

There was a wind driving in from the southwest so strong even the walls of the ravine made no shelter; branches tossed and cracked over their heads. The swing was hitched around a smaller branch as always, a tacit rule of its use. Someone too short or too frustrated by the wind snatching the rope away had added a tether to the end: two feet of braided nylon tied to the knot that served as a handhold. Bo stepped up to go first, as if to prove himself. He didn't look at Raney; he hardly even looked down at the water. He unloosed the rope and pulled it as close as it would come, stretching the line nearly straight. The limb swayed, a band of bark polished to a gleam by a thousand jumpers, the rope nearly grown into the wood. He locked one fist on top of the other, just above the thick swell of the knot. Raney could see dark coiled hair under his arms. She was about to remind him not to make the same mistake again, not to let fear keep him holding on until he passed the moment of safe release, but he was already off—one low grunt as he leaped away from the earth and swung out and down, the weight of him stretching the rope, moving impossibly slow, his knees flexed to his waist until he keened and let go at the perfect, perfect point where physical law carried him just enough forward and then down, down to the deepest point of green-black water. His head disappeared for a moment and then popped up, laughing with the ecstasy of defying death. "All right, little girl," he called out. "Your turn."

Perhaps it was that "little girl" business. Without that, it might have gone differently. Raney might have stuck with the common sense she had always used in these woods and this water, and considered how this rope was changed by the nylon tether. The wind was channeling down the ravine in great bursts strong enough to knock her off balance, and the rope kept trying to lurch away, so she had to hold it by the added tail. She stepped onto the highest root and stretched for the knot, waited for a calm in the wind. Bo squatted on the opposite bank tossing pebbles at the base of the tree crooning her name in a catcall. She could hear the next roar of wind coming, a great whipping in the green crown above and the litter of leaves and small branches rattling toward her along the water, moving so fast the temperature dropped and she began to shiver. She kept one arm locked around the tree until the last second, blocking out Bo's teasing jeer, and then, finally, shoved off in sheer defiance, defying the storm and Bo and the voice telling her this was *not* the perfect, safe moment. She was *not* ready.

The instant of free fall before the rope stretched taut was usually the best—exhilarating and terrifying and dangerously reckless. That few seconds of time stretched into a crystal-clear memory you could use to mark that day in that summer in your life, distinct from all the billions of pointless seconds that blurred into background. But this time Raney began her fall at the instant the wind hit, stinging and wild, pelting her with sticks and leaves so she fumbled and took off spinning. The hard braid of the nylon tether whipped around her arm and doubled over itself and now, *now* was the instant she had to let go or miss the deep pool. She couldn't see Bo, couldn't see the water, but she knew the arc and stretch and plunge so well she let go by instinct, not connected to the part of her brain that sensed the nylon rope coiling around her arm like a venomous snake. Her body fell, then caught and jerked back toward the tree, locked to the rope by the tether until the weakest link, her skin, broke free.

She heard Bo scream. She was lying on her back and Bo was over her, screaming her name, open-mouthed and twisted in excruciating pain—it took a full blessed minute to realize it was her own pain. Fire, worse than fire, seared her arm from her elbow to her shoulder. It scorched down her spinal cord and up her neck like hot poison. She couldn't breathe and then she couldn't stop panting, every muscle rigid with pain.

"I'll go get help," Bo said. "Your granddad. Where's your grandfather?"

Raney opened her mouth and heard a sound come out that wasn't words at all. It sounded like an animal. Bo started to cry. He wadded his T-shirt under her head and stood up.

"No! Don't leave me here." He knelt down again, and for the first time Raney looked at her arm, a bracelet of oozing raw flesh wound in three crossing rings. She remembered a hunting trip with her grandfather, a .22 propped in a notch tracking a raccoon waddling up the riverbank like a broken-hipped cat, Grandpa leaning over her shoulder whispering, "Wait, wait . . . Okay. Now!" Seeing the coon turn a somersault from a standstill and not believing she'd done it. Grandpa had skinned it while she watched, showing her how to work the point of a knife through the fur and in between the skin and muscle to the clean plane of fat and sinew, then use bare hands to slip the sheath of fur and flesh off like a glove. That was how her arm looked.

She grabbed on to Bo's leg. "Don't go. Don't tell him. It won't kill me, not if I don't let it get infected."

"You have to tell him. You need to go to a doctor."

"Just stay here with me." After a while Raney stopped shivering and sat up, holding her arm away from her body so nothing could touch the raw stripes. "What's a doctor going to do? Put Neosporin and a clean bandage on it. Help me up. He's away from the house till at least nine. There's a whole emergency room of supplies in the bunker. He won't notice. Not if I'm careful."

Raney pretended to be asleep when Grandpa came home. Overnight the weather shifted to the west, and then the northwest, and by morning the peninsula was cloaked in a cold rain so she could wear a loose sweater over her bandages. No one seemed to notice that she was suddenly more left-handed than right. By the time Bo was in Connecticut and settled into his new school, the wound had closed, leaving a bright-pink bracelet of scar, and Raney was sure her face had been forgotten behind the rich, pretty girls who went to a school like that.

One morning in early November she came down to breakfast and found the Rubbermaid box of paints and canvases she'd seen in the bunker that day with Bo. She sat down and ate her cereal, got up and washed the dishes, left the house for the school bus, and then turned around and walked back up the driveway to the kitchen door. "Why did you get me that?"

"It's been a while since I've seen you paint. Thought maybe you were out of supplies."

Raney opened the wooden box and ran her fingers across the row of untouched tin tubes. She didn't know if she would have the heart to mar them with dents and smears, almost better to hold them, perfect, for some day when she was ready and deserving. After a long minute Grandpa said, "I met Joy, Grandmama, when she was fifteen. I never told you that, did I?"

"No. She probably did. Fifteen seemed like a long time away to me back then." She looked at him. "Why are you telling me this now?"

He shrugged. "I'm sorry you don't have a woman to raise you."

"I like it the way it is. Us." He didn't answer. It was what it was with no changing it, after all. She could tell he believed her, despite the look of regret on his face that she couldn't explain. She never told Grandpa about the swing; it made her happy to believe she'd spared him any additional worry. It would be another decade before she understood that the bliss and curse of adolescence is the capacity to lie better to yourself than to anyone else, especially your own folks.

· 5 ·
charlotte

Charlotte got to the hospital early the next morning. Felipe Otero had kept Jane stable over the day, and Helen Wong, a new doctor hired just out of fellowship, had managed the patient fairly well until about 3:00 a.m., when Jane's vital signs had deteriorated again. Charlotte looked at the crossing numbers on Jane's flowchart—the Neosynephrine dose going up and her blood pressure declining—and knew she was in for a rocky day again. It was like the child who plays happily at nursery school all day until she senses her mother's approach and begins to wail, but as soon as Charlotte registered that thought, she consciously stepped back from the attachment. She'd been in this job long enough to know it did no one any good—not the family, not the patient, and certainly not herself.

Anne was on duty again—that was a relief. She saw Charlotte recreating the night from the numbers on the chart and said, "Not out of the woods. Lower the dose and she tanks. BUN and creatinine are going up."

"No surprise. We're saving her heart and brain at the expense of her kidneys." Even as Charlotte said this, she looked at Jane, who lay

45

as inanimate as the day before, and knew they were possibly not saving her brain at all. She pulled the sheet down and rubbed her knuckles hard against Jane's sternum.

"Anything?" Anne asked.

"Barely. Could be the high BUN, though." Charlotte wouldn't
consider a diagnosis of brain death until Jane's lab values were nor-
malized. She read Otero's notes and Wong's notes, ticking off what
test results to check and what tests were still to go. Then she read the
nursing notes—brief, often rote phrases that filled in the continuum
of hours between physicians' assessments. Over the years Charlotte
had discovered how much they added to her general sense of her patients' progress, comments ranging from when they were bathed or
how they responded to physical therapy, to what visitor had evoked
some response no white coat ever witnessed. One note in particular
stood out to her this morning. "Who's Blake Simpson?" she asked
Anne.

Anne flipped to the back of Jane's chart and pulled out a card.
"Police? He left this with Jody, the night nurse."

Charlotte picked up the business card. "Jefferson County. Have
they identified her?"

"Jody would have told me. If they told her. Call him."

"After rounds I will. Has Orthopedics been by yet?" She went
over her list of consults and orders with Anne, gearing up for the
day. Her mission for this next phase of Jane Doe's care would be
to identify problems that could be solved. It sounded straightfor-
ward on the surface—what else would a doctor be doing? But the
truth about her job was that much of medicine was still a mystery
and a patient with multiple failing organs could overwhelm one's
capacity to be decisive and effective; it was easier to measure what
was wrong—lungs that couldn't suck enough oxygen out of the
air, kidneys that couldn't balance the blood—than to specify the
cause. And even when the cause was obvious, there was often no
obvious cure. So in the tangle of abnormal labs and scans and tests
Charlotte found clarity in deciding what she was capable of fixing

and going after it "with the fangs of a bulldog," as Otero would say. Charlotte would say that she hoped he was referring to her medical acumen and not her body type, and she herself saw it as a way of buying time. Fix the problems you can fix, do your best not to cause any new problems, and buy time for the brain and body to heal themselves. Then Otero would usually try to begin a conversation about God and fate and Charlotte would spew that God better damn well wait in line for her patients, which Otero seemed to find the best joke of the day, no matter how often he heard it.

A little after nine she called the number on Blake Simpson's card. A woman answered, "Sheriff's office." But when Charlotte asked for Sheriff Blake Simpson there was a pause and the woman asked, "You mean Deputy Simpson? Out in the field. Would you like his cell number?"

Charlotte looked at the card again. "Yes. Sorry. Deputy Simpson," but in the pause that followed, Helen Seras walked into Jane's room accompanied by a photographer and a journalist from the *Seattle Times*. Helen lifted her eyebrows enough to signal that she was all PR mode now, so Charlotte took the number and hung up the phone.

"A moment?" Helen asked, though it was more a statement than a question. "They're running an article about our Jane Doe."

For the next twenty minutes Charlotte fielded questions for which she had few answers—at least not any answers that made the reporters go away. She vacillated between hoping publicity might find out who belonged to Jane (or vice versa), and suspecting these people were niggling her only for some lurid headline to sell more papers. When the photographer focused his camera on Jane, Charlotte grabbed at his arm, startling both of them, and he hesitated, embarrassed, until Charlotte raised her eyebrows and held her hands up in a plea for respect. She whispered, "She's here, you know"—she nodded her head at Jane—"in this room with us."

"So . . . you'd like her to sign a waiver?" the photographer asked, only half sarcastically.

Helen stepped in and said, "They have my permission, Dr. Reese. Drop by my office when you have a minute?"

When she had a minute she certainly would, Charlotte thought. Fortunately, she knew her day would be packed.

The plan was for Charlotte to meet Eric at Flying Fish at seven. He had long ago learned to bring a newspaper or even his laptop with him; he didn't want to add up all the hours he'd spent sitting at the bar with a beer and shooters while Charlotte finished rounds at the hospital. He had learned to make the waiting an exercise in mindfulness—a pocket of uncommitted time to read, to watch the crowd. To be present. It didn't always work—tonight being a case in point. He took a seat at the end of the bar and ordered a beer, but before the bartender turned away, Eric changed it to a manhattan. He skimmed the first few pages of the *Seattle Times*, but his own writing was too much on his mind and every headline seemed either connected or contradictory to his research. Twice he stopped to send an e-mail to himself with a note about the manuscript. The topic of this, Eric's fourth book, was organ donation and transplantation and he'd believed, or fooled himself into believing, that if he mapped out the structure well enough in advance, it should practically write itself. But every time he thought he had broken the damn thing's back, it got away from him again. It had started much like his other books and articles, as an engaging, narrative explanation of a scientific subject for a lay audience, filled with plenty of personal stories so readers could forget they were being educated while they immersed themselves in someone else's drama, sending up thanks to God their own life might be bad but it would unlikely ever be *that* bad. The deeper he explored this current topic, though, the more he became both fascinated and alarmed by the tangled and potentially malicious influences of money over medical ethics and law. He had finally retitled the book *Buy This Body: The Billion-Dollar Business of International Organ Donation*. His publisher loved it. But while Eric was an increasingly lauded travel and science writer, he was jittery about venturing closer to political journalism and understood this book could change the course of his career—not for the better if he blew it—and the sheer awareness of consequence undercut his focus.

The restaurant was filling up, and he remembered it was Friday and that people, who worked in offices with cubicles and managers, who could take Saturday off because someone told them to stay home and weed their gardens or coach their kid's T-ball games—these people knew work as a thing that could be separated from other parts of their life. The work of a writer was too portable sometimes, giving him the freedom to work anywhere anytime, and the attendant curse of never really being free at all. He was always working on the book in some corner of his mind. On that score he envied Charlotte, who kept her pager on but could at least physically walk away from her patients.

At eight twenty he pulled out his cell phone to call her, but at nearly the same moment she put her arms around his shoulders and said, "We have a table," and his book and his looming deadline were temporarily forgotten when he pulled her arms tighter, letting himself remember her face before he turned to look at her.

The place was crowded now. By the time they sat down, the heat of so many bodies had penetrated his light wool jacket, her raincoat. Charlotte pulled off the gloves she wore until Seattle's summer fully arrived in July; her hands were small, perhaps her only delicate physical trait, and perpetually cold. She laid the gloves in the middle of the table and Eric idly picked one up—black leather, lined with fine white rabbit fur. She had been wearing them, or some like them, on their second chance meeting at a friend of a friend's birthday party. She had dropped one and he'd picked it up, mindlessly brushing the downy fur inside the cuff across his lip, and been almost startled by the intimate smell of her perfume. He still remembered feeling a rush of embarrassment as if some private part of Charlotte had been exposed to him. The next day he had detoured through the cosmetics area at Nordstrom pretending he was buying perfume for a girlfriend, disturbed that the confusion of samples left him unable to remember Charlotte's exact scent, which had stayed so pure in his mind all night.

The restaurant was lit with sconces and a few chandeliers that gave off a soft yellow light. Charlotte studied the menu. "I want a beer," she said declaratively.

"You never drink beer."

"I know. Advise me."

"Hefeweizen. Try the Blue Moon."

She scanned the menu for no more than a minute. "Let's split. Whatever you want. Lily Allen is coming to the Paramount next month. Should I get tickets?"

"Sure," he answered. He ordered crab cakes and slaw, caught Charlotte's brow furrowing, and asked if she wanted something else.

"What?"

"You're frowning. No crab?"

"I wasn't listening. Crab is fine. But honestly I'd rather have a bacon cheeseburger. How's the book coming?"

He shrugged, reluctant to detail how stymied he felt in this final draft, especially when she seemed so distracted. "Stalled."

"Still worried about controversy? What's the worst that could happen?" she asked.

"The Chinese mafia could gun me down on the streets of Seattle. That sort of thing."

Charlotte looked up, fully focused on the conversation now. "Seriously?"

Eric was tempted to say yes, just to hold her attention. More and more lately it seemed like her mind was elsewhere. Her patients absorbed her, he knew, particularly when she had one in limbo, not clearly going to survive but not clearly hopeless—and Charlotte was always the last to abandon hope. Plus, her parents had announced they were moving out of the house where Charlotte was raised, which had stirred up a bit of turbulence in her whole family. Sometimes, though, he suspected it was the two of them, their own relationship, that had begun to turn, but every time he thought of some way to flat-out ask her, he wondered if the question alone could derail them. Were they that fragile? "No. They'll probably just throw me into a cell in Mongolia for a few decades. You seem tired. Your new patient doing better?"

"She has a lot of worse to go before we hit better. If we ever hit better. The *Times* was there today."

"So that was her? Hard to believe anyone will recognize her photo, though."

"It's already in the paper?"

Eric pulled the creased newspaper out of his laptop bag and put it on top of Charlotte's empty salad plate. The photograph of Jane staring up at her was worse than the sketch she'd seen the day before. The sketch, oddly, had looked more alive, given that the artist had presumed what Jane might look like without an endotracheal tube. In this grainy portrait Jane's puffy eyes were glazed with lubricant, her bruised and swollen mouth distorted by bands of tape and gauze anchoring the plastic tube that connected her to the ventilator. She looked quite dead, really. Like one of those Victorian memento mori photographs of dead people.

Eric saw the look on Charlotte's face and took the paper back, reading the article below the headline closely for the first time. "You're in here! They quote you."

"Not all of it, I'm sure."

"'Doing everything possible . . . Hope to find her family . . . Time is her best hope.' Jeez, Charlotte. Come to me for copy next time."

She had to laugh. "What could I do? Helen Seras was ready to take my badge and escort me to the street if I didn't behave."

"But you *will* do everything possible. She's lucky she landed at Beacon. Will she make it?" he asked, lowering his voice.

Charlotte shrugged, somber again. "Miracles happen."

"Do they?" Eric lifted his eyebrows and the light caught a look of innocence in him that belied the gray at his temples. In that moment, in that half light, Charlotte remembered the face she had fallen for, when she had first allowed herself to believe they could build a reliable world together. Would that take a miracle too? she wondered.

"Sure," she answered. "Well, no. But if we hook all our machines up to her we might salvage enough of her brain to tell us who's looking for her. Or who ran her over." She thought of the message she'd left for Deputy Simpson and was tempted to check her cell phone for any missed call. Suddenly none of it seemed even mildly humorous—her distress over the photograph and her quotes, her frustration with Helen Seras. She was worried that she would lose this woman, that it might take an actual miracle to save her and she herself was not miraculous. All of it tumbled into a sad, overwhelming fatigue. "You know what? Let's take dinner to go."

"Leave? Now?"

"I'd rather eat in the bathtub."

Charlotte first met Eric at the publication of his second book, which might as well have been his first, as his *actual* first book went out of print not too many years after its release. This second book was a narrative nonfiction that followed three couples through in vitro fertilization. It did reasonably well—won an award from the American Association for the Advancement of Science and garnered a three-line mention in the *New York Review of Books.*

He gave a public reading at the Elliott Bay Book Company. Charlotte saw a mention of it in the *Stranger*, and on a whim, she decided to go. Unfortunately, the reading coincided with a Mariners home game. Every parking place near Pioneer Square was taken; the lots were charging triple. She ended up parking four blocks north of the ferry and getting to the store twenty minutes late, embarrassed about interrupting the author and his audience in the middle of the talk. The bigger embarrassment, though, was that she was one of only five who'd shown up at all, two of whom appeared to be local homeless taking shelter from the drizzly weather. She considered pretending she'd walked into the wrong room, leaving before she was noticed, but he nodded and beckoned her in and she was stuck. She could have guessed, though she didn't know until later, that it was his first public appearance. He read from three long passages in a nervous voice, losing his place twice. Halfway through the third selection one person walked out; Charlotte found her mind drifting to the episode of *The West Wing* that she was missing. And his book didn't even cover artificial insemination. She slipped out the door the second he asked if there were any questions.

The ball game must have let out—the streets were crowded with big-bellied men waving enormous, inflatable hands and overwrought children smeared with mustard and tears. The light changed against her before she could cross, and the swell of bodies and the smell of beer felt intolerable. She looked at her watch, impatient to get back to her car.

Suddenly the crowd took in a simultaneous gasp and then fell silent. There was movement, commotion, a flux of people to the right and back to the left, shifting quick and coordinated as a flock of starlings united in panic. A few solitary voices called for help and the crowd parted like cornstalks falling under a mower blade just before something heavy hit the ground. At the curb, half-sprawled in the muddy gutter, Charlotte saw a big dark slab of a man seizing with arched back and rigid limbs, his supersized plastic Mariners cup rattling against the curb with each rhythmic jerk of his arm.

Charlotte's purse and jacket were down and she was on the pavement between the moving traffic and the man's head, anchoring her small hands on either side of his meaty cheeks to protect them from the cement. A woman called out, "Put something in his mouth." Charlotte looked at her and said, "I'm a doctor. Don't put anything in his mouth. Call 911." She looked for the nearest sober, calm adult and told him to find a cop and get the street blocked off. She checked the man's wrists and neck for a MedicAlert, then she scanned the faces and called out in a voice twice as loud as her own, "Does anyone know this man?"

It ended nearly as quickly as it began. His seizure stopped. Charlotte lifted his jaw to open his airway and leaned over his face to make sure he was breathing. Slowly his body relaxed as if he had been in nothing more than an oddly timed deep nap. When his eyes fluttered open, she put her mouth near his ear and spoke low and soothing, "You're okay. I'm right here with you. We're going to get you to a hospital and everything will be okay."

After the ambulance left she looked down at the front of her dress—splattered with greasy mud and saliva. Her purse and coat were no longer on the curb where she thought she'd dropped them. She brushed her hair out of her face with the backs of her filthy hands, suddenly exhausted and in no mood to deal with her stolen cards and keys and money. And then a man walked toward her from the perimeter of the dispersing crowd, holding her purse and coat in his arms. It was the man who'd given the reading—was it hours ago? The author. It was Eric Bryson.

He asked her if she was all right, which struck her as funny given that she was not the patient. She saw him blush, catching his mistake in her eyes. He asked her if she was a doctor, then immediately added, "Of course you must be," and said he'd interviewed a lot of doctors for his book. Had she gotten much out of his talk? All the while he held on to her coat and purse as if unaware they were keeping her hostage there. When she finally reached for them, he invited her for a drink. Charlotte looked down at the front of her dress and lifted her shoulders as if the answer were obvious. Standing this close she was struck by the contrast between his dark hair, his thick dark eyebrows, and his eyes, which were a comforting gray-blue that reminded her of the sea glass she and her brother had collected on family vacations to the Oregon coast or Ocean Shores.

The weather had begun to clear and the breaking clouds were slashed by a pale twilight sky. They began walking up Alaska in the direction of her car, but then they were turning up Marion, and then at the door to the Metropolitan Restaurant before she thought to question who was following and who was leading and whether she cared. She wiped the front of her dress with a wet paper towel in the women's room and buttoned her coat over it, realized upon looking in the mirror that her mascara had wept black streaks over her cheeks.

They split an antipasto plate and a bottle of Zinfandel, and Charlotte noticed how long and slender his fingers were, the hands of a pianist or painter, like they were intended to have a purpose all their own. Designed, perhaps, for when the job of writing involved a quill rather than a keyboard. She told him a little about her job at Beacon, her house, which she had just bought and was trying to remodel herself after a mishmash job by prior owners. She told him about growing up in Seattle in a family of doctors (her mother a pathologist, her father a surgeon) and how sometimes she wondered if she'd ever given any other occupation a chance. Her brother, Will, had proposed to his wife in college on the condition that she, too, go to medical school, declaring it the only way to stomach the average, gory, Reese-family-dinner conversation. They were both pediatricians now.

Charlotte did not tell Eric about Ricky, the boyfriend she had just broken up with, or the fact that one month earlier she and her sister-in-law, Pamela, had lit a match to Ricky's last and best present to Charlotte, a ticket to Belize, where Ricky was now staying in an oceanfront cottage with the girlfriend he'd originally left for Charlotte. All the better—Charlotte burned under tropical sun and hated how she looked in a bathing suit. She did, however, remind herself that she had sworn on the flames of that ticket that she had nothing more in her to give to a man, romantically at least, and at thirty-five planned to take her life forward alone. But even at the height of her anger she admitted that she hated Ricky more for the years she'd given up to him than for his deceit; she probably wouldn't have dated him at age twenty-two, twenty-four, twenty-eight. So it was herself she should be angry at, right? Regardless, it was only herself she could change.

By the time they finished two tiramisus she knew a lot less about Eric than he knew about her. He'd been a mediocre student but a passionate reader. After college he'd taken a job writing for an airline throwaway, churning out articles about beaches in the airline's small market, tips for getting through TSA, which terminals had the best burgers. Two years into it he put on a backpack, cashed in all of his accumulated frequent-flier miles, and got hooked on traveling for a while. He'd done pretty well as a travel writer for a few more years and then the Human Genome Project took off. One night he drank too much tequila and wrote an editorial for the *New York Times* about the risks of knowing your own genetic code, the impossible-to-answer question of whether a deadly diagnosis would change how you live. His tequila-enhanced spin caught the eye of an editor at *Nature* who commissioned an article, which got noticed by a publisher who bought Eric's first book. There was a hesitancy about the way he told Charlotte that story, a reluctance to answer her questions about what had sparked his passions, for travel or science or, in fact, for writing at all. It was a modesty she found comforting and trustworthy, but then she reminded herself that it was natural to look for those traits after dealing with Ricky's ego for more than a year, so she switched to less probing topics. Thus, it was no accident that Charlotte left the restaurant without a complete picture of Eric. But when she woke up the next morning her first thought was about a comment he'd made. He wanted to be a science writer, he'd said, because he'd lost faith in the public's ability to objectively weigh data: too much zealous opinion, too much TV, too much unquestioned religion, too few questioning minds. It could have sounded bitter, but Eric relayed it like a parent gently tsk-tsking a lazy child, like such delinquency only made his job more critical.

After they'd eaten he'd walked her back down to her aging Saab. "Haven't seen one of these in a while," he said.

"Yeah. It runs. When it's not in the shop. I should ditch it, but I'm attached."

She unlocked her car and stood with one foot inside so the door was between them. Still, he stood close enough that she could smell the soap from his white shirt, could see the shadowed notch of his collarbone above his loosened tie. His eyes moved over her face, lingering on her mouth. "You were good with that man tonight. Kind," he said.

"Thanks. And your reading was good. I'm glad I came."

"My reading sucked. But I'm glad you came too. Got you and two homeless people out of the rain."

Charlotte laughed and started to close her car door. Eric held his hand against it and leaned in. "Why did you come, by the way?" She smiled and shrugged her shoulders. She didn't tell him it was because she had decided that if she was still single on her thirty-eighth birthday, she would consider artificial insemination and raising a child on her own.

· 6 ·
raney

Raney didn't hear a word from Bo from September to July. By December she had quit checking the mailbox. By March she decided she didn't care. By April she convinced herself he'd gone all preppy and would be no fun even if he did come back to Quentin. But by June she was taking the long way home from school every day on foot, just so she could pass Hardy's Store. When she chanced upon him sitting on his aunt's front porch in early July she could see straightaway that she'd been partly right—he was paler and more awkward than in her angriest memory. His arms and legs seemed to have grown six inches but forgotten to notify his brain. She gave him a look intended to show she was trying to recall his name, and when he said, "Hey, Raney," his voice broke high and then dropped onto a low note she would never have recognized.

"Hey yourself."

"Friendly as ever, aren't you?"

"I'm friendly enough. To people that act like a friend. How's *New York*?" She drew the words out in a pretentious drawl.

"Connecticut. It's okay. How's *Quentin*?"

His own pretentious drawl naming this unpretentious town sent a hot flush from Raney's chest up to her face. "No worse for missing you, if anybody did."

But after the rust was chipped away, they found a friendship intact if more tempestuous for reasons Raney could not discern. The year had changed more than his voice and his height. He wasn't as book-ish anymore, and suddenly she wasn't always the one laying down the dare. A splinter of anger seemed to be lodged inside him, working its way to the surface in the violent rocket of stones he hurled off the bluff, or the heights he was now willing to climb to. Sometimes in the way he looked at her. Some days they were friends like they'd been friends the summer before, moving from one adventure to an-other, one joke to the next, fluid as a river flowing downhill without any inkling of consequence. On those days they were a team—a unit of two kids against the grown-up world. But other times Raney saw something else quiver through Bo, something primitive and scary and repulsively attractive at the same time. She attributed it to his parents' divorce or the headaches he complained about—it would be years before she connected the changes in him to what was changing in her too. It was as if, after fourteen years of knowing exactly who she was, some ancient, alien being seeded inside her had awakened to throw the old Raney out on her ear. It brought out something mean in her. It made her want to hurt him in a way she hadn't since the day she stranded him in the seal pup cave. It made her want to cry, which she had not done in a long time.

August started with a week of hard rain, and the stream at the back of Raney's grandfather's property clogged up behind branches and brush until the shallow duck pool became a full-blown pond, thick and olive green. She woke up to Grandpa's cursing in the yard and pushed aside her curtains to see him standing beside a shovel planted in the mud with his hands on his hips, his cap thrown to the ground. Never a good sign. She slid the window open and called out to him but slammed it shut at the first breeze, nearly doubled over with the smell.

A six-point buck had got wedged into the driftwood dam. Grandpa said he probably died days ago, his bloated body drifted downstream by the rain. Raney's idea was to chop up the dam and let him drift down to the neighbor's farm, but Grandpa was already going to the barn to get a pruning saw and rubber gloves. She stood near the back door in her nightgown, bare feet turning blue in the dewy grass. "Get your clothes on," he told her.

She started to ask him what he was expecting her to do, but decided cutting up a decaying deer might be a lesser evil than his mood. At the water's edge the smell was so foul she had to drop her head between her knees. She ran back to the house and found a bottle of her grandmother's Youth-Dew and some handkerchiefs to tie around their faces. Grandpa worked for over an hour getting the legs off so the deer could be rolled up inside a plastic tarp. He wore thigh-high green waders to work a rope under the belly, crimson blood coiled through the nacreous water, and the rising heat of the day brought out swarms of iridescent flies. Even such gore has its own kind of beauty.

Once the deer was trussed up in the tarp, Grandpa said he needed Raney's help to haul it out, but despite their combined weights angling parallel to the slope of the bank, they made no progress. Grandpa looked every year of his age, leaning over his knees with that perfumed robber's mask sucking in and out of his mouth, and Raney could not help but think of the day he had raced Bo uphill and met his own match ticking away inside his own chest. Not five minutes later she heard Bo calling to her from the driveway, turned around, and saw him straddling his bicycle. She felt an inexplicable rush of guilt, as if she'd been caught at the scene of a murder. He walked closer until a breath of wind carried the rank miasma of the rotting carcass in his direction and he covered his face with his sleeve. Raney watched him try to puzzle out the mess they were in. "You need help?"

Grandpa laughed, but Raney wanted to run; some irrational part of her mixing up the smell and the decay and an image of how her hair must look ballooned over the tied handkerchief. All of it jumbled into that unwelcome diffidence she felt when she saw Bo's jeans slung low on his hips or his shirt pulled tight across his shoulders.

"Go get him a kerchief, Raney," said Grandpa.

The three of them were able to pull the carcass over the bank and through a patch of woods to an open pocket of higher ground with good sun. Grandpa said the birds would spot the deer quick, promising that within a few days it would go to its sky burial. He rolled the deer off the plastic and arranged its dismembered legs like it was just asleep, then he folded the tarp into a square, bound and knotted by the bloody rope. He stood straight as a soldier by the body with his head tucked down, and Raney felt Bo's eyes watching her, looking for a sign about what he was supposed to do. Then Grandpa pulled out his camp knife and sliced a rectangle of flesh out of the buck's shoulder. He craned, searching the treetops, and then flung the meat skyward, whistling low when a blue-black wedge transformed into a raven, which in one perfect arc carried the first bit of that dead deer to heaven.

Bo's head turned and followed the bird so far he wobbled and righted himself against a tree. Grandpa wiped his knife blade on a fern bough and walked around the pond to disappear inside the barn. A minute later Raney and Bo heard the creak and whump of the bunker hatch hitting the floor, and the smoke of hay dust swirled and settled beyond the barn doors.

Raney saw Bo press his fingers to his temples. "You're not going to throw up again, are you?"

Bo ignored the question and walked out of the clearing toward the bluff. The light breeze trailed over salted sand and tide pools; Raney took a deep breath and wished she could force the clean air through her skin, turn herself inside out and be rinsed pure. After a minute or so Bo sat cross-legged on the ground, took out his pocketknife, and started whittling at sticks like he buried rotting deer every day in Seattle. "I bet your grandpa was sure the world was ending when Chernobyl blew up."

"You shouldn't laugh at him."

"He did, though, didn't he? I bet he made you spend the whole day in the bunker."

Raney started to deny it but couldn't stare Bo down. He had an edge about him today that kept getting in her way, making her hear her words before she said them, see her own face, her shape when she moved. "It wasn't so bad. I learned how to play poker." But Bo looked like he'd scored a point on her, and Raney's mind raced, looking for a way to get back at him, a name for whatever game this was. "You stayin' out here the whole summer? Seems like your mom would want to spend some time with you before you fly halfway across the planet back to that boarding school," she said.

"My mom's in Mexico hunting ghosts or angels with her boyfriend. So what's a 'sky burial' anyway?"

"That's how the Buddhists bury each other. Buddhists don't believe the body matters, once your soul has left. They carry you to a mountain and chop you up for the birds to eat."

"You believe that?" he asked.

"That I want to be fed to birds after I die?"

"That you have a soul that goes on. Something that outlasts you."

Raney looked up at his face. The sun was directly behind him and her eyes stung. "Grandpa says Buddhists believe in karma. That you come back in another lifetime, better or worse depending on if you've been good or bad. You could come back rich, or a beggar. Or not human at all. Maybe a dog. That's why Buddhists don't kill animals. Even an ant. It could be your own kid from a past life."

Bo was real quiet for a minute. Then he said, under his breath, "Wonder what the hell I did."

Raney couldn't help herself. "Yeah. Your life is so terrible you have to choose which mansion to live in, your mom's or your dad's."

"You can be a b-i-t-c-h sometimes, Renee Remington."

"And you can be a stuck-up pain in the neck. I haven't seen my mom since I was six—for all I know that dead deer was my mom, working her way down the ladder of bad deeds. How should I know what happens when you die? I thought your parents made you go to church. Didn't they give you all the answers?"

Bo was silent and Raney was already wishing she could take her words back. She felt too aware of his body next to her, like he was running a fever, the heat of his skin radiating into her own. She wanted him to stab that stupid knife into his arm. She wanted him to go home, all the way to Seattle. All the way to Connecticut. She wanted him to sit closer on the smooth warm rock, to feel the length of his arm matched alongside hers and discover exactly where her shoulder would fall below his. She wanted him to take two wrong steps and fall off that cliff.

After a long minute Bo hurled the stick out over the water, and they both watched it spin end over end, until it fell below the line of sight and they were still, as if listening for the far-off splash. His back was to her now and suddenly Raney heard, or convinced herself that she heard, her grandfather calling her name. She stood to take the path home, but her foot twisted under a rim of the flat rock and she stumbled, reaching for the only thing within her grasp—Bo. He turned and caught her arm, righted her, and there they were, her eyes just at the level of his mouth, and he did not let her go. She turned her face up—it was an instinct—and now she could see him clearly, his eyes, his thin, angular cheeks, streaked and damp. Bo was crying.

Bo didn't come around much for a few weeks after that. Then, near the end of August, his aunt had to drive to Port Townsend to meet with a banker. Bo suspected his aunt and uncle might be selling the store—just a guess, but his aunt did seem even more taciturn than usual. She wanted Bo to accompany her, and when Raney rode her bike past the Chevron station and saw them gassing up the scuffed red car, Bo invited her along. It was only a twenty-minute drive, but by the time they got to Port Townsend, Bo and Raney were joking in the backseat, listening to Cyndi Lauper and Prince on Bo's Walkman, trading the headset back and forth as if no awkwardness had come between them.

Mrs. Hardy drove up and down Water Street looking for the right building until, with an exasperated sigh, she parked and got out, allowed they could walk out to the beach if they caused nobody trouble.

Being a weekday, the beach wasn't crowded, but it was still noisy and smelled of hot dogs and Coppertone, so it felt like a resort compared with Quentin. While most of the beaches on the peninsula were half rock or half mud, the sand here was fine-grained and silky and so hot they had to dig their feet into the darker sand underneath, still damp from the last high tide. Raney twisted her hair up and pinned it with a driftwood stick, bent over a clear pool, and let the water pour into her cupped palms to wash over her throat and the divots and curves along her collarbone. When she stood up, Bo was watching her. She turned and started down the beach. They came across some kids building a sand castle, and when Bo fell behind she looked back to see him digging away right alongside them. A wave washed in and the entire fortress, at least two feet high, collapsed. One of the kids started crying; Raney laughed until a parent stood up and Bo and Raney took off running. Soon the beach was well below them and it became a game of chase, her after him, then him after her. Raney cut up the asphalt drive and across the stubbled lawn until, nearly winded, she came to the concrete gun batteries built to defend Admiralty Inlet from the Japanese. Bo was far enough behind she only had to duck to lose him beyond a small hill, then circle back into the dark tunnels and wait.

One heard stories about these abandoned military caverns, a maze of dank, underground rooms and hallways—hideouts for killers and thieves, and the spirits of soldiers who'd shipped out and never come home. Certainly more than one girl in the Quentin high school had lost her virginity in here. Raney's footsteps echoed against the walls. She heard Bo running toward her and froze, holding her breath until it hurt. He stopped somewhere near the entrance, then turned in another direction. She waited until it was quiet and stepped around the corner, so far removed from daylight her eyes could not adjust and the blackness made her dizzy, as if gravity, too, had been altered by this midnight in the middle of the day.

She listened for a long time and then gingerly walked forward with her arms extended to find the wall. Even with so much care it still shocked her when she hit it, maybe just to realize the blackness was that profound—her own fingertips beyond her sight. She stepped her hands along the wall in the direction she thought led outside, cringing at a plasticky knob of dried gum, a slick patch of moss. And then a corner, another slab wall—not where she expected it. Her pulse jumped. She didn't know if she should go back or go forward or turn around in open space and stumble in a new direction. It was not a closed box—she had come in through an opening and there was no logic to the terror that someone or something could have shut it off, shut her inside a concrete cell. She turned around and pressed her back against the wall, tried to will her eyes to suck in any point of light, but she might as well have had no eyes. She started to call out—Bo was almost certainly out there, somewhere. Or someone was. She heard shuffling, a subtle quake of movement over the ground, but it had no origin or arc she could make sense of. It moved again, close—very close. A brush of two hard surfaces. An instant later she shrieked when something warm rubbed against her arm and, as if the shriek had told her attacker precisely where she was standing, two hands grabbed her around her waist. She heard another voice shriek then bust up laughing.

It was Bo, goddamn him. *Goddamn* him! He took off, though no faster than any blind person could move, and Raney grabbed his shirt and hung on until a dim gray showed in front of them and, as they neared a corner, full sight returned. She started hitting him, beating him over the shoulders and chest, and would have beaten him directly in the face if he weren't so tall. She wanted to break his nose and send him out into the world with a permanent crooked scar like a branded criminal. And goddamn it, he would not stop laughing. And he looked so cool there in the half-lit room, his black hair splaying in every direction and his shirt pulled half off, holding her flailing arms at bay. He just looked so . . . *good*. She stopped hitting him, but he didn't let go of her. She didn't want him to let go of her, which must have been obvious because he slowly pulled her closer and she was still laughing but it was different now, a nervous laugh, not a little-kid-playing-games laugh but something else. Something she wasn't used to, but she liked it. She liked how his arms were more muscled than hers, and that his head was above hers, leaning over her. And then it happened. He kissed her. Soft and hesitant at first and then more sure of himself, pressing into her mouth and pulling her body against his. Raney didn't know if she was supposed to breathe, and after a minute her head started to spin; she pressed her fists against Bo's chest. He moved away just enough to smile at her—he had the best smile, she thought. He always had, even when she hated him.

It was hard to recall, later, the order in which things happened after that. Raney remembered the look on Bo's face changing, more serious at first and then just odd. Scary odd. His breathing grew short and shallow, more a pant than a breath. He seemed to buckle, his knees bending slowly and his hand reaching toward the floor until, all at once, he was down. Hard. Rigid hard. His legs and back arching and his arms held tight to his chest, his head turned awkwardly to one side and then everything, all of him, all at once in a spasm that seemed to go on and on and Raney was screaming and then running out toward the sun into the open field, blinded by the light now and crying for help.

She was a child again, instantly, wanting any grown-up to rescue them. People started running toward her. It seemed to take forever before one man sprinted to his car and got to a pay phone, and then forever for the ambulance to get back. Two people had gone into the concrete battery to help Bo, and a woman was holding on to Raney, pulling her down into the grass and smoothing her hair, crooning to her like a mother. Raney tried to tell the medics what she'd seen—they didn't seem scared, which made her feel only a little less terrified. She couldn't remember what bank Bo's aunt was in and the woman drove her through town until she recognized it. The woman went in to give Mrs. Hardy the news, seeing that Raney didn't have that courage left in her.

A policeman drove her home. He said it was just a seizure—Bo would be fine. Later Raney heard they took Bo to the hospital nearby, Jefferson General, and from there he went straight back to Seattle. It was near enough the school term she didn't really expect him to come back to Quentin. But she didn't expect to hear nothing from him at all, she had to admit. No answer to the letters she left at Hardy's Store. Not that summer or any other summer. It was like Bo had been snatched back into his natural world and left Raney's completely behind. Forgotten. Best forgotten—the way she wanted it too—she finally convinced herself.

· 7 ·

charlotte

The second time Charlotte saw Eric it was equally an accident. Pamela, Charlotte's sister-in-law, had delivered Charlie just eight weeks earlier and Hugo, then two, had turned into a shipwreck of jealous, inarticulate misery. Charlotte stopped by their home on her way to a nearby birthday party and could hear the competition of wails all the way from the street. Pamela opened the door in her bathrobe, one red swollen breast half-exposed, and Charlotte realized there were three people crying inside the house. She reached over to rub Charlie's back and Pamela put the child into her arms. "I have to find Hugo . . ." and she was up the stairs.

Charlotte danced the screaming baby around the living room in a slow bob until Pamela came back with Hugo arching backward in anger, trapped in her arms. It was overall, Charlotte thought, a Rockwell-perfect portrait of family dysfunction. "Where's Will?" she asked.

"At work! Where I wish I was! Taking care of *other* people's children! They both screamed all night and Will was at the hospital on emergency call." Hugo twisted his way out of her grasp and ran back to the staircase, throwing himself against the baby gate until he gave up and collapsed on the floor with a cry that sounded so hopeless Charlotte wondered how that much dejection and angst could accumulate in two short years.

"Are they sick?"

Pamela sat on the couch, looking almost as dejected as her son. "No. That's about the only thing I feel qualified to know. God sent me this day to punish me for all the times I've told mothers how to manage tantrums."

"Let me watch the baby for a bit." Hugo had given up the fight by now and looked like he was minutes away from falling asleep on the rug. "Go take a nap. I'll be fine with him."

"Sure. Spit-up would do a lot for that silk blouse. Why are you dressed up?"

"Birthday party. Friend of a friend just a few blocks from here. I can be late."

By this time Charlie had become fixated on one of Charlotte's earrings and was quiet, appearing to contemplate how he might master the feat of getting his hand locked onto his target. The sudden peace had the effect of a sedative on Pamela. "You want to take him with you?" she asked. "He'll take a bottle now. Sort of."

It had been ten months since Eric picked up Charlotte's mud-splattered coat and stood apart from the crowd while he witnessed her ministrations over the seizure victim. He had called her three or four times in the weeks that followed, but she was always busy. She was on call, she had too many patients, too little sleep, she had meetings . . . When she told him she couldn't go sailing one Saturday because the dishwasher repairman was coming, he quit calling. He almost didn't recognize her when he opened the door at the birthday party—her auburn hair was longer and blown into a sleek scoop around her face. She had more makeup on. In some ways, he thought later, he'd been more immediately attracted to the drenched and mascara-streaked mess she'd been when they first met.

Oh, yes. And there was the baby in her arms. She had a baby.

. . .

"It's you," he said.

"It's who?" she answered, and then, looking at him closely, "Oh. You. The writer—I'm sorry . . ."

"Eric Bryson. And who's this guy?" But then Charlie cried out in his half sleep and Charlotte bumped him onto her shoulder so she could take off her scarf and gloves, dropping one on the floor as she moved past Eric into the hallway, where her friend Elizabeth swept Charlotte and the baby into the party amid much cooing as Elizabeth made a nest for Charlie in an overstuffed chair. Charlotte didn't intersect with Eric again until she went into the kitchen to put Charlie's milk in the fridge, catching Eric propped against the sink holding a full bottle of beer with the cap still on it and watching her like he was trying to figure out the punch line of a puzzling joke. It was the first time she'd seen him without a sweater, and as lean and tall as he was, she saw now that his middle had the soft fullness of a body surprised to find middle age sneaking up on it. The fluorescent lights bled all the color out of his skin, or perhaps just intensified the color of his eyes, the deep black of his hair. It made her feel awkward, the way he was looking at her. Like she owed him something, and maybe she did. How long had it been since he'd called her anyway? Had she said she'd call back?

"How've you been? You're still writing?" she asked.

"Sure. How 'bout you? You were working at Swedish?"

"Beacon. How do you know Elizabeth?"

"I don't. I came with a friend." He tipped his head to one side and saluted Charlie with his unopened beer. "So. Cute baby."

"Charlie? Yeah—they tend to be, don't they?" A group of distressingly loud guests crowded into the kitchen then, their own drinks emptied and refilled enough times none of them noticed the electricity so thick between Eric and Charlotte it made her neck tingle. She cupped Charlie's warm head into the cove of her shoulder. "He's not used to the party scene. I should get him home soon," she said, heading back to the living room, surprised, herself, at how calculatedly ambiguous she was leaving this.

Not much later, Eric was sitting on the couch across the coffee table from her, four or five people breaking in on each other to make a single braided stream of hyperbolic talk, and Charlie sound asleep and peacefully oblivious. Eric said half as many words as anyone else, but each time—a small joke or political jab—it shifted the conversation like an unexpected gust, and Charlotte found herself waiting for his next comment, glancing at him to see how he reacted to each turning of the topic. When a pause fell among them he smiled at her and she suddenly felt embarrassed at her earlier aloofness. She stood up, gathered Charlie in her arms, and made her good-byes. At the door, though, it was Eric who located her gloves and coat and took Charlie from her while she put them on. He was clearly unused to babies and held him like he anticipated some eruption of noise or body fluid momentarily; she almost moved Eric's hands into a more proper cradle.

"I didn't have any idea, you know, about the . . . I wouldn't have kept calling you."

Charlotte buttoned her coat and took the baby back. "Charlie's my nephew. If you don't hate me, call again. We can grab a coffee or something."

He did call, and they did have coffee, then a few weekend lunches and one quick, early dinner, and afterward she reminded herself how stable her life was. Full, really, with her family, her work, her own plans for her future. The next time he called, she was too busy and then too tired. But each time they talked longer, and one week, when he hadn't called, she called him. Just to talk. He was telling her about his new editor when she interrupted him in the middle of a sentence. "Eric, I really don't have room in my life for a romance. Is that okay?"

There was a long pause. "Why did you call me?"

"Because I like talking to you. I like that part."

"So let's talk on my sailboat this Saturday."

"I'm busy Saturday."

"Sunday."

• • •

It was not her thing, sailing. She got seasick and hated the endless wind and sun, the tactical turns back and forth that took you nowhere and back again. It was too unproductive at the end of the day. But she felt bad about having strung Eric along, if that was what she'd done. It hadn't been intentional, more like a hope they would naturally settle into a dependable friendship and avoid all the "rules" that got attached to romances. Yes, whenever she held Charlie or played with Hugo she could feel the primal ache of maternity, the press of time. And the torched ticket to Belize was long enough behind her that she could reasonably envision herself happily married someday, if it came to that, or at least *pleasantly* married. There were even moments she suspected she *wanted* that someday. After Ricky, though, Charlotte felt done with all the effort it took to get there—a bit like sailing: fighting against the wind only to turn around and land at the same place you started except older, sunburned or shivering, and with a lot less money.

Still, on Sunday morning she changed clothes three times before Eric came by, and when he took her bag of towels and sunscreen and his arm brushed hers, she pulled away like she had been burned. It left her angry at herself and freshly tongue-tied with him—tempted to cancel the date on the spot as if her irritating self-consciousness were his deliberate fault. And whatever she had found attractive when they first met was gone anyway—he was wearing shorts and boat shoes, and his long, pale legs with that black hair looking like something pulled out of a giant web. He looked so . . . so . . . academic, even if his travel stories had sounded fantastic. Maybe *too* fantastic. Maybe he was a product of his own verbal embellishments. She could hardly imagine him wrestling a jib across a bow. And she was letting him take her out on the open sound?

They took her car, as always. Eric didn't even own one, living as he did in the heart of downtown where he could walk or take a taxi and sell the lease on his parking space. He had this habit of asking every cabbie where he was from, why he'd scrabbled his way halfway across the planet to this country, to Seattle, sometimes talking for long minutes with the meter still running. It had annoyed Charlotte at first, particularly when she was already worn out from work and could only think about eating or going to sleep, but she was beginning to find it kind of dear, she had to admit. Once, a driver had answered him with a gruff politically charged retort, and Charlotte left the car fuming, saying Eric shouldn't have tipped him at all, but Eric had only laughed and handed the guy an extra five.

It was the perfect sailing day, according to Eric—sun breaking through in a tease of summer, a steady west wind that could take them leagues without a tack or luff. He was transformed out here, completely at ease so that even the natural gawkiness of his body gave way to a coordinated grace. It was the first time she had seen him or talked to him that she didn't sense a surging current of thought engaging much of his mind. There were boats everywhere, colorful billowing spinnakers and the tilted triangles of a race clustered tight as a flock of white birds. The whole world was out to play. Once they were outside the harbor, she turned her face into the strong breeze and opened her mouth so the air seemed to fill her effortlessly, not just her lungs but her head, her entire torso, fill her to the tips of her fingers and toes as if she were a kite borne aloft, caught in an encompassing, superabundant natural force. She felt giddy, blindingly enlightened—how foolish she was to pretend she or any doctor had power over such unknowable physic.

Eric pushed the tiller and touched her knee in warning; the bow cut an oblique angle, and the boom swung easily over her head. She had put a scopolamine patch behind her ear to prevent nausea, and it was making her mouth dry and her eyesight blurry, but as the hull rose and fell across the steady chop, she felt a small knot tying itself in the middle of her stomach. She knew enough to focus on the horizon, tried to keep its level line her single orientation between the swell and dip of the gunwales, tried to recapture the momentary bliss of epiphany she had seen in that gulp of wind. A gust came over the water; she could see its approach in the rippling shimmer. The boat heeled, and Eric reached across and took her hand to pull her to the high side, stretching his legs across the cockpit to brace himself. His right hand gripped the tiller, and seemingly unconscious of his touch, he wrapped his other arm around Charlotte's waist. And then he became quite conscious of it, his arm more secure and purposeful, and she felt his eyes exploring her face as intensely as she had felt them the first day they met, when he had walked her to her car in the twilight. He eased the tiller so the bow dropped and the boat leveled off a bit. She broke her eyes from the stomach-settling line of sky and ocean and looked at him, gave in to the dizzying electric pull between them. He tilted his head and his arm drew her closer. And at that instant saliva flooded her mouth and she lurched away to throw up over the side of the boat.

He still kissed her for the first time, later that evening. That alone, she thought, might have been what persuaded her to let go and fall in love. So almost a year after she chanced upon a book reading, chanced upon a man falling into a seizure practically at her feet, her life diverged onto a course she couldn't have predicted or planned. A course she would have said she no longer hoped for, in no small part because it depended on someone else.

In the middle of Jane's fourth night at Beacon Hospital she had a grand mal seizure and Otero had to put her into a medically induced coma with phenobarbital, a potent sedative. It was the only way to stop the electrochemical fireworks set off by the injured parts of her brain, and each seizure had the potential to cause even more damage. As much as Charlotte hated it, the phenobarbital coma delayed one pressing dilemma: it gave her the perfect reason not to continue checking her patient for brain death. Deeply sedated, Jane couldn't react to the basic tests of brain function—pain, or noise, or a light brush of her eyes. And if she was brain-dead, all else was pointless. She would expire soon after they stopped the ventilator.

The MRI had confirmed Charlotte's diagnosis of fat emboli— dozens of small lesions were scattered through the cortex of Jane's brain, that thin, tangled neural shell that held higher consciousness.

Her mind. Her *Jane*-ness. No, not "Jane," Charlotte thought, but the woman Jane had actually been. Was. *Is*. The mother, the child, the friend, the artist or mathematician. The atheist or Christian, Democrat or Republican or anarchist. The teacher or bus driver. Or all of those—as complicated as all people are—defined by one thing one day and changed on another. Searching, always, for what lay on the other side of the truth we believe absolutely today. The seat of Jane's soul, whatever a soul was, resided in her cerebral cortex—the rest of her body was little more than the insensate plant that fed it, allowed it a means to see, smell, hear, communicate, move.

Looking at the MRI with the radiologist, hearing the tap-tap-tap of his pencil against the black-and-gray splatter of wounds through Jane's brain, Charlotte had for one dark moment almost wanted Jane to be proved brain-dead so they could stop all the machines and let her go. Better, perhaps, than discovering how little of her might be left if her body survived with just enough brain function to keep her heart and lungs going. Still, when Felipe suggested they lighten her coma every few days to reevaluate, Charlotte argued they should focus instead on what they might be able to fix—her lungs, her liver, her kidneys, all of which were precarious—and give her brain as much time to heal as they could. He didn't argue back. He'd been her partner for too long.

After the first few days, the flurry of media interest had died away, and to Charlotte it seemed like the authorities were passively waiting for someone to claim this lost woman rather than actively working to locate anyone who cared. She had traded phone messages with the deputy investigating Jane's case, Blake Simpson, but hadn't talked to him yet, though she knew through the nurses that he was following Jane's progress—or lack of progress.

On her way back to the ICU after lunch she passed the hospital gift shop and saw a small stuffed raccoon on the shelf, which reminded her of a family camping trip at Crescent Lake on the Olympic Peninsula. She had been about eight, so Will, her brother, would have been ten. They had discovered a nest of baby raccoons in a tree near their campsite, scrambling and crying in the high branches as pitifully as abandoned kittens. Will had braced his back against the trunk so Charlotte could stand on his shoulders, swing her leg over the lowest limb, and shimmy close to the terrified animals. In their panic one had fallen to the ground. She was sure she had killed it, but after the longest minute of Charlotte's young life that kit had stumbled to its four feet and scampered up the neighboring tree. Crescent Lake wasn't too far from West Harbor, the hospital where Jane had been treated after her accident— maybe not far from where Jane had lived. Would hopefully live again. Charlotte put the stuffed raccoon on her hospital account and took it up with her to the ICU, glad that the nurse was out of the room when she put it beneath the sheet, tucked between Jane's casted arm and her comatose body. Charlotte had an ill-placed urge to curl Jane onto her side with one hand folded beneath her cheek in the illusion of natural sleep.

Felipe stopped in shortly afterward. "Did he find you?"

"Who?"

"The policeman, Simpson."

"He's here? Blake Simpson?"

Felipe turned to look down the hall. "Heading for the elevator."

Charlotte checked Jane's monitors and went down the hallway after him. "Sheriff Simpson?" She caught up with him before the doors opened and introduced herself. "Do you have a minute?"

He shook her hand with a small bow. "Dr. Reese, at last. In person instead of in a message. I have all the time you want."

She had expected someone stern-looking, or at least more intimidating. But his smile was so welcoming it was hard to picture him putting anyone in handcuffs. He was an inch or so shorter than her and had a gap the width of a sideways penny between his front teeth that gave him a boyish, approachable face. "Never say that in a hospital." He cocked his head and leaned forward as if he'd misheard her. "That was a joke. About time. Never mind—I'm glad to finally connect with you. You haven't identified her, have you?" and before he could respond she shook her head. "No. Crazy question. I would have heard. Are you getting any closer, do you think?"

"Is there somewhere we can talk?" he asked.

They ended up in the coffee shop in the basement—an establishment that could only survive in a city hospital where hundreds of people were too busy or too tethered to patients to leave the building. It smelled of stale dishwater and burned coffee, and the only natural light came through two narrow, grimy windows high on the wall, with views of feet passing along the sidewalk. She apologized for it, but Simpson said no one in law enforcement could drink coffee that hadn't boiled at least half a day.

"I'm actually a sheriff's office deputy. My official title." He took a sip of coffee and added three teaspoons of sugar. "How much do you know about the accident?"

"Only what was in the emergency room record—so mainly about her injuries. Other than you, no one's been to see her. Except the press."

"Most of the investigation is being handled out in Jefferson County. When the call came in from 911 as a hit and run—*probable* hit and run—my office was notified along with our traffic investigator. This Jane Doe"—he met Charlotte's eyes and paused—"your lady upstairs, was unusual in that the ambulance drivers and the ER staff said she was conscious and talking but couldn't give them a clear story or her name. Maybe because she'd hit her head, or . . ."

Charlotte filled in. "She was hypothermic. That can make people confused. It was lucky she didn't die of exposure before they found her."

He nodded. "So you know all that. I understand she told the ambulance driver a deer was hit and she was trying to save it. But later she said she was blinded by somebody's oncoming headlights."

"So she was driving?"

He shook his head. "No. No, there was no vehicle at the scene. She was probably walking near the road, or crossing it, and was hit by a driver who fled the scene. Or possibly she was a passenger and the driver let her out of the car then hit her and drove off. Could have been hitchhiking. She was found about eight feet off the road in the grass—tall enough a lot of cars passed by for a lot of hours before a trucker spotted her. We don't even know what time the accident happened. There *was* a dead deer, on the opposite shoulder of the road ten feet north of her location. And a second deer too. A fawn, closer to where the victim, your lady, was found. The medics, the ER docs, were paying more attention to her injuries than her story, of course. By the time the traffic investigator got to the emergency room, she'd been given something for pain and was making even less sense. The doctors wanted to take her to the operating room for her leg, which was bleeding pretty bad, and the on-duty deputy decided to let that go forward. Thought he could get more information after she was all fixed up. Of course, things didn't go like everybody planned." He grimaced in a commiserating sort of way. "Not much does."

Charlotte found herself trying to re-create some plausible scene in her imagination: Jane walking down the road and finding the struck deer, bending to help it, and being hit by an oncoming car. Jane hitting the deer herself and sending someone else away in her car to get help—would a person do that for a deer? Wouldn't the person have come looking for her? Or more grim scenarios: Jane kicked out of a car during an argument, Jane kidnapped, Jane fleeing—a husband, a boyfriend, a psychotic stranger, caught and hit and thrown into the weeds and deliberately deserted. "If the driver of her own car, someone she knew, hit her it would have been intentional, wouldn't it?"

"I try not to assume. Everything's considered until it's ruled out."

"Can you trace the car that hit her?"

He took another sip of his coffee and Charlotte thought he was repressing a smile. "All I can say is the car probably had a high carriage, judging by the impact. There were several sets of tire marks nearby—but then an uninvolved car could have braked for the deer and left it for dead before Jane even got there. So . . . hard to know." He did smile then. "It's never quite as easy as it looks on *CSI*."

Charlotte rubbed her temples and laughed. "Yeah. Or on *Grey's*

Anatomy. She had nothing with her that gives any clue? No purse, no suitcase?"

"We found a canvas tote bag with some clothes in the mud a quarter mile down the road—some jeans and T-shirts. Underwear. Bathing suit. All about her size, so probably hers. She had a few hundred dollars in her pocket but no wallet."

"No ID?" It was a stupid question, she knew.

"We combed every square inch of the surrounding area. A lot of marsh out there. The bag of clothes was half-sunk. No matches have turned up in the system, not in the State or National Missing and Unidentified Persons data banks, and her fingerprints aren't on file. We had a sketch made and posted it, locally and on the web. Pretty sparse place, though. My theory is she was moving, or running, *from* somewhere else *to* Jefferson County—if she was from around Kalaloch or Forks, you would expect somebody out there to notice her missing. Only a handful of people live in those towns and most are Native."

Charlotte got home late that evening and discovered Eric in her kitchen taking a lasagna out of the oven. "You cooked! That's sweet of you," she said, kissing him lightly and dropping into a chair at the table.

"Trader Joe's. Vegetarian, though, and I added some fresh stuff. My Internet was down, so I worked here today."

"Get much done?"

He shrugged. "Yeah. Except every new idea makes the book that much longer and the deadline further behind. I decided to add a chapter." He lit a candle stub, poured two glasses of wine, and carried their plates over, sitting across from her and taking her hand, a habit he had of knitting their fingers together for a moment before starting to eat. Funny that all of a sudden it reminded her of her grandmother's reliable preprandial prayer—a ritual so routine no one listened to it. "You look beat," he said.

Hearing Eric articulate what must show in her face made Charlotte feel beyond "beat"—like her last pocket of energy had suddenly deflated. She was too tired to think about explaining her day to him. "So what's the new chapter?"

"I keep coming across stories that spin out of some of these transplant cases: surprises from the genetic testing, unexpected consequences, weird symptoms."

"Such as?"

"Oh, people who claim they inherit memories from their transplanted organs. Food cravings for things the donor ate—a lot of those. Twins who get the same cancer in the same kidney. Some pretty macabre stories, like a bone marrow donor who was accused of a rape when his blood showed up in the crime scene, but, of course, the rapist was the guy who'd gotten his bone marrow."

"Someone he knew?"

"That's the scariest part—he was a Good Samaritan donor; he'd been kind of a delinquent kid and wanted to make amends, but with his record nobody believed him. He almost went to prison for it. And then there was a girl with liver failure. Her dad wanted to donate part of his liver and the tissue typing showed that her real father was—"

"The postman," Charlotte broke in.

"You wish. It was her mother's brother."

"Oh, God. People love stuff like that, though. Maybe they'll make it into a TV serial and we'll be rich, *rich* and famous!"

"Which you would hate," he said, laughing.

"The famous part, maybe. You've got the genetics credentials covered, after your genome article. Does your editor like the idea?"

"I might write it into the book and see what he says after. I'm still tracking down one geneticist in Sweden who never answers his phone or his e-mail."

Charlotte listened, watching the way his fingers played over his wineglass and thinking of how much of her body they had touched. They had made her feel beautiful in a body she did not consider beautiful. She had been with Eric over the course of two other books and numerous articles in their three years together, and she had decided

it was not possible to love a writer until you understood the cycle of
his work. Each phase reflected a different part of the creator as much
as it reflected the developing creation itself. He was always happiest,
or at least the most talkative, in the research phase, the journey of
investigation igniting him from one topic to the next until gradually, intuitively, he discovered how they should be connected. He had
an inherent curiosity fueled by the promise that whatever puzzle he
solved, another question always waited. In that regard he had the perfect job. She envied him that flexibility—medicine could also be described as a quest to solve puzzles, but doctors could not choose the
problems they were required to untangle, nor abandon them when
no solution could be discovered. As he wrote his last draft, though,
Eric would get quieter, as if all his words had to be saved for the page,
ideally distilling his research so that readers were not just enlightened, they were inspired. But then he would turn the project in, meet
his deadline, and immediately swoop her off to a weekend in New
York or San Francisco, as if he wanted to make up whatever ground
they'd lost. He'd talked about Paris this time, if she could get some
extra days off. Out of the blue she caught herself wondering if these
intense celebratory weekends really moved their relationship any further ahead. Ahead of where? Where were they headed? She almost
asked him, in a complete change of mood, but checked herself. She
was tired. And tonight she sensed in him the restless energy of being
ready to be done with the book without being done with it—trapped
in his indecision. How appropriate, she thought, and then hated herself for thinking it.

Eric sat back in his chair holding his wineglass halfway to his
mouth. "Something's bothering you. Things okay with your parents?"

"Not so great. It's stressful to pack up thirty-eight years of your
life," she said, remembering she'd promised her mother she would
help her wrap and box the contents of a china cabinet crammed with
dozens of antique figurines her grandmother had passed down—
dancing dandies and shepherdesses with porcelain lace frocks and
pink-bowed lambs. Although she had been forbidden to touch them

as a child, Charlotte would sometimes turn the skeleton key in the tall, glass-fronted doors of the mirrored cabinet and build a story set of these bisque-faced, rosy-lipped peasants. Sure enough, one day she dropped a coiffed lady in a bell-shaped dress and cracked her head clean off at the neckline. Charlotte had been terrified, but her mother, the least domestic of women, had propped the hollow head on a candlestick from which it reigned over their dinner table for years, decorated with tinfoil crowns for birthdays and Christmas. Her mother hated those figurines, though she wouldn't confess it; just rolled her eyes and repeated, "I promised I would take care of them." The burden would be Charlotte's before long. "Hard to accept that all your junk won't fit into the teeny-tiny suitcase they let you take to heaven. But they're okay. Stuff at work isn't so okay. I see a collision course ahead over my Jane Doe."

"No relatives yet?"

Charlotte shook her head, absentmindedly reached across the table, and pinched out the candle. "I met the sheriff's officer on the case today. They don't have much to go on. Nobody's come looking for her. How can you make it this far in life, our age, and have no one who cares enough to notice you've disappeared?"

"Unless she wasn't expected anywhere yet. Maybe she was headed off for a camping trip in the Olympics."

"Alone? For ten days? And she wasn't dressed for any weather."

"Is she getting any better?"

"On the best of days she's stable—or maybe I should say, stuck."

"Do you think she's brain-dead?"

"We can't even test for it now. Which I'm glad about—she needs more time." There was the edge of a challenge in her voice.

"So what's the collision course?" Eric asked. Charlotte looked at him questioningly and he added, "You said she was on a collision course."

"The hospital has filed for a guardian ad litem for Jane. Next step, the court will assign her a certified professional guardian—someone to act as her next of kin."

"Well, she needs one, doesn't she?" He sounded puzzled; Charlotte knew the distress in her voice was bigger than the facts sounded. It was curious to her as well, this defensiveness she felt, but she was too exhausted to sort it through, or even filter what she should or shouldn't share with Eric.

"Of course, eventually. But Jane has a family out there. Somewhere. And my job, Beacon's ethical duty in my opinion, is to do everything possible to keep her alive until her family finds her and tells us what she would have wanted."

"Even if she's irreversibly brain damaged?" Eric asked.

Charlotte felt angry now, and even though she knew her conflict was with Helen Seras and Beacon's ranks of legal advisers and administrators, she let Eric feel her heat. "Yes. Even then. Maybe she has a living will. How can Beacon be objective about any decision when keeping her alive is costing them twenty thousand dollars a day in free care? But it shouldn't be decided by some court-appointed stranger either."

Eric had seen Charlotte struggle with patients in their final hours. It was part of an intensivist's job. He'd asked her once if she was worried that letting someone go might be construed as a lack of either skill or compassion, particularly since she admitted that she was not an absolute right-to-lifer, even questioned the existence of God. But rather than being either offended or conflicted, Charlotte had readily answered, "My job is to keep people alive as long as possible. Whatever they find on the other side will still be there waiting."

He leaned across the table and put his hand on her arm, a gesture that usually ended with their hands clasped, but tonight, as more often lately, she did not move. "I said it before. She's lucky to have you."

"Well, I'd rather she have a husband. A mother. A child."

He was quiet a minute. "It's something else, Charlotte. You're angry at me."

"Why do you say that? What have you done? Nothing. Made me dinner. You're the perfect boyfriend."

He let out a short, bitter laugh. "Except for my one fatal flaw, you mean."

Suddenly she felt like she might start to cry. It was ridiculous, this outburst. He *was* the perfect boyfriend, despite his occasional moodiness. Despite his preference for gluten-free, preservative-free, suspiciously vegan food. In spite of or maybe even *because* of his "one fatal flaw." Every day with him was perfect—yesterday, tomorrow, next year, next decade. The only thing not so perfect was that time kept moving—a grinding mudslide shoving everything and everyone onward, ready and willing or not. Eric saw her face and dropped his head into his hands, and now the only thought she had about time was a futile desire to take the last five minutes back. "I'm sorry," she said. "I'm . . . I'm just stressed. You all right? It's not your head, is it? Does your head hurt?"

He took a moment to answer and she could see the pain in his eyes—nothing any medicine could fix. "No. My head doesn't hurt. Let's go to bed. Okay? Let's get some sleep."

· 8 ·

raney

Bo didn't come back to Quentin the next summer, or any summer after that. In an age before e-mail, before Facebook, before every child over four had a cell phone, his physical absence had to be explained by Raney's imagined tragedies or intentional rebuffs: his mother had moved him to an ashram; his father had sent him to school in England; he had walked in front of a car; jumped off the Aurora Bridge; been hit over the head by a mugger and had amnesia, forever tortured by the image of her own nameless face.

The obvious solution was to ask Bo's aunt, who walked out the front door of Hardy's Store every morning at seven thirty to sweep the walk, and remembered Raney enough to nod when she came inside the store to buy dog food or passed Mrs. Hardy in the pharmacy. If his aunt had any conscience or heart, Raney thought, she would have noticed Raney's face going eight shades of red and offered some word about her nephew—it was her silence that convinced Raney that Bo stayed away from Quentin because he had found his place in the world and realized it held no room for bastards like Renee Lee Remington.

Raney's best friend, Sandy, finally marched up to Mrs. Hardy and asked her outright where Bo was living and why he never came to visit. Sandy came back outside and said that Mrs. Hardy said, "If my sister and I were still speaking, I guess I could tell you." And then she told Sandy to tell her mother that they had not paid their bill, which was three weeks overdue.

Raney dealt with the disappointment the same way she effectively dealt with the other desertions in her life. She decided that if Bo could forget her, she could forget Bo. She spent most of July flirting with a junior varsity basketball player who'd sat across from her in history class. But after six versions of his game-winning free throw, she spent August with mixed-media watercolors and charcoal pencil. Half the canvases showed a thin, sober-faced boy in various stages of blooming manhood, like an age-progressed image of a kidnapped child on the side of a milk carton.

She thought of Bo less over time, of course. High school ended with the letdown she had come to expect from most beginnings and endings in Quentin, a town that did best when it was allowed to linger in some lazy whirlpool of time, moving nowhere, progressing toward no particular goal. Once you embraced that, it was a decent-enough place to live, and Raney understood without naming it that the mountains and woods and water rooted her soul here as surely as the outside world tempted her away. But at eighteen most of her friends didn't even stay around long enough for a graduation party. They flung their caps into the air and were on a bus to Seattle before they hit the ground. Even Sandy left, headed for Gonzaga University, where she would last sixteen months before she got married and bounced right back to Quentin.

Raney had her chance to leave. On her own eighteenth birthday her grandfather handed her an envelope with $7,000 he had saved working pickup shifts at the machine shop. He said if she was smart she would leave before moss grew over her north side and blackberry vines tangled up her feet. The envelope sat between them on the kitchen table, which had been scrubbed so many times by Raney, by Grandpa, by Raney's grandmother, and probably by her mother, that the green paint had been polished down to the bare wood in places, the gaps chinked with grease and crumbs from a thousand meals. Grandpa's smile looked painfully forced. "It's yours. Go away to college if you want. Go to the Louvre in France. Go see that 'Kadinsky' fellow you like. Up to Vancouver to see that lady painter."

Raney's hands felt heavy in her lap, the distance between her and the money as wide as heaven itself. "There's no need, Grandpa. I'm in no rush to leave you."

"Raney, you've been leaving me since the day you were born. As it should be."

"Be easier to leave if I knew where I was going."

"Hell, stay in the same place and you discover nothing new. Not about the world. Not about yourself."

"Look who's talking. You'll just hide in that bunker all day. Alone. Eating what? Canned beans? Waiting for what?"

"Aliens." He winked at her. "I let the army give me my tour. I'd rather you take yours from me."

But it is not so easy to spend money when you have spent your whole lifetime learning to do without it. She closed her bedroom door and put the envelope on her bedspread. She sat against her headboard hugging her pillow to her chest for a long time before she ran her finger along the seal and pulled out a thick stack of ten-, fifty-, and hundred-dollar bills. No bank check or plastic debit card for her grandfather— ever wary of putting any institution between himself and his money. Raney figured she was lucky he hadn't converted it all to gold nuggets. She laid out the bills in various configurations—by denomination, then in five-hundred-dollar piles, then in interweaving spirals, and last in a single heaped mound she could toss in the air like Barbra Streisand in the movie *Funny Girl*. At last, when the house was quiet and dark, she resealed the envelope and put it in her underwear drawer. Unlimited choice can be as paralyzing as poverty or ignorance.

A year later Raney was working as a receptionist at the marina in Port Townsend, a job she took only because the office window framed the boatyard and docks; the manager had made his offer just as the sunlight caught the angled spires and wedges of a hundred masts and keels, so she said yes. One early summer day she walked by the bookstore on her lunch break and saw a coffee table–sized book on the postimpressionists. She bought it and the next month she enrolled at the Art Institute of Seattle.

On the last day of the first term she planned to find a Christmas gift for Grandpa, then take the six-twenty ferry to Bainbridge Island and from there a bus out to the Olympic Peninsula. It wasn't four thirty yet, but already dark; a billion tiny Christmas lights coated the barren trees along First Avenue—one last blaze before an endless gloomy winter. The shops along the avenue sold useless things: tourist souvenirs and doodads for people who craved much but needed nothing or, like her grandfather, needed much but craved little. The light changed at Union and the wind was fierce with a pelting slurry of rain and sleet. Raney ducked into the closest store—because it was warm, dry, convenient, lit like a jewel box . . . no other reason. She picked up and put down a Tlingit raven's head key fob, a set of etched shot glasses, a discounted Windbreaker with a Seattle Mariners emblem that Grandpa would hate but Raney thought would do, if she scraped off the logo.

She saw him standing across the room on the opposite side of the display cases, half turned away. His hair was cropped short and his nose and cheeks were pink from the cold night—that white skin had never shown mercy. She didn't need to see any more to know it was Bo. Even in a winter coat he was still too skinny, too long-limbed. He was holding a trinket box, flipping the lid open and shut with those long, articulated fingers that she remembered examining starfish and river stones. They still looked out of proportion. Beautiful Frankenstein hands thieved from a woman's grave for a man's body. He was showing the box to a girl; he said something that made her laugh and she smoothed her perfectly smooth hair behind one perfect seashell ear and turned in Raney's direction. Raney moved behind a mirror next to the jewelry rack, which unfortunately gave her a side-to-side comparison of their two faces. As soon as the girl turned away, Raney pulled her collar up and left the store.

The street was crowded now, people clumsy with armloads of Christmas presents, balancing umbrellas over shopping bags so they tangled together and caused pedestrian traffic jams along the sidewalk. She made it two blocks down to Seneca, but when the light turned green, she felt as if all the air had been sucked out of the city. She stood at the curb with the crowd bumping past until the light turned red again. After another missed light she knew she was going to turn around. Considering all the accidents that alter a life, Raney wondered if the agony people put themselves through over every single choice made as much sense as trying to paddle up a waterfall.

Bo and his girlfriend were gone when she went back. The jewelry box was still on the counter; it was quite lovely—covered with tiny cowrie shells. For some reason it made her feel better to know he hadn't bought it for the blond girl with the perfectly smooth hair and the perfectly shaped ear. She opened the lid expecting the tinkle of music or a spring-loaded plastic sea horse. Nothing. Only the private joke he'd told the girl that Raney would never hear. The shopkeeper had his eye on her, apparently waiting for her to filch something. She picked up a large, candy-swirl glass marble and asked him to wrap it up.

All the years of forgetting someone can backfire, Raney discovered that night. All the years of thinking you were not thinking about how he had changed, where he was living, who he was loving; it gave your subconscious free license to build an entire parallel life of might-have-beens. An imagined twin. You don't even realize how much space you've given it until the invented life is blown to bits.

She walked up and down the street pretending to look for a gift but really looking for a tall, ghost-pale young man and his prep-school-pretty girlfriend, whose hair was getting blonder and whose skin was getting peachier by the minute. She saw the girl's face clearer than Bo's, his was mixing up with the long-haired boy of caves and woods and tree swings. After an hour she looked at her watch and saw she'd missed the ferry and bus, called Grandpa from a corner phone booth, and told him she'd come tomorrow or the next day. She walked north against the rain and sleet toward her apartment, through the Pike Place Market, where the stalls were closing; the crash of their rolling metal doors sounded harsh and personal. A block farther up to Starbucks and the smell of hot coffee finally made her more conscious of how cold and hungry she was than how fast a person could disappear in a city the size of Seattle. So she went inside. And there he was. Without the girl.

Raney discovered another lesson that night: in the split-second shock of unexpected meetings you can tell a lot about what a person thinks of you—if you're prettier or uglier than he recalls, if that secondhand coat you're so proud of just makes you look poor, if the sight of your face is a cause to celebrate or a reason to run. You can even make a good guess about whether five long years of silence was an act of disenchantment, dislike, or, worse yet, disinterest. In Bo's face she saw trepidation. As if seeing her again opened a door to problems bigger than he was ready to tackle.

He stood up. "Raney? God, it's you, isn't it? What are you doing here?"

She shrugged as if she could barely remember his name, wondering if she would ever be willing to take her eyes off his own slate-blue ones again. "Christmas," she said, the first word that popped into her head. Her hand closed around the gift-wrapped marble in her pocket and she held it out to him. "Merry Christmas."

He took it hesitantly. Turned it over in his hand and put it into his pocket. "How'd you . . . ? Thank you."

"Open it." She sat down at his small table with his half-finished espresso, the burnt-umber liquid swirled with foam. She never could fathom how people paid so much for something gone in two swallows. She watched him unwrap the present, careful not to tear the paper. Not like a boy, she thought. But most boys would have laughed at the gift of a glass marble. Instead, Bo put his elbows on the table and held it in both hands, balanced on the ends of his fingers so they made a little altar like that marble was the flame of life. He turned it around so the light from the pendant lamp above the table danced along the ribbons of colored glass.

"It's like there's a whole planet inside it," he said, bringing it close to his eyes so it must have looked equally huge.

She leaned over to touch the marble, spinning it on the pedestal of his fingers. "Look there. The way the red and the indigo streamers twist around each other." But he was looking at Raney now, in a pensive sweep over her face.

"Indigo," he repeated.

She pulled her coat closer about her throat and sat back in her chair, crossing her arms. "You quit wearing your hair long."

He rubbed his hand over his close-shaved head. "Yeah. Growing it out again."

"It's not bad short. So are you in school? I always expected you to go away to someplace fancy. Out in New York or something. Yale or something."

"Duke," he said. "Duke University, in North Carolina," adding the state, Raney understood, because he did not expect her to know.

"I'm at the institute."

"The institute?"

"Yeah. The mental institute." He looked almost taken in and she laughed. "The Art Institute. Just up the street. Studying design."

"Painting too? You have to paint all your life, Raney. You have to promise me."

Promise him, she thought. It sounded like something you would put at the end of a good-bye letter.

He was spending Christmas at his mother's house in Laurelhurst; his father had sold the family home on Queen Anne, remarried, and had a new baby on the way, a fact Bo relayed with odd dissociation, like it was irrelevant to his own life. He had traveled a lot, and Raney tried to act like she was plenty used to friends dropping snippets about their semester in Spain or spring break in Greece. Seattle was still Paris to her. But overall he kept skirting questions, turning the conversation back to Raney, and she couldn't decide if that was out of curiosity or because he did not want to be cornered into saying why he never once sent a letter or phone call back to Quentin. Either way, after half an hour they were easing into each other, settling into a common space where they talked as unfettered as when they were fourteen and fifteen.

The barista wanted to close, and they walked out to the street. The rain had turned to a mist so fine it was nearly imperceptible, a fresh nip on her cheeks, a gauze over the Christmas lights woven impossibly thick through every tree. The streets were noisy with partiers, despite its being a weeknight—the holiday more an excuse to break rules than a celebration of tradition or faith. Bo was telling Raney about a puppy he'd snuck into his dorm room to raise. He'd taken it for walks in the middle of the night so the RA wouldn't find out, but the dog had disappeared one weekend after a house party—stolen, Bo was sure. He had posted signs everywhere, though he knew it was useless. They stopped walking and Raney watched his hands stroking the dog's back, caught between real life and imagination. She remembered his hands holding a book in the woods, on the beach, in the bunker, and wondered if he knew he had mastered something rare and was meant to be a storyteller. Once, when they were kids, she had asked him to read aloud to her, more because she was frustrated at being ignored than because she had any actual interest in the book. It worked at first. He had made a different accent for each character and talked slow or fast as the action moved slow or fast, but after a while he was mumbling so that all she'd heard was the rise and fall and punch of his voice. He'd grown oblivious to her as his audience. She'd started to feel jealous of the book that so absorbed him, those petty, vicious English schoolboys and their smelly roasted pig. She had called him out on it and he'd said, she remembered, "Sure, Ms. Vincent van Gogh. Like you give a fart for anybody else when you're painting." After that they would choose the day's spot, Bo with his book and Raney with her tackle box of paints, and be happy enough in silence.

Bo finished the story about his dog and looked around. "Where are we going?"

She pointed to the building behind him. "This is my apartment." She didn't ask him to come in, but he said, "Okay," and then they were climbing the stairs and unlocking her door and then she was throwing clothes into the closet and dishes into the sink and kicking textbooks under the sofa.

"My roommate's already gone home. She's a worse slob than I am—could have at least thrown her pizza box away."

"Who's your roommate?"

"Brittany. She's a photographer. I didn't know her before I got to school, but she's nice enough"—Raney opened the refrigerator—"and she usually keeps beer. Want one?"

"Sure." He tried to twist the cap off, grimacing when the metal ridges scraped his chilled fingers. She brought him a bottle opener and sat next to him on the couch—a ragged paisley piece of junk they'd found at a garage sale and covered with an afghan. "Nice place," he said.

Raney laughed. "No, it's not. Are you gonna stay in the dorms or move someplace you can get another dog?"

"Hmm. I might not go back right after Christmas."

"Why? Semester off?"

He took a sip of beer and looked around the room, either deaf to her question or deciding that it was not worth answering. He pointed with the bottle to the wall covered with Brittany's photographs. "She's pretty good."

"Yeah. She likes buildings, highways, playgrounds—never people. Man-made things without the man that made them." Bo got up and walked close to a grouping of bridges and highways. "How'd she get Highway 99 with nobody on it?"

"They'd closed it off for the St. Patrick's Day race."

"Why does she dislike people so much?"

"Oh, she doesn't dislike people. Particularly if they're male."

Bo was leaning toward the photograph of the bridge, one hand tucked into his hip pocket. From the back his haircut looked ragged, like he'd let a drunk fraternity brother go at him with sewing scissors. "Where's your stuff?" he asked.

"In the bedroom."

"What, so you got banished from the main room?"

"We share the bedroom too. But she's at her boyfriend's most of the time."

"Can I see?"

"The bedroom?"

"Your paintings."

What was she expecting when she opened the door and turned on the light for him? Astonished praise? Stunned silence while he absorbed her genius? Only three people, Grandpa, Sandy, and now Bo, knew both her old work and her new and thus had some measure of how she had grown from a child to a woman through the arc of her art. Was she hoping Bo would see, absorb, and know her now as if he had never stayed away? Whatever she was expecting, she felt something cave in when it didn't come. He scanned the paintings with his mouth pursed. Raney sat down on her bed, waiting, talking herself into not caring. After a long while Bo leaned against the wall, holding his eyes on her face like he was winding up to say something summative and profound. But when he finally spoke he said, as if they had just been talking about her grandfather, "I bet your granddad still goes into that bunker. Does he? Still waiting for the end of the world?"

"Grandpa? Of course. Gotta end someday." She didn't try to hide the sharp edge in her voice, but Bo seemed to interpret it as sarcasm and laughed softly.

"What does he do when the cans expire?"

"He gives 'em to the food bank a month before. Or we eat beans every night for a month. What made you remember his bunker?"

"I always wondered what he expected after an apocalypse. I mean, if everyone you know, your whole town, is decimated, why would you want to survive?"

"Well, those are words spoken by someone who never had to face death." It was a blind lashing, and as soon as she saw his hurt expression, she wished she'd just swallowed her pride about the paintings. She felt confused about why she'd let him come up to her apartment now, smacked by the admission that she had let her hopes build up, as if running into Bo twice in one night was some predestined path carved by more than her own sweat, for once. "Grandpa was a POW in Korea and half the men in his unit starved so I guess he pretty much lived through the end of his world. Besides, I think he sees the end of the world as an opportunity. Like if we have to start all over maybe he'll find some place he fits in." Herself too, a dark voice inside her added. Suddenly she wished Bo would leave, cursing the sleet that drove her inside the gift store and reintroduced his gilded life to her own. She'd been happy enough before measuring her lot against his, hadn't she? Thinking this school, this apartment, these paintings were a step to somewhere else. Her eyes stung with tears and she lay back on the bed so that Bo couldn't keep staring into her face.

A moment later, though, the bed dipped when he sat next to her. He put his hand on hers, cautiously knit his fingers between her own. "You don't have people in your paintings, but they don't feel lonely." His fingers curled around hers, no mistaking their intention to hold on. Raney held her eyes as wide open as she could to keep tears from spilling down her cheeks. "Your paintings feel like everything is connected—the trees, the light, even the missing people . . ." One fat tear escaped with that, slipping across her temple and, she hoped, disappearing into her hair. She felt the bed move as he brought his other hand to her face and stroked the path the tear had made.

"So you don't hate them?" she said, embarrassed she had to ask and asking anyway.

"I don't hate them, Raney. No one could hate them."

Raney could not have said later whether he kissed her or she kissed him, but they kissed then, crossing the mountains between friendship and romance. He tasted different than she'd expected, which made her aware that she had been expecting this kiss. Anticipating and preparing for it. She tasted the coffee, a sweetness of brown sugar and earthy florals. For all his height, his frame fit well with her own, thighs and hips and shoulders, longer, wider, stronger; safely encompassing, though she would not have guessed how much she wanted that. She knew pride in her own body, too, which overtook her shyness—that magic time when smooth skin and clear eyes and supple joints rank with the grandest of natural wonders.

Bo took off his coat and sweater and stretched himself across her so the quick thud of his heart came through her own chest. He hesitated a moment then closed his eyes, slid one hand under her shirt and eased it up, up, working each side higher until it tangled in an awkward band above her bra and Raney had to quit pretending she had no part in this, sat up, and wriggled her arms free. Above her again he ran his hand over her belly and the swell of her breasts and she was surprised that his skin was as soft as her own, like he had never used his hands for anything but turning the pages of a book. She heard him sigh and when she opened her eyes he was looking at her right arm, tracing the bracelet of scar where a thin nylon rope and high wind and adolescent foolishness had nearly cost Raney a limb. He leaned down and pressed his lips into the raised pink flesh, then moved his face lower along the course of her ribs and let one hand trail downhill to her navel, gently pressed his palm against the shallow cove between her hips.

"Have you done this before?" he asked.

"*This* or *it*?"

He blushed and she could see how he hated what it gave away. "You know. It."

Raney shook her head. "I hated every boy in Quentin and haven't met any here I like much better."

"Me neither."

Despite the blush she was surprised. The smooth blond hair and seashell ear of the girl in the gift store flashed into her mind. "No girlfriends?"

"One. For a while—not long enough to, you know . . ."

"Have sex," she finished.

Saying the word broke the tension. Bo laughed and moved off her, bunched the pillow under his arm, and looked at her with a new easiness. "I have an idea."

"What? You ravish me and we both pretend we know what we're doing?"

"Let's go out for breakfast."

Raney looked at the alarm clock. "It's one in the morning. Doesn't anybody care you aren't showing up?"

"No. Mom stays with her boyfriend half the time. I'll call her in the morning. I want to spend the day with you."

She laughed and put her hand over his where it lay on the bare skin of her waist, so safely unself-conscious now she felt older, smarter, funnier. "What? In bed?"

"No. I mean, maybe. Someday." His face got serious again, like he was weighing what to say next.

Raney reached over her head for her shirt and pulled it across her front. "You have a car?" Bo nodded. "Give me a tour. I've lived here six months and hardly left downtown."

When she was a grown and married woman, a mother with her own child to guide, Raney knew that if she had any advice about love it would be to make all the delicious room possible for that time between wanting sex and having sex. The anticipation building like an electrical charge—so strong it binds and forgives all sorts of inadequacies. Inside that window the goal is still the winning of love rather than the maintenance, which takes a more enduring patience. In ways, she and Bo had been waiting since his last summer in Quentin. They talked another two or three hours in Raney's apartment that night, mixing time and topic until a patchwork of missed history began to fill in the lost years. By 4:00 a.m. they were drunk with fatigue and with each other, and Raney made him get under the covers with her, both of them fully dressed. Before they fell asleep he scratched the back of his head and she ran her fingers through his hair. "I think I liked it better long." Bo pulled his head away and reached up to stay her hand. Raney smiled, surprised at his unexpected vanity. "You're cute either way." But instead of relaxing, he moved her hand higher up the back of his scalp, carefully guiding her index finger over a curved ridge of skin.

"What happened?" Raney asked.

"I had to have an operation. In October."

Raney was awake again. She sat up and turned his face away from her, brushing his hair back. Even in the dim light of the street lamp below her windows she could see the crescent of pink tissue arcing across his skull. "Jesus, Bo. Why didn't you tell me that? What for?"

"You remember the day in Port Townsend? When I had the seizure? They found something in my brain. A tumor." Raney couldn't stifle a gasp and Bo touched her lips. "It's okay—it wasn't cancer or anything—I'd probably had it all my life. But it came back, so a few months ago they took it out again."

"They cut into your brain?"

He sat up and crossed his legs so their knees were touching, leaned so close Raney inhaled his own exhaled breath. "Yes. They cut it out, and now it's gone. Forever."

Raney was quiet for a moment. "It seems like I would have known somehow. Known you were in trouble."

"But I'm not. I'm fine now."

"You are? You're sure?" Bo nodded and Raney began to relax again. "What other secrets should I know about you, Mr. Bo?"

"I don't go by Bo anymore. Not at school."

"No? So what do they call you back at Duke University in North Carolina, U.S.A., planet Earth?"

"My middle name. Eric."

"Yeah?" Raney tilted her head, like seeing him from another angle might change how she interpreted him. "Eric's nice. But I'll still call you Bo."

When he woke up, Raney was sitting up in bed with a paintbrush in her hand, shaping the hint of gold cast across Bo's face in the morning sunlight. She hadn't put her shirt on, and blushed when she realized he was awake. "You're painting a person," he said. "See? Not lonely at all." Then he reached for the brush before she could pull away and drew a gold band over the scar on her right arm. "An Egyptian bracelet. For my Cleopatra."

They ate breakfast at Lowell's, carrying trays of thick smoked bacon and fried eggs up the narrow stairs to sit by the window and watch the ferries and the orange-and-black freighters cut through the lead-colored sea. Bo had an old Fiat convertible, which stayed cold inside despite keeping the heat turned on full blast, and Raney rode with her hands tucked between her legs. They drove around Seattle like gaga tourists, him pretending interest in sights he'd seen a thousand times, and her pretending most of them weren't surprises. He took her to a sculpture in Fremont of life-size stone people and a human-faced dog waiting for a bus, each dressed by the neighborhood in Santa hats and red scarves. Even the dog. He cut through blocks of small wood-framed houses and turned underneath the Aurora Bridge where the span of concrete and iron abutted the land and cars and trucks boomed overhead, and in that dark wedge of useless space someone had sculpted an enormous cement troll hulked over a snatched Volkswagen. They drove along the north shore of Lake Union and across the Montlake Bridge, castle-like turrets guarding either end as if the water it spanned were a defensive moat cutting the city into warring halves. They crossed the 520 Bridge and wove south through Bellevue, then west again across the I-90 Bridge and past the Kingdome back toward downtown. All of it was new to Raney, who still spent most of her weekends on the peninsula with her grandfather.

She could tell Bo liked driving. He would rev the engine to the top of each gear before he shifted down, take the turns fast so the little car pulled against the pavement then shot into the straightaway with him holding her close. She had not seen this daring streak in Bo during those two summers in Quentin, and wondered if it had been fired by the life he'd lived between then and now, or by the scare that his life might be cut short. "How long do they make you wait after brain surgery to drive a car?" she asked him, but got no answer. A nineteen-year-old boy will take his revenge on the world wherever he can, she guessed.

Bo wanted to buy her a Christmas present, "to top the glass marble," he said. They parked in Pioneer Square and stood at a stoplight with other Christmas shoppers, dusk already falling and the weather turning to a stinging chill. When the light changed, Bo grabbed her hand and pulled her across the street into Magic Mouse, a toy store that could have come from Grandpa's boyhood. It looked as if a hundred kids had stocked the maze of rooms and shelves. He tried to buy her a paint set, stuffed animals, a globe filled with pale-blue water and when you shook it your fortune popped into a little glass window. When she refused on all, he took her across the street to his "favorite store in all of Seattle," an antique and rare books store that smelled like old paper and leather and paste bindings. Thousands of volumes rose up the high walls on packed shelves, random stripes of color and texture that collectively made a singular body of art. Breathing in their scent, Raney thought of all the readers who'd held these books, turned their pages, and considered their words, then sold and lost all but what could be contained in the space of a memory. She watched Bo roam, pulling out books at random and running his fingers along the titles, the publishers, the authors—most forgotten. He spent a long time looking through one oversize book and then carried it up to the counter and had it wrapped. He didn't give it to her until they were back in his car.

"Bo," she started to protest.

"Too late. Nonreturnable. Go on. Open it." He watched her in silence, pleased and proud.

Raney pulled the book out of the taped brown paper. It was plates of Monet's paintings from Giverny, a cumbersome and sumptuous book bound in faded green cloth worn bare at the corners. She opened it to the center folio where one of his early water lilies paintings spread across both pages with a thread-stitched seam up the middle. Even in this ancient book she could see the saturated greens and blues of Monet's best years, before his eyes began to go bad. She started to thank Bo for it, but he broke in, "It's Claude Monet. French impressionist. You know his work?"

There were many ways she might have taken that question: a conversation opener, spontaneous words that popped out with no thought. But when she looked at Bo she knew he was being serious. She closed the book and ran her hand over the cover, choosing to rush by the small wound his question caused. "It's beautiful, Bo. Thank you."

He kissed her and started the car. "I have to run by my house for something. I know a place we can eat near there."

It was dark by the time Bo pulled into his driveway. He walked around to Raney's door to let her out, as if assuming she'd stayed in her seat expecting that. "I'll wait here," she said, pulling her coat tighter.

"It's cold." After a minute he leaned into the car and added, "No one's home. There aren't even any lights on."

He led her through a maze of shrubs to a side door and into a huge kitchen. Banks of drawers surrounded a marble-topped center island bigger than the whole of Raney's bedroom, and she counted two double sinks, two dishwashers (verified as such by the Clean and Dirty signs stuck to their fronts), and two separate ovens on different walls. He pushed open a sliding door into a butler's pantry between the kitchen and dining room and she followed him through. Heavy, dark beams crisscrossed the ceiling, and one entire wall was a built-in sideboard, glassing in silver platters and pitchers, stacks of plates and bowls ten-high and three-deep. The house was so empty it was hard to imagine this table filled with enough people to make a dent in all that china. In the living room dried-up roses in a crystal vase sat moldering in brown water underneath a giant oil painting of a copse and a meadow. The painting looked old and expensive and lifeless to Raney. Like the roses, she thought. Like the house. She heard a clock ticking somewhere. Bo had disappeared into the entry hall and called to her from halfway up the stairs. "Come up."

"What if your mom comes home?"

"She won't. They went to Lopez Island—her boyfriend has a house out there."

The stairs curved up to a long balcony that was lined with bedrooms and by the time Raney reached the top, all the doors were closed and Bo was nowhere in sight. A strip of light shone beneath one door, and she knocked, waited a moment, and turned the knob. It was plainly Bo's room—a wreck of disorganization compared with the rest of the house. The shelves had books in rows and books stacked on top of the rows and books stacked in front of the rows. His suitcase lay open on the floor and clothes were piled on the unmade bed and draped over the edges of open, empty drawers, as if putting them inside would have taken inordinate effort. Along the windowsill was a line of model sailboats, but otherwise the only iconic vestige of his younger years was a poster of Farrah Fawcett.

She heard him call to her from somewhere down the hall and went in search. She found him in the bathroom off the third bedroom she opened, clearly the master suite.

"Wow. Your mom likes pink."

"Yeah. I think it was her life tragedy not to have a daughter." He turned off the bathroom light, and she saw him put an orange prescription bottle in his pocket. He stood quite still, watching her with a quiet focus that sent an exciting flutter down her spine.

"Get what you need?" she asked.

"Hmm? Not all of it. Not yet." He turned off the bedroom light. She was blind in the sudden darkness. She heard him take a step toward her and she laughed, nervous, uncertain. She heard nothing more but knew he was closer, and then his arms were around her shoulders, moving down her back, pulling the length of her against him and holding her there, so utterly encircled she felt slender and small for the first time in her life, and for the first time in her life she enjoyed the awareness of her lesser size, her lesser strength. His breath was at her temple, then her ear and then on her mouth and he pressed deeply into her, walking them as one backward to the bed so as one they lay across it. He was confident now, more sure of his hands, his lips, his tongue than even half a day ago. Raney felt every nerve concentrated in her mouth, an impelling force determining what her body would do. She had started this kiss six years ago and let it linger half-completed but calling. She felt terrifyingly thrilled, willingly out of control, and understood that this precipice comes only once in an entire life, and so was holy in its own way. She broke away for a moment to catch her breath, to relish this, and even in the darkness she could see Bo smile and had to laugh in wonder that one human being could make another feel this way. She ran her hand up the length of his arm until their fingers enmeshed and she rolled against him and then over him, and this time she was the one to slip her hand beneath his shirt and ease it over his head, sitting astride his waist, marveling at the smoothness of his naked chest. She pulled her sweater off, and when he undid her bra it could have been the first or the hundredth time. She was utterly unafraid of him, of this, of whatever was coming.

The shock of the overhead light, the guttural shriek of Eric's name, the strike of car keys thrown at her back made Raney leap to the other side of the bed.

"Mom!"

"In *my* house? *My* bed?"

"I thought you were on Lopez."

"Up." Raney's sweater hit her in the face. "Get your clothes on. I'll be downstairs."

Bo was whiter than Raney thought a person could get and still be breathing. She put her sweater on and saw the tag hanging out under her chin but could not think through the steps required to turn it right. Bo was still immobilized, staring at the door his mother had slammed shut. "Lopez??"

"She told me . . . It'll be okay. She's just surprised."

"Surprised? Try livid! Is there a back way out?"

"No. You have to talk to her. She's not usually . . ."

"Usually what? What's *usual* about finding you in her bed with a half-naked stranger?"

Raney's purse was still downstairs. She raked her hair straight and licked her fingers to rub off any mascara smears, but a glance in the mirror showed a street urchin—streetwalker, she figured Bo's mother would assume. Bo took a deep breath and closed his eyes for a minute before he started down the stairs. Raney heard his mother harping, shrill and incessant, and Bo's voice getting louder as he tried to cut in. Then his mother was calling, "Raney. Please join us. Now."

Raney stood at the top of the grand spiral staircase for a moment before slowly marching down to meet them; Bo watched her entrance with a mix of adoration and wariness, like a nervous groom. They sat next to each other on the sofa, too far apart to touch. Bo's mother stood in front of the fireplace with one arm clasped tight across her waist as if she'd eaten something rancid, the other at her forehead holding a lit, gold-papered cigarette angled between two long fingers. Raney had a flash image of a unicorn puffing smoke through its golden horn and choked on a laugh.

"This is funny to you?" Eric's mother pinned Raney with her eyes. "You listen to me now. I am not a prude. I understand that Eric's sexuality is"—she drew a design in the air with the cigarette, conjuring her next word—"emerging. That's natural. Most boys experiment. But Eric is not—" She broke off for a minute. "He'll be leaving for college again in a matter of weeks, and . . ."

"Mother . . ."

"You're going back. You have enough in your way as it is, agreed?" She turned back to Raney and now Raney noticed the heavy lag when his mother blinked, a faint slur when she asked, "I don't suppose you know Melissa?"

Raney looked at Bo, certain he was about to leap off the sofa and make it clear that Melissa, undoubtedly blond and peachy and still twinkle-eyed about some sweet joke shared over a trinket box, was history. Instead she saw Bo blush. Before he could muster any words, Raney stood up. "Very nice to meet you, Mrs. Bryson, I appreciate all your hospitality. And I'd like to compliment you on your bed. Mattress is nice and broke in. Just how I like 'em." She walked through the dining room and kitchen, picking up her coat and purse and getting to the car before she exhaled, furious that it was too far to walk back to her apartment. Bo didn't come out for a long time, and Raney could see lights flashing on in other rooms upstairs; once she heard two hard surfaces slam together. She looked at the gables and wings of his house, the equally imposing houses beyond the hedges and across the pointlessly wide street. A whole family could be at home together and never be in the same room.

It was cold and she started to shiver. Finally Bo came out the kitchen door. He turned to say something to his mother and Raney heard her scream, "Go ahead, check her pockets."

He seemed scarily calm once he got into the car, adjusting his mirrors and seat belt and backing out of the driveway with a deliberate silence. When they were blocks away he said, "I'm sorry. It's not about you. She's been like this since the operation."

"Why? You said it's all fine."

"It is. There's follow-up stuff, but . . . No. It's fine. I'm just not sure I want to go straight back to school. And she has plans for me. Or thinks the universe has plans." He shrugged, looking out the window for a moment like whatever he was trying to clarify might be found there. "She's a mother. What can I say?"

"Plans from the universe!" Raney said half under her breath. "I thought she was the Free Spirit, Find Your Inner Being type."

"She is. Was. Until I . . ." He faltered, like he didn't know the answer himself.

Raney only then realized how close she had been to tears again—twice in twenty-four hours. She would not have thought it possible. She moved her hand across the seat and slipped it under his thigh, an apology, though she knew if one was owed it was not by her. He wrapped her hand in his own and they rode the rest of the way to Raney's apartment with no talk at all. He stood close behind her while she fit the key into her lock, and as soon as the door swung closed, he pushed her gently against it, flicking off the light switch. She turned it back on and he turned it off again, trapped her hands behind her, kissing her fully, becoming playful again as if the last hour was easily forgotten. She laughed and wrestled free, crossed her arms between them.

"So who is Melissa?"

"She's a girl I knew in boarding school—she grew up near me."

"And?"

"And she thinks she wants to be my girlfriend."

"Thinks? So you don't think she *really* wants to be your girlfriend."

"I don't think she *really* knows anything about me. Who I am."

"Bet she's giving you more than a marble for Christmas."

"I'm happier with my marble."

Raney thought about the book of Monet folios then, and remembered it was still underneath the seat of Bo's car. At that moment, for some reason, she knew that book would never belong to her. Knew it was a beautiful, rare thing she'd been lucky to hold for a few moments and should content herself with the memory. "Is Melissa who your mom thinks the universe has picked out for you?"

He got more serious with that question, sensing the change in her mood. "I think the universe wants me to be with someone I love. No matter where she comes from." He kissed her again and nothing made sense to her anymore except the kiss; they slid down the door until they were on the carpet, his arm a pillow underneath her head, the room lit by the slice of light from the hall. He was looking at her so seriously, so intently, like he wanted to pull her thoughts out of her mind and absorb them into his own experience. And for an insane moment she wondered if he could, and what he would discover there—what paucity of etiquette and education he would absorb and try to replace with his own.

"I want you, Raney. I love you," he said.

She waited a long time before she asked him, "Do you know the difference yet, Bo?" He pulled back, baffled and guarded. "What did your mother mean, 'check her pockets'?" Bo didn't answer and she pressed him further. "Bo? Check for what?"

"Nothing."

"Tell me." Raney gently pushed his arms away and sat up. "If you care about me, you'll tell me."

She could see him wanting to lie, then push deeper to tell her the truth, and for that she felt a terrible, overwhelming loss even before he answered, "She lost a pair of earrings. She thinks they were in her bathroom."

"And she thinks I took them."

He looked so sad Raney almost wanted to drop it, tell him not to answer her because there was no answer to this that would not punish him for the life he was born to. No matter how fast and far you walk you will always be shaking your boot with one last clinging, stinking vestige of the place you are trying to leave behind—it was true for both of them. She held his sweet, shadowed face in her hands and said, "You know what I think the universe plans for me? I think the universe, this world, rolls over people like me without a backward glance, so I'd better be watching out for myself." The hurt in Bo's face made Raney's chest twist with something spoiled and hard but she kept going, pulling him out of her heart like a thorn. "Where do I fit in your world, Bo? Where would I possibly ever fit?"

· 9 ·

charlotte

Charlotte discovered the nearly invisible scar hidden beneath Eric's hair, a smooth arc of tissue she traced with her fingertips, the first time they made love. He'd brought his hand up to cover hers, at first halting its exploration and then gingerly guiding her forefinger along the course of the healed incision. "No secrets from a doctor, are there?"

They were tangled in sheets; a dim light made it hard to read his expression. "It's a surgical scar, isn't it?"

"Yep. Brain transplant." He laughed, but even in the low light she could see the reticence in his eyes. "I had brain surgery. Three times. First when I was fourteen and the last nine years ago." The medical part of Charlotte's mind was already intruding, dreaming up the worst diagnoses. She waited for him to volunteer more, to be reassured before she had to make him tell her everything. Instead his next sentence was a question: "Want to break up now?"

"No. But I want to hear more. If you want to tell me."

"I had a tumor. Benign—but it grew back. Twice."

"You had a brain tumor? What kind?"

"Pilocytic astrocytoma."

"How come you never told me this?"

"I guess I don't consider it my most marketable feature."

"Marketable? Are we buying and selling something here?" Charlotte was sitting up now. She felt unreasonably annoyed at Eric for not telling her this sooner, as if a patient had withheld some vital fact that might change her treatment plan. "Maybe it's none of my business—just seems like you might have slipped this detail about your life in somewhere between the names of your pets and your favorite bands."

"Well, I'm telling you now."

Charlotte turned on the bedside lamp and stared grimly at Eric for a moment. Then she kissed him so hard it was almost a rebuke. "But you're okay now. It's gone?"

"I have an MRI every year. So far, it's stayed gone."

She rolled on top of him and locked her hands on either side of his head, a surge of relief surprising her with tears. "Don't do that to me again. Promise?"

But an hour later she was wide awake. Promise her what? That he could foretell the future? How many benign brain tumors came back twice? He woke to find Charlotte watching him, propped up on one elbow as if she'd been waiting for him to reveal the rest of his secret in his sleep. "There's more, isn't there?" she asked.

"You didn't look it up?"

"I didn't know your latest computer password."

"It's under my desk lamp. Any diagnostic guesses, Dr. Reese?" He sounded groggy or, more truthfully, a little sad, as if what they said to each other next would send their relationship bumping off in a new direction, for better or worse, and he knew he would miss this time.

"I don't want to guess. I was awake half the night trying to guess."

"I have neurofibromatosis. I had a couple of seizures when I was a kid. They thought it was epilepsy until they found the tumor."

"Neurofibromatosis?" She was surprised, but also suddenly calmer hearing him name it, a disease that could be fairly innocuous. A disease she was at least somewhat familiar with. "I wouldn't have . . . I know it can vary a lot from person to person, but I never noticed anything."

Eric pushed aside the dark hair in the cove underneath his arm; Charlotte saw a cluster of light brown spots on his skin. "Recognize it? My neurologist used to bring his medical students into my appointments to name this."

"Crowe sign? Is that right? I haven't read about it since my pediatric rotations." She touched the most visible freckles under his arm and then ran her hand across his bare chest. "You don't have any other spots? Bumps?"

He shook his head. "I have some Lisch nodules in my iris, but other than the freckles there's nothing you'd see. And my well-meaning mother treated my headaches and first seizures with herbs and diet for a long time before my father stepped in."

"Herbs?"

"Mistletoe, skullcap, goldenseal." He sounded detached from it, almost clinical. Charlotte couldn't get a sense of the confused, ill child who'd experienced it. "How long before you were diagnosed?"

"I ended up in the hospital after a seizure, and my dad whipped me off to a neurologist in Boston."

"Neurofibromatosis is inherited. One of your parents must have it."

"Autosomal dominant. Mom has a few café au lait spots, but she didn't want to get tested. It can be a spontaneous mutation—that's pretty common. And what difference would it have made? I've got it. It's in my genes forever."

"Your mother wouldn't get tested?"

"I started getting sick around the time she and my dad split up. Probably part of the reason . . . it carries a lot of extra baggage for her."

Charlotte studied the steep angles of his high cheeks and nose, all the enviably defined features her own face lacked. She wanted to touch the thickened semicircle where some surgeon had cut through his sweet, fourteen-year-old skin and sawed through his skull into his sweet, fourteen-year-old brain. She wanted to reach through the body of the adult Eric to the boy and comfort him. And whether it was the fourteen-year-old boy she envisioned or the thirty-six-year-old man she held, this sudden confrontation with his mortality broke open a new truth for her. "I think I love you," she said, having given it no thought at all, only opened her mouth to surprise both of them. Eric's eyes darkened for a second before he laughed, more to himself than to Charlotte. "You're laughing at that? *I* don't even know what I mean!"

"You chose the right profession, Charlotte. You love taking care of broken people."

"But you're not broken. Neurofibromatosis isn't even that rare—it isn't life threatening."

"No. Not unless it's causing tumors in your brain."

He didn't return any words about love, and she didn't repeat them. Not for a long time. But things changed as a result anyway. A few weeks later he invited her out to Lopez Island to meet his mother and her longstanding boyfriend. Within the first hour Charlotte knew she had two strikes against her. The first was her figure, not a surprise to her—she would at best describe her own body as "solid." Eric's mother greeted Charlotte appraisingly at thigh level before lifting her gaze and eventually smiling.

The second strike was that Charlotte was a doctor. "You'd like some more beets?" she asked Charlotte, holding the heavy platter above the table with one hand so steadily it made Charlotte's arm ache. They were sitting on a sunny, south-facing porch and Eric's mother had on sunglasses, which obscured the keen direction of her eyes. "I was getting so many red spots on my hands, those spidery blood vessels, before I started eating beets. You can put them in all sorts of dishes, Charlotte." Eric got up and walked into the kitchen.

"Too many sunburns in my life, I guess. I'll have to try that. Eric's a good cook—especially vegetables. He must have learned from you," Charlotte said.

"He had to detoxify all the poisons he was prescribed." She waved her hand, perhaps batting away an insect, an entire past. It was disconcerting not to see her eyes. Charlotte looked through the doors into the kitchen, where Eric was already washing up dishes, with dinner still on the table.

Eric's mother had made up two different rooms for them, Charlotte's at the back of a narrow converted porch, the painted plank floor sloping perceptibly toward the single-paned windows overlooking a cattailed marsh. There were some amateur watercolors tacked to the walls, predictable island scenes of pale water viewed through sea grass or dunes. One, though, was of a pensive boy shadowed in long light, viewed from the high vantage of a bird. Or a god. There was a quality of isolation about the child that seemed both sad and futile and drew Charlotte close. She was surprised to see Eric's mother's signature in the corner and wished she knew how long ago it had been painted. She had been trying to protect him for a long time, Charlotte thought, a maternal fist against a force of nature.

Eric knocked once and she moved to the window before he came in. He picked up her overnight bag. "You should take the double bed."

"No. I like this room. Listen to the birds out there."

"Red-winged blackbirds," he said. "They love these wetlands; nest in the cattails. They're polygynous—one male can have ten females."

"Don't get too inspired! Where did you come up with that trivia?"

"I wrote an article about wetlands four or five years ago. Best thing about my job—I can sound smart without knowing much of anything." The ceiling was so low he held his shoulders hunched like a gangly, self-conscious teenager. Charlotte sat on the narrow bed, remembering the first time she'd snuck up to a boy's room just to see his signed Bruce Springsteen poster—they had both climbed out a window when the boy's mother started up the stairs. Twice that age now and she felt almost as awkward in this house. From the nightstand she picked up a woven reed box with a carved wooden snake on top, coiled to strike. "Is this where your mom keeps her pet scorpions?"

Eric laughed. "It's a Lombok box. I got it for her in Indonesia."

"Ah yes—during your worldwide travels. How full of surprises you are, with all your secret pasts."

Eric closed the bedroom door and sat next to her, pressed one large hand against her chest with little resistance until she was lying across the bed and he stretched above her. "Maybe we should keep some secrets of our own later tonight."

When they got off the ferry the next day, Charlotte asked Eric to drive back to Seattle, forgetting he didn't have a valid license. "You should renew it. You could drive my car."

"I don't drive. You know that."

"No. I know you don't own a car—a cool, eco-conscious choice—but I had no idea you flat-out don't drive."

"Are you going to break up with me over it?"

"You keep asking me that." She pulled onto the crowded highway, edging between eighteen-wheelers and cars filled with kids in bathing suits dangling cigarettes and bare feet out their open windows. "Why hadn't you told her I was a doctor?"

"I don't tell her a lot of things. I should have, I guess. She's a little . . . She hasn't had it easy—grew up with next to nothing and lost her last relative, her sister, nine years ago. I've learned to love her as she is, I guess. She's too old to change."

"There's no such thing as too old to change." There was a long silence between them that Charlotte filled with recalled snippets of backhanded compliments Eric's mother had made over the course of two long days, only now they seemed born more of fear than personal judgment. How deeply can love alter a person? How much choice do any of us have? Insects streaked through the headlight beams like tiny shooting stars, and her contact lenses were beginning to sting. She put the blinker on and a second later pulled across two lanes onto the shoulder through a blare of horns. "Look, I *do* know what I meant. I meant that word. What I said."

Eric was still clutching the dashboard, the car barely at a stop. "Jesus! What are you doing?"

"I'm telling you I love you. It isn't my fault—it's not like you get to vote on these things, is it?"

He let his head fall back and closed his eyes for a moment before taking her hand. "No. There's no voting."

"And?"

"And what?"

"Am I in this alone? Say it. Let me get out now."

He squeezed her hand hard enough she was sure he was letting her know how much he was about to hurt her, distracting her with physical pain before he crushed her heart. "No. You are not alone. I love you too."

"Really? You do?" He smiled at her. "So can we agree your mother has no vote here?"

But Eric was right. It *was* in his genes forever, this nearly invisible disease, this genetic flaw with myriad expressions, so that the articles and textbooks Charlotte read could spin her from placid acceptance to anguish in the course of a few pages. The statistics were overwhelmingly in his favor—until she factored in the seizures, the brain tumor, the cell type, the recurrences. Statistics gave no peace when you hoped to replace a percentage with a name. A face. A single individual who might or might not be the one out of one thousand. At night, in bed, her worry was quieted in the urgent, instinctive drive to bond. Charlotte could almost forget Eric had a permanent, threatening diagnosis so thoroughly enmeshed in his DNA it would be his and half of all his children's and theirs beyond and beyond, until it was extinguished with the last of that cell line. It was, in ways, like falling in love with someone of another race or religion or culture. The blind accommodation of budding love blotted out all obstacles until eventually, inevitably, the outside world would force the lovers in front of a mirror: *Look at you! You think you can make your own rules? What will become of your children?*

She remembered the editorial Eric had first written for the *New York Times* about the peril of knowing the demons in your own genetic code. She understood it in an entirely new way now, how much present-day joy could be crushed by dread of your likely future. Time might loop back on itself in quantum physics, but this surely was example enough of the reason God and nature had never granted people the power to foresee what was coming. For the first time she got it—the unappreciated bliss of ignorance; that the street you cross might not be safe, that the child you carry might not be born whole, but no matter the scope of the tragedy, if you are blind to your fate you can be happy until that moment arrives.

What will become of your children? Could she ask him that? Could she let him go without asking?

One morning, six months after Lopez, she rolled close to him and said it. "I want to have a child someday, Eric."

He stroked her hair quietly for a moment, then kissed her. "I know. I love you. I've never let myself . . . Give me some time." And she loved him, too, so she let that be enough for a while.

A few months later they were with Charlotte's family for her birthday dinner, in the house where she'd grown up. Every adult but Eric was a doctor. Will and Pamela, Charlotte's brother and sister-in-law, were pediatricians; Charlotte's father was a retired surgeon, and her mother had been a pathologist. Charlie was a toddler by then and latched on to Eric after he proved willing to wind up Charlie's toy car a dozen times over without flagging. Charlotte watched them, Eric teasing Charlie with false starts the way you might coax a dog to fetch, Charlie scrunching his small body into a wad of laughter, playing on the tease as much as the racing car. A dozen times Eric let Charlie creep close and launched the car just before the baby reached him. Once, though, lunging before he'd found his balance, Charlie tumbled against Eric's knee and Charlotte saw Eric instinctively pull away before giving Charlie the car to stop his tears. Pamela had been watching their game, and happened at that moment to turn from Eric to Charlotte with a maternal smile, a questioning tilt of her head. Charlotte blushed and only then caught Eric looking across the table at her, looking at Pamela, seeing what he was not supposed to see and no longer playful at all. Her parents were oblivious, retelling one of her father's more raucous hospital stories. In the midst of it Eric abruptly left the table and Charlotte followed him into the kitchen. He was leaning against the wall with his arms crossed and shot her an uncomfortable smile when she asked what was wrong.

"No problem," he answered lightly enough. "I love hearing autopsy details between the bleeding-raw steak and the birthday cake."

"I'm sorry. We forget. I can put your steak back on the grill." She kissed him. "We've always been sweet with our patients—even my mom. And most of hers were in pieces."

He had laughed at that, but she understood that Eric had been a patient too many times himself to divorce the humor from his own history. By the time the evening was over, though, she understood that it was not her parents' graphic stories that drove Eric from the table that night. It was the look on her own face as she watched Eric playing with Charlie.

．． ．

It was Jane's twelfth day in the intensive care unit. Her lungs had stiffened so much the pressure required to inflate them had blown a hole through the delicate alveolar membranes, and they'd had to put a chest tube between her ribs. Orthopedics had one bit of good news: they planned to remove her right arm cast in a few days. Jane was no longer septic, but she had now developed a superinfection in her intestines from all the antibiotics she'd gotten, and her kidney function was deteriorating. Charlotte knew only her patient's relative youth was keeping her alive. She felt trapped in a grim version of whack-a-mole—solve one life-threatening problem just in time to discover another.

Charlotte started the day with her usual list, a computer printout of her patients' names with her own notes penned in the margin—who had a CT scan or procedure scheduled, who was going to the OR, what lines needed to be changed, what critical labs were still pending. She had developed a system over the years, using different-colored pens to highlight different levels of urgency. Jane Doe's name was nearly blotted out by red. Despite some trickles of good news, this morning's lab work showed that she would have to be dialyzed soon if things didn't turn around. And why should they turn around? Charlotte asked herself, then answered, Because sometimes, now and then, despite the APACHE II scores and SOFA scores and Glasgow Coma Scales—despite every imperfect predictor nailing the coffin closed, someone lived.

When their loved ones were unconscious and on the brink, family members would sometimes press Charlotte for any intuition she might have about their survival. She was too clinical to wade into that subjective tease, and saw it as little more than fortune-telling spun by doctors to give families a false sense of control. Instead, she gave them the best statistics she had to offer and tried to walk them through the pros and cons of necessary decisions. But in her heart she knew she *did* have a second sense about patients' survival, something closer to hope than fact. Hope for another day outside, another birthday party, another meal taken through the mouth rather than a feeding tube. She could sense it around some patients like a visible luminescence. And some not—as if they were ready to move on, crumble back to the organic matter and energy they had started with. She knew better than to share this nameless second sense. She had not always been right. And it did not take many miraculous recoveries to decide that her job was *not* to decide when life ended—it was to give nature as much time as possible.

She jumped when Felipe Otero put his hand on her back, then laughed at herself and pulled his arm over her shoulder. "Daydreaming," she said. "And you were the one up all night! How was it?"

"The usual fun. Three a.m. heroin overdose. Want a coffee while I report?"

They walked to the lounge at the end of the hallway and compared their lists, Felipe filling in the gaps from the day and night before, Charlotte adding a different opinion about one patient or another—the ICU beds were completely full this morning and she knew there would be pressure to move someone out. She looked up with a question and caught Felipe smiling at her; he had a dark scruff over his chin and his hair was a mess of luxuriant black waves after working all night. "What's funny?" she asked.

"This is how Bonnie and I trade the boys now, a morning report at handoff."

"Felipe? You didn't tell me. You moved out?"

"Last week. I couldn't say it."

"I'm sorry. I really am."

"I am too. We'll see—nothing definite yet." He rubbed his hand over his face quickly, the brush of skin against stubble at odds with his usually conscientiously groomed appearance, and the humanness of it somehow made his loss more palpable for Charlotte. "You know there's a meeting about Jane today," he said.

"I didn't get an e-mail. Did I? I get too many. What's it about?"

"She has a professional guardian now—I think Helen Seras wants her to meet us. The ethics board too."

"What did Helen do? Look at Jane's hospital bill?"

"Watch out—the walls have ears. My hope is that when they finally identify her, she turns out to be an heiress. They'll name a new wing after her handsome donation."

"The Jane Doe Memorial Wing—I can see it now. When she's identified I wonder if the hospital will call her insurance company before they call her family. Assuming she's insured."

"You assume so optimistically. I'm going to take a shower and shave before the meeting—save me a seat."

There were no seats to save; Charlotte edged behind the filled chairs toward the back corner of the room. Helen smiled at her. "We're a little tight. The larger conference room was booked." It seemed to Charlotte that Helen was always smiling, as if she had been hired to smile—to make it clear how completely at peace she was announcing the hospital's policy decisions, whatever they might be and however the staff might respond. Felipe had enough business sense to appreciate Beacon's perpetually increasing debt and balance

Charlotte's tendency to mistrust their motives, but Felipe wasn't here and this room was already putting Charlotte into a dour mood. It was usually reserved for family conferences and Charlotte had broken too much bad news at this table, guiding wives and sons and daughters across the gap between the possible and the probable, circling surreal definitions of meaningful life.

There were four or five people here from the ethics board, a medical social worker, and some of the nurses who'd taken care of Jane. Charlotte saw Anne trying to look invisible, tucked into a folding chair at the back with her eyes half-closed like she was dozing, though she was likely memorizing every word. Sitting next to Helen was Keith Sonnenberg, Beacon's guardian ad litem, wearing his signature dark tailored business suit and jazzy bow tie, his wiry gray hair sticking out above one ear after he took his glasses off. He'd been to the ICU twice in the last week to see Jane, and something in his contemplative response to Charlotte's medical explanations made her trust him—the way he cupped his hand over his mouth with his shoulders hunched while she described what the fat globules dislodged from Jane's femur had done to her brain, mulling it pensively for a moment before saying, "Hmm. I see," to himself, and then moving on to his next question. Sitting next to Keith was a woman, probably in her early forties, whom Charlotte had never met.

Helen started. "I'm sure you all recognize that Jane is a unique case for Beacon. We've never had an unidentified with us for so long—an unconscious patient with no family. No voice, essentially. It's a difficult position for the hospital. For all of you. Beacon has filed a petition of guardianship and Keith, our GAL, has been able to expedite that with the commissioner. So I . . ."

Anne's hand shot up. "Sorry—in the dark over here. A petition for what?"

Keith looked like he was about to explain but Helen jumped in. "Guardianship. A certified professional guardian, or CPG. Given how critically ill Jane is, at some point she may need someone to speak for her—to address her medical directive."

"You mean whether we should keep going or pull the plug," Anne added, and when Helen went silent, "I'm just trying to be clear about what you're saying."

"We have no idea what Jane Doe—who has an actual name and personal story—would want if she can't recover. It isn't Beacon's place to decide whether she should be artificially kept alive or"— Helen's lips pressed into a tight line and Charlotte knew she was tempted to spit back Anne's own words—"allowed to die naturally. And we aren't there yet. I'm not suggesting that. Keith? Would you like to introduce Ms. Herrand to everyone?"

Keith did not look wholly comfortable being the diversion from this hiccup, but he gave a considered "Hmmm," slowly got to his feet, and explained that the commissioner had reviewed Jane Doe's case and officially designated her as an "alleged incapacitated person, or AIP" (which struck Charlotte as a malignant twist of legalese—anyone who walked into Jane's room would know her incapacity was way beyond "alleged") and, given this official stamp, the commissioner had assigned Jane a CPG.

Now the woman on Keith's left stood up and Keith let her take over the discussion. Christina Herrand wore no makeup, but it suited her well-defined, lightly lined face. Her voice was so quiet everyone in the room stopped moving in their seats or shuffling papers in a collective effort to hear her. "As Ms. Seras said, this situation presents an unusual dilemma. Most Does are identified long before the legal process catches up to the point of designating a CPG, and certainly there's hope that this patient will find her loved ones—well, *they* will find *her*—before any critical decisions need to be made. The legal system can't replace family. You all know that. Even for professional caretakers there can be emotional attachments that feel"—she paused and looked at the faces around her— "offended, for lack of a better word. On the other hand, a complicated case like Jane's can stir different opinions about end-of-life choices within the care team, particularly when there is no family member to advise them on the patient's wishes. My job, as a professional guardian, is to become that adviser. So for now, think of me as Jane's family. The one who can speak for her until she can speak for herself."

Felipe walked in just then, gracefully introducing himself to the whole room and reigniting Helen's smile. That Latin charm—Charlotte had told him more than once that he was wasting his best asset by being a doctor; he should be an ambassador, a Ferrari salesman, or at the least a highly paid gigolo. The conference went on for twenty more minutes as Helen called on various specialists to discuss Jane's multiple failing systems and medical options. From across the room Charlotte watched a patchwork of notes collect on Christina's yellow legal pad, some circled or boxed and connected with lines or arrows. The *Christina Herrand Mind Map of Impossible Decisions Made Simple*, Charlotte thought. Christina didn't look old enough to be in this job. Only someone who had raised children and grandchildren and buried parents could have sufficient wisdom to be a mandated guardian—a stranger yesterday and as powerful as nearest kin today.

Charlotte knew the patient better than anyone here, and when it was her turn to speak, Christina seemed sensitive to that—her face softened; she attended every word. But it was more than that. There was a sympathy in her eyes that reached out to Charlotte, almost an apology, like she knew she was hearing more than clinical facts. Christina asked Charlotte to explain in lay terms what had probably happened during Jane's initial surgery immediately after the car accident. Charlotte went step by step through the evidence that the fat emboli from Jane's leg had caused her brain damage and seizures. "It isn't like a stroke, is it?" Christina asked.

"Sort of. Think of the bits of fat as a shower of sparks hitting the brain, and every spot they hit is injured."

"Permanently?"

Permanently? Charlotte hated that question—nothing about the human condition was permanent. "There is a good chance that parts of her brain will never fully recover. But I think you're asking if Jane could have a meaningful life again and I can't answer that until she's off all the sedatives and her blood chemistry is back to normal. She needs more time. All the time we can give her." And a universally acceptable definition of "meaningful," she was tempted to add.

Felipe was the last to speak, and Charlotte heard the hint of accent that crept in whenever he was tired after a night on call; it lent a sadly romantic note to his discourse on Jane's history and likely future. He explained that the latest complication was her kidneys, initially shocked by the low oxygen levels and low blood pressures she had suffered after her surgery and then, just as they were recovering, she had developed an infection and her blood pressure had dropped again. She would probably need dialysis in the next day or so.

Helen Seras asked, "Can you tell me, Dr. Otero, if she isn't dialyzed, how long might she survive?"

"That is perhaps the only easy question you have asked. Her potassium level will rise about one point a day, and when it exceeds seven, her heart will fibrillate and she'll die. Painlessly."

At noon people began to leave the room for other patients and other meetings. Felipe waited for Charlotte and as they neared the door Christina Herrand intercepted them. "Dr. Otero, what do you think the chances are that Jane will survive this?"

"Survive? There are many ways to survive. Do you mean will she wake up? Go back to her life as she knew it before? Those chances are slim, Ms. Herrand."

"Slim," she repeated the word to herself like that might reveal more than Felipe had said. "Could you make a percentage guess?"

Felipe glanced at Charlotte and she knew what he was feeling—they had been here before with patients, had this same conversation with actual relatives, people who shared blood or name or love with someone so near death. They wanted numbers. Numbers were comforting, numbers were the Dow Jones average and mortgage rates and the statistics of lightning strikes. "Okay," Felipe finally answered. "Eleven percent of slim."

Christina asked Charlotte to introduce her to Jane. The nurse who'd been covering for Anne during the meeting reported that Orthopedics had scheduled Jane's cast removal for the next day. She'd needed to suction Jane's tracheostomy a few times but otherwise the patient was stable. Stable, Charlotte thought, seeing Christina react to her first view of Jane. Stable, meaning no deterioration. No improvement. The downhill tumble arrested but the monumental climb back up barely begun.

Christina walked to the bedside and turned to look at Charlotte, waiting for her. "Why does she have a tracheostomy?"

"We put in a trach anytime a patient needs long-term ventilation—when they'll have to be on the breathing machine for more than a few weeks." Charlotte whispered the words out of habit as much as for any valid concern that Jane might hear them. Early in her career she had seen a supposedly sedated patient open her eyes when an oncologist had described her tumor as "a death sentence." And once, freakishly, a cardiac patient had gone into ventricular fibrillation and been coded for forty-five minutes with chest compressions and electric shocks—as close to dead as a live person can get. He'd survived, miraculously, and the next Christmas, Charlotte got a nice card from him that contained a miracle of its own—a postscript quoting an exact phrase she had used to convince the code team to keep going for just three more rounds, "my lucky number," before they called it off.

Jane's face was pale, flaccid, and swollen from the fight to balance her fluids and blood pressure. The stuffed toy raccoon Charlotte had bought for her had rolled facedown into the corner of the bed. With each delivered breath the coiled plastic tubing that tethered Jane to the ventilator moved like something alive. Charlotte leaned near and said, "Jane, someone is here to meet you. Her name is Christina Herrand." Then she pulled a chair to the bedside for Christina, left the two of them, and started working on chart notes at the computer. After fifteen minutes or so she looked up. Christina was still there, sitting quietly with her head tilted slightly, her hand resting lightly on Jane's casted arm. Charlotte couldn't see her face from this angle and wondered if she might have dozed, she was so still. Finally Christina stood and gathered her purse and briefcase, brushed her fingers against Jane's cheek, righted the toy raccoon, and then walked over to Charlotte. She whispered, "You won't know how much she'll remember about the accident until you can take her off the ventilator?"

"Her MRI showed the fat emboli injured a lot of her brain, as I explained in the meeting. On top of that her blood pressure and oxygen levels were low for a long time." She paused, trying to assess whether Christina understood how critical that was. "We really can't know how much permanent brain damage she has yet. It could take months."

"Or years? Years spent . . . like this?"

She said it kindly, inoffensively, but the phrase piqued Charlotte, as if Christina Herrand were already predicting a contest. Charlotte wanted to give her the benefit of the doubt, though. This case *was* "an unusual dilemma," to quote Christina. This Jane Doe had family, most likely. Somewhere. God forbid they pop out of the woods after Beacon and its legal teams and guardians, these strangers, made an irreversible decision.

Just then an aide came into the room and called out, "Good morning, good morning!" She walked to Jane's bedside. "Hello, Ms. Doe, it is a beautiful sunny Tuesday and it's time for your bath!" She turned on the faucet at the sink and with a clatter of plastic and metal she filled a pink bucket with warm water.

"That's nice—they bathe her?" Christina asked.

"Oh, yes. She gets physical therapy too," Charlotte said. "Christina, may I ask, have you had much intensive care experience?"

"Actually, this is only my second medical case, and the first was for financial guidance."

"Do they give you any medical training? For your work?" Charlotte asked.

Christina seemed to weigh Charlotte's intent. "CPGs work in many different areas, whenever someone needs help with legal decisions because they're too overwhelmed or unstable." She paused. "I have no specific medical training. No. But then neither do most family members."

The aide placed the bucket on the chair Christina had left at the bedside and pulled the sheet back. Christina was visibly startled and took a step toward Jane. "What's wrong with her hand?" Three of Jane's fingers were blue black.

"It's ischemia. When her blood pressure was low for so long, her limbs weren't getting enough flow." Charlotte eased the sheet off Jane's lower body. All of her toes were a mottled purple and the lower portion of her right foot was obviously dead—black sunken skin edged with a serpentine line of bright pink. "It isn't infected, so we're leaving it alone for now. She'll have to have it removed eventually. If she recovers."

Christina brought a hand to her mouth. "My God."

Yes, thought Charlotte. My God, indeed.

Charlotte, Eric, Pamela, and Will had decided to meet for dinner the next evening at a restaurant on the pier. Charlotte arrived late, as often happened, this time held up by a phone call about Jane from the orthopedics team just as she was leaving the hospital. She found them drinking cocktails at a table in the back that overlooked Elliott Bay, all of them bathed in summer sunlight reflected off the water. Pamela hugged her as if they hadn't seen each other in months, though they rarely went a week without talking. Eric stood up to pull out Charlotte's chair; after three years together he still treated her with manners her grandmother would have demanded.

Pamela poured Charlotte a glass of wine from the nearly empty bottle on the table and said, "Eric's telling me about all the quirky genetics stuff he's learned researching this new book. Apparently there's a lot more incest going on than anybody's admitting to—shows up when they do the organ matching. I want to know if they keep a transplant list for cats. Effie's kidneys are going, and the vet says I should think about putting him down. It would kill the boys. And me. God, I've had him longer than I've had *you*," she said, leaning into Will's shoulder. Pamela had a passion for both cats and birds, though an unfortunate intersection of the two had left her currently birdless. Effie was an enormous tortoiseshell—a male, which Pamela swore was so rare he was worth what she paid. He'd nearly eaten Charlotte's own cat alive when she'd boarded him over a weekend.

"Did Eric tell you his book's almost finished?" Charlotte said.

"It is? We have to toast!"

"I still have a chapter to go. And I never toast until after the reviews come in," Eric said.

Charlotte felt compelled to add that he never read his reviews, not even when she screened them first. "But he's close enough to finishing, he's looking at new laptops. He buys a new one for every book. Like they came with a preloaded manuscript."

"What do you do with the old ones?" Will asked.

"I give them to my brothers."

"Where did the youngest decide to go to school?"

"Seattle University. He'll be at my place for a few weeks this summer. He wants me to help him get a dog." Eric started telling them about his half brother's scholarship, the new girlfriend, the plot for sneaking a dog into his dorm room. Eric's voice lifted whenever he was on the subject of his two half brothers, but especially Jimmy, the younger one. He talked faster, easier, with an almost parental pride, understandable given that Eric was practically old enough to be his brothers' father. Suddenly Charlotte became aware of Pamela's probing, almost wistful gaze, begging the question of when Eric and Charlotte would finally move forward and have their own child. Her instinctive response was to change the subject. "Hey, I've got news from Beacon Hospital. My Jane Doe has finally given us a clue about her identity!"

Pamela leaned closer. "She's identified? How did that not make the six o'clock news?"

"Well, no, she isn't identified. But the orthopedics department took off her cast this afternoon and discovered a scar. Unique enough it might match with records somewhere, or at least be recognized by someone."

"I bet she's from the Olympic Peninsula after all—some little town out there and whoever knows her wants her to stay missing. Maybe it will turn into a murder mystery. Attempted murder, at least. Eric can write a book about it. What did they find?" Pamela asked.

Charlotte hadn't seen the scar herself yet, but she'd already called Blake Simpson to give him the orthopedist's description. "Some circular rings wrapping around her right upper arm. The deputy on her case knows about it; it might be in the news tomorrow."

Pamela asked if it could be a tattoo or gang mark and maybe that was why she'd been run down, but before Charlotte could answer, Will asked, "How does that feel? For you, I mean. I have the sense you've been her family so far. It might be strange to have a husband or parent step in and make decisions."

The question stopped her. How did it make her feel? Her job wasn't to be Jane's family—Keith Sonnenberg and Christina Herrand had made that clear. The legal system might be allowed to act as Jane's family, but not her. Not the doctor. For Charlotte the agenda was clear—to use the best of modern medicine to keep Jane alive. To hope that at some point, some part of her mind would recover. It was vague, yes. She meant it to be vague. "At some point" required no time limit. "Some part of her mind" required no measurable parameters. But what if Jane's family believed keeping her alive was futile? Cruel, even? Other doctors at Beacon had said as much. Christina Herrand likely agreed. "I don't know. I guess it depends on how well they knew what Jane would have wanted. But how well does anyone know that about someone else? Even family? Does anyone really know what they'd want until the time comes?"

Pamela said, "Well, doctor to doctor, we both know nobody gets out alive."

Eric was quieter than usual on the walk home. Charlotte wrapped her arm through his, pacing her step to his longer stride out of habit. "Too much medical talk?"

Eric shrugged. "I should be used to it by now. Sometimes too much." He dropped it after that, but his body was less relaxed against her own. He had never discussed his brain tumor with Charlotte's family. She wanted to tell him she understood—to risk burdening him with how much his own medical condition weighed on her too. They could talk about so much together, but never this. The facts, yes, but not the implications. Sometimes Charlotte saw Eric take a Tylenol and she wanted to rush him in for another MRI. It was always there in the background, in the scar on his head barely concealed by his thick black hair, in the extra years it had cost his education, his career, in the missing, broken gaps that nobody but him could mend. And, more and more lately, in the stalled decisions for her own future that seemed to be eroding the love between them. All stolen by a single fractured gene.

"I've never told Will or Pamela about your medical history. Being pediatricians, they would totally get it, but . . . What am I saying? I'm just saying I think it's your decision, not mine."

"No big deal." But he headed for the bathroom as soon as they were back at his apartment. Charlotte heard the medicine cabinet open and close before he took a long shower. She was half-asleep by the time he got into bed, so cautious not to awaken her she knew she would hit either a stone wall or an argument if she tried to talk it out. In minutes he was snoring and she was wide awake. She walked her cold feet up his back until he muttered and let go of the day in a long sigh, rolled onto his side, and breathed quiet enough for Charlotte to let her mind go.

Why could she not love an uncomplicated man? Her mother had done it for forty-two years—found someone smart and sturdy and been plenty entertained by arguing about the pros and cons of lumpectomy over mastectomy, laparoscopic surgery versus open. Their shared careers, two children, and four weeks of vacation (usually to medical meetings in serendipitously tropical locations with suspiciously empty meeting rooms) had kept her parents happy enough. But we love who we love, and how do you fix that if you discover you need different futures? She couldn't think about it without feeling the solid earth split black and gaping beneath her.

Eric was already up when Charlotte woke the next morning. He'd made coffee and put out a plate of French toast for her; his own dirty dish was already in the sink. He sat at his computer, possibly so engrossed in his chapter he didn't hear her come in. More likely upset with her about the half-finished conversation last night, she decided. It frustrated her again, too easily. "Eric, would you just say it? Tell me I was insensitive. That my family drives you crazy." He turned around and looked at her with an expression she hadn't expected, a surprised half smile on his lips but such anguish in his eyes it drilled even deeper into her guilt. "Okay, *I'll* say it. I was thoughtless. I . . ."

"Oh, God, Charlotte. Please stop. This is not . . . I need to go to the hospital with you."

A breath caught in her throat. She saw it all now—how quiet he'd been after dinner, the long shower and something taken from the medicine cabinet before he slept deep and hard. Had he seen his neurologist lately? Had he had his routine scan and kept the results to himself? "Why? What?"

"I need to see your patient."

"My patient?"

"The scar on her arm you described—I need to see it. I think I know who she is."

· 10 ·
raney

Raney didn't totally believe what she said to Bo the night they came so close to making love, that "the universe rolls over people like me." But it was plenty clear the human race considered some people more equal than others, and her words served their purpose. The next day a FedEx truck dropped the book of Monet paintings at her apartment with no return address, no note—like it had been sent to her from the painter's Giverny grave. Other than that Bo didn't make any effort to reach her.

She caught the bus back to Quentin for the holidays; Christmas came and went with no letter, no phone call, no late-night pebbles thrown at her window. It was a vacuum of contact so intentional it made its own raucous noise and crushed even the bit of hope she would admit to. There were nights after Grandpa went up to bed when Raney would finish the dishes and pull a kitchen chair over to the telephone, stare at the infuriatingly mute black box, and think herself through every step of calling Bo: how she'd pick up the receiver, punch in the ten numbers burned so crisp in her memory she knew the page and column they occupied in the Seattle phone book. She could feel the hard circle of plastic pressing against her head and hear the punctuated hum as their lines connected. Her imagination always screeched silent at the moment she should have heard Bo saying hello. She was never going to make that call or put a pen to paper—partly because there were not enough words to make either of them feel right about what had or hadn't happened. But partly, also, to punish herself. As if she needed to be sure she hurt as much or more than she suspected she'd hurt him.

Three days after New Year's an overnight frost laced every twig and tire rut with shimmering crystals and Quentin threw off its blanket of clouds to the bright-blue arctic cold. As always, Grandpa got up and dressed before the sun was above the horizon. He went out to the barn to feed the dogs and hens and did not come back in. Raney was at the kitchen window in her bathrobe when some wrong shape between the sharp shadow of the barn door and the glittering grass caught her eye. It was Grandpa's booted leg. In a breath she was out the door and kneeling over him. The white enamel pan of chicken feed had been dumped and pellets lay scattered in the folds of his jacket and the stubble of his beard like oat-colored hail.

"Slipped," he said. "The ice."

He raised an arm for Raney to help him up, but halfway to sitting he collapsed again. "Grandpa? What is it? Did you break something?" He shook his head and rubbed at his left shoulder, his face the same color as the frost. "Did you fall on your arm?"

"It's not broken. Just . . . hurts." He rubbed it again and then balled his fist into the middle of his chest. Raney bunched an old horse blanket under his head and ran into the kitchen to call 911.

Grandpa stayed in Jefferson General Hospital for two weeks. The doctors told Raney he'd lost 25 percent of his heart. She bit back the question of which quarter was gone—the piece that loved tramping alone through the woods following deer up impossibly vertical paths, or the piece that loved felling and chopping up two great fir trees every summer so they could be self-sufficient with heat for a full winter, or the piece that loved hauling engine parts out of old trucks and cars to refurbish and sell. Or maybe, God forbid, the piece that loved her.

He seemed diminished when he came home, his blusters and gripes punctuated with question marks. After a week or so, when Raney still couldn't goad the fight back into him, she concluded it was less from circulatory weakness than from slamming into his own mortality. But mortality wasn't really the right word. Dependence— that was the demon slipping in like a wintery draft, half-disguised in the pills and capsules they sent home with him.

On the twelfth day, when he'd barely joined into a conversation with her, Raney decided the noise of one steady voice was better than questions answered by silence. She grabbed a book off her bedroom shelf and pulled a rocking chair next to Grandpa's bed, crossed her feet on the end of his mattress, and started reading out loud. "'Chapter One. Third. I've watched through his eyes, I've listened through his ears, and I tell you he's the one—'"

Grandpa interrupted, "Who's the one?"

"I don't know yet. We have to keep reading."

"Sounds like it's about Jesus or something. Religion or something."

Raney flipped the book over and looked at the jacket cover, realized it was one of the books Bo had left at her house the first summer he'd been in Quentin—one of the few she hadn't read. "It's a novel, Grandpa. *Ender's Game* by a man named Card. Orson Card," and she continued reading through the first page until he interrupted her again.

"I just got out of a hospital—I don't want to hear a story about people having operations."

"Well, what *do* you want? *Little House on the Prairie*?"

"At least I'd learn something useful." He pushed a Kleenex box off the bedside table and dug a big paperback out from under a stack of *Auto Trader*s. "Here. Read this."

Raney readjusted herself in the chair and flipped through the book for a minute before she started reading, first to him and then out loud to herself in a tone of disbelief. "'I believe we are the descendants of people who left civilizations among the stars. . . . The world's cities will perish but there need not be another Dark Age. Instead, we can go from our Survival Homesteads on to the stars.' Grandpa? Where did you find this?"

He sat up with more vigor than he'd shown since his heart attack and snatched the book away. "Give it t'me. Look here. Oh, damn—I can't read it without my damn glasses. Look here." He opened the book to a different page and thrust it into her lap.

She saw the title now, *The Survivor*, volume 1, by Kurt Saxon, and read the table of contents: "'How to Make a One or Two Horsepower Windmill from Scrap. How to Make the Best Black Powder. Surviving a Nuclear Winter.' A nuclear winter? The Berlin Wall came down last year, Grandpa, or didn't you hear?"

"And Saddam Hussein is taking over countries left and right. It never hurts to know how to take care of yourself, Renee. By yourself. You never know when you'll be left all alone."

Raney shut the book, stung as sharply as if her grandfather could have known how close to her heart his arrow of personal pessimism had landed. "Take your pills, Grandpa. I'm gonna put dinner on."

"Renee," he called out just as she reached the door. She stopped, her hand still on the doorknob, unable to look at him. After a minute of silence she heard him exhale so deep she had to turn around, worried it was a last gasp, and was almost more startled to see him colored with emotion. "I know it's not easy, the years between leaving one home and finding another. I know it's not easy."

Until the day Raney told her grandfather that she was not going to return to the Art Institute, she'd had only one blowout argument with him. She had just turned twelve, and after much pleading on her part, he agreed to take her on a backpacking trip. When the awaited day came, they hiked eleven miles uphill to the campsite with gear and food and water, her load nearly as heavy as his, and by the time he finally dropped his pack and said they were done for the day, Raney was holding her eyes wide to keep tears from spilling down her dirty cheeks. Grandpa counted five matches into her palm and pointed to the blackened ring of rocks in the middle of a clearing, proof any number of former hikers had readily made fires on this site. Then he started stringing up the rope and tarp that would be their tent as if he didn't doubt they'd be heating chili and warming their stiff hands within the quarter hour.

The sun was below the tree line and mosquitoes emerged in a rank miasma. Her sweat-soaked T-shirt grew cold, reeking of the smoke-and-pepper musk new to her body. She walked the perimeter of the campsite gathering sticks and dead wood, constructing her timber tower with the same careful layering she used for their woodstove at home. But in the woodstove she'd always wadded a brown paper grocery bag under the kindling pyramid. She struck the first match on a campfire rock and touched it to the smallest dry stick, watched the bark glow and flare, then dampen just as quickly when the bark burned away to pulp.

On her next try she collected pine needles dry as old bones, dead aspen leaves, and brittle gray cones. She lit the second match, waited until the sulfur burned away and the tiny wooden stick held a steady blue flame, then touched it to each material in turn. Only the fine spray of pine needles burned. She cupped them against the wind down to the bottom of her pyre, where they dissolved from orange to gray ash without so much as a thread of smoke. Matches three and four died an equally futile death. Her hands grew clumsy and thick with the cold and the fifth match snapped in half, so close to the bulbous tip it burned her fingers when it finally caught and she dropped it into the dirt.

Raney sat down on a rock and glared at the charred skeletons of another man's success as if all her anger might reignite a blaze. Grandpa troweled a shallow ditch around the pitched tarp, whistling through his collection of birdcalls.

Half an hour later he pried the lid off a can of chili and started eating it cold, straight from the tin. He handed her a spoon and gestured for her to dig in. Raney flew into a fury, threw the spoon into the coals, and told him she hated camping and when she grew up she would live in a house with a built-in furnace and a dial thermostat and when she didn't sleep in her own bed she would sleep in a hotel on clean sheets somebody else had to wash. He listened and nodded and then untied his Coleman bedroll and went to sleep, leaving the can of chili with its thick orange jelly of grease on a split log for Raney to eat when she chose. She had stood outside the tent, railing at him until the forest was hushed as a graveyard and she was too spent to care what she ate or where she slept.

The next morning he took her hand and led her into the woods, scanning the branches of the evergreens without even glancing at the ground. "Here," he said, stopping in front of a bough laced with pale blue-green necklaces of moss. "Tease that off the branch. Go around here." He swept his hand in a general circle. "Get three or four handfuls of the stuff." At the base of her virginal pyre he mounded up a nest of moss and handed Raney one more match. The moss caught and blazed at the first touch of the flame, burning long enough to scare all trace of damp and cold from the smaller sticks so they, too, burned and caught and in turn caught those above.

They cooked oatmeal and sausages and hot chocolate and roasted half a bag of marshmallows. Grandpa acted like last night had never happened—talking about camping trips he'd taken with Raney's grandmother before she got sick, a boyhood elk hunt with his own grandfather, "back when we used muskets and flint," and laughed gently under his breath when Raney nodded without so much as a smile. After they ate they carried the dishes to a stream and scrubbed them out with sand and sat still and quiet until all the life that depends on a stream forgot they were intruders and let them witness the ceaseless hunt for food.

After a very long while he said, "Raney, you'll make a lot of choices in your life—some like mine and some different. But you can't know who you are unless you know who you are not. Met your limits and overcome what you can. On your own." He paused, giving her time to digest this. "Do you get my meaning?" At the time, all she could wonder was why he'd put her through a cold, hungry night instead of building the fire himself. But as if assuming her silence begged more explanation, he added, "I suppose a nicer grandfather would make it easy on you—tell you how to get through life instead of make you learn it through living. Sometimes you can't find a new path until you admit you've hit your limit. Doesn't mean you're giving up—means you're smart. Tough."

The second big blowout between them happened the day Raney was supposed to go back to school in Seattle after his heart attack, him still so weak that climbing to his bedroom required two stops on the staircase. She told him she was withdrawing and moving back home, and in a burst of cursing he threatened to kick her out of the house, going as gray and breathless as the day he'd collapsed, humbled finally by a nitroglycerin tablet she stuck under his tongue. That battle too, she understood, was over an unwillingness to accept limitations—it was apparently a flaw they both shared.

For a month or more taking care of Grandpa was a full-time job, half her energy poured into making him believe he was still taking full care of himself. Other than the time he had surprised her with an envelope of $7,000 in cash, Raney had never thought about where Grandpa's money came from or went. Until it was her job to do all of the buying and cooking she had never stopped to consider how much was from their own poultry or garden or Grandpa's barter and trade. But one bitter day in February she poured soap into the tub and left the water running while she put the laundry away, then stripped and stepped into a bath of bubbly, icy-cold water. That afternoon she cashed part of her leftover school money to fill the propane tank and later that night she used a screwdriver to open Grandpa's locked desk drawer, taking care not to leave a mark on the wood, which turned out to be wasted effort as he caught her red-handed going through his papers. "You take a wrong turn at your own bedroom door, Renee?" The boom in his voice so shocked her the bank statements and bills scattered. He stared at her a minute and added, "Don't you look guilty as all hell!"

"I'm just amazed to hear you shout so loud. You must be getting better. I can't find any bank statements from the last two years. How have you been paying your bills?"

"I closed the account down. Didn't pay enough interest to cover the cost of the stamps. Why should I give them my money?"

"Do you have any?"

"You're looking for stamps?"

"Money. Do you have any money?"

"What business is that of yours?"

Raney held her retort and stuffed the outdated papers into the trash can. "Grandpa, how are you getting by? You still get your VA check? Pension?"

He crossed his arms and looked at her over the top of his crooked reading glasses. "For someone who's so worried about money you're mighty wasteful. Whole tub full of bathwater gone cold in there." With that he drew his head up, folded his glasses into his pajama pocket, and shuffled to his bed.

After two more days poking into every place she was not welcome, Raney discovered a row of tin cans in the bunker, each with the bottom cut away so the beans or corn or spaghetti could be replaced with rolls of cash bills. There were potentially, she knew, dozens of such secret caches around the farm, and for weeks she passed time unscrewing the oil and gas caps off the engines of abandoned cars ditched behind the barn, prying back loose wall planks, sitting in the dank, cloistered air of the living room praying for X-ray vision to show her Grandpa's hiding places. Finally she got a job waitressing at Loggers Restaurant and Bar. With the money from the cans and Grandpa's veterans benefits it was enough to keep them warm and fed and for Raney to occasionally buy some new canvases and paints.

In June her college roommate, Brittany, called to say she was on her way to Port Angeles and wanted to stop in to say hello. She had all of Raney's bedding and paintings in the trunk of her car, that and whatever clothing Brittany hadn't appropriated for herself. A bottle of Herbal Essence shampoo had spilled and warped the cardboard box holding Bo's book of Monet colorplates; the pages were gummed together and smelled of all the flowers trapped inside. Raney took it as a sign and accepted that she was back in Quentin to stay.

Grandpa got stronger over time—and more belligerent, either as a result of his heart attack or a source of his improvement. Some days Raney bit her tongue so many times it felt raw. She started taking the truck out to the Dungeness Spit or Lake Crescent to paint—once, on a rare day of spring sun, she drove all the way to Cape Flattery. But that evening great peaks of clouds shoved in, turning the sunset an eerie blood orange. By the time she had hiked back to the truck, the storm had gathered and redoubled above, breaking rain so hard across the highway outside Neah Bay that the worn treads on Grandpa's tires seemed to float more than roll down the road.

She waited out the worst of it drinking coffee in a diner just outside the Makah tribal boundary, the storm shivering the plate-glass window like a laundered sheet whipping in the wind. Three men at the end of the bar kept trying to buy her a beer—loosened up on plenty of their own, it was apparent—so she left even though the rain was still blinding. Thus she got only as far as Clallam Bay by the time it was fully dark, when she began to regret that she had not replaced the truck's burned-out right headlight. She didn't realize she'd missed the junction at 113 until she was all the way to Beaver Lake. No wonder she'd passed so few cars. The single headlight barely nudged the black beyond her windshield. It looked like a county-wide power outage, the modern world ended and any houses either unoccupied or absent even lanterns and candlelight. Disoriented and cursing, Raney did a three-point turn on the narrow road, the rear wheel dropping once off the pavement so that for a brief angled instant she gunned across broken branch and mud to gain traction. One mile back up the road she felt the warbling lurch of a flat tire.

"Damn. Goddamn." She shoved the gearshift into park and searched for a flashlight in the glove compartment or beneath the seat, amazed that for all he had stocked his bunker with every conceivable tool for survival, Grandpa apparently assumed his pickup would be blasted straight into a nuclear winter or fried by the radiation of an alien spaceship. The most useful thing she found in the truck was a bag of chicken feed. The reach of the single headlight through the mist died out a body-length away; Raney could practically spit farther than she could see.

She climbed out and slammed the door. After the last groan of hinge and latch had died, the air hung sodden and silent. She stood with her hands on her hips, straining to see any bit of star or moon or reflection of man-made light on the low clouds. The rhythmic grate of frogs started up from the direction of the lake; she imagined the horde of them, slime-green, squatting with their wide, judgmental frowns, shushed a moment to consider the slammed truck door and her curses but now hunkered back down to the solemn business of mating. They made her angry, this army of frogs, and not one who cared an iota for her predicament. She picked up a rock and threw it toward the chorus, answered only by the briefest swell of their collective croaking.

She opened the truck door again, flicked on the interior light, and began to poke through the general automotive refuse Grandpa had stashed in every chink and crevice. Under a tarp in the pickup bed she discovered a spare that looked older than the truck itself. There was a tire iron and jack behind the seat. She hunted for a stone large enough to wedge under the opposite tire, placed the jack underneath the U-bolt, fit the crank into position, and tried to turn it. Nothing gave. She threw more weight into it, straining so with the effort her pulse hummed inside her skull and her eyes teared. Finally the rust etched into the metal threads gave and the lift began to rise, resisting when it hit the full weight of the truck, but with a few more cranks the level plane of the flat tire relaxed into a curve. Two more revolutions with the last of her strength and the tire hung free of the ground. She felt like Hercules, Athena—elated—until she remembered that she had forgotten to loosen the lug nuts.

Raney had only changed one tire before, when she was already late to meet friends and came running downstairs to find Grandpa had let the air out of the rear wheel. It was a hot summer evening and he was settled on one of the nylon strap chairs beside the pond, his beer on an overturned five-gallon bucket next to a pile of round rocks he was slinging at targets both fixed and on the wing. She'd had her license for three months and had suffered all of his lessons on jumping dead batteries, changing oil, cooling an overheated engine. He talked her through setting up the jack and wrestling off the flat tire, but after ten frustrating minutes, when sweat rings stained her best shirt and she was sure her friends had given her up for the night, she threw a lug nut at his head.

"You're going to need that."

"Why is it you insist on teaching me every goddamn thing in as hard a way as you can make it?"

"Don't cuss. Your grandmother wouldn't have liked it."

The memory of that evening inspired a fresh string of curses shouted out to the dark, swallowed up by the forest, the frogs startled into unified silence for a single lonely moment until one brave bull coaxed them back into song.

Then, beyond the rolling chorus of croaks, she heard something else, something not of the forest or the lake. Another car engine. And then a flicker of light raked between the trees. Headlights taking a curve in the road so they bore steadily at her, blinding as twin search-lights before they disappeared at the next bend. Her first emotion was relief. She wouldn't spend the night huddled under a plastic tarp in the passenger seat eating chicken pellets! But then she considered her circumstances: a mud-splattered young woman stranded beside a de-crepit, hitched-up truck with one hubcap set out like a begging bowl. She tried to recall how long she'd driven off the main road before catching her mistaken turn. She tried to gauge the boundaries of the reservation, how far inside or outside those boundaries she might be.

The truck's interior bulb was dim, but in this wet black nowhere it would surely have been spotted. The car took another bend; lights winked in, then out of sight. Raney pulled the tire iron out of the socket, turned off the interior light, and groped her way around the pickup's bed until she was on the far side. She lost her footing on the embankment but stayed low when she heard the car coming closer, saw the road under the truck glint gray as the headlights shone dead on. She held her breath and listened to the engine, said a prayer when the tone dropped a note as it slowed. "All right, God, I suppose you have a plan and this is part of it but I am asking for a break here, if I have any say at all. Which I probably don't, so why the hell am I bothering to ask?" And so the prayer took its usual course of circular deterioration, if on a more desperate note.

Maybe the car would slow just enough to pull around and go on by. Maybe they would stop and offer help. Most people were nice enough, weren't they? Her grandmother would have said yes, that mean people were mean because too many people had been mean to them, and if you were nice to them for once you might turn the cycle of meanness around to kindness. Her grandfather would have said the world had plenty of mean people in it and it only took one or two, particularly when they were elected into office, to ruin your life and everybody else's, so why expose yourself to any more people than absolutely necessary?

The engine sounded close now, slowing down, not a steady slowness like people gauging how much clearance to leave, but a curious slowness—people assessing this unexpected gift at the side of the road, maybe a road they traveled every day, because this was their land and they had a right to make their own rules and maybe here all that mattered was who caught whom. In the dropping pitch of the engine she could hear them debating. And then the car stopped, hummed a minute more before it went silent—only the tick-tick of contracting metal. Raney heard men's voices, muffled through the window. Her bladder clenched. The car door opened and someone stepped out.

"Thought it was her truck. Engine's warm." There was a scuffle of dirt, metal on rock and the hubcap spun. "Forgot to loosen the lugs before they jacked it up. Fella wouldn't do that. Must be our lady friend."

"Open the door, man. Anybody hiding on the floor?"

Raney felt the truck shift as the driver's door opened and a faint illumination from the overhead light gave shape to the steep slope dropping away inches from her feet. She should roll down the bank and crawl into the woods, lose herself in the pitch. She should bolt down the road, yelling loud enough somebody would hear, wake up, and call for help. She gripped the tire iron with one hand, the other stretched about a great stone, measuring the weight and cut of its angles. Her pulse hammered the base of her brain.

"Only thing hiding in here is a purse. Girl don't go far without her purse." Another car door opened and shut, and Raney heard a third man's voice, one she recognized from the diner. All three sounded too happy at this discovery, too bored with the plain sameness of every night before and after. And then, at the back of the truck, a voice too close. "Hey there! What'd I say?" A light blinded her. "Didn't think you'd wander off." Then a brown-skinned hand reached out and gripped her upper arm.

Raney struck out with the tire iron, swinging in a wide arc until it hit something that gave and crumpled with a pain-searing yelp. The light flashed across the truck and through the canopy of trees, then rolled down the embankment, sinking in the mud where it glowed like a luminescent fish before it died. She crawled forward pawing for the front bumper, the clutched rock cutting into her hand. There was a scuffle of feet and the smell of kicked-up mud and swamp rot, a hoarse call, "Your way. Round the hood," and then she was lifted off the ground, off her feet, striking with the rock blind and wild until it was wrestled from her, and she was pinned against warm, hard sheet metal by two arms, by four separate hands, her head held hard against the hard metal so that when the horn sounded it ached through her teeth, rang through her skull. And then a light, bright enough to see the loose hems of shirts and bulge of jeans.

"Off!" The car shook and groaned. A warp of time, a hesitation. "Off! Now!" An easing, the joints of her elbow, wrist, shoulder looser. Released.

Raney slumped to the ground, wedged as much of her body under the car as she could without losing skin, and even for that she would have felt no pain until she saw gouged flesh. In the visible slice of road she watched a play of feet and legs, a shifting and gathering, a stumble and backing away. Eight legs together, then two apart, sides taken, one outnumbered. Men arguing, something flung into the swamp grass—her purse, she guessed, given her luck. After a paralyzed moment six feet scuffed across the gravel shoulder, three dark figures along the edge of woods soon dissolved beyond the limit of light. And then only two feet left, and the night fallen silent—no sound of men or frogs, not even her own breath, so locked inside her chest it burned.

She saw black boots with a low heel, shiny like they'd been polished, only a fringe of fresh mud from the road lipping the sole. The blue jeans had been hemmed by hand—the stitches even and tidy but the thread not chosen to match the inseam. Should have gone with yellow if he couldn't find gold, she thought, and from a wild corner of her mind came the notion that she should pass that handy tip along before he raped and murdered her. And then a shock of black hair dangled into view. She ducked her head farther out of the light.

"They're gone. Afraid your purse is gone too, 'less it rises on the back of a turtle." Raney stayed quiet. "Not a safe road to be alone on. At night." Then to himself, "I guess she knows that by now."

"Well, now I'm not alone. Got you here. Is that better or worse?"

"Come on out, would you? My back's starting to hurt."

"Yeah? At least it's not seared to the underside of an engine." She flattened her elbows and winged low and slow between the muddy grit of road and the catch of metal out from underneath the car. The man put a hand down to help her up, but Raney rolled away from it and he stepped back, arms held out palms up like you might show a dog you meant no harm. After a moment of standoff she said, "I don't know if I should be thanking you or cursing you."

"Cursing, probably. I offered them a lift back in Clallam. Should have smelled what they were. Your spare is flat, you know."

"Course I know. Makes all the sense in the world to jack your truck up to change one flat for another." The man was no taller than her, shorter if he took off his boots, she guessed; dark eyes, hair, skin, his teeth shone in the big square light he'd left sitting on the hood of the car. They looked clean. Frequently flossed.

"I can give you a lift. Backseat or front, your choice. You can drive, if that's better."

"I don't need a lift from you." The man drew his arms tight around himself and traced a circle with the heel of his boot before he looked up the black, deserted road, waited for her to go on. "Give me your keys."

He nodded once and put his car keys in her hand. "Name's Cleet."

"I don't give a shit what your name is," Raney answered.

Cleet Flores's grandfather had been a strawberry farmer on Bainbridge Island until the early sixties, when a lot of the Filipino communities scattered as land there became too expensive to keep for crops. People wanted houses and stores and restaurants. Supermarkets where you could buy canned and frozen foods. The fields he had cultivated and picked as a child were a high school and a shopping center now. If his grandfather had held on to a tenth of it, Cleet's father and even Cleet and his mother and brother would have been rich. Instead, Cleet's dad was caught betwixt and between—not a farmer but not gentry. Not educated but not able to earn a living with the skills he'd practiced. He took up fishing for a number of years, working out of Alaska in the summers and hiring onto any local boat that would have him the rest of the year.

One fall his father came back from Alaska and found twelve-year-old Cleet at home alone, Cleet's mother and brother packed up and gone back to the Philippines, where, her letter said, at least her own father still owned a house. Cleet had refused to leave. When his father left to fish four years later and never came back, Cleet took stock of his options. He sat in a chair in the middle of their two-room, rented cabin and considered what he had and what he wanted to have. He considered what every person wants, at baseline. How little they really need but cannot do without and thus will always pay for—food, water, warmth, shelter. A good solid bed, a kitchen table and chairs. He looked at his father's life, and at his bank account. And he looked at his hands. He studied the pliant joints and the efficient design of size and strength and flexibility. Hands—a gift of birth, which could not be taken or taxed or licensed. He dropped out of high school and passed his GED, took the money he'd saved from his own fishing work, and enrolled in Gompers Woodworking School to become a carpenter and furniture maker. Now he lived in Port Townsend, building cabinets and kitchens for retirees who were buying up the old Victorian homes, occasionally selling his own handcrafted pieces to tourists in the local galleries.

Raney heard only the bones of his story on the ride back to Quentin, where she stopped the car and got out half a mile from her house so she could remain anonymous and lost to him. His hands had been conscientiously folded on his lap the whole way, like weapons laid down for truce. They didn't look like weapons, she had to admit before they'd even reached the cutoff back toward 113. More like Buddha hands. Calm and intentional. On a surreptitious closer glance she saw the wear of his work across the fingertips and palms, as if they were aging ahead of him, and was surprised to catch herself wondering how they would look in twenty years, stained with wood polish, nicked with scars but just as calm, she thought. Just as calm.

Grandpa wrangled a buddy from the machine shop to rescue the truck, and a week or so later Raney found herself poking through woodworking galleries in Port Townsend. In the third one along, not on Water Street but only a block off, she stopped in front of a simple table just large enough for a lamp and a book, a simple cove along the edge, the wood rubbed so silky you wanted to lay your cheek upon it like a pillow. How could anything so smooth be solid enough to stand on its own? The facing panel had a small bird carved in relief, a heron crouched in sinewy angles like some Asian dancer. Raney asked the clerk for the price and he gave her a quote, adding, "I can discount that some. It's been here a while and we have a new shipment due." He wrote a figure on the back of a card that read "Heron Designs, Cleet Flores." There was a PO box and phone number in one corner. She tucked the card into the back pocket of her blue jeans. She bought a cup of clam chowder and carried it out to the pier, where she sat down and ate, watching freighters skim the line of horizon bellowing smoke like spouting gray whales, and she felt Cleet's card burning through her jeans so hot she wondered if she might discover the mirrored letters of his name branded onto her bottom.

It still took her more than five months to call him, "just to say thanks, you know, for helping me out." She turned him down when he asked her if she'd like to go for coffee or a beer. A month later she found a job in an art gallery down the street from where she'd seen Cleet's table—it hardly paid for the gas it took to drive there and back every day, but it was worth it to be working with other painters, to talk to customers about color and shadow and stroke instead of French dressing versus ranch, baked potato or fries. She was crating a show one evening, alone in the rear of the shop, when the bell rang and she walked out to the desk with her white cotton gloves still on. There he was. Different than she'd remembered but better too. Shanks of black hair angling this way and that, a curl of sawdust caught near his left temple. Nice teeth, still; they looked all the creamier in his soft brown face. She felt herself blush and hated herself for it, which made her face go even hotter. "The door was supposed to be locked—we close at six. What can I do for you?"

"I saw the truck out front. You got it back. That's good."

"Course we got it back." Why had she called him that day, months ago? It was a foolish business all around. The product of loneliness, living in a falling-down house with an old man in a town all her friends had long escaped. He had a cut on his hand, small but still bright with blood, a fresh line in the map of his scars. She took off one white glove and wrapped it about his hand. He stared at the glove for a long moment and she saw him tilt his head, puzzling something out. "Except it cost more to tow it home than we could sell it for. Did you come in here to buy a painting or just to hassle me about my truck?" she said.

"I came in to ask you to go to dinner with me."

"Well, you are just the consummate rescuer, aren't you?"

"I'd hardly say buying you dinner is rescuing. Unless you're starving, which you don't look to be."

For the next year it was a stutter of walks and lunches, chance meetings when Raney was arriving or leaving the gallery, too frequently to be anything but carefully planned. She let it be that way, evasive about commitments, never calling anything a date but more and more often shifting her schedule so that it was predictable enough to intercept.

She locked up late one evening shortly before Christmas and found him waiting beside the truck, wondering if she wanted to go out for some fresh crab. She offered to drive, but he said the restaurant wasn't far. A cold snap had cleared the air and Water Street was crowded with Christmas shoppers, the sidewalks noisy and the bars full and already smelling of stale beer. Cleet pulled Raney close against him when a group blocked the path from curb to storefront, so enraptured by their own conversation they moved as a single, oblivious herd. She kept waiting for him to choose a restaurant, asked where he wanted to eat, and he said just another few blocks down. Finally he cut between two buildings and took a narrow stairway to the beach.

It was another town altogether here, the voices of shoppers and partiers blocked by the buildings, the sound of low surf washing in true and endless. Her feet slipped and dug into the rocky sand, and they had to carve their way around ghost-pale drift logs dropped by higher tides like the toothpicks of giants. Raney saw a point of yellow light ahead and soon they got to a campfire, a cooler filled with cooked crabs, rice, salad . . . Cleet unzipped a duffel hidden behind a log and handed Raney a heavy men's sea coat, then he built up the fire and spread a blanket over the log and nearby sand. He melted butter in a small pot and served the meal on real glass plates.

He must have been cooking and hauling stuff all day, Raney guessed. So this would be the night, then. He would make his move right here on these blankets, probably had a whole other duffel bag packed with pillows and sleeping bags. Her appetite disappeared and she found herself thinking through everything she said before she said it, so the echo of her conversation sounded contrived and pointless. Cleet acted totally relaxed—probably assuming they were both on the same page here. Raney began to shiver inside the coat, not sure what page she was on or even if she and Cleet were inside the same book at all. There was no moon. The cold front had whipped the sky clear as new glass and with the town lights going out, the stars looked like the edge of the universe and close enough to touch. Cleet slid off the log to put more wood on the fire, then stretched out on the blanket with one hand under his head, holding his other straight up to trace out various constellations, some Raney knew—Orion, Cassiopeia, the Dippers— more that she did not know—Hydra, Lynx, Leo. He'd learned them on the boats in Alaska when he'd worked with his dad, he said.

"How often did you go with him?"

"Three or four trips, halibut and sardines. Pay was great—I saved enough in those trips to cover school and set up my shop. Hated every minute of it!" and he laughed. He had a nice laugh. It never sounded forced or polite. Always genuine—a grace note to his general aura of calm coping. Raney got up to pour herself a second glass of wine, but rather than stepping over him to the log, she sat down on the blanket, her crossed leg touching his waist. "Turn out a few more lights in town and we might see some of the Geminid shower, over in the east, near Castor," Cleet said.

"Ah! Castor," Raney repeated, exaggerating the word to emphasize that she had no clue where to find it.

"One of the twins. Castor and Pollux." He tried to direct Raney's untrained eyes. "Castor is white—there. Pollux is darker. An orange star. The myth says the twins protect shipwrecked sailors."

"And were you ever shipwrecked?"

He laughed, more to himself this time, took a minute to answer, "No less than most."

She started pointing to other stars, making up constellations and laughing when he showed her the real ones hidden in her own inventions—she would have made a good shepherd, he said. The fire burned lower; they were both quiet. She knew he would reach for her soon, but she also knew she didn't want to force the night to a close. She wouldn't pretend she hadn't noticed his mouth, its deep, full curves that looked slow and easy. But what would happen after a kiss? She didn't want to risk losing his company just to find out what his lips might feel like. She'd just have to tell him. Make it clear but face-saving—she liked him too much to play any games. Cleet's eyes were closed, and in the firelight his face looked as smooth and proud as one of his polished wood carvings. Her legs were falling asleep and she stretched out; it was warm beside him. She pulled the edge of the blanket up to cover them both, rolling toward him to make it reach fully across. He smelled like cedar. His face was so close . . .

He startled awake, and she saw him recollect where he was. He tried to focus on her, his eyes still lazy with sleep. His full mouth curved into a smile. "Sorry! What time is it?" He held his watch so the firelight illuminated the dial. "We better get going. I have to finish a chair tonight for delivery tomorrow." He shook out the blankets and packed everything into the cooler and duffel, hid them behind a pile of drift, and said he'd get them tomorrow. Then he walked her back to her truck and waved good night from the curb while she got in and drove herself home, feeling like a total idiot.

In May, Cleet took a five-week job in Bremerton, and Raney was startled, annoyed even, to find that she missed him. He dropped by the gallery a few days after he returned to town, and she could tell he recognized that his absence had made a difference to her. It sparked a new confidence in his eyes; for the first time he exuded a masculine purposefulness as subtle as a shift in his scent but there nonetheless, pulling her as invisibly as the moon pulls the tide.

He came by again the next Friday afternoon. "Going for a drive tomorrow—it should be a nice day. I can pick you up—go up the old logging roads back of the park near the ranger station."

"I have a lot to do."

"Name the time."

"Grandpa hasn't been feeling so good."

"We can call him. Check in over the day." He waited only a beat. "Twelve thirty, then. Only you have to tell me your address."

He did not come until twelve forty-five, time enough to check her hair twice, add a braid, and take it out again. She knew him well enough to know that his tardiness was as well planned as the lunch he had packed for the two of them and the six-pack of beer he brought for her grandfather. He knocked at the back screen door and waited while she called upstairs to Grandpa and put the beer in the refrigerator.

"I hoped I'd finally meet him."

Raney glanced over her shoulder and waved a hand in the air. "Oh, he's resting. Better go."

No more than fifteen minutes out of town, Cleet took a right turn down an asphalt road that dead-ended into a webbed network of logging cuts Raney hadn't explored since she'd been a ten-year-old on a Stingray. After an hour of jolting weaves and turns he stopped the car and took the food and beer out of the trunk. "Lumpia," he said, hoisting the cooler.

"Lumpia?"

He laughed—that laugh he had where it was all to himself without shutting her out. "No. No lumpia." He led Raney down an all-but-invisible trail for half an hour until they stood in front of a cabin. Little more than a lean-to, really, with a plank door and wood-shutter windows.

"What is this?" Raney asked.

"Place my dad used to bring me. Me and my brother."

"It's yours?"

"It's no one's. Everyone's. Pretty sure this is park land. My grand-father used to come here too. Way back. Never ran into anyone who wasn't kin to me or a friend, though. Or at least Filipino. Maybe no-body else knows about it. Maybe all our ghosts and dark skin scared them away. Who knows?"

"Ghosts. What ghost stories do you have?" she asked.

"*Multos*—the souls of the dead returning." Raney didn't answer, and after a minute he looked over his shoulder at her with a teasing smile, a shank of hair shadowing his face so the clean planes of his cheek and jaw looked more Asian. Exotic. He was handsome from this angle. Maybe from any angle. "Come in and I'll tell you the story of the White Lady, who only haunts lonely places." He paused a mo-ment before unlatching the cabin door—there was no lock—and when he pushed the door open, the smell of dry dust leaked out like unrecorded days. "Man, it's like nobody's been inside since I came here with my uncle and my father, nine . . . no, eleven years. White Lady must be protecting it, huh?"

It did look untouched. The place had been passed from fathers to sons for three generations or more, but the miracle of it, Cleet told her, the magic, was that it never accumulated more than it ab-solutely needed. Not even after the forestry roads made it possible to drive so close. The structure was built of logs salvaged from the river; there were four fold-down plywood bunks hinged to the walls by steel chain links. A tub and bucket for collecting water. The only thing resembling a luxury was a small woodstove.

They spent the afternoon retracing trails he'd memorized as a child, imagined passages through the dense forest leading to the hol-lowed-out trees and boulders that a boy would be drawn to. Every place had a story, some of little more than a snared squirrel, a fallen bird; some of long weeks surviving here like primitives with no com-merce, only the food they caught or scoured from the woods. He had lived so much of his life in a world of only men, she realized, and at the same moment admitted she had never heard Cleet mention any serious girlfriends.

She was hungry by the time they wound back to the cabin. And cold. Cleet built a fire and they ate quickly until they were full and then more slowly, for the sensual pleasure of it. Something had settled into place between them. Raney felt it, knew it, fought the idea briefly only because it had not originated in her conscious mind or been under her control. But there it was, part of each of them, new but as comfortable as something that had been long present and waiting only to be recognized. Cleet put his beer on the top of the woodstove and turned his body so their crossed knees touched, a pattern of crisscross lines well matched in length. His hands rested palm up and she laid her own within them.

"You didn't want me to meet your grandfather," he said. Raney shook her head. "He wouldn't like you being with a brown skin, would he?" She shook her head again. He put his hands on her cheeks and pulled her face near, slowly tilted his head, and brought his mouth so close their lips almost touched. "I don't care if you don't care."

When he kissed her she was surprised at the gentle insistence of his mouth, urging without demanding. Strong and mindful. It made her feel safe in a way that ached, only because she had not known she was not safe before. He led her to one of the fold-down bunks and unrolled the mattress, covered it with their coats, the room warm now from the fire and the shutters letting in fine slats of light bristled with dust, so that it was an easy thing to take off their clothes and explore each other. When he came into her, she was surprised to discover how much her body already knew, as if remembering a secret carried in her chemistry, waiting and ready.

That part of Raney's life was a time of losing and a time of finding: losing faith that she had been endowed with any inner artistic gift predestined to shake the world awake to her being. Losing any illusion that some shadowy, unnamed father would step into the light and claim her, endow her with a name and bloodline. She used to imagine that, when she was very young—that a tourist's Cadillac or

Mercedes might pull up to the gas pump at Peninsula Foods and spot her hanging around with her best friend, Sandy, pop the passenger-side door open, and wave Raney into the vacant seat so that he could drive her confidently into adulthood. When had that dream died? she wondered.

Three years after she and Cleet were an official couple, Sandy moved back to Quentin for good, having already disposed of two marriages (the first a starter and the second to confirm that she really wasn't much cut out for marriage, she observed). Her second husband had essentially paid his way out of a scandal and left Sandy a tidy-enough sum that when the art gallery in Port Townsend was put up for sale, she could buy it. With Cleet and Sandy and the loose acquaintances they together gathered, at twenty-six Raney finally made a comfortable space for herself in the town she'd grown up in. It was not the home she would have predicted or chosen, but it held room for her painting, and for the woods and mountains that gave her courage to look at the world hard enough to paint it. And more than any other anchor here, caring for her grandfather gave Raney a purpose—something she had never felt before. Though neither would admit it to the other, she was necessary in his life well beyond blood or love.

One jarringly bright afternoon Raney walked into the back office of the gallery, took a quick drag off Sandy's cigarette, and said to her, "He did it. We did it. I think."

"You think? Looks to me like you two been *doin' it* for more than a few years now."

"No. I mean he asked me to marry him. I said yes, I think."

Sandy did not jump on this right away; instead she returned to methodically sorting plastic sandwich bags of earrings and pendants with her back to Raney. "So what's the 'thinking' part? You said yes or didn't you?"

"I kissed him. Then I got in my truck and drove off. Is that a yes?"

"I have known you since you were eight years old, Renee Remington, and this is the first time I have ever heard you question your own mind."

"It seems like the logical next step, doesn't it?"

"I never found marriage to be a very *logical step*." She infused the words with all the detritus left by her two husbands. "Your grandfather pulled it off. Him and Joy. Ask him."

"Don't joke about this, Sandy."

Sandy hefted the bin of jewelry onto a shelf and turned to look Raney full in the face for the first time. "I'm not. If you don't love Cleet enough to accept what your grandfather will say when he hears you aren't marrying someone as white as General Custer, then you don't love Cleet enough to marry him. Honestly I've wondered if it's the only reason you've waited this long."

"That's not it," Raney said angrily. And it was true—she wasn't the least afraid of what Grandpa might say. She would put the question to him, then. Tonight. Before she talked to Cleet again. She drove the twenty minutes home to Quentin arguing out both sides the whole silent trip. Love. Was that what she and Cleet had together? Love? Plenty of other "L" words, for sure. *Like*: she liked him more than anyone else she knew. Maybe more than anyone she'd ever known. *Loyalty*: They had that, didn't they? There was no other man she was the least tempted by and Cleet was as steady as they come. *Lust*: okay, maybe not lust, but sex was comfortable between them. Easy. Then Grandpa's voice broke into her head. *Marriage lasts a long time, Renee. A lifetime. Joy and me had months, years, sometimes, with the two of us against the world. Life's hard enough—you really want to throw race into the fire with it? You love him enough to fight that for fifty, sixty years?*

It's close enough to love to turn into love. And he loves me enough to make it up for both of us, she would answer. And thus her mind spun out the arguments so that she was prepared, she hoped, for whatever her grandfather might throw in her path—had practically painted him into a new suit and tie ready to walk her down the aisle. She burst into the kitchen ready to say it all, and when he wasn't at the table, she ran upstairs to his bedroom hoping to beat any doubts. But his bedroom was empty too. So was the bathroom. She didn't start to worry until she found the barn door open and a single, bloodied, cut-off trouser leg puddled beside the bunker hatch.

Raney climbed into the cab of the truck and had the clutch pushed in before she remembered the keys were in her purse on the kitchen table. She slammed through the back door just as the telephone rang. It was Sandy. The hospital had called the gallery shortly after Raney left. Grandpa had gashed his leg when he tried to cut the padlock off the bunker door with a Sawzall.

By the time Raney drove all the way back to the emergency room in Port Townsend, he was resting on a gurney in his stained nightshirt with a brand-new pair of Jefferson General pajama bottoms covering thirty-two stitches in his left shin. He'd been given a pain pill and had a plastic tube hissing oxygen through his nose. The doctor was nice enough, though to Raney he seemed too young to look so pinched and exhausted. He told her how to take care of the dressing and when the stitches should come out. Then he signaled for Raney to follow him out of the cubicle into the hallway, a look of concern on his face that got her pulse racing.

She started, "I don't know how much his insurance covers here. At the VA, maybe, but—"

The doctor cut her off. "Just call the billing office. They'll work something out for you. How long has he had claudication?"

"I didn't know he had claudication. What's claudication?"

"Pain in his calves when he walks. Atherosclerosis." He must have caught the frown between Raney's brows and tried again. "The blood flow to his legs isn't good—there are plaques, or narrowing in the blood vessels. His wound is going to be slow to heal. Sometimes they don't heal. I'm concerned about it."

"What do you mean, it might not heal? How could it not heal, if I keep it clean, dressed?" He looked so tired she couldn't picture him smiling—like it might take too much effort.

"Hopefully so," he said.

"What happens if it doesn't?"

"Well, let's hope it does."

Raney stayed home from work the next day to take care of Grandpa. Between the pain pills and the pain he still had despite them he was too unsteady to trust on the stairs; he became almost as dependent on her as he had been in the days after his heart attack—and as begrudging. When he wobbled on a step, she grabbed his waist and he tried to pull away, which nearly sent them both to the bottom in a tumble. "Damn, child! I should put a padlock on your bedroom door."

"Don't damn me for helping you, Grandpa. I locked the bunker because it was dangerous for you to be climbing down the ladder alone. And I'm not a child!" She was alarmed at how frail his ribs felt against her, like she could crack him in half. When had he gotten so old? She felt like she'd opened her eyes expecting only a new day but awoke instead to a new era, the last gone before she'd known it was going. She had not talked to him about Cleet yet, and now she knew the real worry was not her marrying a man of a different race. It was her leaving home. Leaving Grandpa.

She pulled an easy chair into the kitchen where he could reach the telephone and refrigerator without letting go of either the chair or the counter, and then drove into town for groceries and, with luck, some crutches. In front of Hardy's Store a state patrol car had parked odd-angled across three spaces, and she imagined the vitriol Grandpa would have spewed about "the law" hogging space that belonged to regular tax-paying Americans. But the joke turned to alarm when she walked into the store, where a crowd of neighbors was gathering. John and Evelyn Hardy, Bo's aunt and uncle, had been killed in a head-on collision with a logging truck on Highway 104. Raney was ashamed at the first thought to enter her head: Bo would probably come back to Quentin for the funeral. She would see Bo again.

Part Two

· 11 ·

raney

The entire town of Quentin packed into the Rising Sun Baptist Church for the Hardys' funeral, even Grandpa. Raney pushed him up the zigzag ramp in a borrowed wheelchair. They arrived so early the sanctuary looked bare, the sparse flower arrangements like lost tropical islands in the chilly white room. Raney told herself that her resolve to be seated and collected early had nothing to do with Bo. She refused to scan the faces gradually filling the pews behind her, tried to concentrate on the folded service program in her hands. It wasn't a given that he would come. It wasn't a given that he was living anywhere near Seattle, or the United States, or, for that matter, that he cared enough about his aunt and uncle to come to their funeral even if he lived next door. At the top of the program page above the scripture from John 11:26 there was a sketch of two entwined angels, which, Raney guessed, were supposed to be Mr. and Mrs. Hardy smiling down on everyone from the hereafter. It had been years since Raney had said two words to either of them, but she for sure knew that neither had been anywhere close to angelic in their lifetimes. She began to sweat, cold as it was outdoors. Then a hard

159

tingle zipped from her scalp all the way down her spine and she knew Bo was in the room.

She didn't actually see him until the funeral was over and everyone had wandered outside into the steady gray drizzle, the ladies' heels sinking through the muddy lawn like golf tees and the men uncomfortable in ties worn only to marry and bury. From the upper yard, near the white walls of the church, a slice of the bay was visible, flanked by the high, evergreen cliffs where she and Bo used to roam. A few fishing boats were anchored out and bucked against their lines in channeled gusts of wind. She studiously focused on the water, leaning over to point out features to Grandpa, barely able to hear her own voice over the thud of her heart. Then she felt Bo's eyes find her and she slowly stood up and turned around. He raised one hand—a wave that was salutation and apology, regret and invitation all mixed into that one single gesture. For Raney it was like plugging in a Christmas tree: one electrical spark that suddenly illuminates not just a tree or a house or a village square but an entire season. An entire faith. Maybe her entire life.

He pulled away from a small group wearing black, which could only be family—no one from Quentin. Bo's mother was not among them. Later Raney learned that his mother had grown so estranged from her sister that even after a sheet of black ice snatched her away at the age of fifty-two, his mother wouldn't cut her Italian ski trip short to attend the funeral, although she did send some crystals to be placed inside the casket.

Bo spoke to Grandpa first, squatting in the damp to shake his hand and ask after the farm and the dogs, careful not to make mention of the wheelchair. And then he rose and faced Raney. He hadn't grown any since she'd seen him almost seven years earlier—still too slim, too wiry. His shoulders had filled out, giving him a more masculine cut—or perhaps it was just the suit riding so squarely out to the sleeve seam and then falling straight and true to his wrists. It looked expensive, his suit. She felt self-conscious about her own consignment-store dress, and a little thought clicked at the back of her brain: how much Cleet had admired it on her.

They couldn't talk long, only enough for the required news. Bo was a pallbearer and had to leave for the graveside service; his cousins were waiting at the hearse. He had already started down the muddy hill when he stopped and came back to say, "I'm here until Thursday morning. Can I see you?" and then his cousin called for him—the other cars were leaving. Bo took one step backward, away from Raney, and perhaps for that, or for the excuse it gave her, she did not mull the reasons it wasn't a good idea to see him tonight, or tomorrow, or ever again. She just answered yes—she'd be home tomorrow. After he drove away, Sandy came up to her and stood there, saying nothing, all of it written on her face.

The first thing Raney did when she got home was call Cleet. "I've got your favorite dress on. Should I drive up to Port Townsend?" He made dinner for her at his tiny apartment—two rooms that had once been the office for a sailmaker's loft, so it didn't even have a shower, only a rubber extension hose that attached to the sink faucet. He'd taken it for the view out over the stormy Strait of Juan de Fuca, and the cheap rent, saying he'd readily trade the hundred-dollar shower for the eight-hundred-dollar view. Raney never stayed the night anyway—she didn't trust Grandpa alone by himself. His leg was stubbornly refusing to heal, and at the last doctor's visit they had hinted that a prosthesis might eventually give him more mobility than a painful, weeping chronic wound. The look on Grandpa's face had made the habitually implacable orthopedic surgeon shrink by two inches right in front of Raney's eyes—well worth the drive all the way to the Tacoma VA Hospital.

After dinner Cleet said he was leaving for the Hood Canal early the next morning to deliver the cabinets he'd made for a Boeing executive's weekend house—the family had offered him space in their guest cottage for the few weeks it would take to install the cabinets and do some other finish work. "You could come with me," he told Raney. "It's right on the water—good clamming there. Be like a little . . . holiday." Had she heard him hesitate? About to say honeymoon instead of holiday? Had she made the substitution in her mind and only then noticed the band tighten in her throat? He had let his proposal sit between them indefinitely decided, as if leaving it undisturbed by more discussion would allow it to shift from a suggestion into something too corporeal to undo.

"I can't leave Grandpa alone."

"No. You shouldn't." Cleet sat beside her on the oversize sofa he used for a bed, took her plate off her lap, and kissed her, eventually, inevitably letting his fingers slip from the nape of her neck to the zipper pull at the back of her dress. "He'll be okay for another hour, or so, huh? I'll miss you."

"I'll miss you too." And she would, she knew, and it made her suddenly want him to stay with her. Be there at her house in Quentin all of Wednesday and into Thursday, too, until well after Bo left the peninsula. They were part of the same world, she and Cleet. Different races, maybe, but each had scraped and gouged and clung to whatever luck happened by until they had carved a common path in this lost corner of the continent. He knew her and knew the life she was born to, because he had been born to it too, had become part of the rhythm of her day—the one person besides Sandy who heard what she *didn't* say almost as clearly as he heard her voice. Years, now, it had taken them to build that—an easy thing to forget to treasure. And after years he knew exactly where to touch her at exactly the right moment in their lovemaking, so there was no need to help or to guide. No danger of one experimental move gone astray.

She told herself all of this again when she got home and checked on Grandpa, then made tea in the kitchen, sitting up long after she was aching for her bed. When the phone rang she put her hand on the receiver without lifting it, the vibrations making her fingers tingle until after twenty-seven rings it finally went silent.

So that was it. She was going to let Bo walk out of her life again—

exactly the right thing to do, she was certain. She repeated it to herself every time she woke up that long night, and worked to remember the way Cleet's voice always made her feel like the world could be at peace even when her mind turned itself inside out looking for terms to settle what felt like an endless fight. She opened her eyes in the dark and saw the velvety shades of Cleet's dark irises, shunned a flash of color at the back of her brain suggesting her own green eyes fell somewhere between Cleet's brown and Bo's blue.

But early the next afternoon when she heard a car pull into the driveway, she no longer felt certain of anything. Out the kitchen window she could see only the front end—silvery blue. Sporty. New. She looped her hair into an unflattering knot and started washing the dishes just to keep her hands busy, drying each one and putting it into the cabinet. He caught her face as he walked by the window and stopped, waited until Raney gave him an almost invisible nod, then came through the back door without knocking.

A mindful of memories flooded in with his slouched gait, his pale, unsettled eyes. Memories fully scented and richly colored: hot-pink Stargazer lilies stolen from his aunt's cutting garden one August afternoon; the illicit odor of burning grass after a day clearing his uncle's yard; seaweed and sand and even that rank, rotted deer. Without looking directly at him she could sense how the man had changed from the boy—an edginess, a sharper definition of self but still not fully at peace. It heightened her own self-consciousness. But no, that wasn't right—it wasn't herself she felt so conscious of. It was Cleet; the easiness of what they were together—no big ups, no big downs—suddenly, disturbingly less palatable to her. Taking care to set the last plate down without a clatter, she turned around and rested her arms behind her on the rim of the sink, hiding nothing about her body. "You came. I didn't expect you to, if I'm honest."

"I never knew you to be anything less than honest."

She offered to make some coffee. "Tea," he answered. "Espresso or tea. So . . . tea. Thanks."

She dumped a kettle of perfectly fresh water down the sink, stuck the spout under the faucet to fill it, and sprayed water all over herself before she thought to take the lid off and fill it through the proper hole. She was annoyed at herself for acting nervous. She was annoyed at him for making her nervous. What did she have to be nervous about? It was all ridiculous—just friends catching up after seven long years. "It's a shame about your aunt and uncle," she said.

"It is a shame. I'm afraid they won't be much missed." Raney raised her eyebrows and he offered an honestly apologetic shrug, which eased the tension.

"Well, sit down," she said. "How can you tell me about seven years' worth of life standing up? I figured you were living in New York City by now. Or London, maybe. Graduate school, for sure. Right? You writing famous novels yet?" Everything came out too fast, words hurrying around some obstacle she didn't want to name. He laughed, and in that quick, self-deprecating exhalation she suddenly saw him at fourteen again, the two of them twisted into their unlikely first kiss, too young to know it mattered, felt him at twenty, nearly seven years ago, the weight of his body pressing her into his mother's bed.

"I'm writing famous three-page stories in *Zeus Air Magazine*, circulation base of five hundred. Best used as coasters or for stashing chewed gum when the stewardess delivers your drink."

"Zeus Air? That's a real airline?"

"Debatable."

Raney relaxed a little more to think that everything hadn't been easy for him, and it made her aware of how many times over these years she had speculated, assumed. She put two cups of tea on the table and sat down across from him. "But you're writing. For a real magazine."

"I do it for the travel discounts mainly—the job lets me cross over with bigger airlines."

"Where do you go?"

"Where do I not go? Far as a plane can take me."

He leaned in a bit, his expression opening up like he needed to tell her the risks he'd taken. He talked about his trips through Southeast Asia, China, Central America. He'd shunned western Europe, and Raney inferred that was as much to define himself in opposition to his parents as to follow his own inclinations. It was like hearing a narration of all those old *National Geographics* she kept stacked in her closet, and she asked him question after question: What was the food like? What color was a tropical ocean—really? Warm enough to swim in? What was it like to stand in an Indian market in the monsoon rains? He never mentioned a single friend on all those trips, and when she asked him if it didn't get lonely he switched the questions to her, when she'd left school, where she worked now, if any of her old friends were back in Quentin too. She leaned forward to reach the sugar and caught his eyes flicker to her chest, pulled her sweater close where it gapped above her breasts, and that, too, she saw him notice. They talked for an hour. No—more than two, she realized when she glanced at the clock. She thought she heard Grandpa stir upstairs and carried up some tea and graham crackers but found him dozing with a pillow over his head, his breathing regular and deep.

When she came back into the kitchen, Bo's face brightened like she'd been away a whole day after years of being steadily together, and without thinking, she kissed his cheek. It was funny, she thought, that a man so out of place in this town and this house could look so at home to her. "Did your grandfather remember who I was yesterday?" Bo asked her.

"Of course. Mind's still sharp as a tack. And you've been okay, right? No more . . ." she raised a hand to the side of her head, hesitant to say it in words. For a second she worried a tightening in his eyes meant bad news, then he ducked his chin like she'd only now reminded him about his surgery.

"Oh—yeah! Totally cured. I still owe you an apology for the way my mother treated you that day you came to my house. No wonder you cut me off."

Raney gave him a sly smile. "I cut you off because you asked me if I'd ever heard of Monet."

Bo's cheeks colored, but then he laughed. "I did? I said that?" He stretched back in his chair, looking truly relaxed for the first time since he'd come in, as if remembering such a comment from his youth made him believe in his new maturity. "I didn't expect you to be living here still. I thought maybe you'd have moved into Seattle. Or gotten married."

Raney could have told Bo about Cleet at that moment—it was an obvious opening to the topic she had skirted. Instead she juggled the words and then shooed them away, told herself it could be said another time. Or not at all; this would likely be their last conversation. Later, when she replayed that day over and over, she knew something had crossed her face. In her memory she could see him pause, deliberate. And in her memory she told herself they both understood the pact they were making.

"But you're still painting," Bo said.

"I still paint. When I have time."

"What blue is this?" he asked, lightly stroking his forefinger over the side of her palm where paint had caught and dried in the fine creases.

"Cobalt. With a dab of carnation—gives it a violet tint."

"Show me."

She shook her head. "It's not ready to show."

"Show me anyway. Please?"

The painting was on the front porch, where the light cut under the eaves for a few hours after dawn and she could stand her canvas out of the rain showers and see across the sloping field all the way to the curl of fog tucked like a baby's blanket over the bay most fall mornings. Bo stood a long time in front of it, looking at the painting, then across the rise and drop of land to the ridge of spiky green forest before the water, then back to the painting. Not once at her. Like the way he had looked at her paintings in Seattle, she remembered— letting his opinion seed and ripen before he spoke. After a while, without a word, he shut his eyes and tilted his face toward the porch ceiling. Then he walked back through the front door into the dark living room and flicked on the overhead light switch. Grandpa had long ago quit using this room for anything but her "gallery"—not that they ever had any guests who were displaced by that choice. The walls were filled with paintings she'd made over the last ten years. They rose from chair back to ceiling, rested shoulder to shoulder across the sofa and against the tables and bookcase. Bo let out a slow, broken breath and Raney recalled all the scenes she had painted while he read his books, back when they were never going to grow up or believed they had already done so; when every day passed without any clock but light or dark, so lost in their own worlds of color and language they started to mix together and she had at times wondered if she was painting the story he was reading. How much of him was still that boy? She looked from the paintings to his face and saw a reaction that made her feel raw—but folded inside out rather than naked, as if two skin surfaces had been scraped down to raw flesh and scarred together. It made her feel like she counted for something in a way she hadn't counted before. He reached for her hand, and she blocked out everything telling her to pull it away. He stood so close she could feel his heat. "I should have come after you seven years ago," he said.

"Bo, I'm engaged, or close to it. I should have told you."

"Close to it? What does that mean?"

What did it mean? To her? "We've been together three years. He loves me. He's a good man. He'll be a good husband." Even Raney heard the empty space that made room for Bo to put his arms around her, weave his fingers through her hair at the nape of her neck so tight she took one step closer at the insistent pressure of his hands. Then she opened her mouth to his and felt all the space between them disappear, all time after this time disappear.

"What do you want, Raney?"

What do you want, Raney? What did she want? Another past? Another chance at him? Whatever it was, it did not reside in conscious thought. He hesitated only a moment, just long enough to allow her to pull away if she chose. "I'm staying in a hotel."

Raney shook her head but made no move to separate until after he kissed her again. Then she took his hand and led him through the kitchen and out across the muddy yard to the barn. Together they pushed aside the hay bales and tugged the black ring latch on the bunker's trapdoor until it gave way. The taint of mildew drifted into the air; hay dust and bits of loose straw stirred and floated into the gaping black hole. Raney wrapped her skirt into a knot and stepped onto the first rung of the ladder. Even with the trapdoor still open to the barn, it was nearly dark in the cavern of a room. She felt along the shelf edge for a flashlight, finding instead a box of matches and emergency candles. She struck a match to one candle and set it on the trunk, then Bo lit a whole row of candles in small glass votives so they pitched at odd angles and the room smelled of paraffin and sulfur and glowed with light from another century. After he pulled the hatch closed, the silence was thick as a comforter. Time didn't matter anymore. Nothing up there mattered anymore. They might open that hatch in two or three hours or two or three days and find civilization—Quentin, Seattle, all of it—had been swallowed up and only the two of them were left, and maybe that was all she wanted. Maybe that was why whatever happened here could be justified. She wondered if she'd known since she first saw his pale face hunched over a book in the woods that they could only be together in some bubble outside the real world.

Bo pulled the mattresses from both cots onto the floor and spread the blankets and pillows and sleeping bags on top of them so the small space was a cushioned nest. The candle flame moved in languid waves over his face and was lost in the hollow coves under his eyes and cheeks. He looked ethereal. Haunted—that much more a mystery to her, and what they were about to do that much less real. He kissed her full and deep and then Raney pushed him away, enjoying the moment of uncertainty she saw cross his face. She took off her jacket and unbuttoned her blouse, let them drop to the floor. Bo slipped his sweater off, disappearing for a moment inside it, then emerging with a static crackle of hair, his body shining pale in the candlelight. They sat without moving for a while, and then he lowered his face toward hers as if to kiss her, but stopped forehead to forehead. "I'm cold," he said.

"Me too."

"No. Never cold." he answered, sure of himself again, moving over her now with his legs locking them into one animal. She felt no shyness with him, no need to prove any point of beauty or sensual talent—she had been here too many times in her imagination, completing an interrupted story. She fought the inevitable comparison to Cleet—tried to believe her body was different with Bo because she had known him so thoroughly before they recognized themselves as sexual beings. Or maybe, she wondered much later, maybe because she could not let herself believe there would be a second chance to learn each other's erotic secrets. There was no permanence to this. Only later did she see the irony in that.

Bo had to leave the next day. He was headed to Mexico for ten days to do a story about deep-sea fishing off some islands, but they decided to meet in Seattle as soon as he got home. Raney would arrange for someone to check on Grandpa and she would pick up Bo at the airport. When she walked him to his car, he pulled her to him with some new reserve she felt but could not place. "Do you love this guy?"

"There's all kinds of love, Bo. There's this kind, what just happened, and there's the marrying kind."

"You're willing to take one without the other?"

The way he said it, it could be taken as a challenge or an aspersion. Or, possibly, an invitation. She wished she could see his eyes. "Are you saying you could give me both?"

He was very quiet for a moment. "Being married to me . . ." He stopped then, as if his rational mind had just caught up with him. A memory. Even the tension in his arms against her back changed into something less fluid—less a part of her own skin.

After a minute she asked, "You'll let me know if your flight changes?"

"I'll call every day—if I can find a phone."

. . .

She thought about many things later, when he did not call her. The first days it was not actual thought, but unadulterated sensual memory, replaying the exact stroke of his fingers over her breasts, her hips, until her skin flushed, aroused so that it was almost a shock to open her eyes and rediscover he was gone. She thought about how there weren't likely to be many telephones on the Mexican island, whose name she could not recall or even guess at despite poring over a world atlas in the Port Townsend library.

Weeks later she relived the minutes and hours after he left the bunker, mapped the interior of her body to determine the minute she knew Jake was with her. Inside her. It eluded her, refusing to be confined to one split second of sperm penetrating egg, DNA from two aligning and dividing into a brand-new individual; maybe, she decided, because the beginning lay well beyond biology.

When Cleet first touched her again, she thought about nothing, her mind emptied like a door automatically shut, splitting Bo from Cleet as completely as her body had in the bunker. As the time came and passed for Bo's return from Mexico and the phone did not ring, Raney learned how much control she had over that door. The room she lived in was Cleet's room, Cleet's future, her grandfather, her art. She was able to almost convince herself that Bo had done it intentionally, set her up for the same rejection she'd put him through seven years earlier and that *this* was the real Bo—a man willing to plot and connive in order to hurt her. But one week more and Sandy caught her squatted in a dark corner of the back storeroom and made her talk.

"You did it, didn't you? Then you thought Prince Charming would come back here and gather you up," Sandy said.

"You can be a mean friend sometimes, Sandy."

"The kind everybody needs most. So what now? I'll drive you to Seattle if you want. Take you right up to his door with my gun in the backseat. Or flowers. I just want it to be you deciding this instead of him."

"Well, some things appear to be already decided." Raney felt the change for certain by then, not in her belly but in the primitive base of her brain where rhythms of breath and heart begin. Like the tiniest pinhole was being blown open to something infinite and all connected; a portal to every bit of soil and air that had ever been part of a human being.

Sandy waited a minute before it began to dawn. "You're kidding. You're on the pill, right? Something?"

"Of course. When I remember."

"And Cleet?"

Raney pressed her hands against her eyes and leaned hard into the wall. After a long minute she shrugged her shoulders. "He'll be happy. He likes kids."

"His own, maybe."

"It could be his own."

"You have choices, Raney. You don't have to get married because of this. It's your life."

Raney wiped her eyes and rolled her head back and forth before she gave a small laugh, then crawled forward so her face was right in front of Sandy's. "It's not about me anymore. I know my choice. And we're gonna be fine. All three of us. Cleet, Renee, and baby Flores."

· 12 ·

eric

Eric loved to drive. With his first paycheck from Zeus Air he put a down payment on two things: a Leica camera lens (which he could at least write off) and a silver-blue Fiat Spider. He was twenty-four years old and, from what he'd seen of life, believed he'd already beaten the beast. He'd *survived*. And that sports car was the sleek machine he planned to spin straight through to the rest of his dreams, with a little extra gas to make up for lost time.

He would spend days following the smallest map lines threaded across Snohomish, Skagit, and Whatcom counties, all the way to the rim of Canada—holding the wheel against the curve, craving the amnesia-inducing openness of a landscape latticed with roads. His mother had fought his renewing his license. She wanted his doctors to block him, but his neurologist wasn't persuaded. Eric had been seizure free for long enough, the doctor said, and he should quit letting the disease *or* his mother define him. So the first day Eric owned his new car he picked up his mother from the Lopez Island ferry and kidnapped her, turning north on I-5 instead of south. When he got near Bellingham he cut west onto Chuckanut Drive, whipping along the coastal road with the top down until her hair was a Medusa frizz

172

and tears arced down her cheeks, driving until he finally caught her smiling.

In his late teens he'd gone through a phase of anger toward his mother, but now that he was well—his brain tumor cut out, destroyed, gone for good, so sure of it he'd skipped his last MRI—he understood that his rage had been against the disease itself, the few glitched amino acids that had likely come from her. Now he just wanted her to forgive herself.

The last time Eric drove a car he was twenty-six. He was on a small island off the coast of Mexico, writing an article about deep-sea fishing. Normally he would have taken buses and taxis, but on this particular trip the delays of local transportation crawled under his skin like a parasite. He had itched to get to a phone since his plane took off from SeaTac; he tried to make a call between transfers and hit his fist into the Mexico City airport wall when he only got a busy signal. Now, with his small hotel still two hours away, he had no patience for the scabbed and skinny boys plucking at his shirt to get him into their father's, their uncle's, their brother's car, so he rented his own. A convertible. Time to celebrate, he could remember thinking, that for the first time in his life he was both healthy and in love.

He remembered many things with precise clarity for a few hours thereafter: the twilight settling in, thick as liquid and seeded with stars; the riotous sounds of an impoverished, close community—barking dogs and blaring radios and car horns, and children everywhere, boiling into the dirty streets—and for the first time in all his travels it did not make him feel more lonely. He could remember pulling to the side of the road, a gleaming sickle of beach where he stripped to shorts and sandals and sent one glorious shout to heaven that the universe had finally turned in his favor. He remembered a wedding party blocking the main road near his turnoff and, it was so odd, he could remember how far away the brake pedal suddenly felt, the strange, elastic expansion of time it was taking to make his foot move from the accelerator, as if his body had changed shape or size.

Everything else became *afterward*—bits of time scattered randomly as broken glass. His first distinct memory from *afterward* was the fingers of his right hand scraping a thin cotton bedspread, a flickering fluorescent light above his head. Later, the Seattle skyline through the window, blue with an early summer sky, his mother reading in the chair beside him. Later still, his fingers moving to the soft bristle of his shorn scalp, the tender edges of a fresh wound. For years images would flash through him at odd times until a vague shape of those lost months began to emerge: a smoldering headache igniting, searing through his eyes, his teeth, the folded matter of his brain; straps binding him, wheels under him, faces upside down; sloshing like so much cargo as he is rolled, lifted, hauled, flown. And always he remembered, would never forget, the sense of some urgent task left unattended so that his rare moments of lucidity had felt desperate. A dream of running through quicksand.

When he was finally moved to the rehab unit two months after his operation, three months before he was able to walk on his own, he got a physical therapist to help him find her phone number. He called three, four, five times, letting it ring until he lost count, then, at last, an old man picked up, the grandfather, a bark in his voice when he told Eric that Raney wasn't there. She lived with her husband now.

Six months after Eric got out of the hospital his father called him from the East Coast and said he wanted to talk to him. In person. He flew Eric to New York, and they met for lunch at a café on Amsterdam Avenue in the middle of a heat wave so intense even the tourists had abandoned the city. Eric had spent the entire flight conjecturing what news his father was about to break—another divorce, another half sibling on the way, some truth about Eric's own prognosis that his mother hadn't been strong enough to tell him. The actual news was both more benign and more mind-blowing: Eric's grandfather had left him a trust fund, which he was to inherit at the age of thirty-five, not enormous but enough to give him options. But his father, the executor, had rewritten the terms so the money would come to Eric now, at age twenty-seven. "Why now?" Eric had asked, and when his father shied from the question, Eric asked him again, goading him to say out loud that he suspected Eric might not have a thirty-fifth birthday. His father looked away, seemingly distracted by the traffic spewing fumes into the miserable air, but Eric caught something— guilt or regret—in his half-hidden face. It was beginning to make Eric mad, watching the pinpricks of sweat stipple his father's upper lip and still he kept his suit coat on. Finally he loosened his tie, his first concession to the coffin of heat making Eric's head pound, and threw the question back. "Why *not* now? You're not mature enough?"

Put to sensible, steady work, the money could be his ticket to a graduate degree, a small house, everlasting comfort if not splendor. It could be there if the day came when Eric couldn't work anymore, or needed extra help. If such a day came. *And then what?* Eric wanted to make his father say out loud. He could afford the luxury of surviving in a life he didn't want to live? The luxurious misery of surviving in a body without a mind? Maybe for that reason alone Eric made it a personal cause to do exactly what his father worried most about—he burned through the money as fast as possible.

He kept the job with Zeus, traveling to the limited reach of its small fleet of 737s, but he began writing freelance, too, keeping a bag packed and ready to go so that whenever the mood struck he could jump on a plane, take his camera and his laptop, and park himself in a hotel where no one knew his name. He sought out the fringes of the tourist routes, looking for niches that hadn't been covered by other travel writers. Rose-petal harvests and camel wrestling in Turkey. An out-of-the way Greek island where the Aegean Sea flowed viscous as saliva, floating effortless even for his skinny body—the salt a life vest. He photographed old women gone frog-faced, their breasts wallowing in simple black dresses as they stood in doorways to observe the world hurtling through change. He tried to imagine them young, virginal; tried to see how young they still were in this ancient, ancient land. He could stand on a bridge, on a subway, on a street corner and watch people for so long he became hypnotized imagining the life they had that he would never witness, and there were moments, scary moments, when he wanted to hurl himself into their existence, turn himself inside out, and become them, become anyone but himself.

When the money was half-gone he sought out more remote places—treks into the Golden Triangle to sleep on mats with tribal groups discovering that the hard authenticity of their lives could be sold to a new breed of tourists rich enough to pay for a week's worth of mosquitoes and mud just to say they'd been there. He burrowed into the slums of Asia and Africa, where cars slipped like fish through the chaotic streets and the smell of life flooded into him and through him until he was saturated. He craved cities where English was not just a foreign language, it was a foreign concept, where everyone seemed to know something he didn't, and the challenge of finding clean water and a safe bed could crowd everything else from his mind. Anonymity became his favorite definition of home. A few weeks in Seattle and he was restless, waking up at night with enough security and empty black silence to remember how much he hated his own fate. The next day he would be scanning the map for any place he'd never been. Even now, a decade later, he couldn't take a taxi without asking the driver to describe the village in Somalia or Ethiopia or Syria where his sisters, his brothers, his cousins, his parents still lived.

Three years into it, Eric was almost through the money when he ran into an old friend from his early days at *Zeus Air Magazine* who worked for Condé Nast now. They ended up in a sketchy bar outside Paris trading stories. The friend had just finished a piece on yachting in the Mediterranean—interviewed a Mexican billionaire on his two-fifty-footer, trying to keep up with him on 1800 Coleccion tequila shots while the guy bitched about his wife forgetting her makeup bag back in Aztec Land so she put him in the "no sex vise" unless their pilots flew the 747 back to fetch it.

They were well into their own tequila rounds when the friend said he'd heard about Eric's car wreck. "My wife's always worried about my dying of malaria, dengue . . . it's the car accidents that kill you over here. Hell, I don't have to tell you that." Eric was ready to brush it off when the friend got too quiet, too fidgety, and added, "Sorry, man. I shouldn't have brought it up." He poured Eric another shot and took a swig of his own. "Listen. They have so many kids down there. I heard that girl had eight brothers and sisters."

There it was. In one sentence. Eric felt so transformed by that inadvertently leaked bit of information he wondered if he had been looking for it ever since his accident—the missing memory that could let him move on. And it did, but not in the way he'd expected. All this time he'd thought he was trying to run away from the smoldering bomb inside his own brain. That was the easy part, he began to understand. He felt almost weightless as it dawned on him, like the next breath he took might lift him off this bar stool, lift him right up over this crowd of happy drunks. As long as he kept his rules straight— kept his boundaries close and stayed out of anyone else's driver seat, when his brain exploded the next time it would destroy only him.

He began to hate the money after that, the cushion it allowed him. For a while he still craved the edge, the risk, wanted to take it, take it, take it all right now before it was over. Strike and get out before he could hurt another soul. He gave away what he couldn't spend—extravagant tips left hidden under his plate, packages that arrived on friends' birthdays with no return address, cash left in envelopes at homeless shelters. And one extraordinary, anonymous donation for a playground and school in a tiny town on an island in Mexico.

The last travel article he wrote was about Cambodia. He trekked three days up to a hill village and dialed his camera into focus on an old man stumbling behind his yoked oxen. He caught the light perfectly on the man's straining, cracked face. Then, a second before the shutter opened, the man looked straight at Eric and for the first time he saw through his lens the true horror of unabating hunger. He was appalled that he earned his living promoting such misery as a tourist attraction. He sold his camera, done with putting its glassy distance between himself and life.

With the money gone he couldn't support himself freelancing anymore and he went back to Zeus full time. Almost on a whim, he pulled out a half-finished essay about the genome project he'd begun that night in Paris after too much tequila. The article eventually turned into a book deal. A few clean brain scans, the meditative calm of losing himself inside his writing—they gave him a way to live again, if only in the present tense. The only dependable tense, wasn't it? Unadulterated by doctored memory, unfettered by anticipation? Over time it became an instinct more than an intentional choice. Finally, at thirty-nine he'd hit a balance that worked—enough giving to counter the taking, enough pause to weigh some risks. There were his parents, his half brothers. There was the legacy of his work if he had any luck. And there was Charlotte. More than any of it, there was Charlotte. But now the description of the faint serpentine scar coiled around Jane Doe's arm felt like it could be enough to tip everything upside down.

The nurse's aide was just starting Jane's bath when they got to her bedside. Charlotte let Eric walk into the room ahead of her and pulled the curtain closed across the glass door. It was the only privacy she could offer them. The aide dropped a washcloth into the bathwater, set the tub between Jane's legs, then removed the foam cushions that protected her heels. Eric had to turn his head at the sight of her blackened toes. The aide bent Jane's knee to wash her calf, her shin, the hollow under her knee, tucking the blue cotton gown under the other leg so that only a small section was exposed. Eric could tell the aide had washed a hundred bodies. She was attentive and daydreaming all at the same time, sloshing the cloth back into the tub, wringing it out, shifting the gown to expose the other leg and beginning there. It must be little different before a wake, he thought, the ritual washing of a body before burial.

She began to wash Jane's right arm, holding it up to scrub the last of the cast plaster away. Her skin glowed under the friction of the cloth and as he watched, Eric saw a band of contrasting tissue emerge, a flushed pink coil encircling Raney's arm between the elbow and the shoulder, like a decorative Egyptian bracelet. *For my Cleopatra*, he remembered telling her. She was the reincarnation of Cleopatra and he had taken her paintbrush away in a friendly struggle to draw a gold encircling line around this scar, turning the injury into a blessing of beauty.

· 13 ·
raney

When Raney was in second grade, Pete Brewer, an obnoxious little boy who ended up in a wheelchair after he ran his Harley into the open door of a parked car, shouted a curse at her on the jungle gym. When she got home she asked her grandpa why the two of them had the same last name. Grandpa was sitting in the yard on a woven plastic lawn chair chipping mortar off some old bricks he'd hauled out of a demo yard, his knees splayed and his elbows braced so the bits of gray cement fell into the weeds. "What? You don't like the name Remington?" he said, without looking up.

Raney sat cross-legged on the damp ground matching up the broken chunks of fallen rock into perfect fitting pairs. "Yes, sir. I like Remington fine."

"And you remember where it comes from?" She did. She could not forget. The day Grandpa taught her how to write her name, he started the lesson with a trip to the storage closet underneath the eaves. He brought out a long wooden box and set it on the kitchen table, swung the tiny brass hasp out from its brass ring, and lifted the lid. A rifle lay inside, fitted into a bed of crimson felt molded to its exact shape, dark with gun oil. The wooden stock was polished to a silky gloss you couldn't help but touch, and the metal barrel and firing mechanism were a fine blue black. He lifted it out of the case and set it across her scrawny knees with solemnity equal to laying the baby Jesus in his manger. "Renee Lee Remington, every time you write your name you think of this rifle. Oldest guns in America."

"This is the oldest gun in all America? Did you take it to the war?"

He bit back a smile. "Oldest gun *manufacturer* in America."

She was afraid to touch it. She kept her hands locked against her chest like two flighty birds until he put it back in the case. For years she thought her ancestors had made all those guns, until she figured out they wouldn't be living like dirt farmers and buying her clothes at Value Village if that were the case.

Grandpa didn't get out the gun again when she told him what Pete had called her on the playground. He just hacked at the ancient mortar clinging like barnacles to those fine red bricks, sending chips flying far afield and spraying dust into the bowl of her school skirt. "I said I like my name," she repeated.

"Then what's your question about?"

"Well, if you are my mama's daddy, why do I have the same name as you? Pete Brewer says I should have my daddy's name. Not yours."

Grandpa put the brick and the chisel down and smiled at her. Then he said something memorable enough for Raney to hold on to until she was old enough to understand it. "Well, it sounds like Pete Brewer is the card-carrying bastard in the Quentin Elementary School second-grade class."

When Cleet walked into the gallery the day he finished his job on Hood Canal, Raney's heart did one wobbly flip knowing that even to look at him was to lie. But after they talked and agreed, she watched him walk back out across the buckled plank floor, seeing a sway in his stride that hadn't been there before. All the words in the world can't make a woman feel as loved as that, she thought, knowing you've changed a man from the inside. And so it was over with Bo. She was

Cleet's again, and part of her could believe she was his even more. She had closed a door to some dangerous place that she hadn't even seen until she'd gone through it and barely escaped. When her mind turned to the color of the child forming inside her body she tried to think only of ten fingers and ten toes, a healthy heart, a strong cry after the first-ever inhaled breath.

Cleet insisted he meet one on one with Grandpa before they set a date. Grandpa had been civil enough whenever he and Cleet had crossed paths, depending on one's definition of civil—Grandpa generally associated that word with all that he distrusted. "What? You're all of a sudden missing your mother's Catholic customs?" Raney asked Cleet when he would not budge.

"Only the ones that serve a purpose. You can't split yourself between the two of us, Raney. Besides, I already know who'd win that fight." She started to retort but he laughed and pressed his thumb to her lips, told her to have the ice packs and bandages ready, and left her waiting on the front porch where she could hear the fireworks. But it was surprisingly quiet behind the closed front door, even when Raney pressed her ear flat to it. When Cleet called her in, she saw two drained shot glasses on the coffee table and Grandpa acting like they'd been discussing how to rebuild a carburetor or what decoy to use on a wood duck, as near to friendship as she'd ever seen him. Later she asked Cleet what he'd said to make a bond. "Bond? I just shut up and listened while he described what he'd do if I ever hurt you."

Pooling the money they had both saved, Cleet and Raney were able to snare a worn-down house in need of Cleet's talent just three hundred yards through the woods from her grandfather's farm, if two miles by car. By the time they were moved in, Grandpa's wound had closed under a shiny purplish patch of thin skin and he had kicked Raney's regular assistance out of his life, although most evenings his truck showed up shortly before dinnertime or they carried their meal to him. The neighborhood was chopped into a disheveled mix of dwellings—a few rotting double-wides, some solid, timeless log cabins, falling-down barns, and a rusting Quonset hut. The neighbors themselves were an equal mix. Some Raney knew from her childhood, and some made it clear they had no interest in new neighbors whether indigenous to Quentin or not. Across the road lived a sprawling family of hard-to-determine relationships, the Wellses, who sent twin four-year-old girls Amelia and Caroline over with a casserole in a shoebox lined with a plastic Rite Aid bag, and thus Raney felt officially graduated to the dubious status of housewife.

The best thing about the area was its proximity to the bluff, where the view faced away from the man-made scruff of Quentin toward the maze of bay and forest and inlets backdropped by snow-capped mountains. Perched above the water was a row of old Victorian-era houses built when the railroad was supposed to make Port Townsend and the Olympic Peninsula the economic hub of the Northwest. A few were abandoned, but some had been purchased by lost tourists in a fit of romance inspired by the view on some sunny summery day, usually left empty more and more days out of each succeeding year. Sometimes she and Cleet would share a picnic on the wide steps of those deserted front porches. Cleet believed the houses made for better property value and maybe it was true—to walk down their street was certainly to walk up the social ladder.

Even before Raney felt the nudge and press of Jake's feet and knees and elbows against the inside of her, she came to a different understanding of her purpose. Rather than her own life as a single book with many chapters, Jake became the title page. The dedication and acknowledgments. The prologue and epilogue. The only lasting thing she might leave behind other than a trunkful of paintings.

They had a snowstorm the day she went into labor, and two giant cedars fell between their house and the highway. Cleet had only cleared one when Raney's water broke. He called 911 and then he called the doctor and made him describe in detail how to deliver a baby at home. The doctor told Cleet to hot-iron a set of new shoe-laces and use that to tie off the cord, then cut it with boiled scissors. Turned out you didn't really need so much to deliver a baby—clean, warm towels, clean water, clean scissors, and a clean shoelace—$17.99 before tax.

And if all of evolution was focused on pushing the human race one step farther through time, then it might barely explain what Raney felt the minute she first touched her baby. Surely no one person could generate that much emotion—it would splinter the mind. When she looked into Jake's scrunched red face poking out of the flannel sheet Cleet had wrapped around him, she knew he had blown in from some old, old star. His mystified, wide-open pupils working so hard to focus—she could see him puzzling out where that stardust had blown him this time around, like he was searching for a bridge between that world and this one. Later that night, while he slept, she wrote him a letter, coaxing his baby-soul to land here for just another eighty years or so—a blink of an eye for an angel, maybe, but scary-crazy for people. His blue-black eyes were the most comforting place she'd ever dreamed of; for Raney they held the wisdom of Buddha, Muhammed, and Jesus combined, just for starters. And his skin was a blend of all three, a perfect balance between Cleet's shade and her own. Cleet had laughed when she first pulled back the bound flannel sheet and ran her hand over Jake's belly and arms and legs and back. "He's all there, I checked," Cleet said, and she couldn't tell him she was crying in relief that after nine months of worry she could begin to let her secret go and forgive herself for what she might have done to him.

At what point did she fully accept that all her intuited conviction had been wrong—that she could see her golden son in Cleet's golden hands and not fear she had both deceived him and conceived their child in that deceit? Whatever day it actually was, she marked it as the day she put Jake into her grandfather's arms and saw him finger-ing Jake's black hair and perfect golden skin, trying to accept that his own blood circulated in the flesh of another race. He stared at Jake for a long, silent time until finally, when Raney thought she would take her baby away and say, "Good-bye! It's Jake or me," Grandpa leaned down and kissed Jake's head. She saw in that kiss what her grandfather must have done twenty-eight years ago when his only daughter put her bastard child in his arms. Maybe it was that kiss Raney's broken mother remembered when she decided Raney was better left behind.

If Raney had loved Cleet incompletely before Jake was born, her love bloomed full-fledged watching him fall in love with his son. Once, in a dream, she bolted awake in a sweaty memory of Bo lighting votive candles down the spine of a broken-hinged trunk, Bo swimming over her, pressing her down into a nest of sleeping bags, Bo's sweat and skin moving through her, and she had cried out in terror that the bare sail of shoulder rising from the bed next to her was his, not Cleet's. She lived the next week in shame at the revived memory. Raney now lived the truth that there *are* all types of love: the kind that hits you like a truck hauling down a highway, the kind that needs as much nurturing as a winter campfire, and the range between. The love she and Cleet depended on was the kind that made life survivable day after day. There was a value in that that might show the tool marks of effort, but for centuries it had put food on tables and kept kids warm and fields planted and doors bolted against the world when a family had nothing but each other for army and justice and church.

As Jake grew he claimed a paler cast of his father's skin, the bold cut of his mother's jaw, the independent will of his great-grandfather—Raney even saw the full, pouted mouth she remembered in her mother. His eyes remained a puzzle for months and finally resolved as two unique colors—the left a rich chocolate brown and the right a shade of gray-blue, as if he would not allow either Raney or Cleet to fully claim that feature.

They had all given him his body. But his soul? She knew that boy's soul had always been his own. His loud energy was enough to over-whelm the small house, and sometimes Raney would ask Cleet two or three times to clear the table or cut up Jake's meat before she realized he had earplugs in. On Jake's fourth birthday Cleet bought him his own set of tools—not plastic ones but real metal and wood, sharp enough to put out his own eye, Raney protested. But then she dug out some blocks of foam core and saw Jake sit engrossed in making a fair likeness of a rocking chair, still and centered on one task for longer than she had yet witnessed. Over the next couple of years Raney learned to take Jake's foam or balsa-wood compositions with her to any school parent conference, so that when the teacher opened with, "So what's going on with Jake, do you think?" Raney could counter with physical evidence, "This. This and a lot more if you show him a little patience."

One evening after Jake was asleep, Raney stumbled in the middle of balancing the checkbook, looking at the bank numbers three times over before going out to Cleet's shop. He was leaning over a cabinet door polishing the last uneven surfaces with fine sandpaper, rubbing his hand over the wood to feel what his eyes couldn't see.

"What's this?" she asked, pointing to a highlighted line.

He squinted at it and went back to rubbing the wood. "Savings."

"No—that's this line here."

Cleet started hunting around for oil and clean cloth scraps, taking up a task, she was convinced, just so he wouldn't have to look her in the eye. She almost wondered if this was where the wife figures out there's another woman, only in Cleet's case it would have been another woodworking tool. Finally he answered her. "It's a college account."

"Okay. College is good." She turned around to leave, but then it boiled over inside her. "We're paying eighteen percent interest on that savings, if you count the credit we're carrying, and I'm not sure he's going to make it out of elementary school. Maybe he won't want to go to college. What then?"

Raney had gotten used to reading twice the meaning into every word Cleet said, but she still didn't see his next thought coming. He set his tin of oil quietly on the bench and rubbed the ache out of his knuckles before he faced her. "He may not. Or he may want to live here in this house, or one like it. Or he may want to buy one of those houses at the end of the bluff. If our son wants to live someplace where people matter—all people—then I intend to give him the means." That was the first and last time Raney heard Cleet hint that he gave a whit about social status. Any battles he'd fought over his darker skin he'd absorbed into his generally tolerant view of mankind, apparently accepting even Grandpa's evident prejudice as an unavoidable flaw that should be overlooked, on a par with acne scars or buckteeth.

Raney believed they might have eked it out, too, if it hadn't been for the Chertoff remodel Cleet accepted when Jake was seven. After the acrimony began she would find herself sitting late into the night drawing charcoal sketches of the old house on the bluff, each from a steeper perspective than the last, so that by the end they felt as haunted and sharp-winged as the bats that twisted from the gabled eaves. The irony of how she and Cleet had played with their own dream-future on that same front porch made the seemingly fated trail to their ruin all the more bitter. Like a trap laid for the amusement of indifferent gods.

The house was famous in their end of town, empty for most of the year because the family that had inherited it lived in New York and were either heedless or barely hanging on to it—the paint and the yard and the roof gradually going more and more wild, green life sprouting from its inorganic gutters. Though it was not quite old enough to have existed in the age of whale-oil lamps, it was built after the fashion of the captains' houses in Port Townsend, tall as a lighthouse with a widow's walk outside the attic, trim boards cut out like fancy cookies. And such windows—four long panes to a frame that a six-foot man might walk through without so much as a nod. Sitting out on the bluff, an old house like that quickly passes from being weathered and charming to being rough and unwelcoming if it is not pampered, and for three years no one with a legitimate right to open the front door ever stepped through it. They did, though. Cleet and Jake and Raney.

After a late summer evening picnic on the overgrown lawn, Jake spotted a half-starved tabby dragging something under the brush near the cellar windows at the back. He came running to his parents already in tears. The mother cat was transferring a litter of kittens through a broken pane of glass and one had fallen—Jake could see it paddling blindly over the basement floor in the wrong direction. Cleet crouched at the window with Jake and invested a lot of breath trying to convince him that the mother would rescue the kitten; interfering would only drive her away and it was unlawful to break into someone else's house even to help a lost kitten. But after further father-son consultation Cleet walked back to his toolshed and returned with a crowbar and various screwdrivers.

If they could blame Jake for luring them into the basement, they had no excuse for wandering around the rest of the house. Whoever had built it had spared nothing—all the more sorrow to see it trundling toward decay, Raney said. Cleet squatted in front of the built-in dining room credenza, walnut with cherry inlay, opening and closing one drawer four or five times just to admire the precision of its dovetailed fittings. "Someone cared about this," he said to himself, with a note of rejuvenated faith in the honor of his craft. "Someone took the time to do it right."

Jake stayed in the basement naming kittens while Raney and Cleet tiptoed guiltily through the first floor, across loomed floral carpets so thick with dust their true color only showed in the impressions left by Raney's bare feet. The doors were all open, which made it easier to pretend they were only looking around one more corner, into one more inviting space: a library filled with the classic titles expected for show, but also plenty of warped paperback mysteries and romances and spy novels; a music room with a grand

piano on bow-squatted legs in one corner and an electric Clavinova
on the other wall. There was a room that held nothing but stacked-
up chairs and end tables and a slashed and stained box spring
canted against the wall.

They didn't move anything. They would never have taken anything. But they went back. Sometimes after a family dinner, a few times
when Jake was at school and they were both at home and her painting
and his joinery had drained them of creative novelty. They would go
out for a walk, and if the walk led them down their road and then to
the bluff and the houses, then it also led them—seemingly without
intent—to the house's open window and back inside the empty rooms.
What did it mean to them, that house? Dreams for a grand home of
their own? A minute or an hour reincarnated to lives they'd missed or
already lived and forgotten?

The Chertoffs bought the house in late fall, long after the kittens
had been weaned and pushed out of the maternal nest. In December
the Chertoffs' Realtor sent Cleet a letter asking if he was available
for a custom cabinetry job and did he have any references and did
he, by the way, know any construction firm who could begin a small
remodeling job within the month?

Raney and Cleet talked it over at the kitchen table after Jake
was asleep, a rare bottle of modest wine open and both their cups
on the second fill. The letter lay in the middle, between them. Cleet
rolled his cup between his palms, shifting right hand forward, then
left, right . . . Finally Raney laid her hand over his cup and stopped
it so suddenly wine splashed through her fingers onto the tablecloth. "You know that house. You know what it needs. Think of it as
a window opening," she said. "Maybe it isn't the ideal time, or even
the ideal window. But if you don't jump through it now, it will be
gone."

"People like them—they're looking for something corporate.
They want custom work at a factory price."

"People like *them*? They're just people. Rich or smart or maybe just lucky. They're just other people. Not so different from us—two legs, two arms, dirty underwear. You should at least consider it. Answer the letter and see where it goes." Cleet tilted his head to the side once—a gesture she'd come to recognize as hinting a crack in his resolve. "Cleet, we can't even afford the college savings anymore."

The project—a new sunporch, bathroom, master suite, and kitchen—took ten months. In that time Cleet bought a new table saw and subcontracted a plumber, an electrician, a drywaller, a painter, and an apprentice carpenter. At the end of the job he handed the Chertoffs' agent, Todd King, his last bill, equal to one-quarter of the sum plus all the unreimbursed expenses Raney and Cleet had paid up front, the last ten thousand out of their own savings while they scraped by on Raney's paycheck.

A month later Cleet sent a second letter, and a month after that he telephoned King five times with no returned call. He drove to the county courthouse to file a lien, and then the crushing potency of the Chertoffs' money was unleashed. Cleet got a certified letter from a lawyer and a hired construction inspector claiming defects and delays totaling $170,000. They offered to settle for $50,000—more than Cleet's salary for the whole job.

"We'll hire a lawyer of our own," Cleet said.

"I talked you into taking this job—it's my fault we're in this. These people have more money than God and they are willing to spend more money fighting you than this whole project cost. We have to walk away from it. If you drop the lien and walk away they won't come after you."

Cleet wouldn't look at her. She sat half in hope he was considering her words, and half in fear that he resented her for not rising up in defiance along with him. The sun had dropped below the trees, and the only light in the room shone from the oven window. She couldn't read his face but would not let go of both his hands until this was seen through. Finally he took in a breath. "My grandparents moved to this country because they believed in the U.S. government. They believed there was a place with justice. For all. If I can get a judge, a court, to hear what I have to say, then we won't lose this."

"Cleet, the lawyer charges three hundred dollars an hour. Every hour. What do we have to pay him with?"

"I'll pay the lawyer after I'm rightfully paid what I'm owed. What I earned."

They went to the first meeting together. The lawyer was in his late fifties probably, ran his office out of a small house in Port Angeles with one secretary, and tended to ramble on about other cases he'd handled, the paucity of good workmen these days. Later Raney wished she'd had the gumption to clarify that he was billing them the same for time reminiscing as for time arguing their case. The lawyer laid out the probable course: the Chertoffs would be deposing their experts to prove the construction flaws, and they would have to find their own experts to counter them. Cleet gave a small nod now and then. But Raney saw every word flow out in vivid greens and golds— a second mortgage, Jake's college money, clothing, groceries, electricity, propane. By noon her shoulders and stomach ached from sitting with every muscle tensed. The long drive home was a conspicuous silence that pounded against her eardrums, interspersed with sharp arguments and tears.

Somewhere along the course, sometime over the next endless months, she let go of the battle. Cleet was fighting devils hot and vivid in his memory and his father's memory and even his grandfather's, back to some root conviction that the soul of a man was ultimately righteous and just and a righteous fight must result in justice. Why could she not believe that? It worked in the movies.

Cleet didn't want her to go to the arbitration, but she insisted. "It's all for show," he said.

"Of course it is. But if your wife doesn't look like she believes in you, why should the arbitrator?"

"No. I mean the whole thing. This whole arbitration is just for show. You were right. They won the day they pulled out their checkbook."

They made Raney sit separated from Cleet, maybe to keep her from kicking his shins so he'd change his answers. Cleet kept his eyes fixed on the opposite wall while the two lawyers took turns asking the experts questions: how they would have run the ductwork or where they would have put the outlets. Should the gap between a counter and a cabinet be an eighth of an inch or a sixteenth? They started at nine and went until five with coffee breaks and stretch breaks and lunch breaks and Raney knew they would be billed for every minute of it. On the second-to-last day the arbitrator looked fed up with the Chertoffs' lawyer's endless dissection of every nail pop and paint drip, which she took as a hopeful sign. The arbitrator asked if anyone needed another break, and she said, "No," too emphatically. It seemed to wake up whatever pinch of humor he had left in his dour soul, and he smiled like it was time to relax and forget this was Cleet against the machine. "You sit still as a sphinx over there," he said, chuckling. "Don't you get restless?"

"We're paying three hundred dollars an hour. That keeps me pretty alert."

Cleet's lawyer was in a barely controlled state of livid after that, but when they got home, after Jake was asleep, Cleet pulled her onto his lap and cupped his wide, rough fingers along the curve of her skull, his body soft and wholly connected to hers for the first time since it had begun. "I love you, Raney. This is why we're a good match, huh? You say what you think and I think what you say."

In his final summary, the prosecuting lawyer said Cleet was skilled and probably well intended, but overestimated his talent, allowed ambition to push his common sense aside. To Raney, that was just another rich man telling the likes of them to stay in their place. But nobody rich ever says that when he's looking for a good deal, she knew.

It took two weeks for the final decision to come in. Raney was in the yard hunting for any tomatoes that had escaped blight; a tremble of bees stirred the lavender and her hand was cupped around the swollen weight of the last fruit—enough joy in one small patch to inspire faith in providence. So when Cleet came to her with the ruling she felt the full ballast of overturned hope.

Cleet's lawyer acted like they'd won the case, saying they should be thrilled to get a fraction of the Chertoffs' unpaid bill, given all the construction claims. And Cleet's lawyer *had* won. They owed him double the award they got.

· 14 ·

charlotte

Two full days had passed since Charlotte sat across from Helen Seras at her sleek glass-and-steel desk and repeated everything Eric knew about Raney Remington's scar. Still nothing had appeared on the evening news or in the papers; no reporters or detectives had barged into the ICU. Nor had any family member. Helen had instructed Charlotte to keep the story to herself until it could be validated. *Validated!* One of those hospital euphemisms like "proper channels" or "organizational challenges" that irritated Charlotte—spineless phrases designed to obscure both the problem and the power behind it.

Helen had listened closely enough, even taking notes while Charlotte explained Eric's memory of Raney's arm caught and stripped raw by the rope swing. But when Charlotte and Helen went to Jane's room together, hours after the bath Eric had witnessed, the blushed and swollen scar had settled back into a faint pink circle of skin and the dramatic revelation seemed less definitive even to Charlotte.

Helen had promised she would notify Blake Simpson that day. Why hadn't he come by? And there should have been at least a phone call from Raney Remington's family, Charlotte thought. If Raney had any living family. If Jane Doe was indeed Raney Remington.

Christina Herrand said nothing about the scar. She came to see Jane every day. She usually brought a book with her, always the same small, leather-bound volume with gold-leaf edging along the tissue-thin pages and a red silk bookmark. Sometimes she brought a bit of knitting, which appeared to be the same rectangle of yarn stitched and unraveled and stitched up again. Charlotte suspected it served best as an excuse to avoid any conversation or eye contact, or perhaps only a purposeful task to fill the hours of waiting—waiting for Jane's condition to change, waiting for some sign that she was destined to live or die so that no one else would be forced to act. Often, though, Christina just sat and watched. Now and then she asked Charlotte questions: What did the Glasgow Coma Scale actually mean? How much could it *really* predict? When might the doctors (and here Charlotte was tempted to remind Christina that she, too, was a doctor, was Jane's primary doctor, in fact) decide if all her toes had to be amputated, all her fingers? And at least twice this: How many people woke up after so much time unconscious on a ventilator? After so many insults to their brain, their lungs, their kidneys, their liver? What quality of life could they hope to come back to?

The second time Charlotte had bitten her tongue for one restrained moment and then blurted, "Maybe better than the average American parked for eight hours a day in front of reality TV." Before she could soften the sarcasm, Charlotte was appalled to hear Christina begin consoling *her*.

Eric was beside himself with impatience, chafing at the idea that he, too, should obey Helen Seras's dictums. He couldn't let it go, as if talking about Raney was all that kept him from physically carrying her back to Quentin, back to whatever life she'd made since he'd left her waiting for his phone call. He spent hours telling Charlotte about his summers in that backwater town, the sense that he had been abandoned there by his parents while they clawed their way through a divorce. He told her about the girl he remembered—

unrecognizable in the comatose creature lying in the ICU: an artist who used charcoal and pigment to show the world both as it was and as it could never be; worldly enough to call him on his prejudices as much as his possibilities even though she'd rarely traveled fifty miles from her own house. "She was always telling me we had nothing in common." He laughed to himself and Charlotte caught a sting of remorse. "Nothing and everything."

After a while Charlotte sat quietly and just let him talk, hearing two separate stories in his history with Raney. When he told her the story of his first kiss, she heard the trauma of his first seizure. When he told her about their two missed chances at love, at age twenty and again at twenty-seven, she heard the timeline of his recurrent brain tumors and surgeries, how they had slashed his youth with precocious mortal terror. And for the first time—how was it possible?—she heard the horrific consequence of his last grand mal seizure and the real reason Eric would never drive again.

She had never been so conscious of how little he had shared about his disease, or how little she'd admitted its effects on him; that the boundaries he had drawn were not just for his own protection. She had fallen in love with him during a blissful window of apparent health, and despite all the textbooks and articles she'd read, for the first time she admitted how unlikely it was to last. It scared her. But what scared her most was that she couldn't tell if she was more afraid for Eric or for herself.

Felipe Otero had been away at a medical conference. Three days after Eric's revelation Felipe stopped by the hospital to pick up his mail and check in, his ten-year-old son, Andy, in tow. The boy looked so much like his father it was easy for Charlotte to imagine that she was seeing Felipe as a child. She dug a handful of quarters out of her pockets for Andy to use at his whim in the vending machines down the hall. Felipe was already pulling up the computer files on the newly admitted patients. Charlotte turned the monitor away so that he had to stop reading and look at her. "Jane has a name," she said.

"Jane Doe? When? I didn't hear anything on the news."

"Ortho took the cast off her arm and discovered a scar three days ago."

"And someone identified her?"

Charlotte almost blurted out that Eric, her Eric, had been the one to recognize the physical mar that distinguished Jane as a unique individual. But suddenly she didn't want to personalize it, at least not here in the hospital. "Well, it isn't certain yet. Helen reported it to the sheriff's office, but she doesn't want the press to know—thinks the photographers would be camped out waiting for the moment of reunion, I guess."

"How could the hospital stop this getting out?"

"Helen could stop the rain if she decided to."

"Charlotte, listen to you. Be careful or they'll give you her job."

"I suppose that would serve me right." He should have laughed with her at that, but there was a look of something closer to sympathy in his eyes that made Charlotte want to change the subject. "The conference was good?" she asked.

"Good enough. Hard to be away from the boys." As if on cue, Andy ran around the corner and slammed into his father's legs with two fistfuls of potato chips and candy bars. "Dr. Charlotte spoils you! And leaves the aftermath of junk food to me." He winked at Charlotte and she felt the co-conspirator with them both, for a moment sweeping away her anxiety about Jane or Helen—even Eric. Felipe had become so much more actively a parent in these last weeks, involved in the small details that must have been handled by his wife before. He seemed quite unconscious of the subtle shift, but Charlotte had an unbidden image of him rousing his three boys in the morning, getting their oatmeal or eggs heated up, their school lunches packed. "I have to get him to soccer practice," Felipe said, putting Andy's head into a mock stronghold. "You're here tomorrow? It's hard to imagine Jane's situation won't become more . . . complicated."

"Complicated? In what way?" She knew he was referring to more than Jane's medical problems. But Andy was already pulling him down the hall.

"Tomorrow. Let's have a drink after work if things don't get crazy."

And following the natural rule that all systems will trend toward disorder, things did get more complicated. By the next day, eighteen days after Jane was airlifted to Beacon Hospital, her kidneys could no longer balance her blood chemistry within the narrow range compatible with life. The level of potassium in her blood was alarmingly high, and Felipe, who was on duty, had to put a large-bore catheter under her clavicle so that Jane could be dialyzed. Her oxygen levels and blood pressure had improved, but the dialysis machine acted like an inert external shunt and worsened both, so she could barely tolerate the full treatment.

Every time Jane's ICU door opened, Charlotte wondered if it would be Christina Herrand with a court order to turn everything off, or Jane's astounded relative, begging for more time. And what if one occurred only a day before the other? When she couldn't stand it any longer, Charlotte went to Helen's office. Helen's assistant was a twentyish girl who had a different-color stripe in her bleached-blond hair every time Charlotte saw her. Today it was sky blue, and somehow the defiance of this distinctly unnatural color cheered Charlotte up. When Helen's office door opened, she grasped both of Charlotte's hands warmly, as she always did, as if she were running into an old friend unexpectedly at a cocktail party. "I'm glad you came by. She's no better, is she? Your patient. I stopped by this morning, but you and Dr. Otero looked busy so I didn't interrupt."

"What's happened since her ID, Helen? I haven't heard anything."

"Oh? I thought Simpson had called you . . . I've been keeping him up to date on Jane's condition." Charlotte caught a hesitation in Helen's eyes before she added, "His office found an address on the Olympic Peninsula. Simpson went out to talk to the husband two days ago."

A husband. There was a husband. Charlotte felt something inside her briefly expand and then utterly collapse, leaving a void of remarkable and unanticipated magnitude. "So she's really Eric's friend, then?"

Helen looked at her frankly, absent her usual placid smile. "What I've said is confidential, Charlotte. Simpson believes she's been identified, but you should wait for him to tell you more. I know her condition is . . . tenuous. You have decisions to make . . ."

"No . . . I just . . . Why hasn't her husband come to see her yet?"

"Well, grief does strange things to people. I called the husband myself yesterday—I didn't get very far. He basically hung up on me when I said I was from Beacon. And I shouldn't have even told you that."

"Why can't I phone him? He might be more open with me—her doctor."

"I'm asking you to wait. Let the law deal with it first. Please."

"We might not have many more days. She's got strangers acting as her family." A pink flush deepened the sun-scarred folds of Helen's thin neck. Charlotte felt her register the extent of Charlotte's disdain and forgive her—a cost of business. "Why don't you want me involved in this?" Charlotte asked.

"Dr. Reese. Charlotte. Remember, this was a hit-and-run accident. Whoever left Jane in a ditch along the highway is likely to be prosecuted. You can imagine how that could escalate if she doesn't survive."

Charlotte was already parked in front of her own house before she dialed Felipe's number; they'd had no time to talk at the hospital. She could see Eric's shadow through the closed window shade— back at work, which was good. The geneticist in Sweden was nearly impossible to reach, and Eric had been forced to write around missing information; he was getting anxious about his deadline, but he'd been too distracted to write in these last few days. She wanted to tell him everything, despite Helen's request. It would be some relief to hear that

Simpson had found the husband, wouldn't it? Give Eric some sense of resolution? She watched his shadow stretching, rubbing his head. *Resolution*. Another hollow word, she thought. A word that worked in poetry and obituaries maybe, but this? Whatever Eric had lost when he discovered Raney felt impossible to name, much less resolve.

He would begin pacing the room right about now, she knew, reading a copy of his day's work out loud and stopping every lap or two to cross something out, make a star beside the good stuff. Even as she had the thought, his shadow reached the end of the coffee table and stopped, hunching over a page for a moment before he started walking again. He was a man of reliable habits, though she suspected he hadn't always been. Certainly not in his wilder traveling days, before she knew him. When Raney had known him.

Charlotte was about to give up on Felipe when he finally answered his cell phone. He was grabbing a burger just a few blocks away—she should drive over, catch up on things. By the time Charlotte got there, he'd already ordered her a glass of Malbec and a plate of calamari. "Eric's probably made dinner," she said.

"Just an appetizer. I heard you met with Helen today and figured you'd need some sustenance."

"What did you hear?" she asked.

"Only that Jane's demise could now be someone's murder charge. That Helen is worried you may not be the most objective member of the care team."

"Helen Seras *said* that?"

"Well, not until I asked her and she admitted it." The flourish with which he said this made Charlotte laugh despite herself. "It's the only way to get the truth from them!" he went on. "So now I'll ask you. Is it true?"

"Which? Murder or my objectivity?"

"You choose. I already know the answers. 'Only machines are objective,'" he quoted her from their past conversations.

"Correct. As for murder . . . I'm not a lawyer. Not my problem."

"As long as you keep the machines going." Felipe's irreverence was his most appealing characteristic in Charlotte's opinion, but the joke sent an uncomfortable shiver through her. "Maybe *Helen* needs to reconsider her own objectivity. She gave me a grilling about starting dialysis—harmless enough, unless she's tallying up the daily cost of Jane's survival. Or maybe Christina Herrand, the hired gun—excuse me, *guardian*—is whispering in Helen's ear. She was there tonight, knitting. Rumi in hand."

"Rumi? I'd assumed she was reading the Bible," Charlotte said.

"I peeked when she went to the ladies' room."

"I know Helen's told her about Jane's ID—I guess she had to, legally. I've avoided talking to her about it. Or she's avoided it . . ."

"I'm sure she's waiting for proof positive. Notarized, no doubt. If it's true they've found the husband I'll miss Christina, in a way. I was hoping that knitting might be a sweater for me. Scarf at least."

"You don't think it's true?" Charlotte asked him.

He shrugged and for the first time looked slightly reserved. "I don't know. Maybe a husband has been found. But did Helen say Jane was, indeed, Eric's friend? It makes for a remarkable coincidence— the doctor's boyfriend being the one to identify the unknown patient. Don't you think?"

"They happen sometimes. We're the only Level I trauma hospital here."

"True. How is Eric handling it?"

Charlotte stumbled for an answer. The startling moment of Eric's discovery felt almost trivial compared with the tremors that continued between the two of them, undiscussed. Felipe was watching her somberly. He said, "We need to do more formal testing on her brain stem, Charlotte. A few more days of dialysis but . . . There could be some tough decisions ahead. Have you talked to him about that?"

Charlotte shook her head. "There's still a lot we haven't talked about." After a pause she asked, "What do you think about the tests?"

"I think I've let you postpone it for too long."

"That's not what I meant. Do you think she's brain-dead?"

"Likely. Which could be the better of two evils."

"She's thirty-nine. Two years older than me."

"You've lost patients younger than this, Charlotte. What's different here?" He had put his fork down and was studying her as if no answer could be wrong except the failure to answer at all.

"I don't know. That she's alone? A victim?" She groped for something more rational, but the truth swept in from somewhere else. "I just feel like she has more to do. I have to give her more time here."

"So you are the immortal twin, come to the rescue." She looked puzzled and he continued. "You've forgotten your school lessons. Castor and Pollux, the twins. One the child of Zeus and one the child of a mortal. When the mortal Castor is killed, Pollux splits his immortality to save him."

"Are you telling me not to try to play God, Felipe? *Really*?"

"I know better than to tell you anything." He laughed. "And we are all Gods within our realms, as my grandmother would have said. Especially doctors, as my mother would have said. Anyway, it worked in the myth. Except, of course, the twins could then live only in the stars."

By the time she got home, Eric had put her dinner under plastic wrap in the refrigerator. He looked up expectantly and she leaned to kiss him—another moment to collect her emotions, to imply without lying that there was still no news. She couldn't talk about it now. What would she tell him? She felt almost as confused about Jane's identity as she had before Eric saw the scar. Why hadn't Simpson called her yet? *A husband. There was a husband.* She heard Helen's words again, tried to imagine what kind of husband could shun his critically ill wife. How would Eric react? She was too tired to think anymore, talk anymore—she had the next day off; there would be time then, after she'd slept. She shut his laptop and coaxed him into bed.

She woke up spooned around him like it was any summer Saturday— as if the stress of these last three days had blown everything out of perspective and a deep, dreamless sleep had set it right again. He pulled her arms tight and said, "Sunny today. Let's get away. Go out on the boat."

She showered, washed her hair, and put a thick conditioner on to soak, as much to linger in the hot water and steam as for any improbable benefit to her unruly hair. After she'd rinsed and turbaned her head she stood dripping in front of an empty linen cabinet. She got back into the shower and called out to the bedroom, "Can you get me another towel? There're some in the dryer, I think."

"Maybe I should hold you hostage for it," Eric joked, like his old self.

"If you make me wait any longer I'll be dry anyway."

He tossed the towel over the shower door and started to shave. Charlotte emerged, tubed in fluffy pink, and stood behind him facing the mirror. "If I move in with you, we are throwing those towels out," Eric said.

"They're great towels. Expensive towels."

"They're pink."

"Expensive pink."

It had been their joke for years, this trading of personal quirks and pleasures they would be forced to relinquish if they lived together. The quips had started as tentative bait dipped into the waters of commitment that the other could snatch or swim by. But by now the jokes felt de-barbed—their way of promising not to leave each other without being obligated to stay. She had assumed it was their tacit agreement to give it more time—the answer would declare itself. She watched him shave and knew by heart exactly where the next razor stroke would begin and end. A comfortingly unchanging habit in a comfortable unchanging relationship. As soon as she had the thought, she remembered her own rule never to greet a patient's family with the words "There's been no change." There was always change, from one breath and one heartbeat to the next. Dying and surviving both required momentum, and in her mind, only a heartless doctor would refuse to measure that change for a family.

A year or so after their first trip to Lopez Island, when his mother's uncalculated rudeness had made Charlotte realize that she was falling in love, her house had become the more commonly shared dwelling. Eric had gradually taken over two drawers in her dresser, the top shelf in the bathroom cabinet that she could hardly reach anyway, and displaced her white sugar with his agave syrup in the kitchen. For another year it had seemed part of a slow, easy stream going somewhere purposeful, no need to predict where, in its own slow and easy time.

Then Eric's editor had come into town. The three of them took a jazz brunch cruise on the *Argosy*—one of those tourist activities you did only when you hosted an out-of-towner—and came away from it freshly reminded of Seattle's unique beauty. After the cruise they'd dropped the editor at his hotel and come back to Charlotte's house. Eric wandered into the kitchen and came back to the bedroom with two glasses of wine, holding one out for Charlotte. She was lying on her back across the bed with her head at the foot so that her hair hung over the edge, still matted and curled from being out on the water. Her hands were folded over her abdomen and her blue jeans were unzipped. She was wearing headphones connected to an iPod and didn't show any sign of hearing him come into the room. "Wine?" he asked.

He walked over and lay down next to her. When she still didn't move he pulled one of the earbuds to his own ear and listened: Joan Osborne's "St. Teresa," the one she always listened to when some pent-up emotional wave was about to break. When the song ended, he rolled above her with one hand beside each shoulder and studied her face looking for a clue. "Hey in there. You okay?" Charlotte nodded, calm enough for him to assume their quite perfect day on the quite perfect Puget Sound had merited Joan. "Jim wants to talk about marketing. Good sign. I told him I'd stop by his hotel before he goes to the airport. Want to come? Or I can get a cab."

Charlotte took out the other earbud and looked into Eric's lovely blue eyes, one of the first things she'd noticed about him years ago. She saw his face as freshly as she had seen the Seattle skyline from the boat this morning. It was handsome to her, even when she reminded herself to focus on the flaws that had disappeared with familiarity—the lean, slightly crooked nose, the hollowed shadows that made him look too serious unless he was smiling. He wasn't that thin, really, but if all you saw was his face you would expect protruding ribs and hipbones, the same skinny, awkwardly tall physique she'd seen in his teenage pictures.

"My period is late," she told him.

She didn't know what she expected from him; she didn't even know what *she* thought about it yet. He seemed to be sorting out the definition of each word as if English were a foreign language and took great concentration. "How late?" he finally asked.

Neutral, she thought. He sounded carefully, conscientiously neutral. "Four or five days."

He nodded. "Okay. Not so much." So. Less neutral now.

She sat up and zipped her jeans. "Yeah. Probably nothing. I think I'll stay here. You go. Tell him bye for me."

He brought Thai food back, three stars for her favorite yellow curry, just the way she liked it. He called to her from the kitchen, and she heard him getting plates out of the dishwasher, filling glasses with ice. When she came in she could tell he'd gone to extra trouble—poured each cardboard carton into separate glass serving bowls and found some chopsticks and cloth napkins. It was late; the light through the window above the sink was dimming, but the kitchen was still warm. As soon as she sat down, Eric started talking about all the plans he'd discussed with Jim, the blurb he was hoping to get from Jared Diamond, book jacket options, the one chapter that would still need revision—he'd decided to trust his editor's judgment on that. Oh, he'd forgotten to tell her that his father had called from Spain. He and his new wife were spending the summer there with the boys. Charlotte said almost nothing. Finally, Eric stopped working so hard to fill the empty space between them. The curry made her mouth burn—a point of focus in a day that had begun to seem surreal. She put her chopsticks down, folded her napkin in the middle of her half-finished plate, and looked at him. "It was a false alarm."

"You got your period?"

"I took a pregnancy test," she said.

He paused, calculating. "You already had a test kit here?"

She shrugged. "I get them free from the hospital. It was negative." And when she could stand to look at his face again she almost cried, seeing his blatant relief.

That was over a year ago—hard to believe, she thought. They could have talked more about it then; he'd taken her hand across the table and made himself open and willing, but she'd only given his hand a squeeze and started clearing the dishes. There was no rush; better when he was less distracted by his book, when they were further along, when the gash of regret left by him and her own body had stopped bleeding.

Eric was already in his boat shoes and on his second cup of coffee, engrossed in the newspaper. Charlotte came into the kitchen and sat next to him, waited for him to look at her. "I need to tell you something. Helen Seras says the sheriff's office located a husband."

He stared at her, as if he had to repeat the words to himself. "You found out this morning?"

She squeezed his hand, but he hardly seemed aware. "Yesterday. I couldn't say it last night—Helen has asked me not to talk about it at all until they know more. I'm not even sure they've confirmed that Jane is Raney. The husband hasn't been very cooperative." The look on Eric's face made it clear he had no doubt Charlotte's patient was Raney. "Eric, she's so sick. Do you understand the tests we need to do?" He got up and walked to the window; after a moment he shook his head.

"When someone's been this badly injured, it's hard to know how much of their brain still functions. Even the ability to breathe. You can't tell when they're on a ventilator—the machine is breathing for them."

"You're talking about brain death," he said.

"Yes. Once she's off the sedatives, once the dialysis machine has balanced her blood chemistry, we need to test her brain-stem function. We check her corneal reflexes, her response to pain. We stop the ventilator and see if she can breathe on her own."

"And if she doesn't react? Doesn't breathe?"

"It means she doesn't have enough functional brain to survive, no matter what we do. It means we're being cruel. Defying nature. We stop the ventilator and let her go. Truthfully, what's harder is if she does blink, or breathes on her own. If she has enough brain to live but not to wake up. How far do we go then? For how long? Who decides that, if there's no living will?"

"Someone who cares, I hope. If Raney has a husband—or a grandfather or anyone else—I'd want them to decide."

"I want the same thing. Even if she isn't Raney."

Eric was so quiet it hurt. Charlotte walked to the window and stood next to him; across the street her neighbor pulled into his driveway and slid open the door to his minivan disgorging a gaggle of children that seemed too numerous to have fit safely inside. Balloons tied to the mailbox—a birthday party, then. Finally Eric said, "She's different for you, even before you found out I knew her."

Charlotte blew a circle of fog on the windowpane and outlined the cluster of colored balloons, as still as a photograph advertising family life in the great American suburbs. She said, "There's no wind today, you know. Bad day for sailing. We could take a ferry ride to the peninsula instead."

"Even after what Helen told you? You're going to walk up and knock on his door?"

"What else can I do?"

"I can knock."

If it was terrible weather for sailing, it was perfect for crossing the sound. The sun was still low on the eastern horizon and every riffle of water flashed a silver-blue mirror. The triangle of Mount Baker pierced the northern haze and the snowy dome of Mount Rainier shouldered the south, like two great pillars holding sea and sky apart for life to play out between them. It made Charlotte feel insignificant and grand all at the same time, so impermanent in the vast landscape that it was blindingly obvious the only way to matter at all was to cling to every moment even as you leaped into the next.

She looked at Eric and felt a rush of love. If she ran to him, told him, "Now. Tonight. Time won't last for us either," would she catch him on this wave? Or was this urgent intimacy just her desire to have what Raney once had: Eric when he could still pretend he would never die.

He looked at her, squinting against the sun. "What?"

"It's just so beautiful out here today."

The docking announcement sounded overhead and they walked back to the car; the hold was chilly and dark and Charlotte turned the heated seat on until they were out on the road and back in the sun. They drove across Bainbridge Island and the small Agate Pass Bridge, which connected it to the peninsula, then half an hour later crossed the massive Hood Canal Bridge, hinged in the middle for the passage of nuclear submarines heading from the Bangor submarine base. The land in this corner of the country was splattered in channels and islands like a messy afterthought of creation. Charlotte had lived in the Northwest all her life and couldn't memorize the puzzle of earth and ocean, only the names of the few towns and beaches that attracted summer tourists and their money. She and Eric should have taken some weekends here, gone hiking or to one of the lodges on the coast. There just never seemed to be enough time. Here and there a finger of tribal land touched the highway, marked by fireworks stands and pickup trucks advertising fresh-caught salmon and fresh-dug clams. Deeper into the peninsula the air was ripe with the stench of dairy cows and horses where massive barns loomed over modest homes. Then the clutter of the town began, sparse at first—a nest of abandoned cars, a small grocery, a bar, a hamburger stand.

Eric got quieter as they neared Quentin. Charlotte tried to imagine what he must be feeling; every time he'd been to this town it had marked some drastic change in his life—broken family, broken love, broken brain. Every memory from here must make the specter of Raney's immobile body more horrifying. For one startling moment she wanted this trip to be a dead end, for Raney Remington to be discovered alive and well, gone fat with a passel of children. A complete stranger hooked up to Beacon Hospital's machines.

"Do I turn here? Do you remember?" Charlotte asked.

"Take a right up there at the gas station. I can find her grandfather's house. It's a place to start."

Quentin had hardly changed, Eric said. It seemed to have shrunk rather than grappled to its spindly legs in the eleven years since he'd been here. He signaled Charlotte to pull up in front of the plate-glass windows of a small building. Hardy's Store was a sign shop now, advertising custom and preprinted plastic, laminated, or metal signs. The interior was dark, despite the Open sign hanging at an angle from a string on the front door. Eric cupped his eyes to the glass and saw walls plastered with No Trespassing, For Rent, For Sale, Logging Feeds Families, Stop the Land Grab. He was quiet and she took his hand.

"Was this where she worked? Raney?" Charlotte asked.

"No. It was my aunt's grocery store. She and my uncle lived up there. And me, for a while." He pointed to the three uncurtained windows above the porch where he had lived for two summers of his unfolding life. "I'm glad it's closed. Don't really want to know all that's happened here since they died."

Charlotte shielded her eyes to look up at the inhospitable dark rectangles. She had been to Eric's childhood home in Laurelhurst once, before it was sold. A grand Arts and Crafts specimen on the crest of a hill overlooking the lake, with gardens spilling across a double-sized lot. His mother and stepfather were in South America, or maybe it was South Africa—they were always somewhere else—and Charlotte and Eric sat in the kitchen at the back of the house where doors led into a butler's pantry and maid's quarters.

The house was chilly with no one home, room after cavernous room above and around them. Or maybe the house was always chilly—it had that aura.

She waited in the car outside the sign store while Eric stood, hands in pockets, somberly looking down the street as if something unexpected might appear. "Where now?" she asked when he finally got in.

"Her grandfather's farm, I guess. If he's still alive. Go straight along this road toward the park." A few miles on he told her to take a left, then right, then turned them around to try another road. After five more turnarounds they crested a hill and he asked her to pull over. He got out and studied the mountains that could be seen from that vantage, the break in the horizon that marked the bay. "It was back there. The first road we took." He directed Charlotte up and down four different driveways before he asked her to stop in front of a small, Hardie board–sided house with six identical neighbors. Th~~~~~~~~~~~~~~~~~~~~~~~~, their patchy lawns dotted with plastic Big Wheels and skateboards. She followed him along a worn dirt path behind the houses until he stopped underneath an enormous bigleaf maple fouled with the scrap plywood of a broken tree house. Eric paced out where the old barn had been, the duck pond, the rusted red car nestled in morning glory and hollyhocks, the farmhouse itself. It had all been turned into a subdivision.

They drove twenty minutes down the highway to Port Townsend, and Eric found the art gallery where Raney had worked, but Sandy had sold it just six months earlier to a transplant from Los Angeles. "Bought it sight unseen and retired to more work than I left behind," the new owner said. Sandy had taken off for the Costa del Sol, or was it Costa Rica? Someplace sunny. But in his files he did have an address for the woman named Renee who had worked for Sandy off and on. Charlotte put the address into her GPS; it was only a mile or so from where Raney's grandfather had once lived. It had to be her.

This time Eric asked Charlotte to park at the end of the road. A muscle twitched in his jaw and Charlotte knew he was contemplating what he might say to the man who answered the door. "I should go," Charlotte said. "I'm her doctor—I have a legitimate reason to talk to him."

"Should you check with the detective first? Are you breaking any law?"

"Raney's my patient, and she can't tell me what she wants." Charlotte looked over the steering wheel down the densely wooded road, no house even in sight. "I guess I don't care. It's the right thing to do and if the law isn't with me, then it should be."

After a minute of silence they decided to go together. But as soon as they rounded the first curve through the green-black trees and saw the only house, saw the broken front door, the grass-grown walk and punched-out windows, they knew it was vacant.

· 15 ·
raney

Love is certainly the least rational state of mind. Love makes babies that were never intended. Love drives knives into perfectly decent if still imperfect husbands and wives. It breaks bank accounts and sends people into rages over slights they'd ignore in a stranger. And it can blind you to changes happening in someone you've lived with and depended on—particularly when they are changes you don't want to face.

Cleet sold his tools after the lawsuit. Raney didn't even know he'd put an ad in until a pickup truck drove straight across their front yard and backed up to his shop. She would have thought they were being robbed if she hadn't witnessed Cleet loading his jointer, shaper, band saw, and most of his routers into the padded bed. She watched, convincing herself it was an empty exercise in spite until the three men bent under the weight of a pristine slab of Honduras mahogany Cleet had owned for eight years—saving it for some piece of furnishing he had yet to imagine. That scared her. She pulled dinner out of the oven before it was warmed through, fed Jake, and sent him across the woods to play with the Wells twins. When Cleet came in she was

waiting at the kitchen table, already worn out from the arguments
she had shouted into the echoes of her own mind.

"It will cost you twice as much to replace them. Even buying
used."

He twisted a bottle of beer open and sat opposite her. She could
smell his sweat, sharper than usual, smelled his unwashed hair. He'd
lost ten pounds since the arbitration, she bet. "I won't be replacing
them. I won't need them where I'm going," he said.

Later, she tried to pin down what she'd assumed he meant by
that—that he was taking a company job? Leaving Quentin? Leaving
her and Jake? "Even if you work with somebody else's tools you'll
need some of your own. Whatever they paid won't make a dent in
what we owe."

"Raney, I've taken a job on a purse seiner. Off the Aleutians out
of False Pass. I leave next week."

She sat back in her chair with the force of it, like a physical blow
in her chest. "You didn't want to talk to me first? How long will you
be gone?"

"A few weeks. Maybe more. Christo got me on. It's good money.
Too good to pass up."

"So where am I in this? What if I say no?"

He looked at her for a long time; his eyes were so dark in the low
light they were all enormous pupil, bottomless. "You won't. Any more
than I would you."

There wasn't time to think about Cleet's choice before he left. Or
maybe that was Raney's best excuse not to think about it—a trick
that had been getting her through the last months pretty well. They
made love five times in four days. In the same four days Cleet and
Jake made a tree fort in the bigleaf maple behind Grandpa's house
and a somewhat wobbly stool, into which Jake carved Raney's initials.
As if he'd been told that seven is the age of reason, Jake brought his
school calendar to the breakfast table the day Cleet was leaving and

made him circle the days he'd be gone, turning any sorrow into a team project the only way Jake knew how. Raney watched Cleet avoid the uncertainty by drawing ever fainter rings along successive days all the way through the month; fading one day to the next with the same gradual paling she saw between their skin tones.

After Cleet left, Raney bought a huge map and thumbtacked it to the living room wall. There was so much more ocean than land in the world, so much more space than people. The Aleutian chain swung halfway to Russia like the curved tusk of a great mammoth, blue water slipping through every island crevice, lapping millions of miles of beach. Great tongues of current forever swallowing the earth.

Cleet sounded upbeat when he called her from Port Moller. The work was grueling, filthy, he smelled rank with fish even when he could shower, but he liked his four crew members well enough. He called twice in the first few days offshore, but then Raney heard nothing for a week. Still, she didn't worry. In some ways it was easier at home, with just her and Jake. They settled into new habits—dinner in the tree fort when the weather was good, walking together through the woods and along the creek bed to Grandpa's every day.

She didn't start worrying until the doorbell rang and through the sidelight she saw a man on the porch with the name of the boat stitched on his jacket. Her very first feeling when he gave her the news was a deep shame for the surreal overlap in time when she had been painting, playing with Jake, cooking and freezing meals for when Cleet came home, and all the time he was already gone.

The net had just closed and they were starting to purse when the boat lurched. The sea was rough that day. Pretty high. Cleet had been at the bow, the others at the stern, so they couldn't say exactly how many minutes passed before they realized he was in the water. They'd sent the skiff over immediately; the coast guard was there within twenty minutes or so . . . The man giving her the news stopped talking after a while, or Raney stopped hearing him. Even by the next day the conversation seemed vague as a fading dream—

someone else's nightmare, surely. She remembered asking the man about a survival suit, or a life jacket—was Cleet wearing one? He'd rushed to say the captain had made them wear some new, high-tech jackets—CO_2 cartridge that inflated if you went over. Gave one to every man, it was that rough. But a survival suit? No—only if the boat was in danger. Then he'd licked his lips and taken a minute to think. She could see his mind turning, weighing, almost stopping himself before he said they'd found all the jackets on board though, in the end. She remembered leaning forward with her elbows on her knees and her forehead on her fists, concentrating like he was telling her the last secret code to save the world and it was her job to memorize it, only it was coming out in a language she couldn't understand.

The day of Cleet's memorial service Raney opened her jewelry box for the first time since he'd gone away and found a business card tucked into the lining of the lid. It was for a law firm, and at first glance Raney thought it was left from the arbitration and nearly tossed it away. She saw Cleet's handwriting on the back of it and looked again—"The Jones Act," he'd written. The card was for Boren, Stack and Jacoby, Maritime Law: Handling Maritime Injury and Wrongful Death.

In a small town nobody gets to have secrets. Everyone accepted Cleet's death as an ironically timed accident, or at least they did Raney the kindness of keeping any doubts to themselves. Sometimes she wished they would quit being so polite and just tell her what gossip they'd heard. She accepted casseroles and flowers left at her door, and hugs—usually sincere. But in the following months she saw their questions. A blush when they surprised her in the cereal aisle, a calculated dance of sympathetic words: *He was a well-meaning man*, when she wanted to hear *Strong. Honest. Right*. Or, worse, *You stood so steady by him during that awful business*, when she wanted to hear them scream what she knew now: *It's money that decides the law in this land. Money trumps right or wrong*.

Was it a gift to her that he put himself to rest in an ocean where she could stand and look over him always? No burial expenses required? She could only wonder if he had been warning her when his hand lingered at the small of her back while she washed dishes, or if she should have noted his momentary pause before he took Jake to task for some forgotten chore. The devil of a suicide, even when it is dressed so carefully as an accident, is the never-ending cry that you should have seen it coming. You should have been able to stop it. It tears you into two people, one unable to forgive the other, and the best you can hope for is some tolerant coexistence and a day when you might at least put your bloody hands over your guilty ears.

Sandy let Raney come back to work full time, even though the gallery barely earned enough for one half-time person. She knew her salary was being paid at the expense of Sandy's own. The shared company of their friendship was hopefully worth something, but Sandy wouldn't even stay in the room when Raney reminded her that *she* ran the cash register, after all, and it was obvious that what they earned did not equal what they spent.

If she was careful—if she filled her mind with all the chores she had to do and the people who depended on her, if she spent each morning with Jake, all day with Sandy, every evening with Grandpa and Jake together—she could usually forget how terrifyingly lonely she was without Cleet. Some nights when she could not sleep the only thing that kept her sane was painting, even if she'd had to go back to using house paint and plywood most of the time.

Jake, though—Jake remained her miracle. Her anchor. Her reason. She could still stand over his sleeping body like a newborn's and be astounded that, for all the garbage in her life, this gift had come her way. He was growing into a leaner version of Cleet, with a narrower face shaped by strong cheekbones—movie-star cheekbones, Raney thought. His skin was a half shade lighter than his dad's olive-brown, with shanks of almost-black hair as untamable as a live creature camouflaged on the crown of Jake's sweet head. And bless his gorgeously odd eyes, one dark from Cleet and one light from her; it was like watching the two of them be alive and together in the living flesh of the boy they'd made. By the age of nine it was clear Jake would be taller than his father. He ate everything he could lay his hands on and seemed to only gain longer arms and legs, until he resembled one of his own construction-toy skyscrapers—all spindles and knobs, his feet as big and awkward as a swan's. That part of his blueprint must have been inherited from Raney's unidentified father, the wild card she'd passed along through her genes.

By third grade it took the patience of saints to coach Jake through his homework, and Raney had quit trying to convince his teachers that maybe two and two didn't always have to equal four. Maybe if they could slow down for one tax-paid minute and *look* at how much Jake already knew about geometry, about angles and space and the pull of gravity . . . it was all there—in the shapes he carved into wood and molded out of clay. But the best she could do was try to make Jake believe it about himself.

Three years after Cleet died, two things were becoming clear to Raney. First, she was likely to lose her house unless the Gateses and the Jobses of the world suddenly decided her paintings were collectible, and as Sandy couldn't sell more than one or two a year, that was unlikely. Second, it was not safe for Grandpa to live alone anymore. The decade-old wound along his shin had reopened and needed dressing changes three times a day; his doctors were pushing him to have the leg removed. More and more often Raney came to Grandpa's house and surprised him asleep in the kitchen because he could not make it up to his bedroom. She and Jake finally dragged the mattress and box spring downstairs and set Grandpa up in a corner of the kitchen with a marine toilet.

Jake spent almost every afternoon there, reclaiming an interest in the plywood tree fort he and Cleet had built together. Now it was Jake and his great-grandfather. Grandpa would sit in the folding aluminum lawn chair with his leg propped up and call out instructions to Jake, fourteen feet overhead with a collection of hammers, nails, and scrap lumber scavenged from the barn. In the course of a few weeks the fort had a roof and two walls. Raney could hardly bear to look up at it wondering when the boughs might reach their limit, though she trusted that a man who could engineer an underground room strong enough to outlast all of mankind could engineer a tree house. She wondered if this room in the sky was his last-minute pitch at optimism.

At every doctor's visit Grandpa got a new pill—one to open his lungs, one to thin his blood, one to relax his blood vessels, one to regulate his heartbeat, his thyroid, his urine flow. At least nobody was foolish enough to try to regulate his temper. When his latest doctor, who looked too young to be out of high school, started writing out another new prescription, Raney rapped her knuckles on the desk. "This is not what he needs."

The boy-doctor blushed and said with faltering confidence, "I understand your concerns, but your grandfather has Class Four congestive heart failure and atrial fibrillation, hypertension, COPD, renal insufficiency, and . . ."

"No. You do *not* understand my concerns. If you did, you would write out a prescription for decent bus service so he could still have a life. A prescription for a house with doors wide enough for his wheelchair. A ramp to his bedroom. Or if nothing else, a prescription for a visiting nurse because things are getting kind of dangerous." Even if she felt a little mean about her sarcasm, the expression on the young doctor's face was worth it. "Tell you what," she went on more softly. "I'll buy him a bigger pill box if you'll make us an appointment with somebody who can help with all the rest of it." All the stuff that might make him want to stay alive, she thought.

The eventual meeting with the medical social worker was both good and bad. Good because he helped Grandpa admit that maybe he *did* need a little extra help now and then, and maybe it *was* hard for Raney to do it by herself—a turnaround that made Raney want to suggest the social worker switch into diplomacy and focus on Afghanistan or Iraq. But bad because he helped *Raney* admit they would need to sell either the farm or her house to pay for a home health aide and Grandpa's rising medical bills. She hardly needed to talk to all three Realtors in town to know they would be listing the farm. Raney's mortgage was so high she might as well be renting her house from the bank. When she broke that news to Grandpa, he didn't speak to her for a whole day, then lashed out that he should never have kept that rifle in the attic. Too many stairs between him and it.

Raney retorted, "Look at it this way. My house doesn't have any stairs."

"Your house doesn't have any room!"

"More than your ground floor—all you can use here. You can sleep in a real bedroom and get yourself into the kitchen without any help." He didn't answer and she leaped into the pause with her last bribes. "Beer in the fridge, Grandpa. And the food will be better—I'll try some new recipes."

Now his face contorted, and even through his thick stubble and smoke-crinkled skin she saw him turn red, which got her worrying about his heart more than his temper. "Goddamn, child. Is this really what you've learned from me after thirty-seven years?"

She could hear him verging from anger into hopelessness. But the full impact of it didn't hit either of them until the sale closed. Grandpa refused to leave his house until the boys Raney hired to move the furniture took everything but the wheelchair he was sitting in. When Raney came back from dispersing the last load, Grandpa was nowhere to be found, his wheelchair butted up against the stairs and his walker missing. The kitchen, the living room, the front porch, and his upstairs bedroom were all empty. She searched the yard, the near woods, even looked for tracks in the shallow mud at the edge of the pond. On a second pass through the barn she found his walker under a tarp and scuff marks leading to the bunker lid. There were guns inside the bunker, she knew. The fact that he'd gotten the trapdoor open was proof he had the strength to use one.

She called his name and heard nothing. She gulped one huge

breath before she pulled up the door. Through the gloom she could see his swollen feet poking out from the bunk. After an unbearable second of silence she heard his ever-present wheezing. When her eyes cleared she climbed down and sat opposite him. "Why are you here, Grandpa?" Her voice broke in the middle, which made it sound more like a challenge than an offer to talk, but in truth that was how she felt. Challenged and angry at him even as she started to cry.

"I came in here to get some things."

"What? Cigarettes? I guess you could make a bomb out of your oxygen tank. You're lucky you didn't die falling down the ladder."

"Or not." He gave her a minute to calm down. "You know why I built this bunker?"

"Sure. The end of the world—TEOTWAWKI. Or a place to prove you saw it coming first." He was quiet, as if waiting for her to get closer to the truth. "When I was little I thought you'd built it to be my playhouse. Grandma said you built it to forget my mother."

"I built it so I would be in control in the end. Of my own end, at least."

Raney's face was wet with tears now, but her voice was steady. "So why didn't you do it?"

"Because I knew Jake would eventually come hunting for me and open that trapdoor. Jake or you." He looked around the room, or maybe just showed enough compassion to look away from her for a moment. Finally he said, "Let's get started home. You're gonna have a helluva time getting me up that ladder."

The buyer was a development company that had offered 40 percent less than the ask, but the deal was so clean, the Realtor said Raney should take it. The market was only going lower. Raney knew they would tear the house down and build some ticky-tacky look-alikes, even though the rep had talked like he was hoping to salvage the old house as part of Quentin's legacy. *Legacy!* Quentin had barely justified its present, much less its past.

She made a last walk through the rooms; there were pale patches on the floor where furniture had sat in the same spot for fifty years. Dust balls the size of rats. If ghosts were real it was clear why they haunted abandoned houses—the rooms reeked of loneliness now that they had no purpose. The last door she opened was to the living room, where twenty-eight years of her own collected paintings were stacked against or hung upon every wall. She hadn't asked the boys to move them, thinking she would move them herself with Jake's help. Or that she'd ask Sandy to store them. Or maybe not thinking at all. Maybe knowing what she was going to do with them for days and weeks, maybe even years before she started taking them down.

One by one she piled and hauled them through the kitchen and out the back door to the swath of raw, packed dirt next to the pond. She got a shovel from the barn and scraped away the duff and weeds within the bare patch and well beyond. Then she balanced frame against frame in climbing concentric rings, a nautilus shell of where she had started and who she had become. Only four small paintings did she save for Jake, including a charcoal sketch of a pale, haunted-looking twelve-year-old boy, less than two years older than her son was now. When the entire structure was five feet high and ten feet in diameter, she went into the bunker and came out with books and magazines and stacks of Grandpa's saved newspapers along with two butane lighters, one as a backup. She twisted a yellowing *Seattle Times* into a stem and lit it on fire. "So," she said, holding the growing flame in front of her face, "see you in the afterlife." She cupped one protective hand around the light and guided it into the open heart of her house of art, setting the pile ablaze.

* * *

Spring came on in languid gasps that year, a week of chill that left everyone despondent and then a few days of rich warm sun that worked its fingers into new leaves of the alder and river birch along the Little Quentin so they at last unfurled into unabashed greens. The sharp break between sunshine and shadow made Raney feel absurdly hopeful, as if she had been holding her breath, waiting without admitting it. The house felt full now, with Jake, Grandpa, and Jenny, the aide who came when Raney was at work plus two evenings a week to help muster Grandpa into the tub. As his muscles wasted, his weight seemed more like misplaced ballast; his bursts of determined effort invariably pulled them both off balance. Jake was good help, too, but he'd begun to complain of new aches and pains—his knees, his shoulders, his back—and Raney sent him off to other chores when it was time to lift Grandpa in or out of bed, in or out of his chair, in or out of the car for one of his many doctor's appointments. She suspected Jake was pained more by witnessing the infirmities of his once imposing great-grandfather than by any growth spurt of his own. Three and a half years out from Cleet's death she still didn't know how to be both mother and father to Jake. Every physical complaint and disobedience felt like a cry for his dad, though she had witnessed few actual tears.

Maybe for that reason she knew the exact day she first remembered seeing David. New faces were sometimes the only entertainment in Quentin, but there was nothing unusually attractive about his—his jowls too full and his eyes too buried between the high ride of his cheekbone and the low set of his brow. He did have a solid, self-assured smile with even, ivory-colored teeth that made people want to smile back, then stop to hear why he was smiling in the first place. His clothes stood out too. Just blue jeans and a button-down shirt—but the jeans were pressed stiff with deep blue crease lines running straight down the fronts of his legs, and the pressed white shirt looked starched. Those were not Quentin clothes. Regardless, if she'd seen him before, it hadn't stuck. The first time Raney *remembered* seeing David was when Jake first saw him.

It was a Friday and Raney planned to leave the gallery early for a date with Jake. With every passing month he seemed to spend more time by himself. The only thing he could concentrate on was what he made with his hands, some vision he couldn't share until it was finished by himself alone. So on Friday she would pick him up after school and take him skateboarding or fishing, or to Dairy Queen and a movie at the Rose, just the two of them, while Jenny stayed with Grandpa. She told Jake to wait for her in the playground behind Peninsula Foods.

She got there less than an hour after school let out, but Jake was nowhere in sight. It was a small playground—a jungle gym made out of plumbing pipes, a sandbox that had been more dirt than sand for years now—not enough to hold an eleven-year-old boy's interest for an hour. She looked up and down the street, went inside the small grocery, and checked the comic book rack, the candy aisle, the bathroom at the back of the store. No Jake.

Lena, the cashier, was making hot dogs for a city family heading home from the national park, three kids with sturdy new hiking boots and Patagonia day packs with pockets and clips and zippers everywhere, their mother with a perky blond ponytail sprouting through the hole at the back of her pink sun visor. How did these women always look so perfect after a day on the trails? They didn't sweat? Lena caught Raney looking and rolled her eyes in solidarity, chasing a hot dog across the greasy cylinders rotating under the heat lamp. "Hey, Raney. What's up?"

"Jake. Has he been in?"

"Jake? Some other kids were here." The hot dog slipped out of the bun onto the floor. "Shit!" Lena exploded, then shrugged at the waiting family. "It'll be a minute," and seemed just as happy when they walked out. She wiped her hands on her stained apron. "Want to use the phone?"

He wasn't at home when Raney called. She checked the aisles again, half expecting him to pop out and surprise her—hoping to scare her into a Coke or a jawbreaker. He wasn't in the car or at his school. She was running out of places to look after half an hour, short of combing the woods and the beach, when she heard Lena call to her, "Raney! He's here."

Jake was crouched in the corner of the store with his arms locked around knees pressed hard to his forehead. A skin-and-bones fortress. Raney sat on the dirty floor and put her arms around him; he shoved her off at first, then leaned into her shoulder.

"He was in the storage closet. I was getting out the mop and there he was," Lena said.

A group of teenagers jangled through the door—Amelia and Caroline Wells prancing their new figures like they alone knew what was what, Jerrod Fielding and his pimply football buddies—all of them louder and braver once they saw Jake. Someone whistled his name low and mocking; Jake wiped his mouth on his sleeve and turned his face into a mask.

When they left, Raney asked, "Hey, Buddy. What's going on?" Jake broke then, hurling a crumpled mess of yellow-and-black plastic onto the floor. It took a moment for Raney to recognize it as the toy dump truck Cleet had bought for Jake's third birthday. For two years he had taken it everywhere—beside him at meals, under his pillow when he slept, the only bath toy he would have. He had almost lost it when he took it to kindergarten, and after its rescue he'd left it on his bookshelf most often. But always on the top shelf, just beside his bed. The last day she'd seen it was around the time Cleet died.

And then Raney became aware of David. He was standing at the counter waiting to pay for something, apparently not impatient with Lena's distraction. He nodded at Raney, and Jake looked straight at him. David smiled at them both. Such a comfortable smile. Lena took his credit card and put his things in a brown paper bag. Raney noticed, she remembered later, that he'd bought a half gallon of milk. Why would that stick in her mind? Because milk is not what a single man would likely drink? Or that a single man might only eat cold cereal for supper? Did she think about him that way, even that first time?

He asked Lena for an extra paper bag, dropped something into it, and walked over to Jake and Raney, leaning forward slightly so that it was clear he was focused on Jake. It would have made Raney nervous if he hadn't looked somewhat embarrassed about it himself. He rolled the top of the bag down and creased it to make a tidy package, then held it out to Jake. "I have something for you. Looked like you could use it—if it's okay with your mom." Jake looked at Raney and she gave him an equivocal nod, which, to a child offered a gift, could only mean yes. David left with a quick good-bye as soon as Jake took the bag. Raney unrolled the top, opening it just enough to glimpse inside. It was a toy truck. Not yellow. And not a dump truck. One couldn't be too picky in a town with no toy store—he'd had only the six aisles of Peninsula Foods to choose from. A red plastic pickup truck.

She fell a little bit in love with David that day. Before she knew his name, before she knew his work or habits or history. She was old enough to know that once you let the possibility of love slip past the radar of mature reason, it can be hard to go back. On the other hand, what love didn't begin as an illusion, the outcome hinged on lucky or unlucky guesses? Maybe we are all best loved depending on how well we keep our secrets.

A few weeks later, Raney drove to Port Townsend to pick up some things at the hardware store and buy Jake a new pair of sneakers. They were done by eleven so she bought him an ice cream, then they walked out to the rocky tide flats at the foot of the pier and threw Saltines up to the seagulls, following them high above and over and behind their heads until they were both dizzy and laughing and the ice cream teetered precariously on its waffle cone. On the drive home she kept glancing at Jake in the rearview mirror. He looked like such a normal kid, chasing every bubble-gum-blue drip along the side of the cone with his tongue. Appropriately dirty and windblown. Why was it so hard for him at school? Who wouldn't want to be his friend?

"Hey, I know a great beach near here. A sand castle beach. Want to go?" She turned the car around and in ten minutes they were parked and shoeless and using coffee cups scrounged from a garbage can to build a castle with a moat and a canal leading all the way to the water's edge. Jake was so focused he didn't mind when his mother brushed the sand from her knees and sat on the log railing along the parking lot, watching waves and sandpipers and lovers. She saw Jake surveying his fortress, narrow-eyed and calculating, his near-black hair cutting at all angles across his face, and suddenly she thought of Bo. For the first time in so long. This was the beach she and Bo had been to the last day of the last summer he'd spent in Quentin, when they were teenagers. It hit her so unexpectedly she thought she might look up and see him. Right there, just near Jake. Piling sand onto the same castle they'd made over twenty years ago. Her first kiss was just across that hill, inside the black caves of the gun batteries.

A shadow fell in front of her eyes, someone standing with the sun behind him. She raised her hand in a shield and squinted, half expecting it to be Bo, knowing it would be Jake. But it was David. In a moment of "right face, wrong place" she couldn't connect who he was or where she'd met him, only that she knew him. And in that awkwardness she was too friendly, too familiar—scrambling through principals' names and teachers' names and gallery customers' names and then, finally, remembering she'd never heard his name. She didn't really know him at all.

"He looks happier today," David said.

Raney looked past him at Jake, who was watching them now. "He is. He got an ice cream—that always helps."

After a long wait he asked if he could sit down. She scooted over, though there was ten feet of log on either side. "You live in Quentin, don't you?" he asked.

Raney nodded. "You too? You new there?"

He shrugged and glanced out at the water, which put her more at ease. "I'm working for the seafood company, down near the bay."

She looked straight at him then, this news putting him on the map of her world. "Really? You fish?"

"Oh! No. Accounting. I do the bookkeeping—temporary work for now." He laughed when he said it, and Raney wondered if her question had insulted him for some reason. He introduced himself then. "David Boughton." She tried to spell it in her mind: b-o-w-t-e-n, b-a-u-t-o-n. She noticed he wasn't wearing a ring. "Did you raise your son there? In Quentin?" He nodded toward Jake.

"All his life. Me too. Not many of us—most people leave as soon as they can drive. I like it, though. I like the bay. The mountains."

"You work in the art gallery." It struck Raney that he didn't ask this as a question. He already knew; he must have been in before.

"You like art?" she asked him.

He waggled his head from side to side, take it or leave it. But then he smiled, that smile, and any answer would have been acceptable. "I like what I like." She heard a flattening of the "I," a southern accent corrupted with travel.

A wave washed over the sand castle's critical bulwarks and Jake stomped through the rest of it, though he looked satisfied with his work and the day. He came over ready to go. "Hey, Buddy. This is Mr. Boughton. Your truck friend."

David held out his hand. "Nice to meet you, Buddy."

"It's Jake," Jake answered without taking his hand in return.

Raney answered, "I call him Buddy sometimes. A nickname." She stood up and took her keys out of her purse. He walked with them to the car and she held out her own hand then. "Well, it's nice to meet you, Mr. Boughton. I'm Renee, by the way. Renee Flores."

He opened her door for her and stepped back, tucking his hands into his pockets. "And nice to officially meet you, Raney."

They were halfway home before it occurred to her that she had not given him the name Raney.

Sometimes running into the same person for a few minutes here and there, over and over, can make you feel like you really know him. You see him going off to work at the same time every day, a short wave from the car, a rolled-down window to say, "The Seahawks sure blew it, huh?" "Weird weather—maybe it's this global warming business." "Your boy must be looking forward to summertime." Bits of disconnected conversation that add up to nothing more than an assumption that someone is considerate, or reliable, or has a good sense of humor. Like a Seurat painting—dabs of paint that only suggest a scene and your imagination fills in the gaps.

David was a good listener. He could ask Raney a question and sit back with his arms crossed over his chest, nodding, smiling, rarely cutting in to say he'd been through something even worse. It was the listening more than the talking that won her—once she joked to Sandy that she might be falling for herself instead of for him. Or maybe, Sandy countered, it had just been a very long time since Raney had someone to talk to.

The facts of David's own life came out almost incidentally. He had a steady job doing bookkeeping and some tax filing for Tom Fielding, the owner of Oceanic Seafoods. David was renting the one-bedroom mobile at the back of Fielding's property. He kept it tidy and beside the front step he had planted a clay pot with some marigolds and begonias. Pretty things you couldn't kill. He drove a six-year-old black Tahoe that he changed the oil in every three thousand miles, religiously, and he had an associate's degree from Oklahoma City Community College. He'd lived in Tulsa for a while, but his boss there had refused to promote him. As David explained, *he* was the one keeping the business afloat behind the scenes, which eventually got embarrassing for the boss and was at the root of their separation. After that he'd preferred smaller towns—Marshall, Texas; Slater, Missouri; Medford, Oregon. Quentin. That was where you found the heart of this country, he said to Raney. In the small towns.

His family was scattered and not on good terms—he hadn't spoken to his brothers or his dad in five or six years, not since they'd accused him of manipulating the books at his father's appliance repair shop. They were talking outside Loggers Restaurant, where David had bought Raney a cup of coffee. "My dad probably meant well," he said. "Well enough anyway. But he needed cash and borrowed against assets he didn't actually own—if I hadn't cleaned up the accounts he would have been jailed for fraud. Tax evasion anyway." Sadly, rather than being grateful, his brothers had used the mess as an excuse to take David's share of the business. "It's a shame when a family falls apart over money, but some things you can't change." He pressed his lips into some conscious resolve, then lightened up, asking Raney how old she was when she got her first set of paints. A few minutes later she said she was late to pick up Jake, so David walked her to her car. "I always wanted kids. Didn't work out for us."

"You were married?" Raney asked.

"High school sweetheart. Crazy—got married at eighteen. She had cancer. Surgery, chemo—the whole works. Finally beat it and then she ran off with my best friend, five years ago." He looked straight into the deepest part of Raney's eyes. "I've been wanting to tell you that."

He came to Raney's house for dinner a few times, and he would always bring something small for Jake—a package of Pop Rocks, Life Savers, a deck of trick cards. He even brought a gift for Grandpa once, a bottle of cognac (which put him so soundly to sleep Raney turned his nighttime oxygen up and sat in his room counting his breaths). While she set the table and finished cooking, David played catch with Jake in the backyard, a carefree smile on Jake's face that she'd missed. She could tell David didn't get much pleasure from the sport itself—he was so careful to keep his shirt clean and tucked in. Watching them, she realized it had been two years since she'd seen Jake catch a ball.

David loved classic movies and had amassed a good collection through garage sales and bankrupt video stores. He feigned horror when Raney confessed that she and Jake had never seen *Metropolis*, and made a special evening of the screening. It was Jake's first silent movie, and when he grew restless, David jumped in with narration so animated Jake enjoyed the story despite losing the plot. Even Grandpa seemed to have a good time that night, though he remained uncharacteristically tight-lipped about David's more frequent presence in their house. Grandpa made just one pointed comment regarding this new friendship, in fact—reminding Raney about the campfire he'd taught her to light using only one match and her own wits.

One morning Raney came into the gallery and found a note from David: he would be in Port Townsend that afternoon and hoped to take her out for dinner after work. Sandy watched her read it but didn't say a word until after lunch when, seemingly out of the blue, she asked, "So why are you seeing this guy?"

"What's wrong with David?"

"Nothing. As far as I can see. But it's hard to see much past that salesman's smile."

"Well, partly because he's the only one asking me out." Sandy gave her a dubious frown. "It's not serious," Raney said. "What? Are you afraid I'll get married and quit before you have to admit you can't afford me? Every time he takes me to dinner I save twenty bucks in groceries, if I bring the leftovers home."

Finally Sandy laughed. "I guess he is the only single man between eighteen and eighty in Quentin. I hope the sex is good."

"Jesus, Sandy! I'm not sleeping with him. I have enough problems in my life." They both laughed then, but something about the whole conversation bothered Raney for the rest of the day. It bothered her even more when she pinned it down—maybe she did want to sleep with David.

It was David's idea to go into the park for Labor Day weekend—all three of them. They could take Jake on a hike and cook hot dogs over an open fire, maybe take Jake's fishing pole. Raney spent Friday making slaw and fried chicken and cramming so much stuff into their packs they could have camped for three days. Jake had been quarrelsome all week, but on Saturday he woke up at six and started asking when they could leave, going through his tackle box to check lines and lures and weights.

David said he'd pick them up at nine. They waited on the front steps with their water bottles and a grocery bag of too much food, the pack between Raney's legs, ready to go. At nine forty-five she called David's cell phone and left a message. At eleven she called again. At one o'clock she fed Jake the chicken and slaw and made him a batch of brownies, then spent the rest of the day playing any video game he wanted. When Jake finally fell asleep after eleven thirty she drove past

David's mobile at the back of Tom Fielding's house. The lights were out and his car was gone.

On Tuesday, Raney took the afternoon off from work and drove back to Quentin, down the marina road to Oceanic Seafoods. If she'd been hurt yesterday and annoyed today, she was furious by the time she parked and went into the building. Fielding was in his office. He'd been a snob to Raney in high school and she still saw the length of his nose when he talked to her, even though Jake had played with both of his boys off and on until a few years ago, when Jerrod Fielding had hit puberty with a mean streak.

"Hey. Is David in the back? Or out for lunch?"

Tom stood up from the corner of his desk with a half-eaten tuna sandwich in his hand. He wiped his mouth on the back of his wrist and shook his head, still chewing. "Boughton's not here."

Raney looked around the small office as if a grown man could possibly be hidden there. "Can I leave a note for him?"

"Sorry. I mean, he doesn't work here anymore. Quit on Friday. Some family emergency came up."

She could almost see a glimmer of pity in Tom's face, and suddenly she wanted to hit him for sneering at her clothes in seventh grade. "Right. I totally forgot he was leaving Saturday. Thanks—sorry to bother you."

David disappeared as thoroughly as if a tornado had blown his house into Oz. A month later Raney took Jake to a movie in Silverdale, leaving Grandpa with Jenny. When they got home, Raney found the Cenex propane bill hanging on the doorknob. She folded it three times over and wedged it deep in her pocket, one step away from throwing it directly into the trash. In two years Jenny's salary had used up what cash her grandfather's farm had cleared, and his medical bills had soared above his benefits. As if he guessed the numbers he wasn't told, Grandpa grew both more belligerent and more dependent, his anger leeching his waning strength.

After Jake and Grandpa were asleep, Raney made a hot chocolate and poured in a big dash of the cognac David had given to Grandpa. She unfolded the bill onto the table in front of her so the corners fit perfectly inside the red-and-white checks of the vinyl tablecloth, as if making that new paper match up with the squares on that old stained cloth might align her prior married life and her current widowed one. She finished the chocolate and got out an envelope, a stamp, and her checkbook. She sealed the check inside the return envelope and walked all the way down the drive in the middle of the night to put it into their mailbox and raise the red flag. She knew it would bounce, but she didn't think they could suck the gas back out of the tank once it had been pumped in.

She talked to the same Realtor who'd sold her grandfather's farm. He spent a long time walking her property and pulling up comps, and then he spent more time showing Raney graphs and tables and explaining the market meltdown that made her mortgage debt higher than any remotely possible sale price. In the end he was blessedly realistic with her. As she was driving away, he stepped out of the office and flagged her, maybe, she hoped, with some ingenious, viable plan. She stopped and rolled down her window. He looked once over his shoulder before he asked if she'd seen any of the recent articles about how long the banks were taking to act on foreclosures these days. On the way home she went to the library to do a Google search; the next month she stopped paying the mortgage and waited.

Raney did not need a medical degree to know what had happened when she went to help Grandpa dress for breakfast. He was still in bed, leaning against the wall. He looked at her speechless and gape-mouthed, as if she had appeared out of a dream. His right eye was half-closed and his right arm flopped like a rag doll's when he reached for her. He seemed oblivious until the medics came, and then he flailed and fought their help with the half of his body that could still move. They got a shot in his arm, and in the space of three or four minutes he changed from an angry man to an overgrown infant that two strong EMTs could fold onto a stretcher and cart away. The thing he feared most had just happened to him.

The next day another new doctor, a neurologist, showed Raney a CT scan of her grandfather's brain—two wrinkled fetuses curled face to face in the womb of his skull. The neurologist pointed to a walnut-sized black pool along the ruffled left edge of one fetal spine. Too much black. Too little gray. Raney didn't need a doctor to tell her that either.

The doctor gave her some percentage odds on Grandpa's functional recovery, quick to point out that they were guesses at best. She explained how much care he would need after he was discharged, that it might be impossible for Raney to keep him at home anymore. Raney could tell she'd had this conversation before. The doctor put the names and phone numbers of the few skilled nursing facilities available to Grandpa into a folder with some preprinted pamphlets about stroke patients and passed it across the desk to Raney.

"I can't do it. Being in the hospital is misery enough for him. If you'd known him before this you wouldn't even suggest it," Raney said.

The doctor leaned forward across her desk and pressed her lips together for a moment before she spoke. "He may not need to be the brave one. At some point *you* will have to decide how much you can do. Sometimes people forget what they're asking their children to go through."

When Grandpa finally came home he had regained some use of his right arm and right leg, but combined with the persistent wound on his left leg, he was effectively bedridden unless Jenny, Raney, and Jake were all there to get him into his wheelchair. His immobility infuriated him. The worst affliction, though, was the loss of his speech, which lagged behind his recovery of the written word. Raney kept a thick legal pad and a large-grip pen tethered at his side and he would scrawl his needs and curses in large block letters. When he did not feel they were attracting the attention they deserved, he would whack the bed frame and any nearby attendant with the hard pad. It was worth the beating if it humored him, in Raney's opinion, though a real fit would leave him wheezing and blue.

For fifty days Grandpa slid further and further from comfort and communication, but death backed away from him like a tease, locking him in the purgatory of his stubborn body. Raney sat in the rocking chair beside him, waiting for him to fall asleep, waiting for him to wake, to swallow, to breathe, to need her; trying to fathom the words locked inside him.

How could he not be afraid? Everyone, it seemed to her, was terrified by the black hole of whatever lay beyond consciousness. Everyone except him. He was looking forward to the adventure—or so he'd always said. Now she saw her grandfather as if he were standing at a train platform, listening to the thunder of the approaching cars, listening to the rising swell of the horn. There's a prepaid window seat waiting, with an unmatched view of untold wonders, narrated by the master of the universe himself, and her grandfather is ready, more than ready, to put down his load and let this train carry it. But the moment he shifts his weight to step on board, he falters. Could the view from this window beat the view from his own backyard, where he knows the shade of every tree and the blooming season of every shrub and the moment the sun will break across his pond? So he picks up his bag and backs away, with the doors still open and waiting, waiting, and there is no other exit.

One night Raney didn't hear him on the baby monitor. It was her habit to check on him once or twice, but she slept for seven hours straight, the longest stretch she'd gotten in weeks. She woke almost panicked in the morning, much as she'd done the first night Jake had slept through as a baby. But she found Grandpa asleep on his side breathing comfortably, his sheets clean and dry. The pad of paper had come loose from its tether and lay on the floor some feet from the bed. She picked it up and saw his large block letters filling one page. "Death is not the enemy. The enemy is a cowardly conscience."

It must have taken him an hour to write that many words, and all his remaining strength to rip the pad from the string and fling it away.

The last week of November the season changed from fall to winter, a north wind swept through, and the temperature dropped so fast the dew froze in a single pane of crystal stars on her windshield; the sky was so blue and clear it seemed too thin to hold air. Jenny reminded Raney that Grandpa was running low on pills, which meant a drive all the way to the Tacoma VA to fill them at the lowest cost. She got Jake off to school early and filled the car with gas and made a day of it. She drove across the Hood Canal Bridge with the sun still rising, catching bare glimpses of Mount Rainier until she hit Highway 5 where the volcano loomed in all her glacial majesty. She wished she had bundled Grandpa into a blanket and brought him along. "She'll make St. Helen's look like a sparkler when she blows. Goodbye, Seattle! What a party that will be!" he would say.

It took more than two hours to fill all his prescriptions. On the drive back from Tacoma she passed a Rite Aid outside Bremerton and pulled into the parking lot. She took the white caps off Grandpa's nine orange plastic bottles and removed from each a single capsule or tablet. She held them in her palm and tried to read the tiny cryptic numbers and letters stamped on them, then closed them in her fist and went into the store. Near the back there were five aisles stacked higher than her head with cold cures and bowel cures and pain relievers, plus a thousand herbal fix-it-alls. She bought twenty nutritional supplements, some Tylenol and baby aspirin, and got back into her car, then back onto Highway 3. Just before the bridge she turned off the road to Kitsap Beach and parked. The entire Olympic range stood across the water, so vivid in the cold air she could make out the trees and boulders on the foothills near her grandfather's former land, as dwarfed by the highest peaks as the farmhouse had once been dwarfed by the foothills.

She took the bag of Grandpa's bottles and the bag of Rite Aid bottles out to a picnic table overlooking the rocky beach, lined all of them up, and took off the lids. There were plenty of good matches.

When she was done she swept the leftover capsules and tablets into the Rite Aid bag and carried it across the open beach to the water's edge. Handful by handful she flung them over the water and watched them float and drift and slowly sink to the bottom. In a few days they would be dissolved into sand, at rest where they could look at those mountains forever.

She took a leave from work and let Jenny go, not wanting anyone but herself to be putting the pills in Grandpa's mouth. Jenny came to the house anyway most afternoons and Raney knew it was more for her than for Grandpa. The last day Raney dozed off in her chair and startled when Jenny placed a hand on her arm, terrified he'd gone while she slept. Instead he was looking straight at her for the first time in months, clear-eyed and present, telling her the words he couldn't make his injured body say, affections shared without words most of their lives together. She took his hand. How much it had changed. Shed of the calluses so familiar to her touch, his skin seemed no more than a likeness of all he had been. Then he sank again into open-mouthed slumber, the regularity of his breath faltering so that at moments Raney did not think another breath would follow. She wanted to call Jake, didn't want him to miss this moment, but discovered she was afraid to let him see, uncertain what she should say. Was death always such a lonely process? She was terrified and knew she was ready and knew she would be no less terrified in a day or a year. Jenny said, "Tell him it's okay. Tell him it's okay to go."

* * *

It snowed five inches three days before Christmas, a rare event in Quentin. And particularly lucky as the snowfall itself made a good Christmas present and Raney had next to nothing for Jake—a framed poster of the newly opened Tacoma Narrows Bridge and two boxes of Red Vines. He'd been begging for the Deluxe Erector Set, but it could be that or a decent Christmas dinner, not both. Like every other parent in the grand U. S. of A., Raney had represented Christmas as a time to celebrate the blessings of spiritual wealth and material poverty, but every kid knew it was about the toys. Even the president had christened shopping a patriotic duty.

Raney made hot chocolate with cinnamon and whipped cream, put two mugs on a tray, and pushed Jake's bedroom door open against a drift of dirty T-shirts and blue jeans. He had barely left his room since school let out for Christmas. "Jake," she said. He jerked, rolled onto his stomach, and pulled his blanket over his head, burrowing back to the coma-sleep of infancy and adolescence. She raked a different pile of clothes off the chair with her foot, releasing a pungent whiff of body odor. "Hey, Buddy. It snowed!" She put the mugs on the chair and sat beside him on the bed, surveying the room to spot the origin of something gone moldy and sour. "It's after eleven, Jake. Snow! Half a foot or more." She gave him a shake and he slammed the pillow over his head. Raney went back to the kitchen, opened the door, and scooped up a handful of snow, came back to the immobile blanketed lump that was Jake, and slipped a large wad of ice under the covers and down his shirt.

Jake yelped, throwing his covers off like they were filled with fire instead of ice. "Jesus, Mom!"

"Watch your language. I brought you a hot chocolate." He finally swung his legs over the side of the bed, and Raney was startled at how hairy they were—when did that happen? He would be twelve next month, an impossible trick of time, surely. In so many ways he had a mind much younger than his years. She pulled his curtains open, and the sight of snow scalloped along his windowsill seemed to brighten him. "Grandpa would have liked it," Raney said. "Anything that made disaster feel closer at hand, huh?"

Jake was quiet, paying extraordinary attention to the job of blowing a tiny ship of whipped cream across the surface of his chocolate. When he looked up she couldn't read him. He brought his hand toward her face and she felt a quick sting at her temple. "Gray hair." He held up a long white strand.

"Hard earned. I'm surprised there's only one."

"It was the only one I could grab quick enough to get away with it," he said.

"They make you smarter, you know."

"Yeah?"

"Yeah. But only if you let them accumulate."

Raney found one of Cleet's oversize fishing sweaters and his rubber boots and gave Jake three pairs of socks, hoping the boots would fit, surprised to discover that his feet were now as large as Cleet's had been. All she could think, watching Jake tramp designs in the deep snow, was how every other boy in his school was out building snow forts and arsenals of snowball bombs, and none of them would invite Jake to be on their team. All right, then. *She* would be his team.

They rolled the white winter yard down to bare black earth in circles and stripes that wound about like a crazy racetrack, ending up with three great mounds of snow it took both of them to pile atop each other, the crown too high for either to reach. Raney brought a kitchen chair outside so that Jake could straddle her neck just long enough to stick on charcoal briquette eyes. They capped him with fans of fir and cedar that draped all the way to his shoulders, and so decided that *he* must be a *she* and found a bright-red leaf of Oregon grape for her mouth.

Jake saw David first. The surprise made him lose his balance and grab on to his mother's forehead so they both ended up in the snow.

"Hi, Jake, how've you been?" David said with his eyes locked on Raney. Then he said her name, *Raney*, at half volume, maybe a greeting, maybe to convince himself she was really in front of him, as stunned as if she'd awakened from a nightmare and discovered it scarier in real life. Or maybe he was already offering a lame attempt at a hopeless apology.

Raney reacted without a moment's planning. She closed her right fist around a pile of muddy snow, packed it hard, and shot it straight into David's chest. He took one step back but made no other move to block the missile, as if he'd conscientiously steeled himself against the natural instinct to even cover his face. Noble son of a bitch! She scrabbled forward on her knees, reared back, hurled the contents of her left hand—a very large and knobby stub of carrot— and saw it bounce off the side of his head despite his last-second corkscrew dodge. She wished it had been a rock, furious that she didn't see blood on his vile face. If she had any guts at all she would grab Jake's hand, get into the car, smash David's Tahoe on the way down the driveway, and leave him here to freeze.

And then the worst happened—a bile that boiled in her throat and made her stomach convulse—the tiniest explosion went off inside her brain and she knew, detested herself for knowing, that she was glad he was back. If he gave any reasonable explanation, she was actually going to forgive him, maybe just to escape the empty space he was already filling.

He pulled a package wrapped in bright-red paper out of his pocket and held it out on his open palm. "Brought the boy a Christmas present."

Even without looking at Jake, Raney knew he was ready to grab the gift that second, before his mother could scold it away. She had made up a lie to cover David's disappearance—not to save David's skin but to spare Jake's. Now she almost wished she'd recruited Jake into her sorry sense of rejection. She finally let herself look at Jake's face—a mix of astonishment at his mother's behavior and obvious longing to get his hands on that red wrapping paper—and she gave in to all of it. "Go on. Put it under the tree, Jake. Save it for Christmas Day." She could do the dirty work of changing her mind and telling David off after Jake went to bed.

"You got your tree already?" David asked.

She nodded toward the forest at the boundary of their yard. "Still out there." She let him hear how brittle she was, ready for him to leave the present and go back to whatever small town or small-town girl he'd bounced back here from. He looked utterly contrite standing there with his hands stuffed into his bright-yellow slicker, her muddy snowball dribbling down his stomach. *Damn.*

"I've missed you," David said.

"Well, apparently not enough to use my telephone number or e-mail in four months."

"You never check your e-mail."

"I answer my phone."

He didn't respond, and they both pretended to be interested in Jake's attempt to identify the gift through the wrapping paper. She was cold. She pulled off Jake's mittens to give him some advantage and said, "Well, come on in. You can help us cut down a tree after lunch."

Jake yanked his boots and jacket off, dumping both in the middle of the kitchen, and walked to the empty corner of the room where they always put their Christmas tree. He placed the red-wrapped gift on the bare floor and sat on the love seat, watching it like it might get away if he closed his eyes. Raney knew the package would look almost as lonely on Christmas morning. How could she explain to him that every day they got to stay in their own house was a gift? "Why don't you watch some TV, Buddy? I'll call you when lunch is ready."

David stood dripping snowmelt onto the floor, looking as awkward and frozen inside the house as he had looked in the yard. Raney gestured to the table and stayed busy scrambling eggs and making toast so that she wouldn't have to talk yet. She felt his eyes following her back and forth from the refrigerator to the sink to the stove, and when she couldn't stand it anymore, she picked up the mixing bowl and turned to him, her fork whipping the eggs so hard and fast the metal sang. "So. You're back."

"I made a mistake, Raney. I was wrong and you have every right to hate me." She could almost swear she saw tears and concentrated on twisting her heart into a cold knot. "I'll leave if you want. But first I'm hoping you'll let me explain, if for no other reason than so you could trust another man someday."

"Oh, that's good. What movie did you steal that line from?"

"*Love Story*. Ryan O'Neal and Ali MacGraw, 1970."

Raney put the fork down. "You're serious?"

"No. I made that up." He crooked his mouth into his half smile—

even more attractive when his eyes looked so sad. "So you'll let me explain before you throw those eggs at me?"

She sat across the table with her hands locked in her lap. "Go on. Give it a try."

The Friday before Labor Day, right before he and Raney and Jake were planning to go to the park, David's ex-wife, Shannon, called him. He hadn't heard from her since the divorce, so he knew it was something bad. She was sick, and wanted him to come home. Raney knew David's ex had had breast cancer, that he'd stuck with her through a year of surgery, chemotherapy, and radiation. As soon as she was pronounced cured, she'd run off with his best friend. But this time David shared everything, talked so freely Raney felt the heat of his humiliated betrayal. The only reason he hadn't waged war on them both, he said, was because he knew it was all a reaction to her disease. Once she'd beaten it she had to purge her life of everything that reminded her of cancer. "Got her chemo port out, got her breast implants, threw away the wig, and then threw me away too."

He took a long pause, the smallest muscles around his mouth and eyes flickering. Then he seemed to collapse a bit and sighed. Shannon had called to tell him the cancer was back—in her rib cage, in her spine, in her lungs. It had erupted so aggressively her doctor started talking about hospice care before he talked about chemo. The boyfriend had walked out on her—no surprise. David's hands were clenched so tight his knuckles blanched. Taut cords ran from his neck to his shoulders. Through the closed living room door the fast spiel of a cereal commercial whined and Raney moved to tell Jake to turn the volume down, but David put his hand out to stop her. "He doesn't need to hear this. Let him be."

Shannon was determined to fight it, David said. He had packed up her house and moved her to a small place near the hospital, staying with her at night while she threw up everything he fed her. He swabbed her bleeding gums with baking soda and mopped up her falling hair. Raney saw David steel himself to say more; instead he exhaled and sank into his seat, as if telling her all had depleted the

last of his strength. "I didn't love her anymore, Raney. I stopped loving her before our divorce was final five years ago. But it's still hard to
watch someone die." His face went suddenly red and he bit his lower
lip, then reached across the table toward her. "Oh, God. I shouldn't
have said that. Not after what you've been through." His hand lay
in front of her, curled palm up like a man begging coins. "I know I
should have called you before I left. I was in such a state . . . I wouldn't
blame you for kicking me out. I'll leave now if you want." Raney
looked at his defenseless hand open on the table and her core went
momentarily weightless, a spin against gravity. It was not *his* hand
she saw—it was the open palm of a man losing family and she could
not do anything but take it in her own, just as she had needed someone to take hers when Cleet died. His story flooded right through the
pores of her skin and drowned her bleeding heart, along with much
of her common sense.

She knew she would never truly love him, not the way she had
ultimately loved Cleet. Or Bo, right from the beginning. She didn't
know if she ever wanted to romantically love a man again—and the
other kinds of love, the 80 percent that made living together easier
than living alone, well, they could be learned and cultivated, like
any worthy skill. But on that day, at that moment, she felt needed by
David, and she had come to a point where that was enough to carry
the rest.

After lunch they tramped through the snowy woods for an hour
hunting for the perfect tree, settling on one until Jake or David or
Raney would catch sight of another, more symmetrical, better filled
out, just the right height. They all looked like Charlie Brown trees in
the end, too starved for sunlight to be more than wisps on one side
no matter how good they looked on the other. Impostors, like all of
us, Raney joked.

She couldn't find the tree stand, so David hammered a square
of plywood onto the bottom of the trunk while Jake hovered over
the baseboard heat register thawing his hands, but the tree leaned

so precariously that David finally tacked three fat dowels against it with picture nails. When that fell over, he stapled kite string into the window frame and tied the tree upright. Jake was duly impressed, obviously comparing David's carpentry skills to Raney's, as if he had forgotten Cleet's. Jake ran to the bathroom and came back with a worn green towel, which he draped around the plywood for a skirt. Then he placed his red package front and center before they even started decorating. She could see it pleased David.

It grew dark outside. They counted down from ten and plugged in the light cord—enchanted that even the scrawniest of trees can muster Christmas if you drown it with enough colored bulbs. Raney suggested creamed chicken soup with green beans and Boston brown bread for dinner, having emptied Grandpa's bunker of cans after they sold the farm. Even a year later they were still eating mackerel. But David wanted to take them out to Fat Smitty's, which sent Jake into food ecstasy, anticipating the french-fry-cheeseburger-milkshake stuff he never got at home.

Highway 101 was a ghost road, the familiar landmarks strange— vague white shapes like the covered furnishings of a summer house closed up for the season. David kept the Tahoe straight in the cleared tracks, slow and even across the ice. They drove all the way to Fat Smitty's and found it dark due to the snow, so they drove all the way home again to eat canned soup and bread, but it did not matter at all. Jake seemed happier than Raney had seen him in weeks. David asked him about his tree fort and his wooden bridges and towers, dropping the questions into a flow of conversation so Jake was never put on the spot. After dinner Jake went to bed, exhausted by the day. David started carrying the dishes to the sink, but Raney told him to sit down.

"No. I should be going." But he sat down anyway. She began stacking dishes and he said, "Renee, come sit here with me, would you? Is it okay if I call you Renee sometimes?" He was playing with the saltshaker, turning it around and around in his hands, which were solid and square and seemed ill-suited to the keys of a calculator or computer. She liked that his fingernails looked so well kept, clean even after a day cutting and hauling a Christmas tree.

"It's okay," she answered.

"Jake seems like a good kid. A loner, isn't he? Like I was."

Raney buffered the truth, grateful David's open-ended question made it easy. "He's been keeping to himself more this year. He's still adjusting to Grandpa's passing."

"Sports can be a good outlet," he said brightly, but he must have seen something in Raney's face, because he quickly backpedaled. "I was never much of an athlete either."

"He's been having trouble with his back. Joint pains. The doctor says he's just growing but I want to get another opinion." There was a long silence between them after that and Raney found her mind going blank. "Seems like I'm always giving him Tylenol or—"

David broke in, "Tom Fielding's offered me my job back. Between Oceanic Seafoods and some extra hours at the dairy I have plenty of work here in Quentin. I get good benefits. Health care, pension. Jim, at the dairy, offered me quarters in back of the office. Not as nice as Fielding's mobile—it's just one room." Slowly, deliberately, he touched her wrist with his index finger. He let it rest there for a moment and then stroked the length of her palm out to the end of her thumb, then each of her fingers one by one. "I could make us a life, Renee. With you and Jake."

Raney didn't pull her hand away. She felt the one point of contact between his finger and hers and wondered how it would be to lie next to him. It was only skin, a small fraction of all that made a whole person. "Are you asking if you can live here with us?"

"I'm asking you to marry me." He looked straight into her eyes now, like he was unafraid of any answer she might have for him and willing to stand his ground. He was not a bad-looking man. His hairline was receding, which did not improve his full face, but he was self-confident enough to keep his hair cut short.

"Marry." She repeated the word, looking at their hands side by side on the checkered tablecloth. His: large, thick-fingered, and soft-skinned. Hers: rough and red as a farmer's, not even elevated by grace notes of oil-paint colors anymore. His left ring finger was still banded with a pale memory of his wedding ring. *Marry*—what did that word mean anyway? People used it like it could seal God's blessing for a guaranteed happy future. Like it could bear the burden of love-struck boys on bent knees and girls pure and trusting in white lace. And then what? Twenty thousand cooked meals and floors to mop and sickness to nurse and three months' bills to pay out of next month's paycheck. All the usual cruelty of the world still thrown in your face. But at least you had some hope of not facing it alone.

Raney told David how many months it had been since she'd paid the mortgage. He was quiet for a minute, and then said he'd guessed as much. They would make it through.

And so she nodded her head and knit her fingers into his. "All right. If it's all right with Jake. Yes."

· 16 ·
charlotte

Raney's house had been empty for weeks, judging by the blackberry vines snaking through the front steps. It looked more than abandoned—it looked . . . abused. The front door had been kicked in, the glass panes smashed. Eric stepped onto the porch and Charlotte followed, hesitant, felt such a penetrating chill she wanted to sprint back to her car. Looking in the windows, she could tell people had lived here recently, and left very abruptly. The kitchen was visible through the broken front door—pots still on the stove, a box of cereal on the table. Jackets still hung on pegs in the hallway. No one had disturbed these things, and yet someone had overturned a cabinet in the living room; books and a few childlike wooden carvings lay scattered among shards of broken vases. She waited for Eric only a moment before walking quickly back down the driveway, but he was a long time returning to the car. He looked somber, his face too still. "You okay?" she asked. He nodded. "Do you think it was her house?"

"I know it was. I found my copy of *Ender's Game* on the floor, in the glass. I gave it to her . . . well . . . more than twenty years ago."

She took his hand, but he barely seemed aware. "Do we go back home, then? Give up after all this?"

"I don't know. Not yet. The police must have an address for her—they found her husband. Can you call the deputy?" he asked.

She'd thought about calling Blake Simpson any number of times, but had the feeling there was a reason he hadn't yet contacted her. She looked up his phone number, but as soon as it rang she hung up. "Are we breaking any laws? Coming out here on our own like this?"

"No," Eric scoffed, as if the idea were ridiculous, but then he added less confidently, "Probably no. How should I know?"

Charlotte dialed again, this time holding until a woman answered—Simpson's assistant. He was out of town that week, but she could put Charlotte on with another officer or take a message. "No. No message," and she hung up without leaving her name.

"Chicken," Eric said. She tilted her head in partial acquiescence. Then she checked her watch and punched in another phone number. "Who are you calling now?"

"Helen Seras."

"You're going to tell her you're here?"

"No way! She's in the weekly utilization meeting—I'm calling her assistant."

All the compliments Charlotte had given to Helen's secretary about her ever-changing hair colors paid off. She was happy to help out after Charlotte explained that she'd stupidly misplaced the address Helen had given her. The secretary located Simpson's file in less than ten minutes and called Charlotte back, completely understanding about how embarrassed Charlotte was to have lost the address in the first place, so of course she wouldn't mention it to Helen.

"She lives in Queets. *Queets*?" Charlotte said, reading the address to Eric.

"Quinault tribal town, I think."

"I got the name of the husband too. David Boughton."

It took them four hours to drive across the Olympic Peninsula to Queets, skirting the national park. They stopped in Sequim for lunch at a small Mexican restaurant, and after that the land began to flatten out so the light came hurtling unimpeded across the strait and the sky was enormous and hopeful. They passed through Port Angeles and Elwha and Fairholm, turning south at Sappho and followed the GPS through Forks on their way to Queets. There were no street signs. They drove past the town in a blink and turned around again. "Are you sure you have the right address?" Eric asked. "Even your GPS is lost."

"Maybe they have a lot of Wolf Ridges." Charlotte looked out the window at a landscape sparse in population or homes of any description. "When did any wolves live around here anyway?" They finally stopped at Queets's only gas station and asked the clerk, who studied the address in consultation with the only other customer, and after some debate, they directed Charlotte and Eric to a road four miles away. There was no name to mark the turn, but they took it anyway, driving more than half a mile along the rutted gravel without seeing any house or intersecting driveway. The road ended at a large brown mobile home, upgraded with a bump-out and a columned porch. Two fat adobe pots flanked the front door, each planted with fading snapdragons and yellowing bolts of dill. Charlotte began to regret her impulsive decision to track Raney down. The trailer had an air of ruined hope about it, as if whoever had tried to turn it into a home had given up. It bore a sad resemblance to the shell of Raney's body, too uncertain of sustainable inhabitance. The GPS voice pinged to life after having led them astray for the last half hour: "You have reached your destination!"

"Pity," Charlotte answered. "There's no car here; maybe we should come back later."

"It could be parked in back. You're not even going to knock?"

"Maybe her husband doesn't live here anymore. We should have called first," Charlotte said.

Eric stared at the house for another minute and then unlocked his door. "I'm going up."

Charlotte put her hand on his arm. "Eric? Remember. We don't know what happened to her. If it was really an accident."

"Right. Well, he didn't shoot her. He's unlikely to drive a car onto his porch and run me over."

"I'm not making a joke."

"I know you aren't. But she did marry him. She wouldn't have married an out-and-out criminal."

They finally decided to go together. The entry was recessed under the added front porch, so it fell in shadow. They reached for the doorbell at the same time and each hesitated, then Charlotte nudged Eric's hand aside—this had been her idea first; if they were criminally trespassing let it be her fault. She pushed the button but heard no sound. She pressed it again, longer, to be sure.

"Knock," Eric said, and then did it himself. The door sounded hollow, insubstantial. Eric put his face to one of the sidelights; Charlotte resisted an urge to pull him back. "Somebody's living here," he said. "Coatrack's full." He rapped on the glass—a thin, rattling sound that reverberated louder than the veneered door. He moved to the other sidelight and cupped his hands around his face.

"I think we should go," Charlotte said, tugging on his sleeve. Suddenly the trip here felt like a dangerous clash between her life as a doctor and her life with Eric, a threat she couldn't name.

Eric rapped the window once more; the sound of it crept under Charlotte's skin and she hurried back to the car. Eric came after her. "You're here for the right reasons, Charlotte."

"Am I? Really? I'm forgetting—am I here for Raney or for you?"

"Charlotte—" and then the front door opened. They turned around almost simultaneously, both of them struck silent.

The man standing in the doorway was nothing like Charlotte had expected, either from her images of the type of man Raney would have married, or from this heartsick trailer at the end of a deserted road on a nearly deserted highway. Even so, she knew it was him. He wore a pressed white shirt and belted trousers over a modestly spreading waistline. His dark hair was barely long enough to comb back with no attempt to conceal his advancing baldness. His arms hung loose at his sides, and through the shirt Charlotte could tell he was not a man who depended on physical strength to earn his living. What does he do out here? she wondered. "Why *are* you here?" the man asked Charlotte, clearly having overheard their argument.

She looked at Eric, then walked back up to the porch and offered her hand. "I'm sorry to bother you like this, Mr. Boughton. I'm Charlotte Reese . . . Dr. Reese. I'm Renee's doctor in Seattle."

He didn't offer his own hand, but stepped onto the porch and closed the door behind him. "Yes. I figured as much."

Charlotte and Eric exchanged a glance. "I wanted to talk to you about Renee's condition . . . what we're doing for her." She had practiced so many conversations with him in her head since she'd learned of his existence. They seemed pointless now—circling the truth with all the usual, open-ended medical caution. "To be blunt, I'm wondering why you haven't been to see your wife yet. Why you haven't returned the hospital's phone calls."

"That's blunt enough. Your lady vice president, Mrs. Seras, has made it clear that Renee is not going to know if I come or if I don't come. So did the deputy, Simpson." He looked from Charlotte to Eric and back, the set of his mouth turning defensive. "They're investigating me, you know. Think maybe I'm the one who ran Renee over with a car and left her to die on the side of the highway . . ." His voice broke and Charlotte saw his back stiffen. "Maybe I shouldn't blame them— a man's wife disappears and he doesn't report her missing. But in case the deputy doesn't share the details with you, Renee packed her bag and walked out on our marriage that night. It is not my habit to go looking for people who don't care to be found."

"I'm sorry. We didn't know," Eric said.

"And you are?"

"Eric Bryson. I'm a friend of Renee's—from a long time ago."

David Boughton put his hands into his pockets with a deliberate calmness and took out a set of keys. "A *friend* of Renee's. Well, I'm late for work and will ask you to leave now." He locked the door and stepped off the porch, following the path that led to the rear of the house. Eric started after him and for a moment disappeared from Charlotte's sight, sending her into near panic before he came back to her car. Boughton pulled around in an old black Tahoe and blocked their way. "And you may give a message to Mrs. Helen Seras. My wife might not have loved me anymore, but I loved her. It's not up to me to decide when she dies. That is up to God."

He drove fifty feet down the driveway and slowed, one arm hanging from the window of the Tahoe, clearly waiting for Eric and Charlotte to get back into their car and leave. Once both cars reached the highway, Charlotte deliberately turned the opposite way, clench-ing the steering wheel so hard her hands hurt. After a few miles she pulled over, shifted into park, and let her head fall against the seat. Eric watched her quietly for a moment. "Are you all right?"

"I'm okay."

She put her hand on the gearshift, but Eric stopped her. "Char-lotte? There's someone else inside the house. I saw someone's shadow through the window. Not Boughton's. It was someone smaller. Did Helen or Simpson, anyone, ever say if Raney has a child?"

"No. Never." But then how many details had Helen shared with her? A quick comment that Simpson had found a husband and a warning to drop it. "Why do you think it's a child? Maybe Boughton has a girlfriend already."

"Because when I followed Boughton around the side of the house, I saw a kid's skateboard."

They drove far enough up the driveway to see the trailer without being heard. "He wouldn't have had time to go and come back, do you think?" Charlotte asked.

Eric shrugged. "Drive on up. You might as well, even if he's there. You know you aren't going to go back to Seattle without finding out."

By now it was late enough that the eastern side of the house was in shadow, and a light shone through the sidelights next to the front door. Eric got out and walked around the house, came back, and told Charlotte the Tahoe was still gone. She climbed the front steps and knocked, watching as shadows moved across the sidelight glass. Two minutes later a brown-skinned, black-haired boy opened the door. He looked from Charlotte to Eric and back again, solemn and darkly composed. Charlotte started to say hello but he cut her off. "I heard you say my mother's name, Renee." He stared, waiting for some sign. Charlotte nodded. "Is my mom going to die?" he asked.

He was not much shorter than Charlotte, but his demeanor seemed younger than his height might suggest, making it hard to guess his age. She held her hand out to him and he observed it without offering his own. "I'm your mother's doctor, Charlotte Reese. I'm taking care of her at a hospital in Seattle," Charlotte said.

"You didn't answer me."

"I'm sorry. It isn't a question I can answer yet. She's still very sick. But we're doing everything we can to help her." He seemed to be calculating the truth in that, his mouth tightened at the corners and his gaze sharpened, holding her eyes with no timidity, as if he might reach through her to his mother. "What's your name?" she asked.

"Jake."

"May I come in?" She moved to follow the boy into the house, but Eric touched her arm. "I don't think we should," he said, but Charlotte felt too invested now to leave it half done.

The television was on and the low rumble of voices in the background made the trailer feel less isolated. If she lived here she would never turn it off, Charlotte thought. Above the set were shelves filled with VHS tapes, classics mainly—and then she saw Bette Davis slink across the screen in black and white. The wall in the hallway displayed several oil paintings that must be Raney's, Northwest landscapes reminiscent of Emily Carr, arresting enough to make Charlotte pause. There was a striking charcoal sketch behind glass that had to be Jake, though the face had been drawn a bit too long. The trailer's added bump-out had been made into a kitchen, and it gave the home an extra dimension that seemed more personal and substantial than she would have guessed from the outside. But the place seemed too orderly for a household in the midst of such a crisis and she remembered David Boughton's crisply pressed white shirt. Where were the toys? A boy's industrious mess? She wondered if Raney herself would have kept the rooms so precisely tidy.

Jake's skin was a lovely mocha—Native American possibly, or Hispanic—and his hair was quite black and so straight it shot at angles across his forehead and cheeks. Maybe the child was adopted. The shape of his face was arresting, clean lines and planes, his nose so narrow it was almost feminine. She could tell he was in that burst between childhood and full adolescence, his facial bones growing with their own odd symmetry, just hinting at how the final composite would gel—a cubist portrait. And then she looked more closely at his eyes. No, it was not an illusion of the light or her imagination. They were, truly, of two different colors. The left eye was a deep brown somewhere between his hair and his skin tone. But the right was distinctly blue. A cool slate-blue eye in this decidedly non-Caucasian boy.

"Jake. I like that name. How old are you?"

"Twelve. In December."

"It must be hard for you, not seeing your mom for so long. I know she misses you."

"Did she tell you that?" Jake asked, his eyes wide with the question so he suddenly looked much younger. She wanted to touch him, a hand on his shoulder or cupping his face, something reassuring.

"She can't talk to us right now. But I talk to *her* sometimes. And sometimes it seems like I hear her voice. I know she thinks about you every day." He watched her without blinking. She knew he recognized the lie, but couldn't tell if the lie made him feel better or worse. His mouth softened a little and she went on, "I think . . . I think she would want me to be sure you are doing okay. Are you?" His face didn't change at first and she saw him glance toward the back window where David's car would have been parked. Eric sat on a chair nearer the doorway with his fists locked under his chin, listening but separated. "Jake, can you tell me what happened?" Charlotte asked.

"They had a fight that night," Jake said.

Charlotte felt Eric's eyes on her. "The night your mother was in the accident?"

Jake was slow to answer. "The night she left here. She wanted to take me to a doctor, in Seattle, and he was mad about it. He was mad about a lot of other things already—all that stuff in Quentin before we left."

Piece by piece Charlotte drew broken parts of a story from Jake that did not all fit together. As she asked questions and drew him out, it dawned on her that Jake had not known his mother was in the hospital until he overheard Charlotte and Eric in conversation with his father, just an hour ago. He seemed disconcertingly relieved about that, in fact. But after a few more questions she realized that David Boughton had convinced Jake that his mother had disappeared from his life voluntarily—run away from both of them.

She saw Eric check his watch, sensed his growing tension, and considered how this scene would transform if Jake's father came home. "Jake, listen. We have to drive all the way back to Seattle tonight so I can keep taking care of your mother. But I'd like to talk to you again."

Jake stood up and Charlotte saw him wince and shift his weight. "I want to come with you. I want to see her."

"I wish we could take you. I want you to see her too. Could you talk to your father about coming to Seattle?"

"He isn't my father."

Eric had been quiet until then. Now he drew close and asked, "Who is your father, Jake?"

Jake went to another room and came back with a photograph of Cleet holding Jake on his lap in front of a commercial fishing boat. "My name is Jacob Remington Flores. And this was my dad."

Charlotte took the picture. "He's a good-looking man. So are you. You look like him." She had heard Jake say "was," and tried to think of a way to ask what had happened. As if he'd read her thoughts, Jake volunteered, "He died. Fishing on a boat like that." Charlotte saw Eric's shoulders sink; he turned away and walked down the hallway.

"Jake, I'll tell your mother I met you. I'll tell her how strong you're being, okay?" As they were leaving, she thought of one more question. "You said your back was hurting. Is that why your mother was taking you to a doctor?" He turned around and raised his shirt, bending just enough for Charlotte to see the lazy S shape curling his spine—not dramatic, easily missed, she knew from experience, but enough to need medical attention.

They were already in the car when Jake came outside and waited for Eric to roll down his window. "My mother would never have left me. You can tell her I know. David is lying."

"I should have asked him if he felt safe. I should have given him my phone number. What if he isn't safe with that guy?" Charlotte asked. She was hunched over the steering wheel, seeing the inside of the trailer more clearly than the road. She'd hardly said a word for the first ten miles, barely aware of Eric's tense posture and silence. The car briefly veered over the centerline and she heard him gasp. "Should we go back?" she asked. When he didn't answer, she broke her eyes from the road and glanced at him—did she actually see a trace of tears on his cheek? She'd been so concerned about Jake she hadn't considered Eric's reaction to seeing how painfully Raney's life had unfolded. "Eric, I'm sorry—I'm so sorry. It must be awful for you, what's happened in her life."

"You didn't see it, did you?" Eric asked.

He sounded acutely aggrieved, beyond rational grief. "See what?" She glanced in the rearview mirror, expecting a mangled animal in their wake. "See what?"

"Jake. His face."

"What did you see? Is he being abused? I should turn around," Charlotte said, pulling the car onto the shoulder and skidding several feet in the gravel before the car came to a full stop.

He answered in a broken voice, "All those stories I told you about Raney and me as kids. In college and after. When my aunt and uncle died and I saw Raney for the last time, I slept with her, Charlotte."

That was it? Charlotte thought. Some surge of guilt was enough to bring him to tears when he had been so stoic this whole wrenching day? He had a look of astonishment on his face, either at whatever she had missed or the fact that she was oblivious to what she had missed. "What are you talking about?"

"I slept with Jake's mother twelve and a half years ago." He waited, watching for a transformation in her expression. "Did you see Raney's paintings? The charcoal sketch of Jake on the wall? I saw you look at it twice. That wasn't *Jake*." Charlotte's jaw was tight. She wanted to get back on the highway and drive away from here, be home in her own small house with her cat and her own bedroom that smelled of down and clean wool. "That was me. Raney made that sketch of *me*. When I was twelve years old."

Charlotte tried to grasp the crisis of conscience he must be experiencing, seeing this woman who had meant so much to him battling death and unable to save her own son. Nothing less could have inspired this delusion. Surely a delusion. Why did it make her feel angry instead of sympathetic? "Are you telling me you think Jake is your child? Did you look at his skin? His father's—real father's—picture? His last name is Flores."

"Yes. I don't know. I can't explain it." Eric's voice was barely recognizable to her, it was so tight with pain. "Raney didn't know her own father. Who knows what race he was."

"It doesn't work like that," she retorted. "She's clearly white—a recessive gene. Why am I explaining this to you—the one who's writing the whole chapter on genetics?" Then she added more to herself, though perfectly audibly, "Because you're more committed to a memory than you are to me, is why."

Eric slumped against the door and for the next sixty miles neither of them said a word.

They didn't see each other for three days after they got back from Queets. Charlotte stayed after work for committee meetings she had ignored all year; she volunteered to take Felipe's shift one night when his son was sick and slept late on her next day off, curled up with the cat, her phone turned off. Eric left a message saying his editor wanted an additional chapter by the end of next week. And what next? Charlotte thought. We'll say we have too much laundry to see each other?

When she wasn't thinking about Eric, she was thinking about Jake. If something didn't break soon, she would have to confess to Helen or Simpson that she had been to Queets. But when she got to the hospital on Friday morning, there was a pink message slip in her mailbox. Blake Simpson wanted her to call him.

"Dr. Reese," he said cheerfully as soon as he heard her voice. "I understand I missed your call. I found a note on my assistant's desk." He lowered his voice so slightly Charlotte suspected it was uncon-scious. "Find all sorts of things on her desk instead of mine."

Charlotte's pulse jumped so she felt almost faint. She'd been careful not to leave her name with the assistant when she made that aborted call to Simpson's office from Quentin. She hesitated until, in the same inclusive sotto voce, he said, "We keep a record of caller ID here, of course."

"I should have thought of that."

"Most people don't," he answered, laughing softly and letting her off the hook. She remembered the appealing gap between his front teeth, the permanent informality it lent to his face, in such contrast to his uniform. He was an easy man to open up to. "Mrs. Seras has kept me up to date on Renee Flores. I hear she's not making much progress."

"She's holding on—some things better, some things not. She's getting dialysis now. But her lungs are a little stronger." She thought of Jake, his solemn eyes when he told her that he knew his mother would never have left him.

Simpson gave her a minute and then prompted the ultimate question. "But she's not waking up."

"We had to sedate her to prevent seizures . . ." Simpson was quiet on the other end of the line. Charlotte was afraid he would ask her about the impending tests for brain death. Now, after meeting Jake, how could she bear confirming that Raney was gone in all but flesh and they must let her flesh follow? She wondered how much Simpson understood about Raney's three possible outcomes: recovery, brain death, or the purgatory of persistent coma—only one of which, the least likely, would give Jake a mother.

"Well, it's a shame," Simpson said. "I guess you know she has a school-age boy."

Charlotte hesitated for a moment and then decided to tell him about the trip to Queets. "Deputy Simpson, I drove out to see her husband last week . . ." She paused, wondering if he might start reading her Miranda rights or something. "I waited three days after Helen Seras called him and he never came to see Raney. Never even called. I . . . It isn't . . ."

"Yeah. Mr. Boughton let me know you'd been to see him. Let me know pretty loudly, in fact. I hope you didn't find him too unpleasant."

Now Charlotte vividly remembered David Boughton's last words to her, the angry defensiveness in his voice when he said only God could decide Raney's fate.

"How did he identify her if he won't come to the hospital?"

"We showed him a picture of her, her scar. He said he didn't want to remember her like that—hooked up to the breathing machine."

"Deputy Simpson . . ."

"Blake."

"Do you know how the accident happened yet? Mr. Boughton said he was being investigated. Are you allowed to tell me? I don't mean to put you in a—"

He broke in, either deciding it was no longer confidential or that he did not care. "I investigated Boughton from here to Oklahoma and twenty towns in between. I checked the car; he cooperated and let me inside both his house and the Tahoe. Keeps it pretty clean—no fabric marks on the bumper. No repairs, no record of any repairs in the shops near there. There's no evidence he's harmed the son—we tried to interview him but Boughton cut it short, which is his legal right. I checked the guy's work history, his landlords. Talked to his estranged family. I turned up a string of lost jobs and broken relationships and not a single good friend. You met the man. What did you think of him?" Before Charlotte could decide what words best described the uncomfortable, almost hostile feeling she'd gotten from David Boughton, Simpson said, "Exactly. I went to the court for a warrant but the judge turned it down—what did I have? Renee Flores was found with a bag of clothes that suggested she was leaving him, just like he told us. Unfortunately, it isn't a crime to be a narcissistic jerk. Which brings me to the point of this phone call. If you *did* see or learn anything you think is pertinent, I'd appreciate a statement."

The question immediately sucked Charlotte back into that trailer in Queets, Jake's angular and cautious brown face that was captured in the sketch on the wall. She saw his cautious eyes watching her, one a soulful, aching brown and the other blue. The same slate blue as Eric's. It was impossible, but impossible to deny the blood she saw in both of them. She felt sick—a caving of the solid, reliable elements in her world. "Deputy Simpson . . ."

"Blake."

"Jake, Raney's son, said his parents had a fight that night, the night of her accident. Boughton told Jake that his mother ran away of her own accord, but Jake says he's lying."

There was silence on the other end of the line for a moment, and Charlotte found herself unimaginably euphoric, hoping that she had offered the key to Jake's escape from his stepfather. Then Simpson answered, "Yes. We know all that. Unfortunately, it's also not a crime to argue with your wife."

Making rounds that morning, Charlotte had to force herself to focus on her other patients. Raney, Eric, Jake, David Boughton—they preoccupied her mind, creeping into any space between thought and action. She went to Raney's bedside last, afraid some fresh complication might have arisen overnight and the end would be too plain to deny anymore. Raney's room looked unchanged, though. No extra pumps or tubes, "no CPR going on"—ha!—the dark joke she and Felipe sometimes used as a one-line summary to start the average "no bad news" day. But she was relieved to find that the rocker Christina Herrand always sat in was empty; her services were no longer needed now that Raney had been identified.

Anne, Raney's usual nurse, was away and everything took more time, more explanation. Diana, the kind, methodical, and very inexperienced nurse who was on duty, seemed increasingly nervous around Charlotte as the morning progressed. When it was time for Diana's break, she was out of the room so fast Charlotte knew she'd done a poor job camouflaging her impatience.

She checked Raney's lines, her medication infusion rates, her urine, her color, her lungs, her heart—the usual daily routine. But the doctor in her couldn't shake off the discordant images of Eric with this woman, as a boy, as an adolescent, as an infatuated young man, as a lover. She glanced at the automated blood pressure reading, then turned Raney's wrist over and placed the first two fingers of her left hand over Raney's radial artery, preferring to diagnose by touch than by machine. They might have taken too much fluid from her in dialysis this morning; her pulse was weak—the slightest compression and it disappeared. Charlotte had touched her often in the course of care, usually with gloves on, always with some clinical purpose. Get in, make a plan, get out. Solve all problems and keep the spark of life going another month, another day, another hour, because without that bridge the rest of a lifetime would never happen. It was not her job to judge where the road led beyond that.

A bottle of lotion stood on the nightstand and Charlotte poured some into her palms, smoothed it over Raney's arm where the flesh was still pink and perfused above the necrotic fingertips. Her arm was a stick of wood, a heavy inanimate weight. Charlotte let the hand fall back onto the air mattress. Damn you, Raney. Tell me if you're in there. Tell me what you would want. The room was empty but for the two of them. She sat down in the reclining armchair provided for family members. She'd never sat in one before, never known any friend or relative who'd been in intensive care. A thousand days—more—she'd paced these rooms and studied the monitors for a numerical history of her patients' courses, always in too big a rush to sit and watch. Just watch. The way husbands and children and sometimes even parents watched and prayed. She tried, for a moment, to clear her mind of medicine; to stop the calculations of perfusion and oxygenation, to sit here like any un-savvy fellow human and pretend that this woman would wake up one day and tell Charlotte her story: how she'd gotten here, where she was right now, one foot in this world and one in, well, who could know? She'd never found an answer to that one in medical school.

One of the monitors alarmed—an IV bag was nearly empty. Charlotte got up and switched it. The fluorescent light above Raney's bed made her face look ghostly, a death mask. Now that the swelling was gone, her chin, her brow, and cheeks were distinctly sculpted. How did family members stand it? Being able to see and touch the one they loved, able to stroke their arm, whisper in their ear and get nothing in return? No confirmation that the touch, the words, a kiss had passed through the shell to the soul inside. Someone had combed her hair, as if a visitor might finally come, or Raney herself might suddenly wake and run her hand over her hair as women do to assure themselves they are presentable. Charlotte swept an errant strand off Raney's forehead and then tucked her own hands into her pockets, thinking. She leaned closer to the bed, close enough to smell the oils in Raney's hair, the scent of her skin. "I'm jealous," she whispered to the comatose woman, and then laughed at hearing this pitiful truth audibly escape. "I'm jealous that you had him when there was still time."

When she got home from work, she washed her hair, poured a large glass of wine, and sat on her deck watching the Friday evening bridge traffic on 520 back up to a near standstill. When the glass was empty she opened her laptop and Googled commercial paternity-testing labs. She wrote three numbers on a sticky note, which she stuck to the side of her wineglass. After the sun had set and the evening began to cool, she carried the glass and her computer inside, shredded the sticky note into confetti, soaked it thoroughly in the soapy glass, and flushed it down the disposal. Then she called Eric. "It's me. I need pizza," she said.

"Margherita?"

"Meat for me. Greasy meat."

They had not gone this long without seeing each other since Eric flew to New York six months ago. When the doorbell rang, she let him in, then opened her bathrobe and wrapped it around them both. In the morning she woke to find him lying on his back staring at the ceiling. They hadn't talked about any of it the night before, and now Charlotte was almost afraid to, as if any rift caused by Jake's paternity might cleave right through the heart of everything they were to each other, even if she didn't understand how those issues were connected yet. He must have felt her eyes, even her thoughts. He didn't look at her and said, "He isn't safe there."

"You think Boughton would hurt him?"

"Physically hurt him? No. There are other ways of ruining a kid."

"Blake Simpson, the deputy, called me," Charlotte said.

"Did you tell him we . . . ?"

"He already knew." She told Eric that Simpson didn't feel any better about Boughton than they had, but no arrest or prosecution was likely to come of it.

Eric asked, "What if you told him you were worried about Jake? Couldn't he do something about that?"

"Based on what? The fact that Boughton didn't welcome us into his home when we rang his doorbell unannounced and accused him of abandoning the wife who had just abandoned him? Jake might not seem happy, but he didn't look abused." She got out of bed and pulled on her blue jeans, agitated now. Maybe she'd called Eric too soon, before she knew what she was hoping for.

"You're still upset, aren't you?" he asked. "Look, forget what I said about being Jake's father. His skin color . . . we both saw the picture of Jake's dad. The real problem is that if no one cared enough to notice Raney was missing for two weeks, who's watching out for Jake now?" Charlotte's face twisted into tears, a rare event in their history together. He got out of bed and tried to hold her, but she pulled away. "Charlotte . . . I'm sorry. You were right—it's gut-wrenching to see Raney like this. To see her son growing up in that place. My imagination . . ."

Charlotte spun around and slammed both of her fists against his chest, sending him back a step with a look of shock. "That's not it. I'm *not* right for once, even when I need to be! Damn it!" She fell against the wall and slid to the floor, wiping her eyes. "I was at her bedside yesterday, looking at her face. You can see bits of her in Jake—her chin, the shape of her eyes." She shook her head as if that might make the truth she saw go away. "But most of him . . . it *is* your face, Eric. I can't explain his skin color, but he's your child. The child you won't have with me. And I am trying not to hate you both for that."

He looked so stunned it made her want to hit him again and then wrap herself around him, hold on and say nothing else. Ever. After a moment he said, "You're hating us for loving each other twelve years ago. Look, you and I both want to help Jake—let's focus on that right now. It doesn't matter where his genes came from, does it?"

"Doesn't it? All last night I thought about my parents, my brother. My nephews. The only people in the world who love me no matter what I do. Even when they hate me." She saw him consider protesting this and shook her head again. "Blood is blood, Eric. Maybe old married people get there too, but if there's any chance you're Jake's father you should find out."

"Well, since that's impossible, I'd rather worry about helping him. A gift to Raney, if nothing else."

"How? What can you do? Send money to David Boughton and hope he starts a college fund with it? Kidnap Jake?"

"I've already thought of something. If the last thing Raney wanted was to get Jake to a doctor about his back, start there. Is it scoliosis? How serious is that?" Eric asked.

"I don't know. Scoliosis can be really bad in kids. It's out of my field, but Will or Pamela would know. They're bringing Hugo and Charlie over later." Charlotte had promised to watch her nephews while her brother and sister-in-law went to a party. She saw his eyes darken and said, "I won't tell them everything, Eric. It's your story to tell if you want."

After a moment he asked, "Is there any change?"

She knew he was asking about Raney, if only by the hopeless note in his voice. She wished she could counter that, say something positive and still tell the truth. "I don't think she's going to make it."

Pamela and Will came by a few hours later. The lingering pall between Eric and Charlotte was obliterated by Hugo's and Charlie's energy; in moments they had overtaken the house. When they could do little more than crawl, Charlotte had started a game of hiding small toys about her house, colored blocks or stuffed animals at first, then Matchbox cars and trucks, balls, Lincoln Logs. An Easter hunt at every visit. Pamela said it spoiled them, but she didn't urge Charlotte to stop. The boys never complained or fussed when Pamela walked out the door.

"Hey, guys!" Charlotte said, lifting Charlie onto her hip and swinging him around. He was so accustomed to the greeting that as soon as she picked him up, he locked his legs around her waist and let go, dropping upside down to dangle above the floor until the centrifugal force of Charlotte's spinning made his hair stand up. "Mind if I give them ice cream?" Charlotte asked Pamela. Pamela flapped a hand in the air—all rules were off at Aunt Charlotte's. Charlotte poured her a cup of coffee and set it on the table with a slice of cinnamon bread.

"Will's waiting in the car," Pamela said, but then she looked at the gooey bread and sat down.

"I have a medical question for you. Scoliosis in a child. What's the usual course?"

"Hmm. It depends on the degree of curvature. And the age of the

child. If it's significant it usually means surgery. Can be a big operation but without it the curve can become pretty crippling. Who has
scoliosis?"

Charlotte felt Eric watching them, listening. "A friend asked me
about it. I said I'd try to help."

They heard Will in the living room. "Pamela? It's *your* office picnic. If you want to go alone . . ." He came to the kitchen door.

Pamela said, "He's the one to ask—the professor. Will, what do
you do for scoliosis? I mean, when do you consider surgery versus
bracing?"

"Depends on the degree of the curve. But first you need a dif-
ferential diagnosis." Hugo heard his father's voice and ran into the
room, slamming into Will's leg like it was a punching bag. Will barely
seemed to notice. He scratched Hugo's scalp with his knuckles and
went right on talking. "Is it congenital? Idiopathic? Part of a syn-
drome? A tumor? The treatment might be the same, but you need to
be sure no other organs are involved." Hugo began to bang on his leg.

"A tumor?" Charlotte said. That hadn't crossed her mind. "Malignant?"

Will bent over Hugo. "Go find Charlie, Hugo. Or jump on your
sweet Aunt Charlotte's big, king-size bed." He winked at Charlotte
but it worked—Hugo bounded into her bedroom. "Not always malignant. Not at all. Tuberous sclerosis. Neurofibromatosis. Those can
cause scoliosis." Charlotte's face flushed and she was careful to keep
her eyes on Will, refused to look at Eric. "I'd be happy to talk to your
friend if she wants," Will continued. "Pamela? Can we go? Please?"

It lay between them like a loaded gun—at the zoo, at the wading pool
in Green Lake, on the swings. The boys played and Eric and Charlotte
took turns being three and five years old again. Being parents.
Teachers. Playing any role that allowed them to be together and still
avoid each other. After Pamela and Will picked up their sons and shut
the door to Charlotte's house, the gun exploded inside her. "You need
to find out, Eric. You need to know. *Jake* needs to know."

"You're running with this, Charlotte. Okay, so neurofibromatosis is one possibility. One remote possibility. So are a dozen other causes. Jake needs to see a doctor—we can try to make that happen. What's the point of going further?"

"It's the right thing to do. The moral thing to do. If you are his father . . ."

Eric brought his palm down on the table with a loud slap, then looked as surprised by his reaction as Charlotte was. He took in a slow, full breath. "Jake has a father. Should I damage that relationship even more? Isn't Jake under enough stress?"

Charlotte's chest felt so tight she couldn't control her voice—torn with frustration and sadness and something bigger. Something hooked deep into the muscle and bone of what she and Eric were together in love. And what they were not. "*Step*father," she said. "Not father. You knew Jake's mother longer than Boughton did."

Eric looked at her for a long, quiet moment. When he spoke, he sounded both sympathetic and defeated. "Boughton is the stepfather Jake knows. And I'm a stranger. You, too, Charlotte. We both are."

They stayed in their own separate homes that night. Charlotte slept badly, reworking all the conversations she and Eric had started and left unfinished over the last day and a half; each time she came closer to some accord but stumbled before she felt certain of her own mind. Half the input was missing, she thought, ready to call him. So when the phone rang at six thirty the next morning Charlotte answered, "Let's go to Alki for breakfast."

After a short silence she heard Blake Simpson say, "I've already eaten, but that's a kind offer. Is this Dr. Reese?" He apologized for calling so early, but he thought she would want to know that Jake Flores had run away from home and was in temporary foster care.

As soon as she hung up, Charlotte drove to Eric's apartment. She knocked once, a single sharp rap on his door, and then let herself in. He was in his study at the computer and when he turned around,

the deep red crease between his black brows made her suspect he'd
been up all night writing. No more restful than her own bad night,
she thought. She told him that Jake had run away from home. Eric
looked so stricken Charlotte felt a rush of empathy. Had she wondered how much it would matter to him?

"Have they found him?" Eric asked.

"He's in temporary foster care, in Port Angeles. He hid in the
back of a pickup all the way to Forks and snuck into a motel for the
free breakfast bar. Someone there called the police. He'd slept under
some bushes all night."

"Port Angeles," Eric repeated. "He's okay? I mean, nothing happened with . . . ?"

"I don't know. I don't think so. Simpson said they would usually
take a runaway back home, but Jake was so adamant they took him to
a shelter until they could talk to Boughton."

"Right. Right," Eric said, obviously not registering the words.

"I want to see him, Eric. I want to look at his back again. If his
scoliosis is serious and I can convince Simpson, maybe the court will
force Boughton to take him to a doctor. Even if that's all we can do
for Jake, it might make a difference."

Eric brushed her hair back from her face and his fingers lingered
a moment. "Sure. Of course."

"You'll come with me?"

He was quiet for a minute. "Can we handle it through the police?
What would Simpson say if he knew we went to see Jake?"

Was he hoping for an excuse not to see Jake again? "Simpson gave
me the address. If I can get Otero to cover for me after rounds tomorrow we could be in Port Angeles by lunchtime."

The red crease between Eric's brows was still visible. It lingered
longer now than it had three years ago, when they were first dating.
The skin above his eyes drooped a bit more and his belt had moved
out one notch. But some of his features had not changed. Never
would, she thought, wondering if she would be around to confirm

that. The sharp angles of his cheekbones, the slender, bony ramp of his nose—they were becoming more handsome as he aged. She couldn't help thinking they suited a mature face more than a child's.

Felipe couldn't take over until noon, so they caught the 2:05 ferry to Bainbridge. Something had gelled within Charlotte overnight: a sense of impelled purpose she had not willed or rationalized and did not know how to justify. Eric sensed her changed mood. It hung between them in the car like a fine but fractured crystal, ready to shatter if it was not handled carefully.

Charlotte had called the foster home the previous evening to request the meeting, and then called back that morning to say they would be late. She'd been tempted to ask to speak to Jake, or ask the foster mother how he'd reacted to the news that they would be visiting. But in the end Charlotte decided to take only the step in front of her, and if that succeeded, then the step after that. Let each step show her where the next should lead.

In only one action did she break from this: just before she left to pick up Eric, she stopped in the hospital gift shop and bought two packages of sugar-free gum in two different flavors—one grape and one bubble gum. She put them into an unsealed letter envelope and dropped them in her purse.

· 17 ·

raney

No one had seen her body since Cleet died—even Raney had stopped looking at herself in the mirror. Who cared as long as your clothes fit and all the parts did what they were supposed to? She could remember being in the changing room of the public pool where Jake was taking swimming lessons, years ago. A senior exercise class was letting out and she'd walked into a shower room crowded with nude elderly women, soaping up. Raney's first thought was of the witches in a movie version of *Macbeth* they'd shown in her junior high English class, the bubbling cauldron stirred by stripped-down, slack-breasted old women. Most of the students had never seen *any* bare breasts, much less on the big screen, and when exam time came, all anybody could remember about Shakespeare's play were those naked witches. But that day in the changing room Raney thought those women—their flesh mottled pink and quivering like jelly under the hot spray—were more beautiful than any of the dimple-free, nubile goddesses used to sell everything from motor oil to Florida vacations. Those bodies had been put to good use: babies and good cooking and hard labor so that strong biceps still muscled underneath their loose arm rolls. They'd given up the fight against grav-

269

ity and looked proud of it; entered an age when, at last, they would be measured by their minds alone. She wanted to paint those women. Wanted to show off her own post-pregnancy belly and say, "Hey! Look what I did!"

She felt none of that the first night she shared her bed with David. His soft, clumsy hands felt alien exploring her body and she faced how little she knew about this man who was now her husband. Sometimes at night Raney lay next to David and felt Cleet there. And even Bo. Her three lovers, each holding the bit of herself she'd given away and her holding pieces of them while she pondered the boundaries of love. Is it a room inside your soul that opens when your lover enters? That still exists once he's gone? Or is it a space that can only survive in the union of two?

Things worked better outside the bedroom. Having a third person in the house muffled some of the preadolescent tension that could crop up between Raney and Jake. While David and Jake didn't always have much to say to each other, they could fill whole evenings going through David's movie collections—from the old James Bond films all the way back to Douglas Fairbanks. They bought a new television set and a used VCR. And for the first time in months Raney could open the mailbox without worrying she'd find a foreclosure notice from the bank. She could see how thoroughly David worked at this new job of being a father, like the right spreadsheet and number juggling could make the balance come out true. Sometimes she wanted to tell him to relax—he's a boy not an accounting puzzle. You can't *make* a tree grow, you just provide the right sun, water, and soil and give it time.

David decided to salvage Jake's dismal school grades by tutoring him in the evenings. When Raney helped Jake with his homework, she always turned it into a game, using dried beans on the abacus of the tablecloth checks, or making up math stories about ninja warriors or bridges spanning Kool-Aid seas between cookie dough islands. It usually made Jake laugh even if his grades kept falling. David, though, was more methodical. After dinner he wiped and dried the table before he lined up two mechanical pencils and a pad of graph paper. He extracted a neatly folded lens cloth from its zippered plastic pouch to polish his reading glasses, then opened Jake's textbook to the day's lesson. By the time Raney and Jake had the kitchen clean, David had read the entire chapter and worked out every problem on separate sheets of paper. Then he pushed the book across the table and told Jake to read the chapter aloud.

Raney would sit in the corner pretending to read or sketch, sitting so that she could see Jake's full face and a shadowed slice of David's, see their legs underneath the table close enough to entangle but somehow never touching. The breadth of David's shoulders stretched the yoke of his cotton shirt across the back when he crossed his arms, listening. Raney could mark the progress of David's frustration by the way his shoulders tensed up while Jake read, making him repeat the sentence if he stumbled. After a few days of this Raney realized that David had memorized the chapter verbatim, would correct Jake even when the word was wrong but the meaning was right.

Then they would start on the problems, Jake taking extra minutes to adjust the pencil lead length and read the equation or question to himself again, his lips moving until he bit the lower one. Finally he put the pencil to the page. David watched, silently reading the numbers upside down from across the table, and when Jake made a mistake David would let out a little "Whup," as if he were reining in a horse. "Tell me your thinking, son." Under the table Raney saw Jake press his knees together. "Tell me your thinking."

"Well, I thought if . . ."

"Not what you *thought*—you thought wrong. Your answer's wrong. Think it out aloud to me before you get to the answer." And that, of course, shut off all of Jake's thinking. By the second week Jake's legs locked tight when David so much as cleared his throat, and at David's first spoken word Jake dropped his pencil and raced to the bathroom.

Raney walked over and put her hands on David's shoulders, pressing her thumbs against the tense ridges of his neck. "It makes him more confused when he's put on the spot."

"Maybe. Or maybe I just don't know how to help him. My dad would have whipped me black and blue."

"You don't become a father overnight. He's always been shy. He needs to see that you care about him, regardless of his grades."

His shoulders gave a little under her hands; she leaned down and put her cheek against his, to be closer to him, or maybe to be sure that Jake couldn't hear. "I can see you care about him. I see it."

They plowed on through another two weeks of it, David's voice getting softer and his shoulders getting stiffer every time he asked Jake to rework a botched equation. At the end of the first term Jake ended up with a C minus on the homework, an F on the exam and a D in the course, and the house began to feel smaller, like the emotional effort of turning them into a family was a fourth stranger who kept stepping on their toes and wedging awkwardly into the middle of their conversations.

David said things would get better for Jake once winter was over. He would be outside more, where a boy should be. The cycle of failing grades that seemed to be crushing him smaller, quieter would stop for a few months once summer came. Maybe even the aches and pains he complained of would go away. On the first day of spring David drove home from work with a load of two-by-fours and plywood on the folded-down seats in the back of the Tahoe. That Saturday he woke up, took a shower, and put on a clean white shirt, like he was going into the office. Then he got Jake out of bed and announced they were going to build another tree house together. Even bigger than the one Jake had built with Cleet on Grandpa's farm. He'd selected the best site already, David told Jake, and marched him out beyond the fringe of forest scrub where the yard blurred into the woods. Three Douglas firs rose from the ground as straight as silos, no more than six feet apart and naked of branches for so many vertical feet it hurt your neck to scout the lowest green boughs. "Up there?" Raney asked.

He smiled at her, then looked at his feet with his hands on his hips. After a shake of his head he said, "I can put it however high he wants it. Nail some struts into the trees and use them to hold the platform." He was already heading back to the toolshed ready to get going, leaving Jake and Raney behind. "What do you think, Buddy? You ready for another tree fort?"

Jake shrugged and sat down on the ground underneath the trees, scooping up handfuls of dirt and pine needles to sift through his fingers. "Looks like David is."

Raney squatted next to him. "It might be fun, having a tree fort here this summer. Get some other kids over to play?" As soon as she said that, Jake put his head on his arms and she knew it was cruel to hope the end of school meant the end of his isolation. "Jake? He's trying to be your friend."

"It's like he read a book: *This Is How to Be a Kid's Dad*! He's not my dad."

"I know he's not your dad. Nobody can be your dad again. But give him a chance to be some part of our family. We're all trying to figure it out." The earsplitting whine of a power saw was followed by the clap of wood hitting the floor. Jake stood up, a grimace crossing his face as if he'd been punched. "What is it? Your back?" Raney asked.

Jake started toward the shed and then turned around, so abruptly angry Raney felt slapped. "We could have made it alone. Just us. I didn't care about losing the house!" he shouted.

That night, after David had spent hours cutting and stacking all the wood without commenting on the fact that Jake was nowhere to be seen in this father-son bonding project, Raney poured a beer into two glasses and sat down at the kitchen table. David was paying bills, and the overhead light gleamed in his balding brow. His reading glasses had slipped down his nose and he kept tipping his head up to read the checkbook and then down again to look over the rims at his calculator, a bobbing marionette head.

"I'm worried about Jake," Raney said. "I want to take him to the doctor."

David tipped his chin down to look at her, took his glass of beer out of her hand, and after a sip began running his fingers over the calculator keys. A piano player couldn't move like that. After a minute he said, "He's seen the doctor, hasn't he?" Raney sat quiet and still, weighing how long she could stay cool. Finally he took off his glasses and folded them into his pocket, as if her boiling silence had gotten his attention. "Hasn't he? I mean, maybe he's seeing the wrong doctor."

Now she was speechless. She'd been prepared for a battle and was surprised to hear him on her side, then chilled to admit how much it surprised her. "That's exactly what I'm saying. I think this is more than growing pains."

"I do too. I think his teachers have been trying to say so for quite a while. Maybe we should listen."

"His teachers? When did they talk about his back pain?"

He blinked and Raney saw something flicker and then settle itself, as if he'd grasped some fact about her he'd missed before and, in a split second, both pitied her and been moved to act. "Raney, I know Jake isn't my own blood. But he is my family now. I'm here to take care of him—to take care of you both." Raney pulled her chin back a notch, wondering if his next words would make her want to thank or curse him. "Don't you think Jake has all the signs of being hyperactive? ADD? His grades, his frustration, his impulsivity? All this pain you talk about, it's a pretty convenient way to get out of hard work."

"I think Jake . . ." She felt acutely conscious of Jake's closed bedroom door just a few feet from the kitchen, and reined back to a sharp whisper. "I think Jake is pretty near perfect. Creative and smart and sad about losing two people he loved in the space of four years. And, yes, a little out of the ordinary. I think his teachers want every kid to be a perfectly square peg who fits into their perfectly square holes—so their own narrow minds don't have to spin in circles until their heads are up their back ends."

"Raney . . ."

"What? He doesn't make their job easy so we slap a label on him?"

The next day Raney picked Jake up from school an hour early and drove him to a different doctor's office—there were only two in town. She parked in back so David wouldn't see her car if he drove past, then waited more than an hour for the nurse to fit them into the schedule. Raney flipped through magazines, all of them months out of date with articles missing where other bored patients had ripped the pages out. Jake slumped in his chair and stared at the TV mounted high in the corner. He was still mad. Mad at David, which meant mad at her, Raney knew. People shoot the target closest to them. Finally the nurse called her up to the desk, but it was to tell her the doctor was not on their insurance list, so the charges would be higher and she had to sign again at yet another red X.

The doctor had practiced medicine in Quentin longer than Raney had been alive; she had a vague recollection of him wrapping her ankle with an Ace bandage at a grade school field day. He was nice to Jake; paternal, which she could tell Jake disliked. The doctor joked with him for a minute, then started asking what hurt, when it hurt, how much it hurt, what kind of hurt? Burning? Aching? Throbbing? Jake skipped out of reach after the first two questions. Sure, his knee hurt if he ran too fast; his shoulder hurt if he threw a ball too hard. The last time Raney had seen him throw a ball was before she married David. The doctor thumped Jake with a rubber mallet and had him walk around the tiny room, then squat and waddle across the floor on his heels. Then the doctor handed Raney a pamphlet on something called Osgood-Schlatter and some home stretching exercises along with directions for how to take Tylenol and Motrin. At the door he signaled her back and asked if there was trouble at home, how Jake was doing in school, if he complained as much in the summertime. For that she was billed $42.

Raney discovered Jake's next school progress report buried at the bottom of his trash can. David got home before Jake that day and found Raney lying across their bed holding the papers clasped on her stomach like they were a poultice against some nauseating illness. "Raney?" He sounded alarmed.

He took the report out of her hands and sat on the edge of the bed with a heavy sigh; Raney prayed it wasn't a breath of relief that the news was not an overdue bill. "You could at least have him tested," David said.

"I don't think he's being straight with *me*. What kind of answers would he give on some test for ADD? It's something else."

"What *else*? He hasn't complained of pain in weeks. He grew an inch last month—of course things hurt."

Raney rolled off the bed as far away from him as she could get, but he reached for her arm. "Look, I've never had kids of my own— Jake is probably as close as I'll get unless . . ." His color deepened. He put his glasses on the bed and pressed his palms over his eyes. "Maybe ditching his report card in the trash is his way of asking for help." When Raney didn't answer, he added, "If he had diabetes would you refuse to give him insulin?" He could have hit her and it would have hurt less.

For a while David dropped the subject. Raney spent more time building models with Jake, slipping questions about his joints and his back in like they were just comments on the structure rising level after level from his floor. She tried to remember her own teenage years when she, too, had been willing to injure herself to gain an ounce of power. It made her sad that Jake was now too long and heavy to rock back and forth at her breast. Did all parents feel so baffled in the storm of their child's adolescence? Maybe David was right. Maybe it was easier to cope with a physical problem than a mental one and she was the one in denial. But now and then she watched through the kitchen window as Jake climbed the ladder to his tree house and she saw him grimace with a hand at the middle of his back.

A month before school let out, the principal called David and Raney in for a conference. Jake had gotten into another scuffle. The only reason he wasn't suspended was because he had clearly come out the loser. The next week David came home from work with the name of a doctor in Chimacum, just outside Port Townsend—a generalist who'd diagnosed a friend of a friend's daughter with MS after three other doctors said there was nothing wrong. He could see Jake for any aches and pains and evaluate his school problems too. And be discreet about it, if that was what worried Raney.

Raney came home from the doctor's visit with a prescription for something called Adderall. The next morning she put the first capsule in front of Jake with a glass of milk. They both looked at it for a moment, then he shrugged and popped it into his mouth. Raney had to bite her own tongue to keep from making him spit it out just before he swallowed.

His mood and habits stuttered for the next few weeks; some days Raney thought she saw a difference in Jake and other days he seemed the same—cranky and slow at his homework. "Kind of the definition of an adolescent, isn't it?" David said. Two weeks later the doctor doubled the dose, seeming pleased with Jake's report on his progress, and at the third visit the dose went up again.

When they got back from the appointment, David was at home, though it was only two o'clock. "Did you come home for lunch?" Raney asked him.

"Yeah," he answered. She glanced around the spotless kitchen. "Actually I picked up a burger. Taking the afternoon off."

"You feel okay?"

"I'm fine. I'm not allowed an afternoon off?" He picked up his jacket and left the house, slamming the door.

She didn't see him again until he tried to slip under the covers after midnight without waking her. Raney rolled onto her back. The moon was so bright it made shadows in the room, turning everything the shades of one of David's favorite black-and-white movies. "Tell me," she said.

After a broken sigh he said his boss Tom Fielding had cut his hours in half. Business was down and Tom was trying to economize "by laying off the very person who might find him a way to increase his profits, the son of a bitch." Raney rolled onto David's shoulder, felt his heart pounding through her own chest. She soothed him as if he were Jake run home from school by bullies. *There would be other work. Business would pick up again.* She was almost asleep when he said, "I'm losing my benefits, Raney. That's where Tom plans to save the money—he'll never take me back full time."

Summer break began in early June. Jake started spending all day outside, in the woods, roaming the cliffs and inlets of the bay. Raney didn't know where he was half the time. David said it was a good sign—Jake was doing what a twelve-year-old boy should be doing. "Probably climbing trees, chasing frogs . . ." He waved his arm around like that might help him recall more of his own boyhood activities. Try as she might, Raney could not picture David doing any of that as a boy. In fact, it was hard to imagine David as a boy—she kept seeing a slightly balding kid wearing a starched white shirt and wing tips, hoping to skewer a slippery minnow onto a hook without getting his clothes dirty. She knew Jake was outside only because David was inside—and *she* was the one who'd let him in. David was home half the time now, restless and looking for squabbles, it seemed.

Every night Raney sat on the edge of Jake's bed and talked to him about her day, who'd bought something in the gallery, what she'd paint once she had some free time—things he used to like hearing. But when she asked him where he'd been and what he'd done and who he'd played with, his answers cut her off: *Around. Stuff. Some guys . . .* Getting even with her, it felt like. She consoled herself that Jake was finally playing with other kids. She'd seen Tom Fielding's son Jerrod walking with him on the road—not her first choice of friends but a friend nonetheless. So she let him be. She went off to work with his lunch ready in the fridge, a kiss on his forehead, and a promise to make good choices. *Good choices.* Good God, she thought—was there a better way to be sure your son *didn't* tell you what was really going on? And then she left. She drove to the gallery in Port Townsend and left Jake alone the whole day. With David.

Then Sandy closed the gallery for two weeks, supposedly to take a vacation, but Raney suspected the bills for keeping the gallery open had tipped the scales against even Sandy's impractical love of the art. When Raney told David, he walked to the window and stared out toward the muddy yard and tangled woods. After a long minute he let the blind fall closed with a metallic clap. "We can't make our mortgage payment this month," he said, like that was a simple asterisk at the bottom of their spreadsheet, and left the house.

Half an hour later she heard a knock at the door and Raney hoped David might have come home with either an apology or a plan. But instead it was the neighbor girls, Amelia and Caroline Wells. They looked so startled to see Raney answer her own door, she half expected them to shriek and run off.

"Are you looking for Jake?" Raney asked. They nodded their identical heads in unison. "I think he's asleep. Do you want to come inside?"

One of them started to giggle, less like nervous laughter than a mean inside joke. They were three years older than Jake, already blossomed into curves Raney had never had—did Jake have a crush?

Amelia and Caroline looked at each other; one of them shrugged and started walking away. The other said, "Nah. Just tell him . . ." She looked back at her sister, who was waiting halfway down the gravel drive. "Tell him Jerrod Fielding is waiting."

"Waiting where?"

The girl was off the porch by then, sassier with every step. "He'll know."

Jake was at the table when Raney came back into the kitchen, his thumbs flying over a cheap handheld game machine. "The Wells twins were here. I'm supposed to tell you Jerrod is looking for you." She took a box of Cheerios out of the cabinet and sat down before she noticed Jake's expression. "Jake? What's up?"

He shrugged and scootched out from behind the table. "Nothing's up." A few minutes later he came out of his room dressed in jeans and a hooded sweatshirt, heading for the front door.

Raney called out, "Did you eat?" He came back long enough to stuff two cereal bars into his back pocket, and then he was gone.

She didn't see him again until well after dinner had been served and gone cold, been wrapped up and put away. David hadn't come home either, and Raney was angry she'd bothered to cook for either of them. When Jake tried to sneak in the front door with his hoodie up over his head, she lit into him. "It's after ten—I was about to call the police." He was hunched in his sweatshirt with his hands stuffed in the front pocket like some street thug. She remembered the snide laugh Caroline or Amelia had tossed off . . . *Jerrod Fielding is waiting.* "Jake, what's going on?"

He tried to bolt to his room, but she blocked his way. He stood hunched inside the hoodie as if he wanted to hide, wanted her to see. She pulled the sweatshirt off his head and felt her gut go hollow—a suffocating vacuum of breath. The left side of Jake's face was so swollen his eye was buried in a puffy red slit. Blood leaked from his nose. "Oh, my God! Jake . . . Baby . . ."

"He won't tell me who hit him," Raney repeated to David when he finally came home, long after she'd put Jake to bed with Tylenol and an ice pack. David was pacing the kitchen, his hands jammed into his pockets like he might tear into something if he let them loose. Raney was glad Jake wasn't awake to witness it, even if his stepfather's temper was roused for Jake's own defense. "I went to the Wellses' house to talk to Amelia or Caroline. Trina said they were asleep and she didn't want to wake them."

"Do you have to pull the whole neighborhood into it?"

"Well, the girls obviously know something. Their dad used to be a policeman—I thought he could help. If Jake's in some kind of trouble . . ." She stopped, reluctant to make David even madder by repeating what Trina Wells had said. But he halted in his pacing and faced her, hearing the unfinished warning in her voice. How to put it?

"Trina said . . . It made no sense. She called us a 'bunch of drug push-ers' and said she didn't want Jake near the girls anymore."

David's face went white. He started down the hallway, but Raney pulled him back. "It doesn't mean anything. If Jake won't tell me the truth, then he won't tell you. Let him sleep. Maybe he'll say more in the morning."

"It's an insult to this whole family. All of us."

"It's kids. Mean kids picking on someone who's different." Raney knew David had had his own turn with bullying as a child, the humil-iation made worse by the fact that his brother was the bully and his parents did nothing more than tell the boys to work it out between themselves.

He held his fists clenched together as if they might strike out blindly. "You know who hit him. We both know."

"You can't be sure, David. There are other kids who . . ."

"I don't give a shit about Tom Fielding right now—who he is or who he knows or if he fires me."

David left the house and drove away angrier than Raney had ever seen him. When he had not come home by midnight, Raney called Sandy and told her about Jake. "Why would Jerrod Fielding hit him?" Sandy asked, still groggy from sleep. "He's looking at a football schol-arship. Why would he risk it by hitting a kid two years younger than himself?"

"I don't know. Because Jake is . . . different? Dark, for one thing. Or maybe just because Jerrod is his father's son. David ran out of the house so mad I almost called Tom Fielding to warn him."

Sandy didn't say anything for a minute; then, sounding more awake, "David came by my house around eleven, Raney. I could see he was upset but I thought maybe you two . . . He picked up your paycheck." She hesitated, then asked, "Is he on the run?"

Raney sat down with the phone held tight to her ear, her pulse roaring. The house felt empty and unsound, the walls expanding and contracting. "I don't know what to do."

"Well, to hear that from you is to wonder what this marriage has damaged. You and Jake can come here, you know. You can have my house."

Raney rocked back and forth, wanting any place of calm. "Thanks. It's okay. I know you don't like David, but he has a lot of good in him. He wouldn't hurt us." Even saying it she wasn't sure she believed it anymore. She finished with the one thing she knew was true: "David's either left us or he's got a plan that includes us."

"I should tell you this now, just in case. I'm selling the gallery. I talked to the buyer and you can have a job—for a while at least." A sad laugh escaped her and Raney could hear the years of cigarettes and wine. "Until *he* goes broke too."

"What will you do?" Raney asked.

"Go away. South. Another country, maybe. I need a change—before my money runs out. I'm keeping the house, though. It's yours if you need it."

Around 3:00 a.m. Raney saw headlights sweep the wall and heard the Tahoe, the ping-ping of the alarm before he finally shut the door. He took a long time to walk up to the porch and come inside. Slow, heavy steps. He went straight to the kitchen and opened the refrigerator. She heard the cap pop off a bottle of beer. He might not have seen her on the sofa, waiting. But after a while he came into the dark living room and sat down next to her. Too quiet. Too controlled. "You went to see Tom, didn't you?" she said.

He set his beer on the coffee table with a paper towel folded neatly around the bottom of the bottle. "How could I not, Renee? How could I sit in that man's office for the last year, tallying up his money and listening to his jokes about blondes and Jews, bragging about Jerrod making first string and how much the Fielding family donated to his church's capital campaign? How could I know that about him and know what his son did to Jake—to our son—and not make him own up?"

Raney tried to see his face, but the light from the hall only cast him in more shadow. "What happened?"

"He's insulted us. Our family."

"Was it Jerrod? Tom told you?"

David took a long drink from the beer. "Tom accused Jake." He paused. "He said Jake has been selling those pills at school. The Adderall. That he badgered Jerrod to join in—that Jake started the fight."

"That's crazy! Jake is too shy to even dream that up." But she tried to remember the last time she'd actually witnessed Jake taking a pill, how many times she'd refilled them. "You don't believe him, do you?"

"No. I don't know. I don't know what I believe."

"Did you quit?"

"Raney, if you think about that question after what I've just told you, you will understand that staying was not a choice." His anger sounded closer to belittling sarcasm now, attacking her along with everyone else. He picked up the beer and walked into the kitchen, where she heard him dump it down the sink and rinse the bottle. He came to the doorway, took a folded envelope out of his pocket, smoothed it out, and put it on the hall table. "Here's your pay. You should get Jake up and pack some clothes. We're leaving here in the morning, as soon as it's light."

"Today? This will blow over. You'll find work in Port Townsend. Or Sequim. At least we have this house. We can't just run away—you know it's a lie. We'll fight it. Legally, if we have to."

"Like you and Cleet fought his lawsuit? Look at Jake's face and tell me you want to stay in this town." He looked around the living room, at the water-stained ceiling and rotting window frames. "We can't keep the house anyway. We can't afford it anymore."

"What did you do, David?"

"This town is toxic, Raney. I want a new start."

"Tell me. What did you do?" Her jaw clenched so that it was hard to say the words. The entire night seemed separate from her life, a cartoon bubble misplaced in time—an event she was remembering or foretelling but couldn't possibly be living through. "Are you in trouble with the law?"

His face was a stone. "I know too much about Tom Fielding's

business to be in trouble with the law. He would never risk it. But he'll be hot for a while."

How could she tell Jake? Walk in there at four in the morning, take the ice pack off his bruised face, and say, *Pack a bag! Pack your clothes, your pictures, your childhood! We're leaving everything you've ever known. The house your father, your real father, raised you in for seven years before he decided in a moment of madness that you were better off without him?* "Shouldn't we know where we're going before we leave? Have some plan?" she asked David.

"I'll land on my feet. I always do. If I don't find good work we'll come back after this blows over."

· 18 ·

charlotte

It was after five by the time Charlotte and Eric reached Port Angeles. The house, a one-story wood frame painted blue with white-trimmed windows, was on a small street near the end of town; there was a Cyclone fence around the perimeter. The yard was cluttered with plastic trucks and push-toys, a seesaw with smiling frogs for seats, all originally bright yellow and orange, now faded from the sun. The toys looked tired and dirty, but at least more kid-friendly than anything Charlotte had seen at the trailer.

An older woman answered the door. Not the face Charlotte had anticipated, but only then did she realize that she had, ludicrously, been expecting some facsimile of Jake's own mother, Raney. The woman introduced herself, "Louise, the mom around here," and showed Eric and Charlotte through a cramped entry hall to a paneled room that combined dining, TV, and games and stretched the full width of the house. One entire wall was a bulletin board covered with crayoned and finger-painted pictures of houses and cats and bubble-shaped trees; stick-figure families held hands on stripes of green lawn, but few of them showed the classic arrangement of two parents and three children in graduated height. The shelves were filled with puzzles and DVDs and books—*World Book* and Harry Potter, Goose-bumps and Judy Blume. A dozen children from ages two to fifteen could live here, but the rooms above and around them were silent.

Louise offered them lemonade. They declined. She took a chair opposite the sofa where Charlotte and Eric sat side by side, settling herself calmly as if no words were necessary and they might all spontaneously begin a hand of cards, or were awaiting other guests. The sofa smelled faintly of fermented juice and baby lotion. Louise was a heavy woman. It was difficult to read her expression; her eyes were embedded deep in her full face, lines erased by full flesh. The great bulk of her thighs pushed her knees apart, and her skirt planed into a wide, shallow bowl. After a few moments of uncomfortable silence Charlotte began to wonder if Louise understood why they were there.

Finally Louise readjusted herself in the chair and said, "This young man, Jake, is a curious soul to me."

"How do you mean?" Charlotte asked.

Louise cocked her head a bit and Charlotte knew she was being assessed, the untested boundaries of trust established. "He says very little, but what he says is well worth paying attention to. More than I usually encounter in a child this age, and I have known a lot of children." She leaned forward and opened a glass candy jar on the coffee table, held it up for Eric and Charlotte to accept or refuse, then took out a strawberry-wrapped piece. She put the jar down and dropped the wrapped candy into a deep pocket on the side of her skirt. "Deputy Simpson tells me that you are Jake's mother's doctor, over in Seattle. I called him after I heard from you, of course." She waited for Charlotte to acknowledge this with a weak smile before she went on. "He tells me Jake's mother is not doing well, and I find myself thinking that perhaps you've driven all the way here from Seattle to tell him difficult news."

It began to make sense to Charlotte now. Louise was the wall of defense here. Drawing her line in the sand before she would allow Jake to be damaged one more time. "Ms. . . ." Charlotte realized Louise had never given her last name. "No. That isn't why we're here."

And then Charlotte looked at Eric, lost for words that might explain why they *had* come all the way from Seattle to see a boy they barely knew. "When we saw Jake in Queets he told me that Raney, his mother, wanted him to see a doctor—about his back pain. If I can help out . . . Well . . . with all that's happened I was concerned about him. We just want him to know someone else cares."

Louise gave this a long moment of consideration, then heaved to her feet and lumbered to the bottom of the staircase, where she called for Jake. When he came into the room he had the same cautious, observant expression Charlotte had been struck by when she met him in Queets. He wore a faded Mariners T-shirt that looked way too big—likely from Louise's shelves.

"Hi, Jake. Remember us? Charlotte and Eric?" Charlotte was unsure whether she should offer Jake a handshake or whether that might be enough to send him running back upstairs.

He looked solemnly from Charlotte to Eric and back to Charlotte, as if he were trying to recall their faces, or perhaps deciding if he should tell them *anything* he did or did not recall. Louise stood between Jake and the sofa, far enough away to let Jake be in charge, close enough to intervene. After a while Jake nodded and Louise met his eye, then gestured for him to sit in the chair she had occupied. She leaned over him, her great bosom a deep black crevice. "Jake? I'm right here in the kitchen, son. Makin' your dinner. Pigs in a blanket."

The silence became awkward again after she left the room; Charlotte could feel Louise watching them through the open kitchen door. Charlotte smiled and asked if Jake liked Port Angeles all right; if he'd met any other kids here. He studied her quietly with his arresting eyes. Now that he was directly across from her, now that she'd allowed herself to consider the impossible, Eric's features were blatant in Jake's face. She felt foolishly exposed, as if Louise, Boughton—anyone who saw both Eric and Jake—must know the truth immediately—only she had missed it. She glanced at Eric, and even in the poorly lit room he looked too pale, too solemn. After a while she stopped trying to draw Jake out with her pointless questions, and as if he had been waiting for that sign of respect, he asked her, "Is my mother still alive?"

"Yes. She's still very sick, Jake. She would come herself if she could." Still, he looked so cautious, so skeptical. Was it anger? Doubt? A mistrust of all adults after what he'd been through? She leaned closer. "She wants to be here with you, Jake. You believe that, don't you?"

She heard Louise clear her throat. Jake glanced over his shoulder at her in the kitchen and Charlotte saw her stop in her work, wait for a sign from him that all was okay. He looked straight at Charlotte again and said, "Tell my mother I was on my way to Seattle when they caught me. I'm not going back. I won't live with David."

"Okay, I will." She hesitated a moment, then asked, "Jake? Did you leave because David hurt you?" Charlotte knew she was stepping near a line, and for a moment she wondered if Louise might suddenly loom up and snatch Jake into her great arms, carry him out of the room, tall as he was.

But Jake had an answer ready. "He's too smart to hit me. If he had, the police wouldn't make me go back." Charlotte's throat tightened, but Jake's face didn't change—still composed and preternaturally wise. Indeed, he looked so undisturbed it seemed peculiar, given where he was, until she realized that here, for the first time since his mother disappeared, Jake had some hope that his life might change.

The smell of broiling sausage drifted into the room. Somewhere a faucet dripped, or perhaps it had begun to rain. After sitting silently through it all, Eric leaned forward on the sofa so his face was closer to Jake's. "I didn't get a chance to tell you something the other day, but I'd like to tell you now." Charlotte could see Eric trying to smile, to keep this easy despite Jake's wariness. "I knew your mom when she was a girl. Not much older than you. We used to play together down in the ravine near where your great-grandpa lived. I knew him too. One time—when I first met your mom—she tricked me into looking for seal pups in a cave under the bluffs. When the tide came in I was stuck. I spent half the night in that cave!" He looked down at his hands for a moment. "She's a special person. She was a wonderful friend to me. You look a little like she did, back then."

Jake was fixed on Eric's face, more engaged than Charlotte had seen him all evening, the color and light in his eyes brightening and darkening. She could see him turning Eric's story over, calculating the likelihood of such an event. If Jake decided it was a ruse to gain his trust, would he walk out? She wished Eric had waited until Jake seemed more comfortable with them—if they had to leave now, there would be no second chance. She was about to change the subject, hunting for something light to say, when Jake tilted his head and asked Eric, "Did my mom used to call you Bo?"

Louise walked in with a stack of plastic plates and set the table for four, including Eric and Charlotte without any apparent invitation or question. She brought out an enormous platter of sausages wrapped in biscuit dough, baked to gold, followed by potato salad, pickles, and snap peas. Jake got more talkative as dinner progressed, asking Eric to tell him more stories about his mother when she lived on the farm— he, too, it turned out, had snuck cigarettes from the bunker, at the shy age of eight, and been required to eat one when his great-grandfather caught him, which appalled Charlotte but made both Eric and Jake howl in commiseration. Every time he laughed he seemed younger, less precociously guarded.

It was nine fifteen by the time they finished eating. Jake yawned a few times. Louise got up to make some tea and Eric started clearing the dishes. Only Jake and Charlotte were left at the table. She could hear Eric and Louise talking in low voices through the open kitchen door. Charlotte leaned closer and whispered conspiratorially, "I brought a treat for you, Jake. Something small." She rummaged through her purse and pulled out the white envelope and packages of gum. "I didn't know what flavor you like, so I bought two kinds. Grape and bubble gum. You can try them both and tell me which one is the best—I'll bring more the next trip." She unzipped the plastic tape from the grape pack and shook one piece up for Jake to take. He slid it out, unwrapped its white paper sheath, and crumpled the entire piece into his mouth. "Chew it some before you decide. They lose their flavor pretty quick." After he'd given it a good go she opened the second pack. "Now try the bubble gum—my favorite." She took a stick for herself and Jake unwrapped his own, rolling it into a tight curl before he started to put it into his mouth. "Wait," Charlotte said, taking a clean napkin from the wire rack on the table. "Spit the grape out first or you can't tell." He spit the gum neatly into the napkin Charlotte held open across her palm, a silver trail of saliva included. Then he put the second piece in his mouth and chewed with concentration worthy of a sommelier. Charlotte emptied the contents of the napkin into the clean white envelope and folded it closed before slipping it into her purse. "You can keep both packs if you want."

Louise and Eric came back into the room. "Jake, you and I need to hit the sack, huh?" Louise said. She looked at Charlotte with an expression more grave than her words sounded. "Dr. Reese told me she might be able to help you with your back pain, son. Case it's a while before we get you to the doctor. How about you let her have a look?" She helped him pull the Mariners T-shirt over his head with a static crackle, his hair clinging to the neckline so it stood straight up for a moment. He seemed unself-conscious about partially undressing, relaxed around them now.

Charlotte asked him to walk toward the far wall and back, then she had him lean over and touch his toes. The curvature was more obvious to her this time, his pelvic crests clearly asymmetrical in height. She wished she knew more about the problem and could give Louise specific advice, if indeed Jake was allowed to stay here. It had been fifteen years since she'd studied either orthopedics or pediatrics, but something about Jake's clinical picture nagged her. Was it the degree of the curvature? The rapidity with which it must have developed, given that no prior doctor or school nurse had caught it? She picked up his shirt and crinkled it into a sleeve to go over his head. "Thank you, Jake. I know some doctors in Seattle who might help you feel better. Would you be willing to talk to them? If Louise and Mr. Simpson said it was okay?"

"If they can make it stop hurting."

He put his arms up for his T-shirt but Charlotte stopped when it was halfway over his head. "Just one more part of the exam, do you mind?" She placed her hand softly against his rib cage and turned his body so the lamplight illuminated him from the side. With her fingers, she parted the fine pubescent hair just beginning to grow in the hollow of his armpit, and there in the deep golden cove she saw a scatter of dark freckles. The dermatologic signature of neurofibromatosis. Just like Eric had.

Charlotte felt drained. They checked the ferry schedule and realized they were likely to miss the midnight sailing back to Seattle from Bainbridge; it would be quicker to drive around through Tacoma. After an hour and a half on the long stretches of empty highway Eric was sound asleep and she drifted into a half-formed dream of Raney pulling her IV lines out, rising from her ICU bed dressed in jeans and a Mariners T-shirt, looking no more than twelve years old. A light flashed—a car passing—Charlotte jerked awake and swerved hard to the right in a panic. The wheels dropped onto the gravel shoulder and spun with no traction; Eric cried out when his shoulder struck the door. The Saab ended up facing backward on the opposite side of the deserted highway; the headlights sparked on fragments of broken glass, glittering reminders of past tragedies.

They found a motel outside Tumwater and checked in. The room felt damp and close, the carpet uncomfortably nappy. Eric used the toilet and rinsed his mouth, then stripped to his shorts and slid under the bedcovers. He lay on his back with his hands crossed over his chest. How could someone sleep in that position? And yet she knew he would hardly move the rest of the short night. She didn't take her shoes off until she was sitting on the edge of the bed, then tucked her feet up before they could touch the carpet. She was exhausted but wired, too fatigued to drive or think clearly and too agitated to sleep. The streetlights over the parking lot cast a yellow glow through the windows, and in her buzzing semiconsciousness the room was a television set, she and Eric and Jake and Raney inside while David watched—the one in control was the one least invested.

After a while she turned on to her side, facing Eric, studying his profile in the unnatural, intrusive light. His eyes were still closed, but she knew he was awake. "Are you going to tell me what the gum is for?" he said.

"I wondered if you saw that. Do you need to ask?"

Eric sighed and opened his eyes, staring at the ceiling. "Can they really get a DNA sample from gum?"

"Aren't you the one writing about all the latest genetics research? Yes. Usually. Unsweetened is best."

"And were you going to get my sample the same way?" He crossed his arms under his head and turned to look at her, but with the light behind his face she couldn't make out his expression. "Or were you planning to drug me and swab my cheek?"

Charlotte reached over to his chest and ran her fingers over his skin. Pale. Smooth. Almost no hair. "I was hoping you would give it to me. Willingly." She pressed her fingers softly against the flesh under his arm where the freckles of neurofibromatosis marked him, where she had seen the same sign on Jake. "Will you?"

He pulled her hand away. "Have you asked yourself what you'll do with the results? Either way? A match, no match? You can help him just by being a doctor. Being a friend. We both can. If Jake has scoliosis, even if he has neurofibromatosis, we can help him get treatment."

"How can you question it now, with the axillary freckles?"

"Because sometimes we see what we want to see. Not just you—everyone. And the question still begs—if he has the disease, does it matter where he got it? Does it change anything?"

"It feels wrong not to know. Not to take responsibility for it. You know what it's like to live with this diagnosis. You could help him—as more than some anonymous friend." Eric stared at the ceiling, his jaw set. "Maybe the real question you should be asking is why you're so scared to find out if Jake is your son."

He was quiet for a moment; then, too restrained. "Look at me, Charlotte." She held her eyes wide in mock exaggeration. "No. *Look* at me." He sat up in bed and turned his back to her, parted his thick hair to expose the pink rind of his scar. "Teach Jake how to live with it? The opposite is more likely. You think he needs to watch one more parent . . . There is no cure for this, Dr. Reese."

"You've had an unlucky course. An unusual course for NF."

"Yes. We don't choose our luck, do we? Or our parents. Except in this case, maybe Jake can."

"And is that true for us too? You're waiting for me to choose so you don't have to? Choose to give up on marriage and children so you can pretend you would have ever given those a chance? We're stuck, Eric. Stagnating. The only risks you're willing to take are ones that don't include people."

He was still turned away from her, his feet on the floor ready to get up, dress, and walk out. She almost didn't know if she cared anymore, which scared her more than the fear he would leave. Then his head sank into his hands with a sigh so close to a sob she wished she could see his eyes, wanted to touch him but couldn't cross over. After a long time he lay down and said in a resigned voice, "All right. I'll do it. I'll take the test."

Charlotte let Jake's chewed wad of gum air dry, as the instructions said, and mailed it to the genetics lab she had chosen, practically at random, from the hundreds advertised on the Internet. The customer care representative told her not to send Eric's sample until they were certain they could get an adequate DNA extraction from the gum. She would send Charlotte the necessary buccal swab test kit if the extraction succeeded.

Three days later a small package arrived in Charlotte's mailbox. The contents looked so innocuous: an envelope, a clear bag, and two sticks that looked much like home pregnancy tests.

Eric read the instructions and slid the cover back to expose a white fabric-like surface on one end. He scraped it against the inside of his cheek a few times, then closed the cover and put the stick into the bag. He repeated the steps with the other stick. Charlotte put the test sticks into the envelope and wrote the date on the flap, filled in the form, and sealed the envelope. It was done. Two minutes for the test, a lifetime to muster the courage, she thought but did not say aloud. It would only take forty-eight hours; the results should arrive on Saturday. It felt like forty-eight days to Charlotte.

And in the course of that time Raney began to improve.

Charlotte woke early on Saturday. By the time Eric came out of the bedroom she was immersed in a cleaning frenzy, the living room furniture pushed askew so she could mop in places no one looked or cared about, least of all her. He was wearing a flannel shirt so faded it looked like a chamois, exposing skinny bare legs, his hair going in every direction except straight up.

"You're cleaning," he said.

"Sherlock!"

"You're anxious. You only clean like this when you're anxious."

She looked at him sharply and drove the mop hard at a stubborn spot of ancient grime. He walked back to the kitchen and poured a cup of coffee.

As noon approached she found herself at the front window, watching for the postman. But when the small slot beside her front door at last slid open and the day's mail plopped onto the hall carpet, she made Eric pick it up. He brought the pile of envelopes into the living room and sat next to her. It was there, second from the top. So thin. So innocuous. How could so many lives be so permanently changed by the few words inside it?

Eric handed it to her. She could tell he was nervous, perhaps as much about her as about any test result. "Do you want me to open it?" he asked.

"Yes. Open it."

"Do you want to read it with me?"

"No. You read it."

Eric slit the envelope crease with his thumb and pulled out a pamphlet and a few sheets of paper. He scanned the first page, turning it over, and then put the second one on top. Charlotte detected the slightest tightening around his eyes. The concentration on his face made it obvious this page held the results. He put the paper on the coffee table and took her hands. She almost stopped him, felt she had to be ready for the answer, but in what way? He was right—what difference should it make? Wouldn't they help Jake either way? She closed her eyes and told him to say it.

"I'm not Jake's father. We don't match."

Charlotte felt like a cannon had exploded through her middle, splintering this moment, this day, every day to come. Splintering hope she didn't even know she'd nurtured. What had she been thinking? How had she let herself slowly, unconsciously, become so utterly convinced that the result would be positive? Eric pulled her into his arms. "Hush. Hush. It's okay, babe. It's okay."

· 19 ·

raney

They drove around the Olympic Peninsula for two weeks, staying at cheap motels, or in sleeping bags on beaches or in campgrounds, leaving before the park rangers came by to collect a fee; they spent a few nights in the back of the Tahoe while the rain hammered the roof and the truck shivered in gusts of wind. David would pick up the local papers and read the want ads, applying for anything that remotely resembled bookkeeping. They stopped in every public library so he could use the computer to hunt for jobs. There was nothing locking them into Washington—Raney said he should look all over the country, on the Internet at least. But whether for pride or sheer compulsiveness or because he felt as rejected as these sparsely populated counties seemed, he insisted on exhausting the peninsula before they moved on.

As Raney saw it, she still had a full-time job. Now she had to make Jake believe this move was an adventure. A summer vacation touring the bleak towns in the farthest, forgotten corner of America, scattered along the broken two-lane roads like lost pennies collecting dust under sofas—not worth the trouble to retrieve. Sometimes, she told Jake, you have to believe in fortune—the world will give you what you need when you need it. Things will work out. Jake promptly reminded her of the last history lesson he had studied in school— Robert Scott's disastrous expedition to the South Pole, how he nearly died en route only to discover a Norwegian flag already planted, and then *actually* died eleven miles from getting back home.

Three weeks after leaving Quentin they stopped outside Queets for coffee and gas just south of Kalaloch on 101. Raney waited beside the gas pumps, unwashed and unkempt and braced against the biting rain, watching Jake kick an empty beer can down the side of the highway until a logging truck whooshed past and crushed it. David came out of the store after paying, and she pulled him around the building behind the Dumpsters where Jake couldn't witness or overhear. "We need a home, David. A house, a trailer, a single room and a hot plate. No more fast food, no more roadside Sani-Cans."

David put his wallet into his back pocket and scanned the sky, squinting in the single sun ray that darted through a cloud break and then vanished again. Looking for heavenly guidance out of this hell, Raney thought, like he might honestly believe heaven or hell cared what happened to their three vagrant souls—specks in the chaff of the universe. But she could see him bending to her ultimatum—or trying it, at least. "Well, there's the job at the lodge. Hourly—no benefits." He paused. If he was giving her a chance to change her mind he could wait forever. Let him freeze in the rain beside these putrid garbage bins while she and Jake took a bus back to Quentin. "I'll drive on over and tell them I'll take it. For now." He smiled at her. His smile still made her want to trust him, for one more mile. One last mile. The way some flowers inevitably follow the sun; their biology gives them no choice in the matter.

They got into the car and turned around, heading back to the coastal resort in Kalaloch. Raney stared out at the landscape—wind-blown trees, bent by the Pacific gales. She missed the lushness of Quentin—horizons hemmed so close by the forests and hills the world felt smaller. Something you might cope with. But there was a beauty here that she could imagine settling with, if they stayed for a while. If they had a place to live and a way to pay for it. And at almost the same moment that thought entered her mind, a red-and-black sign caught her eye—vivid in the spectrum of natural golds and greens. It was a For Rent sign, pointing up a gravel road that could have led to the moon, it was so empty. Nothing visible from the highway. She told David to stop the car and back up. They looked at the sign for a minute, and then turned up the rough drive.

After a quarter of a mile with no man or man-made structure in sight, David was ready to turn around. But Raney was determined. "The sign didn't look that old, and the road's been used." And then through the brush and cattails they saw a trailer, so brown and squat it popped into view like a nesting ground bird brooding her eggs. The image alone made Raney feel like it could be turned into a home. It was locked—they had to stand on stacked cinder blocks to see through the windows. The owner had built a lean-to along the front and busted out the wall so that it had more corners and rooms than a simple rectangle. They could see two small bedrooms; a tiny galley kitchen with a two-burner cooktop. A bathroom with a shower and double sink.

Raney felt her first spark of hope since seeing her own house disappear in the Tahoe's side-view mirror, and she made David hurry back down the driveway to copy the phone number off the sign, worried someone might rent it before they could call. "Oh, right!" he said. "There's probably a backup on the highway waiting to get that phone number." They had to drive four miles to find a cell signal. David let it ring ten times before he hung up, but Raney made him call back and try again, despite his smug protest that it was a waste of energy and they should keep driving. But this time someone answered. Raney held her breath.

David asked a long string of questions about the trailer before Raney heard him ask if it was still available. He kept shaking his head and asking the owner to repeat his answers—"Barely understand his accent," he whispered to Raney. Finally he asked what the rent was;

she saw him wince. He told the owner he'd think about it and call back.

"I don't care what the rent is. Take it." Raney caught Jake's eyes in the visor mirror—he looked ready to jump whichever way she called it. "Will he rent to us by the month?" David nodded. "Okay, then. This month is yours. If the job doesn't work out, we'll move back. We could be home before school starts."

The owner was a Korean grocer down in Aberdeen. The rent was pitifully low, but so was their money, and when he called the owner back, David wangled a way to work part of the rent off by doing some bookkeeping for the store. They had to drive to Aberdeen to sign the lease and pick up the keys. Before they left, David wanted to look at the trailer again, in case there were any obvious leaks or damage he might leverage into lower rent.

Jake and Raney roamed the wide-open land that stretched un-inhabited in every visible direction, only a few twisted barbed-wire fences marking the boundaries of what must be acres of property. The land had been clear-cut at some point in recent time, exposing a contour of marshy swales and hillocks gouged by logging trucks. Thorned blackberries and the forlorn stumps of decapitated trees stood in weedy patches aflame with fireweed and Indian paintbrush. Jake walked over the uneven turf with his hands in his Windbreaker pockets, scanning his new territory. There would be no worries about bullying neighbors here. There were no neighbors.

Raney caught up to him, and they walked toward the closest marsh until the soaked earth sucked at their shoes and Jake got her laughing at the flatulent sounds. They picked cattails, broke open the felted brown rods, and threw the moist fluff in the air and on each other. He leaned over, trying to snare the largest reeds without falling knee-deep in mud, and Raney saw his hand fly to his back.

"Jake? Is it your back?"

"I'm fine, Mom," he said, his good humor turned sour.

"No, you're not. You've been lying about it, haven't you? Why?"

"Why complain? So David can say I'm just trying to get out of hard work?" He stormed ahead of her, his Windbreaker slung around his shoulders so his T-shirt was drawn taut against his spine. Raney wove toward drier ground to follow him, but when she looked up, she saw something so plainly she wondered if she'd been blind for the last weeks. Jake was limping. She walked faster, marking the fit of his blue jeans and the lay of his cotton shirt—it was suddenly obvious. One hip was riding higher than the other, as if his legs were uneven.

David was waiting for them. After Jake got into the car and shut the door, she pulled David aside and told him what she'd seen. "I want to take him to a pediatrician in Aberdeen."

"*Another* doctor? And pay for it how?"

"Some doctors take charity. We can sign up for Medicaid now. He's limping. Like one leg is shorter, or something."

"Legs don't shrink overnight. You're under a lot of stress, Raney. So is he."

David started to open the car door, and Raney shut it again. "Something is wrong with him. I know it. I can feel it."

"Well, he hasn't been taking his medicine, for one. Maybe he never took it. Started selling it from the beginning."

Raney was speechless, a band constricting her chest. "You think he did it, don't you? You believe Jerrod and Tom Fielding more than your own . . ." David went a shade paler and stammered a word before Raney cut him off. "He needs a decent doctor. I'm taking my son to a doctor."

David looked out toward the wind-swept marsh. After a chilled moment he nodded. "Okay. We'll see. Tomorrow might not be the best day. We'll see."

The grocer asked them to meet him at his store at nine the next morning. It was only a few hours' drive to Aberdeen, but once in the city they would have to pay for a motel, so David pulled into a rest stop eight miles north and hauled out the sleeping bags and tarp. He hunted out the smoothest stretch of grass and kicked the larger rocks aside, then spread the tarp and arranged the sleeping bags side by side. Shortly after they fell asleep it began to rain so they shoved the wet tarp under the car, folded the seats down and made a pallet out of the three sleeping bags, then tried hopelessly to fall asleep again. They were back on the road at four forty-five, pulling into Aberdeen before daylight.

They stopped at a McDonald's for coffee and two breakfast sandwiches to split among the three of them. When David went to the bathroom Raney asked the cashier how to get to a marina or park where they could take a coin shower. Raney had turned her last pair of underwear inside out to last another day, but if she could wash her hair, she could tolerate the rest. One more day and they would have beds to sleep in. Hot water. She could stand anything for one more day.

The marina was well outside town, and the shower was locked. A sign read "Open 8:30 a.m. to noon, 6:30 p.m. to 10:00 p.m." She checked the windows to see if one might have been left unlatched. The whole city was still asleep. Along the docks metal halyards clanged against metal masts in broken music. It sounded so lonely in the gray mist of dawn. The space between her ears buzzed, as if so many nights of bad sleep had garbled the circuitry inside her brain. They all walked back to the car and sat inside with the doors locked and the radio on, waiting, until Raney said, "Just drive to the grocery store and park. Maybe he'll get there early."

It was not a big city, but they still drove the wrong way up a one-way street and through a stop sign searching for the store. By the time they found it, they'd quit talking to each other—their collective patience used up. David pulled into the lot behind the store and parked, put his seat back as far as it would go, and slapped a T-shirt over his face. Raney said she was taking Jake with her to find a bathroom, beyond caring if David was still awake to hear. Let him worry if he woke to an empty car.

They tried a gas station at the end of the block, but the bathroom was for customers only and the clerk showed no sympathy when Raney asked for the key. She stood on the corner looking for another option, then started up a hill toward a large, well-lit building—so many lights had to mean a lot of people, who must all, at some point, use a toilet.

It was a hospital. For the first time in months, Raney felt like her luck had turned. She combed her filthy fingers through her hair and tried to do the same to Jake before he could pull away, then she followed the signs to the emergency room. She left Jake in a chair near the TV and found the registration desk, waited while an elderly couple in front of her dug out their insurance cards and filled in three pages of forms before they finally moved aside. When it was her turn, though, she had no idea what to say. Why was she here? Whatever Jake had, it wasn't an emergency.

"I'm new here. In Aberdeen. Well, not even Aberdeen—up the coast . . . We . . . I . . ." She stopped. The nurse blinked and folded his hands—Raney could tell he'd seen it all. She took a breath and leaned so close she was surprised the man didn't back away. "Look, something is wrong with my son. His back, his joints—he hurts all the time and it's getting worse." She stopped for a minute to gauge whether he was taking her as seriously as he should. He raised his eyebrows, apparently ready for whatever came next. "He's started to limp. I've taken him to three doctors. I am tired of being told it's stress or depression or growing pains or ADD." With the last word Raney's voice broke and tears brimmed in her eyes—she wondered if she would hit the man if he turned her away.

Instead, he nodded. He put a fresh form on a clipboard and made some Xs at the places she was supposed to sign. The emergency room doors whooshed open and two medics rushed past with a wailing child on a gurney; an IV bag swung wildly on a silver pole when they turned the corner. Raney stopped reading and handed back the clipboard. "I shouldn't be here—in an emergency room. What I need is advice. A doctor's name. A specialist. I don't know where to go." A woman walked up and stood quietly behind the nurse, listening. "I might as well tell you now, I don't have any insurance. I don't have Medicaid," Raney said. "I'll pay over time, whatever it takes." There it was. All her cards on the table for the closed club of those privileged to give and receive the best medical care in the world. Jake's fate was theirs to consider and decide.

The man looked at the woman. "You want to take this?"

She told Raney to take a seat in the waiting room, then she disappeared through a door at the far end of the corridor. Raney checked the time: seven thirty. Through all of this, Jake had kept his eyes fixed on the television set, which was tuned to some political talking heads—God alone knew what rage or pain had kept him awake through that. She changed the channel to cartoons and noticed that no one else in the room seemed any less enthralled by *VeggieTales*. She jumped, half-dozing, when the woman sat down next to Jake.

"Ms. Boughton? I made up a packet for you." She opened a large white envelope and pulled out a sheaf of papers. "All the applications you'll need for Medicaid and TANF—Temporary Assistance for Needy Families. It takes a while to get through the system, as you can guess." She handed Raney another page. "This is a list of doctors in the county—addresses and specialties. Phone numbers. Sometimes it's hard to get an appointment if you're on assistance, so call soon." She looked at Jake. "Did I hear you say it's his back?"

Raney answered, "Yes. Jake, can you stand up?" He hesitated for a minute, like he might be poked with something sharp. "She's not going to do anything. Just show her your back." Jake stood up, facing the woman. He looked solemn and resigned, and maybe, Raney thought, ready to end this game. The nurse asked him to turn around and Raney helped Jake pull off his filthy T-shirt.

"Touch your toes for me, would you, Jake?" the woman said. He leaned over and let his hands dangle, then grabbed the toes of his tennis shoes. She stood directly behind him, scanning the bony knuckles of his skinny spine. Raney saw her face change—little more than a light leaving her eyes, a hint of doubt in her confident-nurse smile. "Thank you. That's fine." Then she turned to Raney. "I'm not allowed to give you any medical advice, since you aren't registered in the ER. But if, say, I ran into you in the park or the grocery store and you asked me about a good doctor for our friend here, I would tell you to see this man." She took a Sharpie out of her pocket and circled one name. James Lawrence, MD. Pediatric orthopedic surgeon. She smiled at Jake then, and Raney saw her tilt her head and look more closely. "You have a handsome son," she said. She was looking at his eyes, Raney knew. People were always struck by Jake's eyes.

When they got back to the car, it was empty. For a minute she felt bad about leaving David without a note, worried he was out searching for them. Or maybe a cop had seen him sleeping there with his unshaven face and dirt-streaked clothing and taken him in for vagrancy. Then she noticed the door to the grocery store was open. She told Jake to get in the backseat and wrap up in a sleeping bag, hoping he could fall asleep.

There were no customers inside the store. The lights weren't even on yet, only the white ghost-glow from the refrigerated cases. She called David's name softly and walked down the middle aisle. At the back was an open, lit doorway. A small office with a desk and chair— little more than a broom closet. David wasn't in there, but someone else was—a dark head bent over papers, half-hidden by a computer screen. Raney took a step backward, wishing she'd just waited in the car. "Mrs. Broughton? You Mrs. Broughton? Good, good! Please. I like you sign too." The grocer was half a head shorter than Raney, a round man with a smile that buried his eyes in his cheeks. David had already been in and filled out the rental forms. He had waited awhile, then gone out to look for his wife and son. "He look you," as their new landlord put it.

Raney tried to make small talk. He seemed happy they were renting the trailer, but it was hard to pretend she felt anything but tired and dirty. His accent was so thick she had trouble understanding and gave answers that left him flummoxed once or twice, turning their conversation in circles.

Finally Raney said, "Why don't I go ahead and sign the lease and then I'll hunt for David. My husband, Mr. Boughton. Let you get back to work." The grocer looked concerned, but after a moment he smiled and pushed the lease across his desk. She scanned the pages, looking for the lines David had already signed, assuming she should just sign underneath. At the bottom of the second page a box caught her eye. It was for references. Six references with phone numbers and addresses. Six. Given all the bridges they had burned in Quentin, Raney was amazed to see that David had filled every one in. He had put Sandy's name down first, of course, and Marina—the glassblower from the gallery who Raney barely knew, the only people he could be sure wouldn't jinx the rental. He'd listed Jim, the owner of the dairy David had done a little work for. She suspected that had not ended on good terms—David had been vague when she asked why Jim never called him anymore. Then two names in Oregon, probably from when he'd lived in Medford. A name on the last line had been partially crossed out and written in again, the lines of ink doubled over each other for clarity against the cross-out so they indented the page. Shannon Boughton, in Florida. *Shannon Boughton*. David's ex-wife. I'll be damned, Raney thought. David had given the name of a dead woman as a reference. Had they really ended up with so few friends?

When she got back to the car, David was in the driver's seat with the key in the ignition. "Where were you? I looked all over," he said.

The envelope from the hospital was in Raney's purse. She wasn't sure why she didn't take it out and show it to him. It should have made him as relieved as it did her. A place to start. The faintest glimmer of hope that Jake might get care without their having to sell the car. She thought about that later—her reluctance to tell him what she was planning. What part of her brain was already connecting dots to outline the face she was only beginning to see clearly?

"The marina shower opens soon. Can we stop there before we drive home?" she said.

He shook his head, his nerves frayed, she could tell. "I just want to go. We can take a shower in our own bathroom tonight." He looked in the rearview mirror at Jake. "Right, Buddy? Want to shower in your own bathroom for a change?"

Jake was quiet. Raney could feel him glaring back at David's eyes in the mirror. Then Jake said, "My mother calls me Buddy."

Raney started to make a joke, impelled to lighten the impact, but she didn't have the heart. How could she make David feel better about it without making Jake feel worse? She slid her hand across the seat so it rested against David's thigh. He tensed and kept his hands on the steering wheel.

The drive home seemed to take hours. Twice as far as they'd come. She was not consciously thinking about the rental application—they were almost to Queets when it hit her. It was so obvious she felt nauseous in the face of her own stupidity. David hadn't given the name of a dead woman as a reference. Shannon Boughton was no more dead than Raney was.

When they finally bumped down the rutted driveway and parked in front of the trailer, Raney told Jake to take the key and choose which room he wanted, resting her hand on David's arm to stay him. After Jake was inside she said, "You want to explain?" The heat in her voice made it clear what she'd seen. He slumped against the car door with his eyes focused somewhere between the windshield and the dark hovel in his soul that had generated his lie. After a long time Raney asked, "So are you actually divorced from her? Or was that a lie too?"

He rubbed his hand over his face; the slack fold of his jowl was dark with stubble. "Shannon called and told me she'd broken up with her boyfriend. She begged me to give us another try. Christ, she'd been my wife for eleven years—I thought I owed her a second chance. After two months we were worse together than we'd been before. I didn't know a woman could be that . . . All I could think about was you, Raney. I should have told you the truth. But I thought I'd lose you."

· 20 ·
charlotte

A notepad filled with Felipe Otero's small, even script lay on the desk in Raney's ICU. Her numbers. Felipe must have gotten here early—it was his habit to handwrite each patient's information, though he could as easily print it from the computer. He said it helped him organize his thoughts. Once, Charlotte had found a list of personal goals inadvertently tucked beneath the medical lists: "Try to go to bed at the same time, clean one bathroom every Saturday morning, read one book in common each month, count to ten . . ." After skimming it, she'd been embarrassed to realize it referred to his struggling marriage. She'd found it months before she knew Felipe and his wife were separating, and she remembered thinking she could have written the same list for her own relationship with Eric. Well, were any human relationships so very unique?

The numbers Felipe had written today were remarkably good— they must be Raney's post-dialysis blood work—another miracle of modern medicine doing its superior, computer-calculated job. But it was the ventilator readings that got Charlotte's attention. Raney's pulmonary pressures were out of the danger zone. Her respiratory gases were normalizing.

She knew. It was time. They would stop her sedation and check her reflexes, then take her off the ventilator and see if she had enough brain-stem function to breathe.

She saw Felipe coming down the hall. He broke into a smile, so genuinely pleased to see her it made her particularly glad that today, of all days, she would not have to make every medical decision alone. "You saw her creatinine?" he asked.

"Looks good. They didn't land her potassium quite as perfectly as usual. Still a bit high." It was another joke they had, comparing dialysis to technical marvels such as Mars landings or the Chunnel.

"She wasn't dialyzed today. Those are her own kidneys back at work. She's getting an MRI this morning—it's been a while," Felipe said.

All her lab values were normalizing, in fact. The antibiotics had battled the most malevolent bacteria to a standstill. The last residual hepatic toxins appeared to be out of her system. The inflammation in her lungs had subsided. It was all good news. Heartening. Charlotte began to hope, to pray, that the healing of Raney's body foretold a healing of her brain, but when she looked at Raney's MRI and saw the shrunken folds, too small for the encasing skull, like a child's hand inside a woman's glove, Charlotte knew how permanent the damage was.

She stood with her hands in her deep lab coat pockets, looking at her patient. *Her patient.* A gifted artist, an orphan, a widow, a wife. Her lover's ex-lover, the mother of a boy she felt committed to, rationally or not. How odd to know someone's history, body, home, child—and never have heard her voice, never have seen her open her eyes.

Felipe stood quietly behind her for a moment. "I can write the orders." Charlotte nodded. "Are you okay?" he asked.

She lifted one shoulder. "At least we'll have an answer, even if it's not an easy one. At least Christina Herrand isn't here to share the moment with us," and with that comment she managed a small, disingenuous laugh.

They stood together at Raney's bedside. Charlotte lifted Raney's eyelid and brushed a clean Q-tip softly across her cornea. In the first spontaneous movement she had made in almost three weeks, Raney reflexively blinked—a sign that despite all she had suffered, the most elementary animal functions had survived. She turned to Felipe, not caring if he saw how deeply affected she was. "Tell me. If you were twelve, would you rather learn your mother had died, or see her live in an endless coma—almost as unreachable. Would you rather visit a grave marker or . . ." she gestured toward Raney but her hands ended up covering her face. Felipe put his arms around her and she completely gave in to him, unconcerned that anyone might walk through the open door. "I know better, after all these years. I know better!"

"Charlotte, Charlotte. You're *better* at this job because you care. Because you let yourself care." He rocked her quietly, waited until she was ready to let him go. "There's still a chance, you know. It happens."

"Yeah. But it won't. Not for her. We've both seen her brain scan."

"You did the job you set out to do, as well as any doctor I've ever known. No one can heal a broken mind, Charlotte. None of us."

By the next day they were ready to see if Raney could breathe without a machine. At the moment they disconnected her ventilator, Charlotte inhaled deeply and froze. For three, four, five, six minutes she watched Raney's still chest until she saw the faintest expansion, a butterfly wing of breath. And when it became apparent over the next few hours that Raney's lungs had indeed healed enough to sustain her, Charlotte exchanged the respiratory therapist's high five. Then she walked down the hall to the conference room and scooted a chair against the door, stood beside the window looking over the tarred and graveled roof of the hospital, and cried.

Her job was largely done now. Raney would be transferred to a chronic care facility and her ICU cubicle would soon house some other person on the cusp of life. With Charlotte as the lead doctor, they had cured Raney's body—or at least helped it cure itself. Her liver made proteins again; her heart beat with steady, sustainable pressure; her stomach absorbed the nutrients her tissues demanded;

and now her lungs expanded and contracted with suppleness, gathering oxygen from invisible air. In the end even the root of Renee's brain had rallied to its job, pulsing the rhythm of circling blood and flowing breath—like a power station left behind after the apocalypse, still churning electrons with no one to flick the light switch. How brilliant a body was, Charlotte thought. More than a century after Thomas Edison and nobody had built anything close to such a marvel out of metal and wires.

When Eric came to her house later that evening Charlotte was on the porch watching the evening settle, every solid shape backlit. She barely turned when he bent to kiss her. "What is it?" he asked. "Jake? Is he all right?"

She was surprised by his question—to know that Jake was so much on Eric's mind even when the two of them seemed fatally split over how to help him. "Raney," she answered. "We took her off the ventilator today. She's breathing on her own."

"She is? Do you think there's a chance she'll wake up?"

Charlotte shook her head. "I don't think she'll ever talk. Move. Communicate in any meaningful way."

"How long could it go on like that?"

"Until some new problem happens—some caregiver forgets to wash his hands, forgets her blood thinners, doesn't watch out for bedsores . . . Ask Sunny von Bülow. Is it what you'd want?" She looked at him closely for the first time since he'd come in. "No. Me neither. And I'm the one that put her there."

"He's trapped now, isn't he?"

He was talking about Jake again, she realized. "I don't know. Maybe they'll let him stay with Louise—or find another home for him."

"Charlotte, if he has NF . . . If he needs an operation . . . Whatever he needs . . . I want to pay for it."

She laced her fingers through his. So much he couldn't change about himself, wasn't there? It was true for her, too, of course. Everyone. But harder, probably, when you had skated so close to death so many times. It must be its own sort of prison. It made her both love him more and broke her heart, to see him stretch so far for this one small step, offering his money if he couldn't give his soul. So generous, but not generous enough. Not for her, at least. She understood now why the paternity test had meant so much to her. Some irrational corner of her love had believed that maybe, conceivably, if Eric knew his genes were already inextricably embedded in this child, maybe he would take a risk with the rest of himself too. With her. With another child. But as Felipe said, no one can heal a broken mind. Not even one you love. "We'll both pay, okay?" she said. This at least, they could do together.

As pediatricians, Pamela and Will were the obvious ones to turn to first—Will was on staff at Seattle Children's and would not only be able to recommend the best pediatric orthopedist, he'd get the appointments back-to-back tomorrow if they asked him.

"Jeez, it's as nepotistic as Hollywood," Eric said.

"Only at the front door," Charlotte countered. "Everyone's equal after they get in." One boon of academic medicine over private practice, she knew, was the wall between the patient and their payment. No one outside the billing office would care if Jake had insurance. If anything, the extraordinary nature of Jake's diagnosis would have specialists clamoring.

They invited Pamela and Will for dinner, but they already had plans and said they'd come by on their way home. Dessert, then. So Charlotte and Eric ate dinner alone. He stood next to her in the kitchen, chopping tomatoes for spaghetti. "Are you going to tell them everything?" he asked.

"About Jake? As much as we have to. They'll need to see him—Will, at least—and I'm not sure how to make that happen."

Eric was quiet for a while after that, brushing off her offer to help him cook. She took the knife out of his hand and touched his face. "There's no need to tell them about your disease, Eric. Or the paternity question. The urgent problem is his back—the scoliosis. They'll test Jake for neurofibromatosis and everything else as part of his workup." Despite how much she'd educated herself about NF since they'd fallen in love, Charlotte had told none of her medical family about Eric's brain tumors. They couldn't see the scars hidden by his hair like a secret tattoo. She'd tried to respect his privacy—it was his decision to tell them if he chose. And what sane person could sit through all those family dinner discussions and feel remotely inclined to become the next intriguing topic for dissection? But for the first time it occurred to Charlotte that the real reason she hadn't told her family was that they might ask the questions she couldn't face herself.

It was after ten when the doorbell rang. Charlotte had fallen asleep on the couch. "Sorry we're so late," Pamela said. "We have to make it quick—the sitter charges twelve dollars an hour. I remember being happy with seventy-five cents."

Charlotte put some cartons of ice cream on the table and began the story at the safest place she knew. "You remember my patient—my Jane Doe. They were able to identify her by the scar on her arm." Pamela started to break in, but Charlotte said, "I shouldn't be telling you any of this. The story's complicated because the husband's been under investigation. And . . ." She struggled to find the right bridge to their discovery of Jake at the trailer in Queets. "My patient has a child, a son, and I met him. He's complaining of back pain. I think he has scoliosis and he's not getting any medical care. I'm hoping you can help." There it was. The critical one percent of the surreal story that she hoped might win Jake the golden ticket to see the top specialists in Seattle.

Will was watching her intently—he'd been able to see through her B.S. since they were squabbling preschoolers. "This is the child you were asking me about the other day?" Charlotte nodded. "I'd be happy to help—Children's has some great spine people." He paused a minute, considering her face closely enough to make her flush. "You hadn't told me it was a boy. You're sure he's having back pain?"

"He told me he was. He said his mother was trying to get him to a doctor, but the stepfather wouldn't let her."

"Will his mother recover enough to take care of him?"

Charlotte shook her head. "No. I don't think so."

"So, it won't be easy to get him seen," Will said. "It could take a court order if his stepfather refuses."

"It could take time," Charlotte answered. "He's in a temporary foster home right now."

Will nodded, pursing his lips the way he did when he was getting worried and trying to hide it. "Because, the thing is, scoliosis is more common in girls. And typically it doesn't hurt, it's so gradual. Both of those mean you have to think about something more serious. A growth on the spinal cord. Something that shouldn't wait."

Eric had been sitting at the far corner of the table ignoring the ice cream, slowly spinning his empty wineglass while they talked, sinking further into the shadows outside the chandelier's light until he was a mere observer to their "familial medical grand rounds," as he'd often called the Reese dinner table conversations. So they all turned when Eric cleared his throat and said flatly, "Charlotte thinks Jake could have neurofibromatosis."

"So it is more serious," Will said. He looked at Charlotte again and she felt transparent, as if he were counting the cogs spinning in her brain. She had never been a good liar. "Why do you think he has NF?" Will asked her.

She started to tell him about the freckles under Jake's arm, hoping that would be enough. But it was Eric who answered again. "Because I have it. And Charlotte thought, we thought, for a while, that Jake might have inherited it from me." Pamela's mouth dropped open and Charlotte felt a quickening in her chest, for a moment wishing she had never invited her brother and his wife into this private crisis.

Eric drew his chair closer to Charlotte before he began his own story. "I identified Raney's scar. She was a friend of mine, when I was growing up. We hadn't seen each other in more than ten years." He seemed to purge himself through the retelling, moving back and forth in time until, at the end of half an hour, Pamela and Will knew almost everything. Even the extinguished possibility that Jake might have been the product of Eric's single coital episode with

Raney—how Eric and Charlotte had both been persuaded by the remarkable resemblance Jake bore to Eric: the shape of his nose, the jagged lay of his hair, even the single blue eye. The only thing Eric didn't tell them was how devastated Charlotte had been when the paternity test did not show a match.

"Those mail-order paternity tests can be wrong. Maybe you should do a blood test," Pamela said.

Charlotte answered, "They're not wrong very often. And how could we get a blood sample from him? Besides, the whole idea was crazy. Raney's first husband, Jake's father, was Filipino and Jake has his skin color. And at least one of his brown eyes!" Charlotte laughed telling this part, needing some thin element of humor.

"He really has two different eye colors? Like my cat—Effie. Maybe he's a chimera."

"A chimera? You mean as in the mythical beast?" Charlotte said.

"Well, no. I was joking. But the other kind—the nonmythical kind—is a genetic glitch. Twins that fuse together. If it happens early enough, before the cells differentiate, they can grow into a completely normal-looking person. Only the person has two different cell lines, one from each fertilized egg. Kidney from one twin, liver from another . . ."

"You're kidding. That exists?" Charlotte said.

"For sure in animals. Marmosets. Tortoiseshell cats—that's how I know about it. Calicoes and tortoiseshells are almost always female, but one in a few thousand is a male, like Effie, and those can be a chimera."

"But not in people . . ." Charlotte said.

Will said, "I've read about it. It happens in people. Rarely. Or maybe not so rarely—no one's testing for it, so who knows? They'd look normal, or something as subtle as different-colored eyes." He smiled, but when he looked at her, Charlotte caught a hint of something sad crossing his face, as if he'd begun to appreciate how Jake's story related to his sister's romantic relationship. He shifted the conversation to the topic at hand. "Listen, I'll get the boy into our spine clinic if you can work on getting the permission from the foster home or his stepfather. Maybe our social workers can help. You'll call me?"

After Will and Pamela left, Eric seemed sober, depleted. He said he wanted to go to his apartment. He had more work to do on his last chapter, and anyway, it was office hours in Sweden, where his genetics resource lived. Charlotte could tell he was upset. Pamela and Will had been circumspect about Eric's medical history but still, it was out there now. So this would be their own last chapter, then. Everything finally out in the open just before they separated. She tossed with an unsettled mind, half-dreaming of being asleep and waking in disappointment that the dream was only a dream. She startled in jagged alarm when she heard Eric's key in the lock. It was just after two in the morning, 11:00 a.m. in Stockholm.

He looked so somber it worried her; her first thought, as always, was that his headaches were back, a tingling in his arm or blurring of his vision that might warn his tumor was recurring. "Eric? What is it? Are you sick?"

"I'm fine. Stop worrying about my head." He pulled away, agitated. "Do you remember what Pamela was talking about. Jake's eyes?" She didn't answer, not following him. "Will is right. They aren't freaks or myths."

"What? Who's not a myth?"

And then she heard why Eric had been so quiet at the end of the evening, why he had left so abruptly. He told her about the chapter he'd been working on, and the quirky path of research it had turned up: a kidney transplant patient whose blood was matched against her three sons, hoping one might be a donor. The DNA tests "proved" two of her boys could not be her children. But when they tested cells from different parts of the mother's body they found genetic prints from two different individuals. Different parts of her had arisen from different fertilized eggs. Twins fused into one person. "The woman was a chimera. I called Fikkers, the geneticist in Sweden. He's seen it—people who have two different blood types. Different tissues with unique cell lines. Hermaphrodites sometimes—he even talked about people with different eye colors, like Jake."

"It sounds too crazy. Why haven't I heard about it before?"

"No one knew about this before we were tissue matching. Most would look completely normal."

Charlotte said, "Are you saying Jake is the product of two fathers? You and . . . ?"

"Cleet. Raney's first husband. The man she married a month after I made love to her." He waited for some sign from Charlotte—excitement or astonishment or utter disbelief. "We need to get different tissue from him. We have to test Jake's blood."

It took two days to find Jake. Louise didn't answer her phone or return Charlotte's message—she should have been there if Jake was still living with her, Charlotte thought. She began to wonder if he'd been sent back to his stepfather's. She was ready to call Blake Simpson when Eric called from her house. "Louise telephoned here. She wants to talk to you. She doesn't have Jake anymore."

"Did she say where he is?" Charlotte asked.

"She won't tell me. She *can't* tell me. 'Confidentiality police,' as she put it. But since you're Raney's doctor she can tell you—I think she's using that as an excuse to tell either of us anything."

Charlotte could almost see Louise's broad face as soon as she heard her voice on the phone. Louise began with a deep, plaintive sigh in which Charlotte heard the trials of Jake and all the hundreds of children who'd come before him. "A lot of children spend a few days with me and feel ready to look at their homes and their folks with fresh consideration," Louise told Charlotte. "They shake off all the angry words that made 'em run. You know how it is, that age. Kids keep the last argument spinnin' around and around—mouse on a wheel. But after some time they start to miss things—their room, friends, Mom's food, Dad's jokes. Eventually, usually, even Mom and Dad. I'm talking about kids like Jake, now. Not the ones with the real horror stories.

"I met Mr. Boughton. Read all the records from the social worker.

There's nothin' there that would excuse us for taking Jake out of that household."

Charlotte was holding the phone with two hands like a strong grip might change what she heard. "But Jake told me he didn't want to go back to his stepdad," she said. "He was clear about that. Did anyone—the social worker, I guess—do a thorough investigation? I mean, not all abuse is physical."

Louise let out a sympathetic laugh. It could have felt belittling except that Louise sounded almost grateful for Charlotte's naïveté—a reminder, perhaps, that not everyone had seen so many ruined lives. "David Boughton isn't the best man, but he isn't necessarily a bad man. The mother's accident has been a trauma to both of them—him and Jake. The main reason Jake ran away was to get to her. Boughton could be a decent father in the long run." She paused. "You would tell me otherwise, if you had any facts?"

"I think Jake has scoliosis—maybe something even more serious. He said his mother wanted him to see a doctor."

"Boughton says Jake has seen at least three doctors in the last few months," Louise said, pausing as if she hoped Charlotte had something more.

"If Jake doesn't want to live with him . . ." Charlotte said.

"I asked if you had any facts."

Charlotte bit her lip. What *facts* did she know about David? "So does Jake have to go back to him? There's no option?"

"Actually, there is one option. Our twelve-year-old boy, who sometimes has trouble stringing a dozen words together, has filed dependency proceedings. With some help from DCF—Department of Children and Family Services. He's asking to be permanently removed from David Boughton's care."

"A child can do that? A minor?"

"Yes. And there's a chance the judge will listen to him. Jake doesn't seem to be budging and Boughton isn't begging to get him back." Louise drew her words out cautiously, which made it sound less like the victory Charlotte was starting to hope for.

"Well, wouldn't that be better for him if he doesn't like his step-father?" she asked.

Louise took a long time to answer. "May I ask, is there any chance, from what you can tell, that Jake's mother will make it home?"

Suddenly Charlotte felt like she was back in the conference room again, crying not with thankfulness that Raney had survived when they turned off the ventilator, but with regret. "In my opinion? No."

"Do you know if she, or Jake's father, Flores, has *any* living relatives? Outside of the Philippines?"

Charlotte began to understand where Louise was going. "No. Not that I know about."

"Dr. Reese, have you known many children who grew up in foster care?" It was clearly a rhetorical question. "There are many fine people helping kids like Jake. But you might read up on the statistics before you assure yourself that he's better there than with Mr. Boughton. Placing an adolescent boy is not easy. Sometimes the best choice is not a perfect choice."

"Is there any chance Jake could stay with you?" Charlotte asked.

Louise's reply was preceded by another heavy sigh. "I'm sixty-eight now. My home is for urgent intervention. Short term." She paused. "Boys like Jake make that my own hard choice."

"Right. I understand."

"Do you think Jake should see his mother? Even if they can't talk?" Louise asked.

Charlotte saw Raney in her mind, immobile, unresponsive, her muscles wasted—as if demonic magical creatures had stolen the real mother away and replaced her with a false image. How would he react to that? Was it better to see her in the process of letting go? Or to remember what she'd been? "I don't know the answer to that. Maybe no one does."

Louise said she would try to let Charlotte and Eric know how Jake was faring, but she herself was unlikely to be involved much longer. They were about to hang up when Charlotte asked, "Louise? What if . . . What if someone related to Jake turned up? What then?"

"Well, the judge always prefers to place a child with a relative."

"What if they don't even know each other?"

"Even then. Blood over water." Louise was quiet on the other end of the line. "What kind of relative are you referring to?"

Charlotte took a full breath and held it a moment. "What if Jake's biological father was another man. Not Flores. Someone Jake had never met."

"Someone Jake had never met," Louise repeated in a solemn and carefully objective voice, and Charlotte saw Eric and Jake sitting side by side at Louise's dinner table, their faces so strikingly similar. "Well, like I said," Louise continued, "the court always prefers blood. Jake will be assigned a GAL—guardian ad litem—for the dependency proceedings. They'll know."

"Ah," said Charlotte quietly.

"They could be sure any paternity claim was handled right. Legal proof and all." She gave Charlotte a minute to say something, then sounded like she'd resolved any question in her own mind. "I'll get that name for you. Should know in a few days. I'll make sure you're in contact."

Over dinner Charlotte told Eric about Jake's dependency hearing and the disappointing news that he could not stay with Louise. But she didn't share the conversation about paternity. She wanted to talk to the guardian ad litem first. She wanted to be sure. They talked a lot, however, about whether Jake should be brought to Seattle to see his mother. The entire conversation left them both depressed, realizing they were attached to a child legally beyond their reach. The only good outcome of foster care, they agreed, was that someone other than David would handle Jake's medical problems. *If* Jake's plea for foster care was approved. *If* the foster home took him to the right doctor.

Eric pushed his half-eaten meal away. "Did you ask Louise if it's possible to get a blood sample from Jake?"

She hesitated before she said, "No." Which was the truth, if not all of it.

"I don't guess that would be an easy request to explain, would it?"

The next day, though, Charlotte got a second phone call about Jake. This one from Katherine Hemling, Jake's court-assigned guardian. Louise had asked her to call. Jake's dependency hearing would be coming up next week.

"Do you know where he would live if the judge lets him leave his stepfather's?" Charlotte asked her.

"Not yet. We'll wait for the order before we start that hunt. We have a shortage of foster parents in Jefferson County—as you might guess."

"Ms. Hemling, Jake has been having problems with his back. When I saw him—it wasn't a formal exam, of course—but I think he has scoliosis. Maybe something worse. He needs to see a specialist as soon as possible. Will someone, whoever he lives with, be able to get medical care for him?"

"Oh, the state would *pay* for care." She said it with a mix of both assurance and pessimism. "They do their best, Dr. Reese. But even at their best it's a cumbersome responsibility for most homes."

Now, thought Charlotte. Now, before she hangs up. "I have another question. What if Jake had a blood relative?"

"We've already looked. Believe me—we would always prefer that to foster care."

"What if someone could prove he was Jake's biological father?"

Katherine was quiet for a moment. "Well, can he? If so, if a DNA test proved it, he could file a paternity claim requesting custody. Or are you just asking to ask?"

Charlotte told her, then, about Eric and Raney, the timing of their romance with Jake's birth, the physical similarities. The relatively rare genetically inherited disorder they both likely shared. And when Katherine suggested a simple buccal swab, Charlotte told her why it would not be that simple. She told her about chimeras. After she had explained it all—down to the cats—Charlotte asked if the court might order a blood sample from Jake. Possibly other tissue if that was not definitive.

"Frankly," Katherine answered in a politely curt voice, "that sounds pretty close to crazy. But yes. If you could give reasonable cause, I suspect the judge would approve it. But the biological father would have to file a paternity claim first. And he should do it before the hearing."

That night Eric made love to Charlotte with an intensity that portended an acceptance of finality, or so she imagined. She didn't tell him about her conversation with Katherine—she didn't know how.

When Charlotte went to work the next morning and discovered Raney's bed empty, she rushed to the nursing station in a near panic. But it was nothing unexpected—a spot had opened up at the chronic care facility across the street, so Beacon had moved her. They needed the ICU bed. Within the hour Charlotte was busy taking care of the new occupant, a ninety-four-year-old man in congestive heart failure. Eric surprised her with grilled steak that night—a food she loved and he considered just shy of poison—putting it out on her favorite china with silver cutlery and a good Cabernet. It was funny how often he seemed to predict she might need a boost, had some uniquely personal pleasure waiting even before he'd seen her face or heard her voice.

"What is it?" he asked when she gave up on the fillet halfway through. She told him about Raney's transfer, hoping that would be enough, but he knew her too well. "Something else is bothering you. Is it about Jake?"

It should be an easy thing to tell him, Charlotte thought. A simple rule of law, which he could take or leave. It was his decision. His right. She had to let it go. "I need to know something," she said. "I want you to think about it before you answer. How does it change things if you know you're genetically related to Jake?"

He looked puzzled. "He's more likely to get the medical care he obviously needs. We have more leverage if I can prove he's mine, whether he's in a foster home or with Boughton. We've been over all this."

"Agreed—we might have more leverage. But that's a different question. I'm asking, How will it matter to *you*?"

"Oh, Charlotte," he said, sounding sad and resigned and almost—it broke her heart to hear—pitying. "I don't know. I can't answer that until it happens. Maybe just what you said in the motel that night. It's the moral thing to do, isn't it? If he has NF, he got it from me. I'm responsible for it."

Charlotte tried to keep her voice steady. How could it be so hard to say something to someone you knew so well? "I talked to the guardian ad litem helping with Jake's court case. We can get a blood sample. The court can order one. But you would have to file a paternity claim before the judge would order the test."

"A paternity claim? What, stating that I think I could be his biological father?"

"No. A paternity claim means you intend to *act* as Jake's father. A *real* father. That you intend to raise him."

Eric stood up and walked to the kitchen door with his back to her. She could hear him breathing slowly, like he was counting breaths to calm himself. "Raise him. That's a lot more than we've been talking about."

The resigned tone of his voice ripped through her. She knew she couldn't let it go—not again. "Have we talked about it? Have we even admitted what we should really be talking about? This is more than Jake. This is years old, and we keep pretending we have forever to decide. Or I do. This is about us, Eric."

"What?" He turned to face her. "I haven't stood by you in this?"

"You stand by me always. You stand by me, but we're standing still. In the same place. Where are we going? What are we together?"

They both felt it, the chill slipping into the air, slipping between them. Charlotte was ready to turn away, say, Forget this. I'm just tired—worn out. I meant nothing. Without any effort she had been doing that for years—moving from one day to the next, loving him from one day to the next, knowing that all human plans are subject to the whim of the universe. What was there, in the end, to hold on to? Why count on anything more than *now*—this one infinitesimal point in time? So they had lived and loved as if one day could forever turn into any other. How had she forgotten the first rule of biology? That survival depends on continuous change. Stand immobile in one place and you will starve, freeze, or burn; oxygen will not enter or exit, cell division will cease. Because time will go forward with or without you, implacable and unceasing, glacially grinding down anything that won't move at its pace.

Her voice broke. "You may have a son, Eric. The child you could never decide, never commit, to have with me."

"How is it fair of me to have a child? Even Jake? Do you know what it's like to wonder how long you'll be here?"

"How long will anyone be here? Would Raney have given up having him if she'd known what was going to happen to her? Okay, you have a disease. You might die at fifty. Or tomorrow. Does that mean you and I don't matter? That a child we make is a mistake? If you die before me or get sick again, will it hurt any less because you wouldn't commit to me?"

He looked at her and she saw the wound she had made. Saw it and felt cruel and more wounded herself. "Please, Eric. I can't keep choosing between you and the rest of my life. Stop protecting me from losing you. Oh, God, I've probably lost you already."

He seemed paralyzed for a moment and Charlotte wanted to leave, run from the room and the house and the memory of it all. Then he moved close enough to touch her, ran his hands across her tear-streaked face and around her arms to pull her close. She resisted him at first, then slowly let him hold her until they both calmed. "And what do we do if the test says I'm his father?" he asked.

"Then you'll be his father. We'll raise your son. We will raise him together."

· 21 ·
raney

David refused to go to the orthopedic surgeon in Aberdeen with Raney and Jake. As a man who worked hard for his own living, he couldn't excuse taking up a doctor's time when there was no way to pay him. "There was a boy in my school in Oklahoma who had curvature. Doctor made him wear this metal brace for years. He hated it—finally just threw it away. Ended up doing fine without it," he told Jake. Raney put dinner on the table without a word, using the last of her self-control to keep Jake from witnessing the bitterness two married adults were capable of. Later, in bed, David put his arms around her and whispered, "I know it's hard. If you can just wait until I get a job with benefits. If he isn't getting better in a few months I'll go along with it."

The next morning she slid out of bed, dressed in the dark, and carried David's trousers into the kitchen before she fished through the pocket for the car keys. She shook Jake awake, quieting his mouth with one calm hand. "Breakfast on the road today, Buddy."

After they left Dr. Lawrence's office, Raney drove straight to the Dairy Queen for Yukon Cruncher Blizzards. Neither of them had said much since leaving the exam room—Jake, she figured, because he was pondering how many needles or shots lay ahead. Raney, though, was turning the surgeon's words inside out, hunting for any certainty in the *possiblys*, *probablys*, and *remotelys* he had used. She tried to discount the scariest medical terms—*tumor, cancer, steel rods, transfusion*—against the friendlier ones—*benign, good prognosis, recovery*—but she couldn't clearly remember what he'd said about the actual likelihood of any of them. For all that, she had liked the surgeon. He let Raney know that he had all the time in the world for their questions, even though she could hear ten screaming children through the walls.

"So what did you think of him?" she asked Jake.

"I liked the candy." In this last year of too many doctor's visits, Jake and Raney had both bemoaned the apparent collusion between dentists and doctors who rewarded children with only Batman or My Little Pony stickers after a needle stick.

"What do you think about going to see the doctors in Seattle?"

Jake put his cup on the sticky metal table and popped the top of his straw through the wrapper, pushing the paper down to a crinkle before anointing it with a drop of water so the paper wriggled into a long white worm. How did such things get traded down through every generation of children? she wondered.

Finally Jake answered, "Okay. If we can go to the Space Needle."

"Sure. We can go to the Space Needle." Raney drew two round eyes on the end of another straw and made her own worm. "But what did you think about what the doctor said? About your back?" Jake pretended to be too absorbed in his paper menagerie to hear her. She caught the next falling drop of water in her palm. "Talk to me, Jake. I know it's scary. But if he's right, maybe we could get your back fixed. It wouldn't hurt anymore."

Jake's eyes looked dangerously red-rimmed and she could see he was trying hard not to blink. She was ready to tell him it was all right to cry, an adult would cry about it too, when he said, "Just us, right?"

Raney tilted her head, not wholly following him. "I'd be there the entire time, Jake."

"And not David."

Was this, then, Jake's greatest worry? Was he willing to have surgery if it meant he could separate his mother from David, the man she had voluntarily turned into Jake's stepfather? Raney felt her center drop away, shamed and guilty. She had made any number of wrong turns in her life and knew it could be easy to see that you were in the wrong place but still impossible to know what wrong turn had taken you there. This time she did. She had grabbed hold of people instead of life itself, and expected them to save her. She had grabbed hold of David and expected *him* to save them all. She touched Jake's cheek and said, "If you don't want David there, then he won't be there."

Jake let her hold his hand on the way to the car, even with a crowd of skateboarders hanging around the parking lot. On the way out of town she saw the exit for Highway 109 and the coastline, and cut the wheel so fast Jake asked if there was something wrong with the car. "No. Something's wrong with the day," she said. "There's not enough fun in it yet."

They drove past clusters of weathered, neglected beach shacks, a few newer homes decorated with glass buoys and driftwood carvings of mermaids and fishermen. A surf shop. A burger shack. And then only empty, sand-swept road, the Pacific Ocean hidden by a tidal stream and low dunes. She parked by a yellow tsunami warning sign and helped Jake jump over the gully. They took off their shoes; the sand was so hot they had to climb the shallow rise by digging their feet through the loose surface into the cool underlayers. Raney could tell Jake was favoring one hip, but otherwise he moved with a loose freedom she had missed. Sweeps of blond sea grass clustered like gossiping girls and Jake hid himself among them, thrilled to see his mother worried before he stood up and waved. They sat together on the crest of the dunes and marveled at the beach, a prairie of beiges and browns stretching to a scallop of sea foam, a stripe of ocean, and more sky than Jake had ever seen. Yes, the world was indeed round. Only a sphere could be this infinite.

Jake had spent only one day on the Pacific since he was a toddler—

a weekend trip they'd taken with Cleet. "Do you remember it? Dad found that dolphin skeleton and you were too afraid to touch it?" Jake squinted, as if that might bring some vague recollection into focus. She felt bad about not getting him out of Quentin more often, always counting on more time and more money ahead of them. She picked up a handful of sand and trickled it over his bare leg. "You know what makes sand? Millions of animal shells, ground up by waves over millions of years." But what does a million years mean when you are twelve? she thought when he didn't answer.

What had Jake been thinking when Dr. Lawrence described how he would go to sleep for his operation? Did they have to describe it with the same words they'd use to put a lame dog down? "Jake, did I ever tell you that I knew the very second I was pregnant with you? I couldn't see you or touch you or feel you, but I knew you were there. And I was right." Raney saw a smile play at Jake's lips and decided to forge ahead. She picked up a sand dollar and ran her finger around the disk. "I guess I think about life the same way—a circle. It doesn't have a start and a stop any more than you didn't start the day you were born and you won't end when your body dies. And neither did your dad. His soul is still around us. His love." She watched Jake turn this over, probing it for the solid elements he could hold on to, the hollow parts that left him doubting.

"Just because *you* believe it, that doesn't make it true," he said.

She almost wished God himself would walk out of the ocean with an answer. Did he for some people? The sky was cloudless; two gulls shrieked and dove after the same silver splash. She turned Jake around to face the horizon, "What's out there, Jake? What land would I hit if I could fly straight west?"

"Mom!"

"Come on. You know. Mrs. Bywaters taught you. What country is out there?"

"China?"

She had to think for a minute. Was it Taiwan or Japan? "Doesn't matter. Asia, right?"

He laughed at her, "Asia isn't a country."

"Okay, so I would have flunked Mrs. Bywaters's geography. But if we could both hop on the backs of those seagulls and fly far enough, we would hit some country in Asia, right?"

"Right."

"So you totally believe me?"

"Totally."

"Would it still be there if you didn't believe in it?"

"You're teasing me now."

She turned him around to face her and ran her fingers through his damp, iron-straight hair. The mixed color of his eyes, one blue, one brown, were all the ocean and earth she wanted. "No, Jake. I'm just saying that something can be real even when the only proof you have is your own faith."

David was sitting at the kitchen table when they got home, a half-empty Corona in his hands. Raney sent Jake to his room—it was well after ten o'clock. "Did you eat?" she asked David. "I left you some chicken." She opened the refrigerator and saw the plate still wrapped in Saran, untouched. She dropped her purse on the table and faced him, her hands bracing her against the kitchen counter. "I took him to the orthopedist. It took longer than I expected. I'm sorry."

"I got a call about a job in Amanda Park. They wanted someone today. I told them I'd drive over as soon as I had a vehicle."

"Well, that's a shame. I'm sorry." She opened the refrigerator again and took out the plate, peeled the plastic back, and set it on the table with a fork. "You should eat. I don't like to waste food."

"I don't have much appetite at the moment."

"Do you want to know what the doctor said? Do you care?"

"Care? I'm trying to find a job, Renee. To support us. This family."

She paused one beat before she said it: "You wouldn't need a new job if you hadn't lost your temper with Fielding."

He pushed halfway out of his chair and in one furious sweep

knocked her purse and the plate of food off the table. Coins and ChapStick and pens flew like shrapnel; the glass shattered. "I wouldn't have lost my temper if your son hadn't started selling speed to his classmates!"

Had she known that she hated him before that moment? The word had been rolling loose and quiet in the corners of her mind, audible only when it woke her in the middle of the night, as unreal as a bad dream by morning. "I'm taking him to Seattle tomorrow," she said in a low, hard whisper.

"Come again?"

"I'm taking Jake to Seattle tomorrow. I'll need money."

"Money? Hard to earn it with no car. I couldn't even pick up my check today."

"We can take a bus. Just get us to Aberdeen. Or drop us on the highway and we'll flag down the local. Keep the car. Stay and look for work." She walked down the hall, saw Jake curled on his bed—he would have heard everything through the paper-thin walls. "Jake?" He didn't answer. "Pack a bag, Buddy. Okay?" He gave the smallest nod. Raney went to their bedroom and began throwing clothes into an empty canvas shopping bag—T-shirts, a bathing suit, her best dress—whatever she saw that was hers and not his.

A moment later David filled the doorway. "You got a credit card filled with imaginary dollars? I'm only asking you to wait until . . ."

"I'm driving to Kalaloch to pick up your check. There'll be a morning bus—you can take us there before you go to work." Every muscle was tense, braced to defend herself or grab Jake and run.

But instead of the violent reaction she anticipated, David slumped against the doorframe, his voice collapsing so solidly Raney half-expected the walls to shudder. "Oh, God. Oh, Raney," he said, so bereft she was almost taken in. She looked at him— dark sweat rings staining his usually crisp white shirt, wisps of hair lank against his perspiring skin. She saw him so clearly at this mo- ment—so worn out and weak that her decision to ever follow him anywhere mystified her. What had taken so long? How could she ask Jake to forgive her?

He would drive to Kalaloch to get the check—the night clerk wasn't likely to cash it for her anyway. He asked her to come. The car ride would give them some time to talk—no, not to change her mind—to talk through what should happen next. For them. For Jake. Better to talk where he couldn't hear it all, right?

Raney went to Jake's bedroom, but when she sat next to him he rolled away. He had his shirt off and the abnormal curl of his spine felt like a scold for every mistake she'd ever made. She put her hand on his shoulder. "Jake? You awake?" He didn't move but he didn't have to. She knew he heard. "I'll be back, Buddy. Get some rest."

"Mom? I didn't sell the drugs."

She kissed him. "I never thought you did."

She threw the canvas bag into the front seat; David walked around to the driver's side, so apparently humbled it looked like his coat had suddenly grown too large for his stooped shoulders.

At night the land out here was isolated to the point of forbidding. Black sky and black fields lit only by their headlights; tunnels of wind-twisted trees and brackish marsh so dense with cattails the boundary between solid earth and drowning pool dissolved in a treacherous maze. Tsunami warning signs pointed the way to higher ground but anyone who lived out here understood the two-lane road could not carry them all to safety. The silence between David and Raney hung like ignitable gas; they drove without speaking all the way to Kalaloch, where he cashed his check. He handed the whole wad to her, and she stuffed it into her pocket.

She wanted to leave with Jake on that bus tomorrow with no question they would not be coming back to him. "I'm sorry, David," she said, willing to take her own blame. "We rushed into this marriage. We should have taken more time. It's nobody's fault."

He stared at the road, rolling his fists over the steering wheel.

"Fault." he repeated. "A family falls apart and it's no one's fault—like it's a natural disaster or something?" His tone was bizarrely calm; it set Raney on edge.

"I'd hardly call us a family, David. Jake is sick, and all you've done is stand between him and help." The car was gradually speeding up, the road so sparsely traveled their headlights seemed to end at the rim of the known world.

"You have a short memory, Raney. Remember how I found you? On the brink of losing your house? Your son flunking out of school?"

She could hear him winding up, knew he was probing for a way into her—anger followed by apologies followed by hopelessness, circling back to anger again. Any button he could push. Funny she had never realized before now—at this late age—that an argument could still connect two people after tenderness had worn itself out. She decided to say nothing, tried to soothe herself by imagining the bus trip tomorrow. Maybe the hospital could help her find a place to stay, maybe they'd have a job . . .

"Are you listening?" he said.

"I'm listening." Maybe Jake's schoolwork had been affected by his back pain. Seattle would have more choices of schools anyway. Maybe he'd never needed any medicine—she'd never seen any difference in him, off or on. Couldn't tell from his behavior which days he'd taken it and which he'd forgotten. Or when he'd run out. She looked at her husband's profile—rigid, scowling, likely mulling the next taunt. Had it ended this way with Shannon, his last wife? She knew nothing about him, did she? Nothing at all. This was how he did it, she realized. This was his malignant gift. Someone with no conscience can tell any lie and never be detected—no blush, no averted eyes. "What do you know about Jerrod and Jake?" she asked. "Why would Fielding cover up whatever happened in his office that night? You said he wouldn't go to the police. What was going on with his books?"

David's brow twisted into an expression of mock pity. "Is this how it went with you and Cleet? You finally made him feel worthless enough to . . ."

"At least my dead husband isn't alive and well in Florida. I want to leave tonight. Get Jake. We'll sleep in the bus station. We'll sleep on the road." She twisted her wedding ring off her finger and flung it at him.

"That's what this is all about, isn't it? Shannon. No matter how much I explained. This isn't about Jake. This is about revenge for a lie I only told to protect you." David's jaw clenched hard between his sentences. The road leaped faster under the hood of the car, curving as they neared an empty intersection and the sky was blotted out by a copse of sea-stunted trees. "You're above a lie, Renee? The poor widowed mother? Lost her husband in a 'freak boating accident.'" He had one hand off the steering wheel now, stabbing his finger toward her face.

The rest of Raney's conscious life flashed like a strip of film with missing frames, jumbled and distorted. She saw a deer at the boundary of their headlights, and screamed; David must have thought it a howl against his rage. Then she was out of the car, kneeling on cold concrete holding a doe's massive head, her great neck twisting in fear, the black pool of her eye so close, so huge, Raney saw the dome of the night sky there, the black orb of unending time. There was an agonal scramble of hoof against pavement and then the fawn—there was a fawn—poised to spring after its mother despite Raney's own cry, the shouts of a man, the gunning of an engine. Something solid landed in the nearby marsh with a splash and Raney saw taillights. But then headlights again, a rocket of white light . . . when? A second later? Moments? The fawn, locked in the blinding glare, so close, almost inside her reach . . . We expect so much more, don't we? she thought. How funny that we expect so much more.

· 22 ·
charlotte

Raney was readmitted to Beacon Hospital in less than a week. Charlotte was at home; Felipe called and asked if she wanted to come in. Raney's chest was gradually filling with fluid—an aggressive, drug-resistant pneumonia—some bug almost certainly spawned in the bacterial miasma of Beacon's own ICU, which had flourished with exponential reproduction in the soup of her damp lungs. "Her saturation is eighty-four percent," Felipe told her. "I thought you'd want to be here." She knew what he was saying. They would need to put her back on the ventilator and put in a chest tube to save her life. *To save her life*, she repeated to herself. Words so loosely defined. *Save*—implying kept for later? Rescued from a known and terrible fate? *Life*—that one was easily enough defined by those who were living, perhaps analogous to prisoners describing the mind of God as a locked cell.

Eric was carrying another load of books to the attic room he was converting into his office; he saw Charlotte in her white lab coat, fumbling through the drawer for her keys, her wallet. Usually by the time she had that coat on she was already transformed into the con-fident, collected clinician—as if the coat itself held transformative properties. Instead, she was clearly distressed, tearing her purse apart in her search for the keys. He waited, the box of books balanced on his shoulder, until she looked up at him. "I can't do it," she said. "Find them, I mean. I can't . . . Would you come with me to the hospital?"

In the elevator Charlotte talked without leaving any space for Eric to respond: "How could they have screwed up so soon? One week and she's got an empyema! Were they looking the other way? Maybe it started before she was transferred—maybe we missed the first signs . . ."

Even from the ICU doorway, even with no medical education, Eric could see how wrong Raney's color was—her skin was the blues and grays she had painted him with twenty-five years ago. Twenty-five. He counted the years again, was it possible? Her mouth and nose were covered with a misting green mask. The monitor above Raney's bed showed lit-up numbers in blue and green and red, one flashing: 82, 80, 77 . . . Felipe was holding Raney's wrist in his gloved hands, a small syringe aimed like a fine dart at the pulse just above her thumb. Charlotte went to his side and talked to him for a moment, too hushed for Eric to hear. When she came back, she explained that they were running out of time—the tube would have to go in now if they had any chance to save her. Charlotte picked up the telephone and dialed a number. Then, before she said a word, before anyone answered, she hung up. "I shouldn't do it to her, should I?"

Eric held her eyes for a minute, enough time for her to make the call if she knew it was right. She waited, looking at him for confirmation now, or support, or just to know he would be there when it was done. Finally, when she was ready, he said, "Maybe it's time to let Raney choose."

· · ·

The Jefferson County courtroom looked nothing like Charlotte had expected—a small room at the back of the old Port Townsend courthouse with no throne of a judge's bench, no tiered box for jurors. The judge himself was a nondescript man of late middle age.

The single impression Charlotte had was that his body type would always make him look a bit overweight unless he was a bit too thin. Theirs was only one of many cases on the docket that day—all manner of contested family combinations awaited. She passed part of the long delay studying the women and men and children milling around the waiting room and the grassy lawn that looked over the sound, guessing who might be related to whom. Then Jake walked into the room with Katherine and another woman—Jake's lawyer, it soon became clear.

Suddenly, after so many dragging days and hours, it all moved too quickly. *This* should be the drawn-out part of it, Charlotte thought. Stamping every moment with the full weight of the lives in balance.

Jake barely glanced at her. She felt a rush of blood to her feet, a moment of panic—had she and Eric spent enough time considering it from Jake's side? Eric tensed when Jake was led to the front of the room. He wrapped her arm in his and gripped her hand so hard the bones were pressed uncomfortably against the wooden bench. The judge paused between cases, read the papers handed to him by Jake's lawyer, nodding once or twice, exchanging words. They spoke too low to be heard. Charlotte tried to read the judge's face across the floor. Then, at last, the judge called Jake Remington Flores's name. And then he called Robert Eric Bryson.

The judge looked at Jake. "Young man? You understand what we are here for?" Jake nodded. "You have to speak up, son. For the record."

"Yes, sir. I do." He wore khaki pants so new the creases across the thighs and calves were still crisp. Someone had combed his hair straight across his forehead with a neat part; illogically tidy for a kid. If he were mine, thought Charlotte, I would muss it up.

The judge continued. "If the court found reason to place you in Mr. Bryson's custody"—he lifted the papers in his hand to indicate Eric—"would you be willing to go?"

Jake looked at Eric with the same solemn expression Charlotte had noted at the trailer in Queets and at Louise's foster home in Port

Angeles. It reflected his worldview, Charlotte decided. Appraising, considering—revealing nothing until he was ready. She was sitting so still the bench beneath her seemed to drift in space, gravity a matter of perspective. Finally, after a long moment of apparent consideration, Jake nodded again, and then said, "Yes."

The judge sorted through the papers on his bench and unfolded a single sheet, smoothing it flat. He read the test result aloud and then, for the first time, he smiled. And when Charlotte saw Jake's face, when she saw his own smile, she knew it would be all right. They would be all right.

*"I must be willing to give up what
I am in order to become what I will be."*
—ALBERT EINSTEIN

Acknowledgments

While the events and characters in this novel are fictional and drawn from my imagination, all the medical detail and genetics I've incorporated are scientifically factual.

No acknowledgments is complete without a huge shout of thanks to you, readers! It is the dynamic confluence of readers, knowledgeable booksellers, and libraries that keeps novels a living part of our culture.

For all that the author's name is the one on the cover, no novel gets published without the work of many minds, and I am indebted to the entire Simon & Schuster team. My editors Marysue Rucci and Jonathan Karp have been true partners on *Gemini*. How often you saw the forest when I was lost in the trees. Jonathan Evans and Emily Graff, your meticulous attention to detail was my life raft through those final drafts. Thanks also to my agents, David Forrer and Kimberly Witherspoon at Inkwell Management. You know when to hold my hand and when to push me harder.

It took three years and months of research to wrestle this book to a final draft. I depended on the expertise of many people without whose generous gifts this fiction would have none of the solid weight of facts. Thanks to Dr. Anna Beck for her general medical expertise and wisdom in hospice care and oncology; Dr. Karen Hanten for her wealth of pediatric advice and experience; Dr. Lorrie Langdale for details on intensive care and trauma; and Drs. Michael Souter and Lynne Taylor for those first illuminating conversations. For their unending patience explaining details of genetics and neuroscience, I thank Drs. Kurt Benirschke, Manuel Ferreira, Clement Furlong, Stan Gartler, Sidney Gospe, Lee Nelson, and Virginia Sybert. Additional medical details were contributed by Drs. Terry Clark, Farrokh Farrokhi, David Feldman, Bernard Fikkers, Terri Graham, Anna Harvey, Bill Healey, Chris Kuhr, Dana Lynge, Tom Malpass, Mette Peters, Peggy Sargeant, Sam Sharar, and Brad Watters.

All the Googling in the world could not replace the legal details provided by Deputy Gary Simpson; also Lieutenant Mark Hanten, Sergeant Roy Frank, Criminal Identification Specialist Kaycee Leaonard, and Crime Analyst Sandy Curry. Mr. Keith Thomson, King County guardian ad litem, put up with infinite questions with the best humor, as did Heath Fox, GAL Paula Martin, Debra Madsen, LuAnne Perry, and Briana Rogers of DNA Identifiers.

Paul Svornich, thank you for your intimate familiarity with commercial fishing. Other facts included in *Gemini* are thanks to Barbara Blackie, Elena Giorgi, Gloria Sayler, Joan Hanten, Carole Ober, Jennifer Olanie, Shawn Otorowski, Nancy Johnson, and Rhona Jack.

Many dear friends read early drafts of this work and their forbearance, faith, and forgiveness led to a far better book. Thanks to Erica Bauermeister, Randy Sue Coburn, Claire Dederer, Anne Gendreau, Sherry Larsen-Holmes, Martha McLaughlin, Zan Merriman, Suzanne Selfors, Jennie Shortridge, Gail Tsukiyama, and, for her brilliant painter's eye, Martha Burkert. And to the most fabulous writing group on the planet and their commitment to supporting literacy, thank you Seattle7Writers!

This book was born, revised, and completed at Hedgebrook Writer's Retreat on Whidbey Island. I am forever indebted, and so grateful to be one voice in your phenomenal community of radical hospitality.

My research included conversations with intensive care physicians, oncologists, hospice caretakers, cancer-stricken friends, biblical scholars, spiritualists, and books ranging from neuroscience to *Proof of Heaven* to *The Tibetan Book of Living and Dying*. In all of them, perhaps not surprisingly, I found more similarities than differences. A special note of remembrance is offered to my friends whose lives came prematurely to their physical end during the course of writing this novel. Anna Harvey, you are remembered, and some of your words are in these pages. As you once said, "Death is the ultimate act of our humanity, because it is the last thing we do as humans." Kay Monahan, Annette Moser-Wellman, Marta Wagner, Chris Bernards, Susan Thompson, and Lucie Rose Gendreau, we miss you.

And last, first, and ahead of all else, thanks to my family: Kathie and Ray Wiley, Ellen Bywaters, and Marilyn Wiley. My children, Sara, Will, Julia, and Elise—in you I witness miracles every day of my life. Steve Cassella: twenty-two years and counting, plus all the love that's at the heart of this book.

Charity Suggestion
for Book Clubs

Rose Grant

If your book club is interested in contributing to a charity related to some themes in this book, consider donating to the Rose Grant. Established in memory of Lucie Rose Gendreau, the Rose Grant funds classes, lessons, or tuition for teens who need an extra show of community support during a time of personal struggle. Helping teens succeed in an area of their own positive passion can stop a downward spiral and carry them through difficult years to thrive as wiser adults. For more information email: rosegrant@ bainbridgeyouthservices.org.

GEMINI

CAROL CASSELLA

When an unidentified Jane Doe, the victim of a hit-and-run, arrives in Dr. Charlotte Reese's intensive care unit, she brings with her mysteries—both medical and personal. As Charlotte cares for Jane, she becomes increasingly caught up in the questions of her patient's identity and what led to her accident. Why has no one stepped forward to claim Jane? What will happen if she doesn't wake up? When Charlotte's search for answers reveals links between Charlotte and her patient, the repercussions will forever change her life and her understanding of what love can make possible.

Questions for Discussion

1. Why does Charlotte feel such a strong sense of responsibility for Jane Doe? How does she balance her protective feelings for Jane with her practical understanding of Jane's prognosis?

2. From the moment she first sees Bo, Raney is acutely aware of the differences in their circumstances. How does her sensitivity about her background affect their relationship over the years? In what ways do they have more in common than she thinks? Why is their childhood attachment so enduring?

3. Charlotte sees her job as giving nature "as much time as possible" (117). In practice, what does that mean? How does it influence her feelings about Jane's care and the appointment of a guardian ad litem?

4. How does the small town of Quentin, with its natural beauty and financial struggles, shape Raney's life? In what ways does she identify as a small-town girl, and in what ways does she resent that role?

5. Charlotte and Eric's relationship is haunted by her desire to have a child, and his reluctance to do so. Why is the subject so difficult for them to discuss? Why does Charlotte feel they have stalled?

6. What reasons does Raney give for marrying Cleet? Would she have made the same decision if she were not pregnant? How is her understanding of love and loyalty shaped by her marriage to him?

7. How does Eric's awareness of his neurofibromatosis and the brushes with death it caused, influence his life? What choices does he make as a result? What boundaries does he lay down? Are his boundaries intended for his own protection or for that of others?

8. As a child, Raney makes do with scavenged house paint for her art. How does that same make-do attitude manifest in her adult life?

9. What is the significance of Raney burning her paintings when her grandfather's farm is sold? Why is this a turning point in her life as much as her grandfather's?

10. Does Charlotte go too far by seeking David out and by trying to uncover Jake's paternity? Does her involvement with Raney compromise her objectivity?

11. When she was a child, Raney's grandfather taught her to light a campfire "with one match and her own wits" (229). Does Raney take his lesson about self-sufficiency to heart? At what points does she fail to follow his advice?

12. What prompts Raney to marry David? Why does she ignore her growing misgivings and stay with him? Do you think David was responsible for the hit-and-run?

13. Why do you think the author chose *Gemini*, the zodiac sign represented by twins, as the title of the novel? How does she develop the theme established by the title? What characters or events are "twinned"?

14. *Gemini* contains several mysteries: Jane Doe's identity, whether the hit-and-run was accidental or intentional, Jake's parentage,

and others. Was there a particular revelation that you found most surprising or satisfying? What devices did the author use to maintain suspense?

15. Discuss the role of genetics in the novel. How does Eric's "fatal flaw" link the characters? Eric wrote in his editorial that knowledge of your genetic code could be more damaging than helpful; is that true for Jake? Would you rather know if your genetics carried a fatal flaw or not?

16. *Gemini* raises challenging questions about our fear of death and our willingness to confront or discuss it. Did you react differently to Jane Doe's situation than you did to that of Raney's grandfather? How would you answer the question that Eric poses to Charlotte: "Should quantity of life always trump quality?" (9). Did reading *Gemini* stir you to look more closely at your own feelings about death?

A Conversation with Carol Cassella

What was the genesis of *Gemini*? Did you begin with an idea about a character or plot point? Or something else?

After writing two novels told from a doctor's point of view, I knew it was time to give the patient a chance to speak, so that was the first step in creating Raney. Then I needed to decide what the mystery would hinge upon and I turned to the world of genetics, which is rich with possible storylines.

As a mother of twins, and as a doctor, I've long been interested in how much of our lives is dictated by the genes we land here with—a blueprint over which we have no control. But my identical twins (who share the same DNA and upbringing but have very different personalities) have also confirmed that who we are and how we respond to events in our lives is far more complex than either nature or nurture can explain.

Once I had those starting points decided, my characters began to emerge and the novel grew into a story that encompassed those elements, but also much more. Truly the most fun part of writing a novel is watching it take on a life of its own as it grows and changes over time.

In your first novel your main character was an anesthesiologist, your own specialty; in *Gemini* your main character is an intensive care physician. How did you approach writing from the perspective of this specialty? How are the demands of this job different from anesthesiology?

Intensive care medicine and anesthesiology overlap quite a lot—they both focus on acute care situations rather than long-term problems, and to do them well you need to love physiology—the mechanics of how the heart, lungs, kidneys, and liver keep us alive. They are both fast-paced patient-care settings where things can change very, very quickly, so they tend to attract similar personalities. In fact, many intensivists begin with a residency in anesthesiology before doing a fellowship in intensive care medicine. So Charlotte's work was more familiar to me than, say, a pediatrician's or an oncologist's. On the other hand, it has been years since I worked with patients who were as sick as Raney, and I depended on several ICU experts to get the details I needed. The biggest difference between the two specialties is that in the ICU the patients arrive very, very sick, and the intensivist has to try to turn that ship around. In the operating room, most of the patients arrive reasonably healthy—or at least stable—and our job is to keep them that way.

The title of the novel is the zodiac sign for twins. Why did you choose to highlight that theme?

The title *Gemini* was suggested to me by an editor, so I can't take full credit. It doesn't fully make sense to the reader until the end of the book, when all the pieces of the mystery come together, but once you see the novel as a whole, the title seems perfect! The Gemini myth of Leda the swan and her twins Castor and Pollux—one mortal and one immortal—plays perfectly into Jake's life, both biologically and metaphorically. Does life really end at our deaths—either spiritually or physically? The unique codes within our DNA contain far more similarities than differences, so we are all connected to one another regardless of how we define "family."

But there are other "twin" stories at work in the novel, too: Raney and Charlotte, for all their differences, share similar personalities. They are both gritty, skeptical of the status quo, independent, yet loyal to those they love. I imagine they would have been friends if they had been born into more similar circumstances. And in the course of the novel they are both faced with wrenching decisions about how far to go when caring for a terribly ill person they care about. I even saw Eric's life in twin terms—the boy he was before his diagnosis usurped his belief that he could ever live a normal life, and the man he became afterward.

The settings of the novel help define your characters and contribute to the novel's conflicts. Was it important to you to have parts of the novel set in the Olympic Peninsula? Did you base Quentin on a specific place?

If you have visited the Pacific Northwest you know that our natural beauty is unparalleled. (Yes, I am prejudiced!) One day of sunshine here is well worth the ten days of rain that pay for it. It is such a joy to describe our landscape that I can never resist setting parts of my novel within it. But it also reflects much about *Gemini*'s characters and their conflicts—particularly Raney's. The Olympic Peninsula, home to Olympic National Park and the rainforest, is completely unspoiled in areas, but many of the towns and the reservations are struggling with poverty and unemployment. In ways, it is only four hours but ten light years from Seattle. This has a huge affect on Raney's life, of course. What would she have been able to do if she had been born into a more privileged family? How would that have changed the decisions she made?

On a more thematic level, contrasting the natural world of Raney's woods and coast against the highly technical setting of an urban hospital's ICU made a good backdrop for a novel that raises questions about natural death versus using every possible intervention at the end of life.

The novel deals head-on with moral and ethical questions about death and life and when and how it should be extended by medical means. What prompted you to confront these questions? Do you find your own answers to these questions changing with new experiences from your work or life?

I don't think you can be a doctor in this day and age and not struggle with these questions. We have all seen miracles result from new medical discoveries and interventions—people who are given another chance to hold new grandbabies or hug their spouse. But we have also stood at the bedside of patients tethered to a ventilator, going through a long and drawn-out death that none of us would want and that causes the patient's family extraordinary grief. Too often we, the doctors, are to blame, because we weren't strong enough to advise them honestly. And as medicine has become more complex, we need more and more specialists involved with critical patients, each focused on their own organ system rather than the complete picture. Sometimes families hear conflicting messages, but no one physician is taking the time to listen closely, answer questions, and help them come to difficult decisions. It isn't that doctors don't care; it's often that a rushed and fractionated healthcare system inadvertently neglects that hand-holding component. I often worry that we have raced forward in inventing medical marvels, but our ethical framework and guidance hasn't had time to catch up.

More critically, though, in the last four years this question has become quite personal because several close friends and family members have become gravely ill or died. Being at someone's bedside as a family member, rather than as a doctor, has had a profound effect on my thoughts about end-of-life care.

As our technological ability to extend the end of life increases, do you think understanding the implications of that ability is as challenging for doctors as it often is for individuals and families?

Absolutely. We are approaching the question from different angles—doctors who are deeply invested in saving lives and becoming skilled in the tools that accomplish that, and families who are mired in grief, remorse, and longing as they struggle with end-of-life decisions. Only fifty years ago, less even, death happened more naturally. There was nothing we could do but console. Now we sometimes have to make very hard decisions, and the outcome of those choices isn't always predictable. Will they lead to a few more days or months of good quality life, or a very uncomfortable, even more tragic death? These conversations are extremely difficult for doctors to initiate. They take time and need to happen early and frequently, and there is little leeway in the fast-paced healthcare system to support that.

It's critical for doctors to remember, though, that we must not only be shepherds of good health and long life, we must also be shepherds of good deaths. Death is not a failure—it is the natural and inevitable transition we all make at the end of our lives, just as we made the natural transition through birth into the beginning of life.

What sort of research did you do for the novel? Do you research as you write, or beforehand?

The research for *Gemini* was extensive and broad—maybe that's why my acknowledgments run two-and-a-half pages! But I love that part of writing. Before I begin a novel, I have to know that the topic interests me enough to hold my attention and curiosity for the two or three years it takes to finish it. I spoke to neuroscientists, geneticists, intensivists, medical ethics specialists, forensic specialists, law enforcement officers, lawyers, and protective guardians. Then there's the Internet, which can become a drowning ocean of valuable facts. I usually do several months of research in advance, which gives me the nuts and bolts of the mystery twists, then I augment that with focused research questions as plot points or dialogue. I'm sure I still miss some details, but it is really important to me that my novels are grounded in solid science. While I want my novels to be entertaining, I also enjoy translating the fascinating world of medical science into words that anyone can understand and appreciate.

Your books always contain intriguing medical quirks or situations. Have you always been interested in these unusual details? Do you find yourself collecting them, making note of them for future books?

The best part about medicine is the mystery—the challenge of taking a collection of symptoms and physical findings apart and tracing them back to the root problem—hopefully one we can fix. There are so many more mysteries in medicine than confirmed facts that it never gets boring, particularly when they involve all the social and emotional layers that affect our health and well-being.

I've been a fiction writer and reader since I was very young (though I didn't fully dive in until my forties), so I tend to walk through the world looking for ideas. If some new and startling fact intrigues or puzzles me, I figure it will intrigue and puzzle readers, too, so I write it down or make a voice memo for later reference. Now if only I could live long enough to use them all. . . . Ah, but that dilemma goes right to the heart of this novel, doesn't it?

Would you describe where and how you like to write? In the mornings or evenings? With music or without? How do you transition from parent or doctor mode to writing mode?

Here is my ideal writing life: every single morning I get up and put on my soft baggy sweat pants and fleece, make a *huge* latte, sit in front of the fireplace by the windows and let my imagination spin out on the keyboard for two or three hours before I tackle the less creative tasks of my life, such as e-mail or those dirty dishes. Here's the reality: I leave for the hospital at six and come home too tired to do anything but eat and go to bed, or (on the days I'm not in the operating room) I get pinged with critical meetings or messages about children, the business side of being a novelist, or the business side of medicine, and I'm lucky to get an hour or two somewhere in the day to create a bit of fiction. To compensate I often spend two or three days locked in a room where I do nothing but write.

Unfortunately I need total silence to write, though I love music and find it very inspiring. I usually try to take a break and go for a long walk or run with music, and I always come home with fresh ideas. Movement and exercise are important for generating creative work. It can be difficult to transition from parenting or doctoring to the quieter, inner world from which my stories arise. But that's a problem all of us face, isn't it? I'm so often asked how I balance the different roles in my life, but truthfully I don't know many people—especially women—who aren't constantly juggling all the obligations in their lives.

If there's one thing you'd like readers to take away from *Gemini*, what would it be? What do you look for in fiction?

A good book needs to linger much longer than the time it takes to read it. I want readers to come away from all my novels with more questions than answers—questions that spark conversations and richer internal thought about issues we all face. In *Gemini*, I'm hoping to spark a conversation about what, for each of us, constitutes a good and meaningful death. Those answers will be different for everyone, but they are key to another question I'm raising in these pages: What constitutes a meaningful life? How do we approach love and art and work, and our own definition of family, so that our lives are as rich and fulfilling as they can possibly be and we fully appreciate each of the finite days we are granted on this earth?